KEN FOLLETT

EYE OF THE NEEDLE

PAN BOOKS

First published in Great Britain 1978 by Futura Publications Ltd

This edition published 2009 by Pan Books
an imprint of Pan Macmillan, a division of Macmillan Publishers Limited
Pan Macmillan, 20 New Wharf Road, London N1 9RR
Basingstoke and Oxford
Associated companies throughout the world
www.panmacmillan.com

ISBN 978-1-4472-8523-6

3 5 7 9 8 6 4 2

A CIP catalogue record for this book is available from
the British Library.

Typeset by SetSystems Ltd, Saffron Walden, Essex
Printed and bound by CPI Group (UK) Ltd, Croydon, CR0 4YY

EYE OF THE NEEDLE

Ken Follett was only twenty-seven when he wrote the award-winning *Eye of the Needle*, which became an international bestseller. He has since written several equally successful novels, including *World Without End*, the long-awaited sequel to the worldwide bestselling *The Pillars of the Earth*, an epic of family drama, violent conflict and vaulting ambition set around the building of a great cathedral. Ken Follett is also the author of the non-fiction bestseller *On Wings of Eagles*. He lives with his family in London and Hertfordshire.

www.ken-follett.com

Also by Ken Follett

The Modigliani Scandal
Paper Money
Triple
The Key to Rebecca
The Man from St Petersburg
On Wings of Eagles
Lie Down with Lions
The Pillars of the Earth
Night Over Water
A Dangerous Fortune
A Place Called Freedom
The Third Twin
The Hammer of Eden
Code to Zero
Jackdaws
Hornet Flight
Whiteout
World Without End
Fall of Giants

The Germans were almost completely deceived – only Hitler guessed right, and he hesitated to back his hunch . . .

A. J. P. Taylor
English History 1914–1945

My thanks to Malcolm Hulke

for invaluable help, generously given.

Preface

Early in 1944 German Intelligence was piecing together evidence of a huge army in south-eastern England. Reconnaissance planes brought back photographs of barracks and airfields and fleets of ships in the Wash; General George S. Patton was seen in his unmistakable pink jodhpurs walking his white bulldog; there were bursts of wireless activity, signals between regiments, in the area; confirming signs were reported by German spies in Britain.

There was no army, of course. The ships were rubber-and-timber fakes, the barracks no more real than a movie set; Patton did not have a single man under his command; the radio signals were meaningless; the spies were double agents.

The object was to fool the enemy into preparing for an invasion via the Pas de Calais, so that on D-Day the Normandy assault would have the advantage of surprise.

It was a huge, near-impossible deception. Literally thousands of people were involved in perpetrating the trick. It would have been a miracle if none of Hitler's spies ever got to know about it.

Were there any spies? At the time people thought

they were surrounded by what were then called Fifth Columnists. After the war a myth grew up that MI5 had rounded up the lot by Christmas 1939. The truth seems to be that there were very few: MI5 did capture nearly all of them.

But it only needs one . . .

We know that the Germans saw the signs they were meant to see in East Anglia. We also know that they suspected a trick. And we know that they tried very hard to discover the truth.

That much is history, and I have discovered no facts that aren't already in history books. What follows is fiction.

Still and all, I think something like this must have happened . . .

Camberley, Surrey

PART ONE

ONE

It was the coldest winter for forty-five years. Villages in the English countryside were cut off by the snow, and the Thames froze over. One day in January the Glasgow to London train arrived at Euston twenty-four hours late. The snow and the blackout combined to make motoring perilous: road accidents doubled, and people told jokes about how it was more risky to drive an Austin Seven along Piccadilly at night than to take a tank across the Siegfried Line.

Then, when the spring came, it was glorious. Barrage balloons floated majestically in bright blue skies, and soldiers on leave flirted with girls in sleeveless dresses on the streets of London.

The city did not look much like the capital of a nation at war. There were signs, of course; and Henry Faber, cycling from Waterloo Station toward Highgate, noted them: piles of sandbags outside important public buildings, Anderson shelters in suburban gardens, propaganda posters about evacuation and Air Raid Precautions. Faber watched such things – he was considerably more observant than the average railway clerk. He saw crowds of children in the parks, and concluded that evacuation had been a failure. He marked the number of motor cars on the road, despite petrol rationing; and he read about the new models announced by the motor manufacturers. He knew the significance of night-shift workers pouring into factories where, only months previously, there had been hardly enough work for the day shift. Most of all he monitored the movement of troops around Britain's railway network: all the paperwork passed through his office. One could learn a lot from that paperwork. Today, for example, he had rubber-stamped a batch of forms which led him to believe that a new Expeditionary Force was being gathered. He was fairly sure that it would have a complement of about 100,000 men, and that it was for Finland.

There were signs, yes; but there was something jokey about it all. Radio shows satirised the red tape of wartime regulations, there was community singing in the air-raid shelters, and fashionable women carried their gas masks in couturier-designed containers. They talked about the Bore War. It was at once larger-than-life and trivial, like a moving-picture show. All the air-raid warnings, without exception, had been false alarms.

Faber had a different point of view – but then, he was a different kind of person.

He steered his cycle into Archway Road and leaned forward a little to take the uphill slope, his long legs pumping as tirelessly as the pistons of a railway engine. He was very fit for his age, which was thirty-nine, although he lied about it: he lied about most things, as a safety precaution.

He began to perspire as he climbed the hill into Highgate. The building in which he lived was one of the highest in London, which was why he chose to live there. It was a Victorian brick house at one end of a terrace of six. The houses were high, narrow and dark, like the minds of the men for whom they had been built. Each had three storeys plus a basement with a servants' entrance – the English middle class of the nineteenth century insisted on a servants' entrance, even if they had no servants. Faber was a cynic about the English.

Number six had been owned by Mr Harold Garden, of Garden's Tea And Coffee, a small company which went broke in the Slump. Having lived by the principle that insolvency is a mortal sin, the bankrupt Mr Garden had no option but to die. The house was all he bequeathed to his widow, who was then obliged to take in lodgers. She enjoyed being a landlady, although the etiquette of her social circle demanded that she pretend to be a little ashamed of it. Faber had a room on the top floor with a dormer window. He lived there from Monday to Friday, and told Mrs Garden that he spent weekends with his mother in Erith. In fact he had another landlady in Blackheath who called him Mr Baker and believed he was a travelling salesman for a stationery manufacturer and spent all week on the road.

He wheeled his cycle up the garden path under the disapproving frown of the tall front-room windows. He put it in the shed and padlocked it to the lawn-mower – it was against the law to leave a vehicle unlocked. The seed potatoes in boxes all around the shed were sprouting. Mrs Garden had turned her flower beds over to vegetables for the war effort.

Faber entered the house, hung his hat on the hall-stand, washed his hands and went in to tea.

Three of the other lodgers were already eating: a pimply boy from Yorkshire who was trying to get into the Army; a confectionery salesman with receding sandy hair; and a retired naval officer who, Faber was convinced, was a degenerate. Faber nodded to them and sat down.

The salesman was telling a joke. 'So the Squadron-Leader says, "You're back early!" and the pilot turns round and says, "Yes, I dropped my leaflets in bundles, wasn't that right?" so the Squadron-Leader says, "Good God! You might've hurt somebody!" '

The naval officer cackled and Faber smiled. Mrs Garden came in with a teapot. 'Good evening, Mr Faber. We started without you – I hope you don't mind.'

Faber spread margarine thinly on a slice of whole-meal bread, and momentarily yearned for a fat sausage. 'Your seed potatoes are ready to plant,' he told her.

Faber hurried through his tea. The others were arguing over whether Chamberlain should be sacked and replaced by Churchill. Mrs Garden kept voicing opinions then looking at Faber for a reaction. She was a blowsy woman, a little overweight. About Faber's age, she wore the clothes of a woman of thirty, and he guessed she wanted another husband. He kept out of the discussion.

Mrs Garden turned on the radio. It hummed for a while, then an announcer said: 'This is the BBC Home Service. *It's That Man Again*!'

Faber had heard the show. It regularly featured a German spy called Funf. He excused himself and went up to his room.

Mrs Garden was left alone after *It's That Man Again*: the naval officer went to the pub with the salesman, and the boy from Yorkshire, who was religious, went to a prayer meeting. She sat in the parlour with a small glass of gin, looking at the blackout curtains and thinking about Mr Faber. She wished he wouldn't spend so much time in his room. She needed company, and he was the kind of company she needed.

Such thoughts made her feel guilty. To assuage the guilt she thought of Mr Garden. Her memories were familiar but blurred, like an old print of a movie with worn sprocket-holes and an indistinct soundtrack; so that, although she could easily remember what it was like to have him here in the room with her, it was difficult to imagine his face, or the clothes he might be wearing, or the comment he would make on the day's war news. He had been a small, dapper man, successful in business when he was lucky and unsuccessful when he was not, undemonstrative in public and insatiably affectionate in bed. She had loved him a lot. There would be many women in her position if this war ever got going properly. She poured another drink.

Mr Faber was a quiet one – that was the trouble. He didn't seem to have any vices. He didn't smoke, she had never smelled drink on his breath, and he spent every evening in his room, listening to classical music on his radio. He read a lot of newspapers and went for long walks. She suspected he was quite clever, despite his humble job: his contributions to the conversation in the dining-room were always a shade more thoughtful than anyone else's. He surely could get a better job if he tried. He seemed not to give himself the chance he deserved.

It was the same with his appearance. He was a fine figure of a man: tall, quite heavy around the neck and shoulders, not a bit fat, with long legs. And he had a strong face, with a high forehead and a long jaw and bright blue eyes; not pretty, like a film star, but the kind of face that appealed to a woman. Except for the mouth – that was small and thin, and she could imagine him being cruel. Mr Garden had been incapable of cruelty.

And yet at first sight he was not the kind of man a woman would look at twice. The trousers of his old worn suit were never pressed – she would have done that for him, and gladly, but he never asked – and he always wore a shabby raincoat and a flat docker's cap. He had no moustache, and his hair was trimmed short every fortnight. It was as if he wanted to look like a nonentity.

He needed a woman, there was no doubt of that. She wondered for a moment whether he might be what people called effeminate, but she dismissed the idea quickly. He needed a wife to smarten him up and give him ambition. She needed a man to keep her company and for – well, love.

Yet he never made a move. Sometimes she could scream with frustration. She was sure she was attractive. She looked in a mirror as she poured another gin. She had a nice face, and fair curly hair, and there was something for a man to get hold of . . . She giggled at that thought. She must be getting tiddly.

She sipped her drink and considered whether *she* ought to make the first move. Mr Faber was obviously shy – chronically shy. He wasn't sexless – she could tell by the look in his eyes on the two occasions he had seen her in her nightdress. Perhaps she could overcome his shyness by being brazen. What did she have to lose? She tried imagining the worst, just to see what it felt like. Suppose he rejected her. Well, it would be embarrassing – even humiliating. It would be a blow to her pride. But nobody else need know it had happened. He would just have to leave.

The thought of rejection had put her off the whole idea. She got to her feet slowly, thinking: I'm just not the brazen type. It was bedtime. If she had one more gin in bed she would be able to sleep. She took the bottle upstairs.

Her bedroom was below Mr Faber's, and she could hear violin music from his radio as she undressed. She put on a new nightdress – pink, with an embroidered neckline, and no one to see it! – and made her last drink. She wondered what Mr Faber looked like undressed. He would have a flat stomach, and hairs on his nipples, and you would be able to see his ribs, because he was slim. He probably had a small bottom. She giggled again, thinking: I'm a disgrace.

She took her drink to bed and picked up her book, but it was too much effort to focus on the print. Besides, she was bored with vicarious romance. Stories about dangerous love affairs were fine when you yourself had a perfectly safe love affair with your husband, but a woman needed more than Barbara Cartland. She sipped her gin, and wished Mr Faber would turn the radio off. It was like trying to sleep at a tea-dance!

She could, of course, ask him to turn it off. She looked at her bedside clock: it was past ten. She could put on her dressing-gown, which matched the nightdress, and just comb her hair a little, then step into her slippers – quite dainty, with a pattern of roses – and just pop up the stairs to the next landing, and just, well, tap on his door. He would open it, perhaps wearing his trousers and singlet, and then he would *look* at her the way he had *looked* when he saw her in her nightdress on the way to the bathroom . . .

'Silly old fool,' she said to herself aloud. 'You're just making excuses to go up there.'

And then she wondered why she needed excuses. She was a mature adult, and it was her house, and in ten years she had not met another man who was just right for her, and what the *hell*, she needed to feel someone strong and hard and hairy on top of her, squeezing her breasts and panting in her ear and parting her thighs with his broad flat hands, for tomorrow the gas bombs might come over from Germany and they would all die choking and gasping and poisoned and she would have lost her last chance.

So she drained her glass, and got out of bed, and put on her dressing-gown, and just combed her hair a little, and stepped into her slippers, and picked up her bunch of keys in case he had locked the door and couldn't hear her knock above the sound of the radio.

There was nobody on the landing. She found the stairs in the darkness. She intended to step over the stair that creaked, but she stumbled on the loose carpet and trod on it heavily; but it seemed that nobody heard, so she went on up and tapped on the door at the top. She tried it gently. It was locked.

The radio was turned down, and Mr Faber called out: 'Yes?'

He was well-spoken: not cockney, or foreign – not anything, really, just a pleasantly neutral voice.

She said: 'Can I have a word with you?'

He seemed to hesitate, then he said: 'I'm undressed.'

'So am I,' she giggled, and she opened the door with her duplicate key. He was standing in front of the radio with some kind of screwdriver in his hand. He wore his trousers and *no* singlet. His face was white and he looked scared to death.

She stepped inside and closed the door behind her, not knowing what to say. Suddenly she remembered a line from an American film, and she said: 'Would you buy a lonely girl a drink?' It was silly, really, because she knew he had no drink in his room, and she certainly wasn't dressed to go out; but it sounded vampish.

It seemed to have the desired effect. Without speaking, he came slowly toward her. He *did* have hair on his nipples. She took a step forward, and then his arms went around her, and she closed her eyes and turned up her face, and he kissed her, and she moved slightly in his arms, and then there was a terrible, awful, unbearable *sharp* pain in her back and she opened her mouth to scream.

He had heard her stumble on the stairs. If she'd waited another minute he would have had the radio transmitter back in its case and the code books in the drawer and there would have been no need for her to die. But before he could conceal the evidence he had heard her key in the lock, and when she opened the door the stiletto had been in his hand.

Because she moved slightly in his arms, Faber missed her heart with the first jab of the weapon, and he had to thrust his fingers down her throat to stop her crying out. He jabbed again, but she moved again and the blade struck a rib and merely slashed her superficially. Then the blood was spurting and he knew it would not be a clean kill, it never was when you missed with the first stroke.

She was wriggling too much to be killed with a jab now. Keeping his fingers in her mouth, he gripped her jaw with his thumb and pushed her back against the door. Her head hit the woodwork with a loud bump, and he wished he had not turned the radio down, but how could he have expected this?

He hesitated before killing her, because it would be much better if she died on the bed – better for the cover-up which was already taking shape in his mind – but he could not be sure of getting her that far in silence. He tightened his hold on her jaw, kept her head still by jamming it against the door, and brought the stiletto around in a wide slashing arc that ripped away most of her throat, for the stiletto was not a slashing knife and the throat was not Faber's favoured target.

He jumped back to avoid the first horrible gush of blood, then stepped forward again to catch her before she hit the floor. He dragged her to the bed, trying not to look at her neck, and laid her down.

He had killed before, so he expected the reaction: it always came as soon as he felt safe. He went over to the sink in the corner of the room and waited for it. He could see his face in the little shaving mirror. He was white, and his eyes were staring. He looked at himself and thought: *Killer*. Then he threw up.

When that was over he felt better. He could go to work now. He knew what he had to do: the details had come to him even while he was killing her.

He washed his face, brushed his teeth, and cleaned the washbasin. Then he sat down at the table beside his radio. He looked at his notebook, found his place, and began tapping the key. It was a long message, about the mustering of an army for Finland, and he had been half way through when he was interrupted. It was written down in cipher on the pad. When he had completed it he signed off with: 'Regards to Willi.'

The transmitter packed away neatly into a specially designed suitcase. Faber put the rest of his possessions into a second case. He took off his trousers and sponged the bloodstains, then washed himself all over.

At last he looked at the corpse.

He was able to be cold about her now. It was wartime; they were enemies: if he had not killed her, she would have caused his death. She had been a threat, and all he felt now was relief that the threat had been nullified. She should not have frightened him.

Nevertheless, his last task was distasteful. He opened her robe and lifted her nightdress, pulling it up around her waist. She was wearing knickers. He tore them, so that the hair of her pubis was visible. Poor woman: she had wanted only to seduce him. But he could not have got her out of the room without her seeing the transmitter; and the British propaganda had made these people alert for spies – ridiculously so: if the Abwehr had as many agents as the newspapers made out then the British would have lost the war already.

He stepped back and looked at her with his head on one side. There was something wrong. He tried to think like a sex maniac. If I were crazed with lust for a woman like Una Garden, and I killed her just so that I could have my way with her, what would I then do?

Of course: that kind of lunatic would want to look at her breasts. Faber leaned over the body, gripped the neckline of the nightdress, and ripped it to the waist. Her large breasts sagged sideways.

The police doctor would soon discover that she had not been raped, but Faber did not think that mattered. He had taken a criminology course at Heidelberg, and he knew that many sexual assaults were not consummated. Besides, he could not have carried the deception that far, not even for the Fatherland. He was not in the SS. Some of *them* would queue up to rape the corpse . . . He put the thought out of his mind.

He washed his hands again and got dressed. It was almost midnight. He would wait an hour before leaving: it would be safer later.

He sat down to think about how he had gone wrong.

There was no question that he had made a mistake. If his cover were perfect, he would be totally secure. If he were totally secure no one could discover his secret. Mrs Garden had discovered his secret – or rather, she would have if she had lived a few seconds longer – therefore he had not been totally secure, therefore his cover was not perfect, therefore he had made a mistake.

He should have put a bolt on the door. Better to be thought chronically shy than to have landladies with duplicate keys sneaking in at night in their bedwear.

That was the surface error. The deep flaw was that he was too eligible to be a bachelor. He thought this with irritation, not conceit. He knew that he was a pleasant, attractive man, and that there was no apparent reason why he should be single. He turned his mind to thinking up a cover that would explain this without inviting advances from the Mrs Gardens of this world.

He ought to be able to find inspiration in his real personality. Why *was* he single? He stirred uneasily: he did not like mirrors. The answer was simple. He was single because of his profession. If there were deeper reasons, he did not want to know them.

He would have to spend tonight in the open. Highgate Wood would do. In the morning he would take his suitcases to a railway station left-luggage office, then tomorrow evening he would go to his room in Blackheath.

He would shift to his second identity. He had little fear of being caught by the police. The commercial traveller who occupied the room at Blackheath on weekends looked rather different from the railway clerk who had killed his landlady. The Blackheath persona was expansive, vulgar and flashy. He wore loud ties, bought rounds of drinks, and combed his hair differently. The police would circulate a description of a shabby little pervert who would not say boo to a goose until he was inflamed with lust, and no one would look twice at the handsome salesman in the striped suit who was obviously the type that was more or less permanently inflamed with lust and did not have to kill women to get them to show him their breasts.

He would have to set up another identity – he always kept at least two. He needed a new job, fresh papers – passport, identity card, ration book, birth certificate. It was all so *risky*. Damn Mrs Garden. Why couldn't she have drunk herself to sleep as usual?

It was one o'clock. Faber took a last look around the room. He was not concerned about leaving clues – his fingerprints were obviously all over the house, and there would be no doubt in anyone's mind about who was the murderer. Nor did he feel any sentiment about leaving the place that had been his home for two years: he had never thought of it as home. He had never thought of anywhere as home.

He would always think of this as the place where he had learned to put a bolt on a door.

He turned out the light, picked up his cases, and crept down the stairs and out of the door into the night.

TWO

Henry II was a remarkable king. In an age when the term 'flying visit' had not yet been coined, he flitted between England and France with such rapidity that he was credited with magical powers; a rumour which, understandably, he did nothing to suppress. In 1173 – either the June or the September, depending upon which secondary source one favours – he arrived in England and left for France again so quickly that no contemporary writer ever found out about it. Later historians discovered the record of his expenditure in the Pipe Rolls. At the time his kingdom was under attack by his sons at its northern and southern extremes – the Scottish border and the South of France. But what, precisely, was the purpose of his visit? Whom did he see? Why was it secret, when the myth of his magical speed was worth an army? What did he accomplish?

This was the problem that taxed Percival Godliman in the summer of 1940, when Hitler's armies swept across the French cornfields like a scythe, and the British poured out of the Dunkirk bottleneck in bloody disarray.

Professor Godliman knew more about the Middle

Ages than any man alive. His book on the Black Death had upended every convention of medievalism; it had also been a bestseller and published as a Penguin. With that behind him he had turned to a slightly earlier and even more intractable period.

At 12.30 on a splendid June day in London, a secretary found Godliman hunched over an illuminated manuscript, laboriously translating its medieval Latin, making notes in his own even less legible handwriting. The secretary, who was planning to eat her lunch in the garden of Gordon Square, did not like the manuscript room because it smelled dead. You needed so many keys to get in there, it might as well have been a tomb.

Godliman stood at a lectern, perched on one leg like a bird, his face lit bleakly by a spotlight above: he might have been the ghost of the monk who wrote the book, standing a cold vigil over his precious chronicle. The girl cleared her throat and waited for him to notice her. She saw a short man in his fifties, with round shoulders and weak eyesight, wearing a tweed suit. She knew he could be perfectly sensible once you dragged him out of the Middle Ages. She coughed again and said: 'Professor Godliman?'

He looked up, and when he saw her he smiled, and then he did not look like a ghost, more like someone's dotty father. 'Hello!' he said, in an astonished tone, as if he had just met his next-door neighbour in the middle of the Sahara Desert.

'You asked me to remind you that you have lunch at the Savoy with Colonel Terry.'

'Oh, yes.' He took his watch out of his waistcoat

pocket and peered at it. 'If I'm going to walk it, I'd better leave now.'

She nodded. 'I brought your gas mask.'

'You are thoughtful!' He smiled again, and she decided he looked quite nice. He took the mask from her and said: 'Do I need my coat?'

'You didn't wear one this morning. It's quite warm. Shall I lock up after you?'

'Thank you, thank you.' He jammed his notebook into his jacket pocket and went out.

The secretary looked around, shivered, and followed him.

Colonel Andrew Terry was a red-faced Scot, pauper-thin from a lifetime of heavy smoking, with sparse dark-blond hair thickly brilliantined. Godliman found him at a corner table in the Savoy Grill, wearing civilian clothes. There were three cigarette stubs in the ashtray. He stood up to shake hands.

Godliman said: 'Morning, Uncle Andrew.' Terry was his mother's baby brother.

'How are you, Percy?'

'I'm writing a book about the Plantagenets.' Godliman sat down.

'Are your manuscripts still in London? I'm surprised.'

'Why?'

Terry lit another cigarette. 'Move them to the country in case of bombing.'

'Should I?'

'Half the National Gallery has been shoved into a bloody big hole in the ground somewhere up in Wales. Young Kenneth Clark is quicker off the mark than you. Might be sensible to take yourself off out of it too, while you're about it. I don't suppose you've many students left.'

'That's true.' Godliman took a menu from a waiter and said: 'I don't want a drink.'

Terry did not look at his menu. 'Seriously, Percy, why are you still in Town?'

Godliman's eyes seemed to clear, like the image on a screen when the projector is focused, as if he had to think for the first time since he walked in. 'It's all right for children to leave, and national institutions like Bertrand Russell. But for me – well, it's a bit like running away and letting other people fight for you. I realize that's not a strictly logical argument. It's a matter of sentiment, not logic.'

Terry smiled the smile of one whose expectations have been fulfilled. But he dropped the subject and looked at the menu. After a moment he said: 'Good God. *Le Lord Woolton Pie.*'

Godliman grinned. 'I'm sure it's still just potatoes and vegetables.'

When they had ordered, Terry said: 'What do you think of our new Prime Minister?'

'The man's an ass. But then, Hitler's a fool, and look how well he's doing. You?'

'We can live with Winston. At least he's bellicose.'

Godliman raised his eyebrows. '"We?" Are you back in the game?'

'I never really left it, you know.'

'But you said—'

'Percy. Can't you think of a department whose staff all say they don't work for the Army?'

'Well, I'm damned. All this time . . .'

Their first course came, and they started a bottle of white Bordeaux. Godliman ate potted salmon and looked pensive.

Eventually Terry said: 'Thinking about the last lot?'

Godliman nodded. 'Young days, you know. Terrible time.' But his tone was wistful.

'This war isn't the same at all. My chaps don't go behind enemy lines and count bivouacs like you did. Well, they do, but that side of things is much less important this time. Nowadays we just listen to the wireless.'

'Don't they broadcast in code?'

Terry shrugged. 'Codes can be broken. Candidly, we get to know just about everything we need these days.'

Godliman glanced around, but there was no one within earshot, and it was not for him to tell Terry that careless talk costs lives.

Terry went on: 'In fact my job is to make sure *they* don't have the information they need about *us*.'

They both had chicken pie to follow. There was no beef on the menu. Godliman fell silent, but Terry talked on.

'Canaris is a funny chap, you know. Admiral Wilhelm Canaris, head of the Abwehr. I met him before this lot started. Likes England. My guess is he's none too fond of Hitler. Anyway, we know he's been told to mount a major intelligence operation against us, in preparation for the invasion – but he's not doing much. We arrested their best man in England the day after war broke out. He's in Wandsworth prison now. Useless people, Canaris's spies. Old ladies in boarding-houses, mad Fascists, petty criminals—'

Godliman said: 'Look here, old boy, this is too much.' He trembled slightly with a mixture of anger and incomprehension. 'All this stuff is secret. I don't want to know!'

Terry was unperturbed. 'Would you like something else?' he offered. 'I'm having chocolate ice-cream.'

Godliman stood up. 'I don't think so. I'm going to go back to my work, if you don't mind.'

Terry looked up at him coolly. 'The world can wait for your reappraisal of the Plantagenets, Percy. There's a war on, dear boy. I want you to work for me.'

Godliman stared down at him for a long moment. 'What on earth would I do?'

Terry smiled wolfishly. 'Catch spies.'

Walking back to the college, Godliman felt depressed despite the weather. He would accept Colonel Terry's offer: no doubt about that. His country was at war; it was a just war; and if he was too old to fight, he was still young enough to help.

But the thought of leaving his work – and for how many years? – depressed him. He loved history, and he had been totally absorbed in medieval England since the death of his wife ten years ago. He liked the unravelling of mysteries, the discovery of faint clues, the resolution of contradictions, the unmasking of lies and propaganda and myth. His new book would be the best on its subject written in the last hundred years, and there would not be one to equal it for another century. It had ruled his life for so long that the thought of abandoning it was almost unreal, as difficult to digest as the discovery that one is an orphan and no relation at all to the people one has always called Mother and Father.

An air-raid warning stridently interrupted his thoughts. He contemplated ignoring it: so many people did now, and he was only ten minutes' walk from the college. But he had no real reason to return to his study – he knew he would do no more work today. So he hurried into a Tube station and joined the solid mass of Londoners crowding down the staircases and on to the grimy platform. He stood close to the wall, staring at a Bovril poster, and thought: But it's not just the things I'm leaving behind.

Going back into the game depressed him, too. There were some things he liked about it: the importance of *little* things, the value of simply being clever, the meticulousness, the guesswork. But he hated the blackmail and the treachery, the deceit, the desperation, and the way one always stabbed the enemy in the back.

The platform was becoming more crowded. Godliman sat down while there was still room, and found himself leaning against a man in bus-driver's uniform. The man smiled and said: 'Oh to be in England, now that summer's here. Know who said that?'

'Now that April's there,' Godliman corrected him. 'It was Browning.'

'I heard it was Adolf Hitler,' the driver said. A woman next to him squealed with laughter, and he turned his attention to her. 'Did you hear what the evacuee said to the farmer's wife?'

Godliman tuned out and remembered an April when he had longed for England, crouching on a high branch of a plane tree, peering through a cold mist across a French valley behind the German lines. He could see nothing but vague dark shapes, even through his telescope, and he was about to slide down and walk a mile or so farther when three German soldiers came from nowhere to sit around the base of the tree and smoke. After a while they took out cards and began to play, and young Percival Godliman realized they had found a way of skiving off and were here for the day. He stayed in the tree, hardly moving, until he began to shiver and his muscles knotted with cramp and his bladder felt as if it would burst. Then he took out his revolver and shot the three of them, one after another, through the tops of their close-cropped heads. And three people, laughing and cursing and gambling their pay, had simply ceased to exist. It was the first time he killed, and all he could think was: Just because I had to pee.

Godliman shifted on the cold concrete of the station platform and let the memory fade away. There was a warm wind from the tunnel and a train came in. The people who got off found spaces and settled to wait. Godliman listened to the voices.

'Did you hear Churchill on the wireless? We was listening in at the Duke of Wellington. Old Jack Thornton cried. Silly old bugger . . .'

'From what I can gather Kathy's boy's in a stately home and got his own footman! My Alfie milks the cow . . .'

'Haven't had fillet steak on the menu for so long I've forgotton the bally taste . . . wine committee saw the war coming and bought in twenty thousand dozen, thank God . . .'

'Yes, a quiet wedding, but what's the point in waiting when you don't know what the next day's going to bring?'

'They call it Spring, Ma, he says to me, and they have one down here every year . . .'

'She's pregnant again, you know . . . yes, thirteen years since the last . . . I thought I'd found out what was causing it!'

'No, Peter never came back from Dunkirk . . .'

The bus driver offered him a cigarette. Godliman refused, and took out his pipe. Someone started to sing.

A blackout warden passing yelled
'Ma, pull down that blind—
Just look at what you're showing,' and we
Shouted 'Never mind.' Oh!
Knees up Mother Brown . . .

The song spread through the crowd until everyone was singing. Godliman joined in, knowing that this was a nation losing a war and singing to hide its fear, as a man will whistle past the graveyard at night; knowing that the sudden affection he felt for London and Londoners was an ephemeral sentiment, akin to mob hysteria; mistrusting the voice inside him which said 'This, this is what the war is about, this is what makes it worth fighting'; knowing but not caring, because for the first time in so many years he was feeling the sheer physical thrill of comradeship and he liked it.

When the all-clear sounded they went singing up the staircases and into the street, and Godliman found a phone box and called Colonel Terry to ask how soon he could start.

THREE

The small country church was old and very beautiful. A dry-stone wall enclosed a graveyard where wild flowers grew. The church itself had been there – well, bits of it had – the last time Britain was invaded, almost a millennium ago. The north wall of the nave, several feet thick and pierced with only two tiny windows, could remember that last invasion; it had been built when churches were places of physical as well as spiritual sanctuary, and the little round-headed windows were better for shooting arrows out of than for letting the Lord's sunshine in. Indeed, the Local Defence Volunteers had detailed plans for using the church if and when the current bunch of European thugs crossed the Channel.

But no jackboots sounded in the tiled choir in this August of 1940; not yet. The sun glowed through stained-glass windows which had survived Cromwell's iconoclasts and Henry VIII's greed, and the roof resounded to the notes of an organ which had yet to yield to woodworm and dry rot.

It was a lovely wedding. Lucy wore white, of course; and her five sisters were bridesmaids in apricot dresses. David wore the Mess uniform of a Flying Officer in the

Royal Air Force, all crisp and new for it was the first time he had put it on. They sang Psalm 23, The Lord's My Shepherd, to the tune *Crimond.*

Lucy's father looked proud, as a man will on the day his eldest and most beautiful daughter marries a fine boy in a uniform. He was a farmer, but it was a long time since he had sat on a tractor: he rented out his arable land and used the rent to raise racehorses, although this winter of course his pasture would go under the plough and potatoes would be planted. Although he was really more gentleman than farmer, he nevertheless had the open-air skin, the deep chest, and the big stubby hands of agricultural people. Most of the men on that side of the church bore him a resemblance: barrel-chested men, with weathered red faces, those not in tail coats favouring tweed suits and stout shoes.

The bridesmaids had something of that look, too; they were country girls. But the bride was like her mother. Her hair was a dark, dark red, long and thick, shining and glorious, and she had wide-apart amber eyes set in an oval face; and when she looked at the vicar with that clear, direct gaze and said 'I will' in that firm, clear voice, the vicar was startled and thought, 'By God she means it!' which was an odd thought for a vicar to have in the middle of a wedding.

The family on the other side of the nave had a certain look about them, too. David's father was a lawyer: his permanent frown was a professional affectation, and concealed a sunny nature. (He had been a Major in the Army in the last war, and thought all this business about the RAF and war in the air was a fad which would soon pass.) But nobody looked like him, not even his son who stood now at the altar promising to love his wife until death, which might not be far away, God forbid. No, they all looked like David's mother, who sat beside her husband now, with almost-black hair, dark skin and long, slender limbs.

David was the tallest of the lot. He had broken high-jump records last year at Cambridge University. He was rather too good-looking for a man – his face would have been feminine were it not for the dark, ineradicable shadow of a heavy beard. He shaved twice a day. He had long eyelashes, and he looked intelligent, as he was, and sensitive, which he was not.

It was idyllic: two happy, handsome people, children of solid, comfortably off, backbone-of-England type families, getting married in a country church in the finest summer weather Britain can offer.

When they were pronounced man and wife both mothers were dry-eyed, and both the fathers cried.

Kissing the bride was a barbarous custom, Lucy thought as yet another middle-aged pair of champagne-wet lips smeared her cheek. It was probably descended from even more barbarous customs in the Dark Ages, when every man in the tribe was allowed to – well, anyway, it was time we got properly civilized and dropped the whole business.

She had known she would not like this part of the

wedding. She liked champagne, but she was not crazy about chicken drumsticks or dollops of caviar on squares of cold toast, and as for the speeches and the photographs and the honeymoon jokes, well . . . But it could have been worse. If it had been peacetime Father would have hired the Albert Hall.

So far nine people had said, 'May all your troubles be little ones,' and one person, with scarcely more originality, had said, 'I want to see more than a fence running around your garden.' Lucy had shaken countless hands and pretended not to hear remarks like, 'I wouldn't mind being in David's pyjamas tonight.' David had made a speech in which he thanked Lucy's parents for giving him their daughter, as if she were an inanimate object to be gift-wrapped in white satin and presented to the most deserving applicant. Lucy's father had been crass enough to say that he was not losing a daughter but gaining a son. It was all hopelessly gaga, but one did it for one's parents.

A distant uncle loomed up from the direction of the bar, swaying slightly, and Lucy repressed a shudder. She introduced him to her husband. 'David, this is Uncle Norman.'

Uncle Norman pumped David's bony hand. 'Well, m'boy, when do you take up your commission?'

'Tomorrow, sir.'

'What, no honeymoon?'

'Just twenty-four hours.'

'But you've only just finished your training, so I gather.'

'Yes, but I could fly before, you know. I learned at Cambridge. Besides, with all this going on they can't spare pilots. I expect I shall be in the air tomorrow.'

Lucy said quietly: 'David, don't,' but she was ignored.

'What'll you fly?' Uncle Norman asked with schoolboy enthusiasm.

'Spitfire. I saw her yesterday. She's a lovely kite.' David had consciously adopted all the RAF slang, kites and crates and the drink and bandits at two o'clock. 'She's got eight guns, she does three hundred and fifty knots, and she'll turn around in a shoebox.'

'Marvellous, marvellous. You boys are certainly knocking the stuffing out of the Luftwaffe, what?'

'We got sixty yesterday for eleven of our own,' David said, as proudly as if he had shot them all down himself. 'The day before, when they had a go at Yorkshire, we sent the bally lot back to Norway with their tails between their legs – and we didn't lose a single kite!'

Uncle Norman gripped David's shoulder with tipsy fervour. 'Never,' he quoted pompously, 'was so much owed by so many to so few. Churchill said that the other day.'

David tried a modest grin. 'He must have been talking about the mess bills.'

Lucy hated the way they trivialized bloodshed and destruction. She said: 'David, we should go and change now.'

They went in separate cars to Lucy's home. Her mother helped her out of the wedding dress and said: 'Now, my dear, I don't quite know what you're expecting tonight, but you ought to know—'

'Oh, mother, don't be embarrassing,' Lucy interrupted. 'You're about ten years too late to tell me the facts of life. This *is* 1940, you know!'

Her mother coloured slightly. 'Very well, dear,' she said mildly. 'But if there is anything you want to talk about, later on . . .'

It occurred to Lucy that to say things like this cost her mother considerable effort, and she regretted her sharp reply. 'Thank you,' she said. She touched her mother's hand. 'I will.'

'I'll leave you to it, then. Call me if you want anything.' She kissed Lucy's cheek and went out.

Lucy sat at the dressing-table in her slip and began to brush her hair. She knew exactly what to expect tonight. She felt a faint glow of pleasure as she remembered.

It was a well-planned seduction, although at the time it did not occur to Lucy that David might have plotted every move beforehand.

It happened in June, a year after they had met at the Glad Rag Ball. They were seeing each other every week by this time, and David had spent part of the Easter vacation with Lucy's people. Mother and Father approved of him: he was handsome, clever and gentlemanly, and he came from precisely the same stratum of society as they did. Father thought he was a shade too opinionated, but Mother said the landed gentry had been saying that about undergraduates for six hundred years, and *she* thought David would be kind to his wife, which was the most important thing in the long run. So in June Lucy went to David's family home for a weekend.

The place was a Victorian copy of an eighteenth-century grange, a square-shaped house with nine bedrooms and a terrace with a vista. What impressed Lucy about it was the realization that the people who planted the garden must have known they would be long dead before it reached maturity. The atmosphere was very easy, and the two of them drank beer on the terrace in the afternoon sunshine. That was when David told her that he had been accepted for officer training in the RAF, along with four pals from the university flying club. He wanted to be a fighter pilot.

'I can fly all right,' he said, 'and they'll need people once this war gets going – they say it'll be won and lost in the air, this time.'

'Aren't you afraid?' she said quietly.

'Not a bit,' he said. Then he covered his eyes with his hand and said: 'Yes, I am.'

She thought he was very brave, and held his hand.

A little later they put on swimming costumes and went down to the lake. The water was clear and cool, but the sun was still strong and the air was warm. They splashed about gleefully, as if they knew this was the end of their childhood.

'Are you a good swimmer?' he asked her.

'Better than you!'

'All right. Race you to the island.'

She shaded her eyes to look into the sun. She held the pose for a minute, pretending she did not know how desirable she was in her wet swimsuit with her arms raised and her shoulders back. The island was a small patch of bushes and trees about three hundred yards away, in the centre of the lake.

She dropped her hands, shouted 'Go!', and struck out in a fast crawl.

David won, of course, with his long arms and legs. Lucy found herself in difficulty when she was still fifty yards from the island. She switched to breaststroke, but she was too exhausted even for that, and she had to roll over on to her back and float. David, who was already sitting on the bank blowing like a walrus, slipped back into the water and swam to meet her. He got behind her, held her beneath the arms in the correct lifesaving position, and pulled her slowly to the shore. His hands were just below her breasts.

'I'm enjoying this,' he said, and she giggled despite her breathlessness.

A few moments later he said: 'I suppose I might as well tell you.'

'What?' she panted.

'The lake is only four feet deep.'

'You rogue!' She wriggled out of his arms, spluttering and laughing, and found her footing.

He took her hand and led her out of the water and through the trees. He pointed to an old wooden rowing-boat, rotting upside-down beneath a hawthorn. 'When I was a boy I used to row out here in that, with one of Papa's pipes, a box of matches, and a pinch of tobacco in a twist of paper. This is where I used to smoke it.'

They were in a clearing, completely surrounded by

bushes. The turf underfoot was clean and springy. Lucy flopped on the ground.

'We'll swim back slowly,' David said.

'Let's not even talk about it just yet,' she replied.

He sat beside her and kissed her, then pushed her gently backwards until she was lying down. He stroked her hip and kissed her throat, and soon she stopped shivering. When he laid his hand gently, nervously, on the soft mound between her legs, she arched upwards, willing him to press harder. She pulled his face to hers and kissed him open-mouthed and wetly. His hands went to the straps of her swimsuit, and he pulled them down over her shoulders. She said: 'No.'

He buried his face between her breasts. 'Lucy, please.'

'No.'

He looked at her. 'It might be my last chance.'

She rolled away from him and stood up. Then, because of the war, and because of the pleading look on his flushed young face, and because of the glow inside her which would not go away, she took off her costume with one swift movement, and removed her swimming-cap so that her dark red hair shook out over her shoulders, and knelt in front of him, taking his face in her hands and guiding his lips to her breast.

She lost her virginity painlessly, enthusiastically, and only a little too quickly.

The spice of guilt made the memory more pleasant, not less. If it had been a well-planned seduction then she had been a willing, not to say eager, victim, especially at the end.

She began to dress in her going-away outfit. She had startled him a couple of times, that afternoon on the island: once when she wanted him to kiss her breasts, and again when she had guided him inside her with her hands. Apparently such things did not happen in the books he read. Like most of her friends, Lucy read D. H. Lawrence for information about sex. She believed in his choreography and mistrusted the noises-off: the things his people did to one another sounded nice, but not that nice; she was not expecting trumpets and thunderstorms and the clash of cymbals at her sexual awakening.

David was a little more ignorant than she; but he was gentle, and he took pleasure in her pleasure, and she was sure that was the important thing.

They had done it only once since the first time. Exactly a week before their wedding they had made love again, and it caused their first row.

This time it was at her parents' house, in the morning after everyone else had left. He came to her room in his dressing-gown and got into bed with her. She almost changed her mind about Lawrence's trumpets and cymbals. David got out of bed immediately afterwards.

'Don't go,' she said.

'Somebody might come in.'

'I'll chance it. Come back to bed.' She was warm and drowsy and comfortable, and she wanted him beside her.

He put on his dressing-gown. 'It makes me nervous.'

'You weren't nervous five minutes ago.' She reached for him. 'Lie with me. I want to get to know your body.'

'My God, you're brazen.'

She looked at him to see whether he was joking, and when she realized he was not, she became angry. '*Just* what the *hell* does *that* mean?'

'You're just not . . . ladylike!'

'What a *stupid* thing to say—'

'You act like a – a – tart.'

She flounced out of bed, naked and furious, her lovely breasts heaving with rage. 'Just how much do you know about tarts?'

'Nothing!'

'How much do you know about women?'

'I know how a virgin is supposed to behave!'

'I am . . . I was . . . until I met you . . .' She sat on the edge of the bed and burst into tears.

That was the end of the quarrel, of course. David put his arms around her and said: 'I'm sorry, sorry, sorry. You're the first one for me, too, and I don't know what to expect, and I feel confused . . . I mean, nobody tells you anything about this, do they?'

She snuffled and shook her head in agreement, and it occurred to her that what was *really* unnerving him was the knowledge that in eight days' time he had to take off in a flimsy aircraft and fight for his life above the clouds; so she forgave him, and he dried her tears, and they got back into bed and held each other tightly for courage.

Lucy told her friend Joanna about the row, saying it was over a dress David thought to be brazen. Joanna said that couples always quarrelled before the wedding, usually the night before: it was the last chance to test the strength of their love.

She was just about ready. She examined herself in a full-length mirror. Her suit was faintly military, with square shoulders and epaulettes, but the blouse beneath it was feminine, for balance. Her hair fell in sausage curls beneath a natty pill-box hat. It would not have been right to go away gorgeously dressed, not this year; but she felt she had achieved the kind of briskly practical, yet attractive, look which was rapidly becoming fashionable.

David was waiting for her in the hall. He kissed her and said: 'You look wonderful, Mrs Rose.'

They were driven back to the reception to say goodbye to everyone, before leaving to spend the night in London, at Claridge's; then David would drive on to Biggin Hill and Lucy would come home again. She was going to live with her parents: she had the use of a cottage for when David was on leave.

There was another half-hour of handshakes and kisses, then they went out to the car. Some of David's cousins had got at his open-top MG. There were tin cans and an old boot tied to the bumpers with string, the running-boards were awash with confetti, and 'Just Married' was scrawled all over the paintwork in bright red lipstick.

They drove away, smiling and waving, the guests filling the street behind them. A mile down the road they stopped and cleaned up the car.

It was dusk when they got going again. David's

headlights were fitted with blackout masks, but he drove very fast just the same. Lucy felt very happy.

David said: 'There's a bottle of bubbly in the glove box.'

Lucy opened the compartment and found the champagne and two glasses carefully wrapped in tissue paper. It was still quite cold. The cork came out with a loud pop and shot off into the night. David lit a cigarette while Lucy poured the wine.

'We're going to be late for supper,' he said.

'Who cares?' She handed him a glass.

She was too tired to drink, really. She became sleepy. The car seemed to be going terribly fast. She let David have most of the champagne. He began to whistle *St Louis Blues.*

Driving through England in the blackout was a weird experience. One missed lights which one hadn't realized were there before the war: lights in cottage porches and farmhouse windows, lights on cathedral spires and inn signs, and – most of all – the luminous glow, low in the distant sky, of the thousand lights of a nearby town. Even if one had been able to see, there were no signposts to look at: they had been removed to confuse the German parachutists who were expected any day. (Just a few days ago in the Midlands farmers had found parachutes, radios and maps; but since there were no footprints leading away from the objects, it had been concluded that no men had landed, and the whole thing was a feeble Nazi attempt to panic the population.) Anyway, David knew the way to London.

They climbed a long hill. The little sports car took it

nimbly. Lucy gazed through half-closed eyes at the blackness ahead. The downside of the hill was steep and winding. Lucy heard the distant roar of an approaching lorry.

The MG's tyres squealed as David raced around the bends. 'I think you're going too fast,' Lucy said mildly.

The back of the car skidded on a left-hander. David changed down, afraid to brake in case he skidded again. On either side, the hedgerows were dimly picked out by the shaded headlights. There was a sharp right-hand bend, and David lost the back again. The curve seemed to go on and on forever. The little car slid sideways and turned through 180 degrees, so that it was going backwards; then continued to turn in the same direction.

Lucy screamed: 'David!'

The moon came out suddenly, and they saw the lorry. It was struggling up the hill at a snail's pace, with thick smoke, made silvery by the moonlight, pouring from its snout-shaped bonnet. Lucy glimpsed the driver's face, even his cloth cap and his moustache; his mouth was open in terror as he stood on his brakes.

The car was travelling forward again now. There was just room to pass the lorry if David could regain control of the car. He heaved the steering wheel over and touched the accelerator. It was a mistake.

The car and the lorry collided head-on.

FOUR

Foreigners have spies: Britain has Military Intelligence. As if that were not euphemism enough, it is abbreviated to MI. In 1940, MI was part of the War Office. It was spreading like couch grass at the time – not surprisingly – and its different sections were known by numbers: MI9 ran the escape routes from prisoner-of-war camps through Occupied Europe to neutral countries; MI8 monitored enemy wireless traffic, and was of more value than six regiments; MI6 sent agents into France.

It was MI5 that Professor Percival Godliman joined in the autumn of 1940. He turned up at the War Office in Whitehall on a cold September morning after a night spent putting out fires all over the East End: the Blitz was at its height and he was an Auxiliary Fireman.

Military Intelligence was run by soldiers in peacetime, when – in Godliman's opinion – espionage made no difference to anything anyhow; but now, he found, it was populated by amateurs, and he was delighted to discover that he knew half the people in MI5. On his first day he met a barrister who was a member of his club, an art historian with whom he had been to college, an archivist from his own university, and his favourite writer of detective stories.

He was shown into Colonel Terry's office at ten a.m. Terry had been there for several hours: there were two empty cigarette packets in the waste-paper bin.

Godliman said: 'Should I call you "Sir" now?'

'There's not much bull around here, Percy. "Uncle Andrew" will do fine. Sit down.'

All the same, there was a briskness about Terry which had not been present when they had lunch at the Savoy. Godliman noticed that he did not smile, and his attention kept wandering to a pile of unread signals on the desk.

Terry looked at his watch and said: 'I'm going to put you in the picture, briefly – finish the lecture I started over lunch.'

Godliman smiled. 'This time I won't get up on my high horse.'

Terry lit another cigarette.

Canaris's spies in Britain were useless people (Terry resumed, as if their conversation had been interrupted five minutes rather than three months ago). Dorothy O'Grady was typical: we caught her cutting military telephone wires on the Isle of Wight. She was writing letters to Portugal in the kind of secret ink you buy in joke shops.

A new wave of spies began in September. Their task was to reconnoitre Britain in preparation for the invasion: to map beaches suitable for landings, fields and roads which could be used by troop-carrying gliders, tank traps and road blocks and barbed-wire obstacles.

They seem to have been badly selected, hastily mustered, inadequately trained and poorly equipped. Typical were the four who came over on the night of 2–3 September: Meier, Kieboom, Pons and Waldberg. Kieboom and Pons landed at dawn near Hythe, and were arrested by Private Tollervey of the Somerset Light Infantry, who came upon them in the sand-dunes tucking in to a dirty great *wurst*.

Waldberg actually managed to send a signal to Hamburg:

> ARRIVED SAFELY. DOCUMENT DESTROYED. ENGLISH PATROL 200 METRES FROM COAST. BEACH WITH BROWN NETS AND RAILWAY SLEEPERS AT A DISTANCE OF 50 METRES. NO MINES. FEW SOLDIERS. UNFINISHED BLOCK-HOUSE. NEW ROAD. WALDBERG.

Clearly he did not know where he was, nor did he even have a code name. The quality of his briefing is indicated by the fact that he knew nothing of English licensing laws: he went into a pub at nine o'clock in the morning and asked for a quart of cider.

(Godliman laughed at this, and Terry said: 'Wait – it gets funnier.')

The landlord told Waldberg to come back at ten. He could spend the hour looking at the village church, he suggested. Amazingly, Waldberg was back at ten sharp, whereupon two policemen on bicycles arrested him.

('It's like a script for *It's That Man Again*,' said Godliman.)

Meier was found a few hours later. Eleven more

agents were picked up over the next few weeks, most of them within hours of landing on British soil. Almost all of them were destined for the scaffold.

('*Almost* all?' said Godliman. Terry said: 'Yes. A couple have been handed over to our section B-1(a). I'll come back to that in a minute.')

Others landed in Eire. One was Ernst Weber-Drohl, a well-known acrobat who had two illegitimate children in Ireland – he had toured music-halls there as 'The World's Strongest Man'. He was arrested by the Garda Siochania, fined three pounds, and turned over to B-1(a).

Another was Hermann Goetz, who parachuted into Ulster instead of Eire by mistake, was robbed by the IRA, swam the Boyne in his fur underwear, and eventually swallowed his suicide pill. He had a torch marked 'Made in Dresden'.

('If it's so easy to pick these bunglers up,' Terry said, 'why are we taking on brainy types like yourself to catch them? Two reasons. One: we've got no way of knowing how many we *haven't* picked up. Two: it's what we do with the ones we don't hang that matters. This is where B-1(a) comes in. But to explain that I have to go back to 1936.')

Alfred George Owens was an electrical engineer with a company that had a few government contracts. He visited Germany several times during the thirties, and voluntarily gave to the Admiralty odd bits of technical information he picked up there. Eventually Naval Intelligence passed him on to MI6 who began to develop him as an agent. The Abwehr recruited him at about the same time, as MI6 discovered when they intercepted a letter from him to a known German cover address. Clearly he was a man totally without loyalty: he just wanted to be a spy. We called him 'Snow'; the Germans called him 'Johnny'.

In January 1939 Snow got a letter containing (i) instructions for the use of a wireless transmitter and (ii) a ticket for the cloakroom at Victoria Station.

He was arrested the day after war broke out, and he and his transmitter (which he had picked up, in a suitcase, when he presented the cloakroom ticket) were locked up in Wandsworth Prison. He continued to communicate with Hamburg, but now all the messages were written by section B-1(a) of MI5.

The Abwehr put him in touch with two more German agents in England, whom we immediately nabbed. They also gave him a code and detailed wireless procedure, all of which was invaluable.

Snow was followed by Charlie, Rainbow, Summer, Biscuit, and eventually a small army of enemy spies, all in regular contact with Canaris, all apparently trusted by him, and all totally controlled by the British counter-intelligence apparatus.

At that point MI5 began dimly to glimpse an awe-some and tantalizing prospect: with a bit of luck, *they could control and manipulate the entire German espionage network in Britain.*

'Turning agents into double agents instead of hanging them has two crucial advantages,' Terry wound up. 'Since the enemy thinks his spies are still active, he doesn't try to replace them with others who may not get caught. And, since *we* are supplying the information the spies tell their controllers, we can deceive the enemy and mislead his strategists.'

'It can't be that easy,' said Godliman.

'Certainly not.' Terry opened a window to let out the fug of cigarette and pipe smoke. 'To work, the system has to be very nearly total. If there is any substantial number of genuine agents here, their information will contradict that of the double agents and the Abwehr will smell a rat.'

'It sounds tremendously exciting,' Godliman said. His pipe had gone out.

Terry smiled for the first time that morning. 'The people here will tell you it's hard work – long hours, high tension, frustration – but yes, of course it's exciting.' He looked at his watch. 'Now I want you to meet a very bright young member of my staff. Let me walk you to his office.'

They went out of the room, up some stairs, and along several corridors. 'His name is Frederick Bloggs, and he gets annoyed if you make jokes about it,' Terry continued. 'We pinched him from Scotland Yard – he was an inspector with Special Branch. If you need arms and legs, use his. You'll rank above him, but I shouldn't make too much of that – we don't, here. I suppose I hardly need to say that to you.'

They entered a small, bare room which looked out on to a blank wall. There was no carpet. A photograph of a pretty girl hung on the wall, and there was a pair of handcuffs on the hat-stand.

Terry said: 'Frederick Bloggs, Percival Godliman. I'll leave you to it.'

The man behind the desk was blond, stocky and short – he must have been only just tall enough to get into the police force, Godliman thought. His tie was an eyesore, but he had a pleasant, open face and an attractive grin. His handshake was firm.

He said: 'Tell you what, Percy – I was just going to nip home for lunch – why don't you come along? The wife makes a lovely sausage and chips.' He had a broad cockney accent.

Sausage and chips was not Godliman's favourite meal, but he went along. They walked to Trafalgar Square and caught a bus to Hoxton. Bloggs said: 'I married a wonderful girl, but she can't cook for nuts. I have sausage and chips every day.'

East London was still smoking from the previous night's air raid. They passed groups of firemen and volunteers digging through rubble, playing hoses over dying fires, and clearing debris from the streets. They saw an old man carry a precious radio out of a half-ruined house.

Godliman made conversation. 'So we're to catch spies together.'

'We'll have a go, Perce.'

Bloggs's home was a three-bedroom semi in a street of exactly similar houses. The tiny front gardens were all being used to grow vegetables. Mrs Bloggs was the pretty girl in the photograph on the office wall. She looked tired. Bloggs said: 'She drives an ambulance during the raids, don't you, love?' He was proud of her. Her name was Christine.

She said: 'Every morning when I come home I wonder if the house will still be here.'

'Notice it's the house she's worried about, not me,' Bloggs said.

Godliman picked up a medal in a presentation case from the mantelpiece. 'How did you get this?'

Christine answered. 'He took a shotgun off a villain who was robbing a post office.'

'You're quite a pair,' Godliman said.

'You married, Percy?' Bloggs asked.

'I'm a widower.'

'Sorry.'

'My wife died of tuberculosis in 1930. We never had any children.'

'We're not having any yet,' Bloggs said. 'Not while the world's in this state.'

Christine said: 'Oh, Fred, he's not interested in that!' She went out to the kitchen.

They sat around a square table in the centre of the room to eat. Bloggs was touched by this couple and the domestic scene, and found himself thinking of his Eleanor. That was unusual: he had been immune to sentiment for some years. Perhaps the nerves were coming alive again, at last. War did funny things.

Christine's cooking was truly awful. The sausages were burned. Bloggs drowned his meal in tomato ketchup, and Godliman cheerfully followed suit.

When they got back to Whitehall Bloggs showed Godliman the file on unidentified enemy agents still thought to be operating in Britain.

There were three sources of information about such

people. The first was the immigration records of the Home Office. Passport control had long been an arm of Military Intelligence, and there was a list – going back to the last war – of aliens who had entered the country but had not left or been accounted for in other ways, such as death or naturalization. At the outbreak of war they had all gone before tribunals which classified them in three groups. At first only 'A' class aliens were interned; but by July of 1940, after some scaremongering by Fleet Street, the 'B' and 'C' classes were taken out of circulation. There was a small number of immigrants who could not be located, and it was a fair assumption that some of them were spies.

Their papers were in Bloggs's file.

The second source was wireless transmissions. Section C of MI8 scanned the airwaves nightly, recorded everything they did not know for certain to be ours, and passed it to the Government Code and Cypher School. This outfit, which had recently been moved from London's Berkeley Street to a country house at Bletchley Park, was not a school at all but a collection of chess champions, musicians, mathematicians and crossword-puzzle enthusiasts dedicated to the belief that if a man could invent a code a man could crack it. Signals originating in the UK which could not be accounted for by any of the Services were assumed to be messages from spies.

The decoded messages were in Bloggs's file.

Finally there were the double agents; but their value was largely hoped-for rather than actual. Messages to them from the Abwehr had warned of several incoming agents, and had given away one resident spy – Mrs Matilda Krafft of Bournemouth, who had sent money to Snow by post and was subsequently incarcerated in Holloway prison. But the doubles had not been able to reveal the identity or location of the kind of quietly effective professional spies who are most valuable to a secret intelligence service. No one doubted that there were such people. There were clues: someone, for example, had brought Snow's transmitter over from Germany and deposited it in the cloakroom at Victoria Station for him to collect. But either the Abwehr or the spies themselves were too cautious to be caught by the doubles.

However, the clues were in Bloggs's file.

Other sources were being developed: the boffins were working to improve methods of triangulation (the directional pin-pointing of radio transmitters); and MI6 were trying to rebuild the networks of agents in Europe which had sunk beneath the tidal wave of Hitler's armies.

What little information there was, was in Bloggs's file.

'It can be infuriating at times,' he told Godliman. 'Look at this.'

He took from the file a long radio intercept about British plans for an expeditionary force for Finland. 'This was picked up early in the year. The information is impeccable. They were trying to get a fix on him when he broke off in the middle, for no apparent reason – perhaps he was interrupted. He resumed a few minutes later, but he was off the air again before our boys had a chance to plug in.'

Godliman said: 'What's this – "Regards to Willi"?'

'Now, that's important,' said Bloggs. He was getting enthusiastic. 'Here's a scrap of another message, quite recent. Look – "Regards to Willi". This time there was a reply. He's addressed as "Die Nadel".'

'The Needle.'

'This bloke's a pro. Look at his messages: terse, economical, but detailed and completely unambiguous.'

Godliman studied the fragment of the second message. 'It appears to be about the effects of the bombing.'

'He's obviously toured the East End. A pro, a pro.'

'What else do we know about Die Nadel?'

Bloggs's expression of youthful eagerness collapsed comically. 'That's it, I'm afraid.'

'His code name is Die Nadel, he signs off "Regards to Willi", and he has good information – and that's it?'

' 'Fraid so.'

Godliman sat on the edge of the desk and stared out of the window. On the wall of the opposite building, underneath an ornate windowsill, he could see the nest of a house-marten. 'On that basis, what chance have we of catching him?'

Bloggs shrugged. 'On that basis, none at all.'

FIVE

It is for places like this that the word 'bleak' has been invented.

The island is a J-shaped lump of rock rising sullenly out of the North Sea. It lies on the map like the top half of a broken walking-stick; parallel with the equator but a long, long way north; its curved handle toward Aberdeen, its broken, jagged stump pointing threateningly at distant Denmark. It is ten miles long.

Around most of its coast the cliffs rise out of the cold sea without the courtesy of a beach. Angered by this rudeness the waves pound on the rock in impotent rage; a ten-thousand-year fit of bad temper which the island ignores with impunity.

In the cup of the J the sea is calmer, for there it has provided itself with a more pleasant reception. Its tides have thrown into that cup so much sand and seaweed, driftwood and pebbles and seashells, that there is now, between the foot of the cliff and the water's edge, a crescent of something closely resembling dry land, a more-or-less beach.

Each summer the vegetation at the top of the cliff drops a handful of seeds on to the beach, the way a rich man throws loose change to beggars. If the winter is mild and the spring comes early, a few of the seeds take feeble root; but they are never healthy enough to flower themselves and spread their own seeds, so the beach exists from year to year on handouts.

On the land itself, the proper land, held out of the sea's reach by the cliffs, green things do grow and multiply. The vegetation is mostly coarse grass, only just good enough to nourish the few bony sheep, but tough enough to bind the topsoil to the island's bedrock. There are some bushes, all thorny, which provide homes for rabbits; and a brave stand of conifers on the leeward slope of the hill at the eastern end.

The higher land is ruled by heather. Every few years the man – yes, there is a man here – the man sets fire to the heather, and then the grass will grow and the sheep can graze here too; but after a couple of years the heather comes back, God knows from where, and drives the sheep away until the man burns it again.

The rabbits are here because they were born here; the sheep are here because they were brought here; and the man is here to look after the sheep; but the birds are here because they like it. There are hundreds of thousands of them: long-legged rock pipits whistling *peep peep peep* as they soar and *pe-pe-pe-pe* as they dive like a Spitfire coming at a Messerschmitt out of the sun; corncrakes, which the man rarely sees, but he knows they are there because their bark keeps him awake at night; ravens and carrion crows and kittiwakes and *countless* gulls; and a pair of golden eagles which the man shoots at when he sees them, for he *knows* – regardless of what naturalists and experts from Edinburgh may tell him – that they *do* prey upon live lambs and not just the carcases of those already dead.

The island's most constant visitor is the wind. It comes mostly from the north-east, from *really* cold places where there are fiords and glaciers and icebergs; often bringing with it unwelcome gifts of snow and driving rain and cold, cold mist; sometimes arriving empty-handed, just to howl and whoop and raise hell, tearing up bushes and bending trees and whipping the intemperate ocean into fresh paroxysms of foam-flecked rage. It is tireless, this wind; and that is its mistake. If it came occasionally it could take the island by surprise and do some real damage; but because it is almost always here, the island has learned to live with it. The plants put down deep roots, and the rabbits hide far inside the thickets, and the trees grow up with their backs ready-bent for the flogging, and the birds nest on sheltered ledges, and the man's house is sturdy and squat, built with a craftsmanship that knows this wind of old.

This house is made of big grey stones and grey slates, the colour of the sea. It has small windows and close-fitting doors and a chimney in its pine end. It stands at the top of the hill at the eastern end of the island, close to the splintered stub of the broken walking-stick. It crowns the hill, defying the wind and the rain, not out of bravado but so that the man can see the sheep.

There is another house, very similar, ten miles away at the opposite end of the island near the more-or-less beach; but nobody lives there. There was once another man. He thought he knew better than the island; he thought he could grow oats and potatoes and keep a few cows. He battled for three years with the wind and the cold and the soil before he admitted he was wrong. When he had gone, nobody wanted his home.

This is a hard place. Only hard things survive here: hard rock, coarse grass, tough sheep, savage birds, sturdy houses and strong men. Hard things and cold things, and cruel and bitter and pointed things, rugged and slow-moving and determined things; things as cold and hard and ruthless as the island itself.

It is for places like this that the word 'bleak' has been invented.

'It's called Storm Island,' said Alfred Rose. 'I think you're going to like it.'

David and Lucy Rose sat in the prow of the fishing-boat and looked across the choppy water. It was a fine November day, cold and breezy yet clear and dry. A weak sun sparkled off the wavelets.

'I bought it in 1926,' Papa Rose continued, 'when we thought there was going to be a revolution and we'd need somewhere to hide from the working class. It's just the place for a convalescence.'

Lucy thought he was being suspiciously hearty, but she had to admit it looked lovely: all windblown and natural and fresh. And it made sense, this move. They had to get away from their parents and make a new start at being married; and there was no point in moving to a city to be bombed, when neither of them was really well enough to help; and then David's father had revealed that he owned an island off the coast of Scotland, and it seemed too good to be true.

'I own the sheep, too,' Papa Rose said. 'Shearers come over from the mainland each spring, and the wool brings in just about enough money to pay Tom McAvity's wages. Old Tom's the shepherd.'

'How old is he?' Lucy asked.

'Good Lord, he must be – oh, seventy?'

'I suppose he's eccentric.' The boat turned into the bay, and Lucy could see two small figures on the jetty: a man and a dog.

'Eccentric? No more than you'd be if you'd lived alone for twenty years. He talks to his dog.'

Lucy turned to the skipper of the small boat. 'How often do you call?'

'Once a fortnight, missus. I bring Tom's shopping, which isna much, and his mail, which is even less. You just give me your list, every other Monday, and if it can be bought in Aberdeen I'll bring it.'

He cut the motor and threw a rope to Tom. The dog barked and ran around in circles, beside himself with excitement. Lucy put one foot on the gunwale and sprang out on to the jetty.

Tom took her hand. He had a face of leather and a huge briar pipe with a lid. He was shorter than she, but wide, and he looked ridiculously healthy. He wore the hairiest tweed jacket she had ever seen, with a knitted sweater that must have been made by an elderly sister somewhere, plus a checked cap and army boots. His nose was huge, red and veined. 'Pleased to meet you,' he said politely, as if she was his ninth visitor today instead of the first human face he had seen in fourteen days.

'Here y'are, Tom,' said the skipper. He handed two cardboard boxes out of the boat. 'No eggs this time, but here's a letter from Devon.'

'It'll be from ma niece.'

Lucy thought: That explains the sweater.

David was still in the boat. The skipper stood behind him and said: 'Are you ready?'

Tom and Papa Rose leaned into the boat to assist, and the three of them lifted David in his wheelchair on to the jetty.

'If I don't go now I'll have to wait a fortnight for the next bus,' Papa Rose said with a smile. 'The house has been done up quite nicely, you'll see. All your stuff is in there. Tom will show you where everything is.' He kissed Lucy, squeezed David's shoulder, and shook Tom's hand. 'Have a few months of rest and togetherness, get completely fit, then come back: there are important war jobs for both of you.'

They would not be going back, Lucy knew; not before the end of the war: but she had not told anyone about that yet.

Papa got back into the boat. It wheeled away in a tight circle. Lucy waved until it disappeared around the headland.

Tom pushed the wheelchair, so Lucy took his groceries. Between the landward end of the jetty and the cliff top was a long, steep, narrow ramp rising high above the beach like a bridge. Lucy would have had trouble getting the wheelchair to the top, but Tom managed without apparent exertion.

The cottage was perfect.

It was small and grey, and sheltered from the wind by a little rise in the ground. All the woodwork was freshly painted, and a wild rose bush grew beside the doorstep. Curls of smoke rose from the chimney to be whipped away by the breeze. The tiny windows looked over the bay.

Lucy said: 'I love it!'

The interior had been cleaned and aired and painted, and there were thick rugs on the stone floors. It had four rooms: downstairs, a modernized kitchen and a living-room with a stone fireplace; upstairs, two bedrooms. One end of the house had been carefully remodelled to take modern plumbing, with a bathroom above and a kitchen extension below.

Their clothes were in the wardrobes. There were towels in the bathroom and food in the kitchen.

Tom said: 'There's something in the barn I've to show you.'

It was a shed, not a barn. It lay hidden behind the cottage, and inside it was a gleaming new jeep.

'Mr Rose says it's been specially adapted for young Mr Rose to drive,' Tom said. 'It's got automatic gears, and the throttle and brake are operated by hand. That's what he said.' He seemed to be repeating the words parrot-fashion, as if he had very little idea of what gears, brakes and throttles might be.

Lucy said: 'Isn't that super, David?'

'Top-hole. But where shall I go in it?'

Tom said: 'You're always welcome to visit me and share a pipe and a drop of whisky. I've been looking forward to having neighbours again.'

'Thank you,' said Lucy.

'This here's the generator,' Tom said, turning around and pointing. 'I've got one just the same. You put the fuel in here. It delivers alternating current.'

David said: 'That's unusual – small generators are usually direct current.'

'Aye. I don't really know the difference, but they tell me this is safer.'

'True. A shock from this would throw you across the room, but direct current would kill you.'

They went back to the cottage. Tom said: 'Well, you'll want to settle in, and I've sheep to tend, so I'll say good-day. Oh! I ought to tell you: in an emergency, I can contact the mainland by wireless radio.'

David was surprised. 'You've got a radio transmitter?'

'Aye,' Tom said proudly. 'I'm an enemy aircraft spotter in the Royal Observer Corps.'

'Ever spotted any?' David asked.

Lucy flashed her disapproval of the sarcasm in David's voice, but Tom seemed not to notice. 'Not yet,' he replied.

David said: 'Jolly good show.'

When Tom had gone Lucy said: 'He only wants to do his bit.'

'There are lots of us who *want* to do our bit,' David said bitterly. And that, Lucy reflected, was the trouble.

She dropped the subject, and wheeled her crippled husband into their new home.

When Lucy had been asked to visit the hospital psychologist, she had immediately assumed that David had brain damage. It was not so. 'All that's wrong with his head is a nasty bruise on the left temple,' the psychologist said. She went on: 'However, the loss of both his legs brings about a trauma, and there's no telling how it will affect his state of mind. Did he want very much to be a pilot?'

Lucy pondered. 'He was afraid, but I think he wanted it very badly, all the same.'

'Well, he'll need all the reassurance and support that you can give him. And patience, too: one thing we can predict is that he will be resentful and ill-tempered for a while. He needs love and rest.'

However, during their first few months on the island he seemed to want neither. He did not make love to her, perhaps because he was waiting until his injuries were fully healed. But he did not rest, either. He threw himself into the business of sheep farming, tearing about the island in his jeep with the wheelchair in the back. He built fences along the more treacherous cliffs, shot at the eagles, helped Tom train a new dog when Betsy began to go blind, and burned-off the heather; and in the spring he was out every night delivering lambs. One day he felled a great old pine tree near Tom's cottage, and spent a fortnight stripping it, hewing it into manageable logs, and carting them back to the house for firewood. He relished really hard manual labour. He learned to strap himself tightly to the chair to keep his body anchored while he wielded an axe or a mallet. He carved a pair of Indian clubs and exercised with them for hours when Tom could find nothing more for him to do. The muscles of his arms and back became grotesque, like those of men who win body-building contests.

He refused point-blank to wash dishes, cook food or clean the house.

Lucy was not unhappy. She had been afraid he might sit by the fire all day and brood over his bad luck. The way he worked was faintly worrying because it was so obsessive, but at least he was not vegetating.

She told him about the baby at Christmas.

In the morning she gave him a petrol-driven saw, and he gave her a bolt of silk. Tom came over for dinner, and they ate a wild goose he had shot. David drove the shepherd home after tea, and when he came back Lucy opened a bottle of brandy.

Then she said: 'I have another present for you, but you can't open it until May.'

He laughed. 'What on earth are you talking about? How much of that brandy did you drink while I was out?'

'I'm having a baby.'

He stared at her, and all the laughter went out of his face. 'Good God, that's all we bloody well need.'

'David!'

'Well, for God's sake . . . When the hell did it happen?'

'That's not too difficult to figure out, is it?' she said bitterly. 'It must have been a week before the wedding. It's a miracle it survived the crash.'

'Have you seen a doctor?'

'Huh – when?'

'So how do you know for sure?'

'Oh, David, don't be so boring. I know for sure because my periods have stopped and my nipples hurt and I throw up in the mornings and my waist is four inches bigger than it used to be. If you ever *looked* at me *you* would know for sure.'

'All right.'

'What's the matter with you? You're supposed to be thrilled!'

'Oh, sure. Perhaps we'll have a son, and then I can take him for walks and play football with him, and he'll grow up wanting to be like his father the war hero, a legless fucking joke!'

'Oh, David, David,' she whispered. She knelt in front of his wheelchair. 'David, don't think like that. He will respect you. He'll look up to you because you put your life together again, and because you can do the work of two men from your wheelchair, and because you carried your disability with courage and cheerfulness.'

'Don't be so damned condescending,' he snapped. 'You sound like a sanctimonious priest.'

She stood up. 'Well, don't act as if it's my fault. Men can take precautions too, you know.'

'You can't take precautions against invisible lorries in the blackout!'

That was a silly, feeble excuse, and they both knew it, so Lucy said nothing. The whole idea of Christmas seemed utterly trite now: the bits of coloured paper on the walls, and the tree in the corner, and the remains of a goose in the kitchen waiting to be thrown away – none of it had anything to do with her life. She began to wonder what she was doing on this bleak island with a man who seemed not to love her, having a baby he didn't want. Why shouldn't she – why not – well, she could . . . Then she realized she had nowhere else to go, nothing else to do with her life, nobody else to *be* other than Mrs David Rose.

Eventually David said: 'Well, I'm going to bed.' He wheeled himself to the hall and dragged himself out of the chair and up the stairs backwards. She heard him scrape across the floor, heard the bed creak as he hauled himself on to it, heard his clothes hit the corner of the room as he undressed, then heard the final groaning of the springs as he lay down and pulled the blankets up over his pyjamas.

And still she would not cry.

She looked at the brandy bottle and thought: If I drink all of this now, and have a bath, perhaps I won't be pregnant in the morning.

She thought about it for a long time, until she came to the conclusion that life without David and the island and the baby would be even worse because it would be empty.

So she did not cry, and she did not drink the brandy,

and she did not leave the island; but instead she went upstairs and got into bed, and lay awake beside her sleeping husband, listening to the wind and trying not to think, until the gulls began to call, and a grey rainy dawn crept over the North Sea and filled the little bedroom with a cold, cheerless, silver light, and then at last she went to sleep.

A kind of peace settled over her in the spring, as if all threats were postponed until after the baby was born. When the February snow had thawed she planted flowers and vegetables in the patch of ground between the kitchen door and the barn, not really believing they would grow. She cleaned the house thoroughly and told David that if he wanted it done again before August he would have to do it himself. She wrote to her mother and did a lot of knitting and ordered nappies by post. They suggested she go home to have the baby, but she knew that if she went she would never come back. She went for long walks over the moors, with a bird book under her arm, until her own weight became too much for her to carry very far. She kept the bottle of brandy in a cupboard David never used, and whenever she felt depressed she went to look at it and remind herself of what she had almost lost.

Three weeks before the baby was due, she got the boat into Aberdeen. David and Tom waved from the jetty. The sea was so rough that both she and the skipper were terrified she might give birth before they reached the mainland. She went into hospital in Aberdeen, and four weeks later brought the baby home on the same boat.

David knew none of it. He probably thought that women gave birth as easily as ewes. He was oblivious to the pain of contractions, and that awful, impossible stretching, and the soreness afterwards, and the bossy, know-all nurses who didn't want you to *touch* your baby because you weren't brisk and efficient and trained and *sterile* like they were; he just saw you go away pregnant and come back with a beautiful, white-wrapped, healthy baby boy and said: 'We'll call him Jonathan.'

They added Alfred for David's father, and Malcolm for Lucy's, and Thomas for old Tom, but they called the boy Jo, because he was too tiny for Jonathan, let alone Jonathan Alfred Malcolm Thomas Rose. David learned to give him his bottle and burp him and change his nappy, and he even dandled him in his lap occasionally, but his interest was distant, uninvolved. He had a problem-solving approach, like the nurses; it was not for him as it was for Lucy. Tom was closer to the baby than David. Lucy would not let him smoke in the room where the baby was, and the old boy would put his great briar pipe with the lid in his pocket for hours and gurgle at little Jo, or watch him kick his feet, or help Lucy bath him. Lucy suggested mildly that he might be neglecting the sheep. Tom said they did not need him to watch them feed – he would rather watch Jo feed. He carved a rattle out of driftwood and filled it with small round pebbles, and was overjoyed when Jo grabbed it and shook it, first time, without having to be shown how.

And still David and Lucy did not make love.

First there had been his injuries, and then she had been pregnant, and then she had been recovering from childbirth; but now the reasons had run out.

One night she said: 'I'm back to normal, now.'

'How do you mean?'

'After the baby. My body is normal. I've healed.'

'Oh, I see. That's good.' And he turned away.

She made sure to go up to bed with him so that he could watch her undress, but he always turned his back.

As they lay there, dozing off, she would move so that her hand, or her thigh, or her breast, brushed against him, a casual but unmistakable invitation. There was no response.

She believed firmly that there was nothing wrong with her. She wasn't a nymphomaniac: she didn't simply want sex, she wanted sex with David. She was sure that, even if there had been another man under seventy on the island, she would not have been tempted. She wasn't a sex-starved tart, she was a love-starved wife.

The crunch came on one of those nights when they lay on their backs, side by side, both wide awake, listening to the wind outside and the small sounds of Jo from the next room. It seemed to Lucy that it was time he either did it or came right out and said why not; and that he was going to avoid the issue until she forced it; and that she might as well force it now as live in miserable incomprehension any longer.

So she brushed her arm across his thighs and opened her mouth to speak – and almost cried out with shock to discover that he had an erection. So he could do it!

And he wanted to, or why else – And her hand closed triumphantly around the evidence of his desire, and she shifted closer to him, and sighed: 'David—'

He said: 'Oh, for God's sake!' He gripped her wrist and thrust her hand away from him and turned on to his side.

But this time she was not going to accept his rebuff in modest silence. She said: 'David, why not?'

'Jesus, Christ!' He threw the blankets off, swung himself to the floor, grabbed the eiderdown with one hand, and dragged himself to the door.

Lucy sat up in bed and screamed at him: 'Why not?'

Jo began to cry.

David pulled up the empty legs of his cut-off pyjama trousers, pointed to the pursed white skin of his stumps, and said: 'That's why not! That's why not!'

He slithered downstairs to sleep on the sofa, and Lucy went into the next bedroom to comfort Jo.

It took a long time to lull him back to sleep, probably because she herself was so much in need of comfort. The baby tasted the tears on her cheeks, and she wondered if he had any inkling of their meaning: wouldn't tears be one of the first things a baby came to understand? She could not bring herself to sing to him, nor could she with any sincerity murmur that everything was all right; so she held him tight and rocked him, and when *he* had soothed *her* with his warmth and his clinging, he went to sleep in her arms.

She put him back in the cot and stood looking at him for a while. There was no point in going back to bed. She could hear David's deep-sleep snoring from the living-room – he had to take powerful pills, otherwise the old pain kept him awake. Lucy needed to get right away from him, where she could neither see nor hear him, where he couldn't find her for a few hours even if he wanted to. She put on trousers and a sweater, a heavy coat and boots, and crept downstairs and out into the night.

There was a swirling mist, damp and bitterly cold, the kind the island specialized in. She put up the collar of her coat, thought about going back inside for a scarf, and decided not to. She squelched along the muddy path, welcoming the bite of the fog in her throat, the small discomfort of the weather taking her mind off the larger hurt inside her.

She reached the cliff top and walked gingerly down the steep, narrow ramp, placing her feet carefully on the slippery boards. At the bottom she jumped off on to the sand and walked to the edge of the sea.

The wind and the water were carrying on their perpetual quarrel, the wind swooping down to tease the waves and the sea hissing and spitting as it crashed against the land, the two of them doomed to bicker forever because neither could be calm while the other was there, but neither had any place else to go.

Lucy walked along the hard sand, letting the noise and the weather fill her head, until the beach ended in a sharp point where the water met the cliff, when she turned and walked back. She paced the shore all night. Toward dawn a thought came to her, unbidden: It is his way of being strong.

As it was, the thought was not much help, holding its

meaning in a tightly clenched fist. But she worked on it for a while, and the fist opened to reveal what looked like a small pearl of wisdom nestling in its palm: for perhaps David's coldness to her was of one piece with his chopping down trees, and undressing himself, and driving the jeep, and throwing the Indian clubs, and coming to live on a cold cruel island in the North Sea . . .

What was it he had said? '. . . his father the war hero, a legless joke . . .' He had something to prove, something that would sound trite if it were put into words; something he could have done as a fighter pilot, but now had to do with trees and fences and Indian clubs and a wheelchair. They wouldn't let him take the test, and he wanted to be able to say: 'I could have passed it anyway, just *look* how I can suffer.'

It was cruelly, hopelessly, screamingly unjust: he had had the courage, and he had suffered the wounds, but he could take no pride in it. If a Messerschmitt had taken his legs the wheelchair would have been like a medal, a badge of courage. But now, all his life, he would have to say: 'It was during the war – but no, I never saw any action, this was a car crash, I did my training and I was going to fight, the very next day, I had seen my kite, she was a beauty, and I *would* have been brave, I know . . .'

Yes, it was his way of being strong. And perhaps she could be strong, too. She might find ways of patching up the wreck of her life so that it would sail again. David had once been good and kind and loving, and she might now learn to wait patiently while he battled to become the complete man he used to be. She could find new hopes, new things to live for. Other women had found the strength to cope with bereavement, and bombed-out houses, and husbands in prisoner-of-war camps.

She picked up a pebble, drew back her arm, and threw it out to sea with all her might. She did not see or hear it land: it might have gone on forever, circling the earth like a satellite in a space story.

She shouted: 'I can be strong, too!'

Then she turned around and started up the ramp to the cottage. It was almost time for Jo's first feed.

SIX

It looked like a mansion; and, up to a point, that was what it was: a large house, in its own grounds, in the leafy town of Wohldorf just outside North Hamburg. It might have been the home of a mine owner, or a successful importer, or an industrialist. It was in fact owned by the Abwehr.

It owed its fate to the weather – not here, but two hundred miles south-east in Berlin, where atmospheric conditions were unsuitable for wireless communication with England.

It was a mansion only down to ground level. Below that were two huge concrete shelters and several million Reichsmarks worth of radio equipment. The electronics system had been put together by one Major Werner Trautmann, and he did a good job. Each hall had twenty neat little soundproofed listening posts, occupied by radio operators who could recognize a spy by the way he tapped out his message, as easily as you can recognize your mother's handwriting on an envelope.

The receiving equipment was built with quality in mind, for the transmitters that were sending the messages had been designed for compactness rather than power. Most of them were the little suitcase sets called Klamotten which had been developed by Telefunken for Admiral Wilhelm Canaris, the head of the Abwehr.

On this night the airwaves were relatively quiet, so everyone knew when Die Nadel came through. The message was taken by one of the older operators. He tapped out an acknowledgement, transcribed the signal quickly, tore the sheet off his notepad and went to the phone. He read the message over the direct line to Abwehr headquarters at Sophien Terrace in Hamburg, then he came back to his booth for a smoke.

He offered a cigarette to the youngster in the next booth, and the two of them stood together for a few minutes, leaning against the wall and smoking.

The youngster said: 'Anything?'

The older man shrugged. 'There's always *something* when he calls. But not much, this time. The Luftwaffe missed St Paul's Cathedral again.'

'No reply for him?'

'We don't think he waits for replies. He's an independent bastard, that one. Always was. I trained him in wireless, you know: and once I'd finished he thought he knew it better than me.'

The youngster was awestruck. 'You've *met* Die Nadel?'

'Oh, yes,' said the old-timer, flicking ash.

'What's he like?'

'As a drinking companion, he's about as much fun as a dead fish. I think he likes women, on the quiet, but as for sinking a few steins with the boys – forget it. All the same, he's the best agent we've got.'

'Really?'

'Definitely. Some say the best spy ever. There's a story that he spent five years working his way up in the NKVD in Russia, and ended up one of Stalin's most trusted aides . . . I don't know whether it's true, but it's the kind of thing he'd do. A real pro. And the Führer knows it.'

'Hitler knows him?'

The older man nodded. 'At one time he wanted to see all Die Nadel's signals. I don't know if he still does. Not that it would make any difference to Die Nadel. Nothing impresses that man. You know something? He looks at everybody the same way: as if he's figuring out how he'll kill you if you make a wrong move.'

'I'm glad I didn't have to train him.'

'He learned quickly, I'll give him that.'

'Good pupil?'

'The best. He worked at it twenty-four hours a day, then when he'd mastered it, he wouldn't give me a good morning. It takes him all his time to remember to salute Canaris.'

'*Ach du meine Scheisse.*'

'Oh, yes. Didn't you know – he always signs off "Regards to Willi". That's how much he cares about rank.'

'No. Regards to Willi? *Ach du meine Scheisse.*'

They finished their cigarettes, dropped them on the floor, and trod them out. Then the older man picked up the stubs and pocketed them, because smoking was not really permitted in the dugout. The radios were still quiet.

'Yes, he won't use his code name,' the older man went on. 'Von Braun gave it to him, and he's never liked it. He's never liked Von Braun either. Do you remember the time – no, it was before you joined us – Braun told Nadel to go to the airfield in Farnborough, Kent. The message came back, quick as a flash: "There is no airfield at Farnborough, Kent. There is one at Farnborough, Hampshire. Fortunately the Luftwaffe's geography is better than yours, you cunt." Just like that.'

'I suppose it's understandable. When we make mistakes we put their lives at risk.'

The older man frowned. He was the one who delivered such judgements, and he did not like his audience to weigh in with opinions of its own. 'Perhaps,' he said grudgingly.

The youngster reverted to his original wide-eyed role. 'Why doesn't he like his code name?'

'He says it has a meaning, and a code word with a meaning can give a man away. Von Braun wouldn't listen.'

'A meaning? The Needle? What does it mean?'

But at that moment the old-timer's radio chirped, and he returned quickly to his station; so the youngster never did find out.

PART TWO

SEVEN

The message annoyed Faber, because it forced him to face issues which he had been avoiding.

Hamburg had made damn sure the message reached him. He had given his call-sign, and instead of the usual 'Acknowledge – proceed' they had sent back 'Make rendezvous one'.

He acknowledged the order, transmitted his report, and packed the wireless set back into its suitcase. Then he wheeled his bicycle out of Erith Marshes – his cover was that of a bird-watcher – and he got on the road to Blackheath. As he cycled back to his cramped two-room flatlet, he wondered whether to obey the order.

He had two reasons for disobedience: one professional, one personal.

The professional reason was that 'rendezvous one' was an old code, set up by Canaris back in 1937. It meant he was to go to the doorway of a certain shop between Leicester Square and Piccadilly Circus to meet another agent. The agents would recognize each other by the fact that they both carried a Bible. Then there was a patter:

'What is today's chapter?'

'One Kings thirteen.'

Then, if they were certain they were not being followed, they would agree that the chapter was 'most inspiring'. Otherwise one would say: 'I'm afraid I haven't read it yet.'

The shop doorway might not be there any more, but it was not that which troubled Faber. He thought Canaris had probably given the code to most of the bumbling amateurs who had crossed the Channel in 1940 and landed in the arms of MI5. Faber knew they had been caught because the hangings had been publicized, no doubt to reassure the public that something was being done about Fifth Columnists. They would certainly have given away secrets before they died, so the British now probably knew the old rendezvous code. If they had picked up the message from Hamburg, that shop doorway must by now be swarming with well-spoken young Englishmen carrying Bibles and practising saying 'Most inspiring' in a German accent.

The Abwehr had thrown professionalism to the wind, back in those heady days when the invasion seemed so close. Faber had not trusted Hamburg since. He would not tell them where he lived, he refused to communicate with their other agents in Britain, he varied the frequency he used for transmission without caring whether he trod all over someone else's signal.

If he had always obeyed his masters, he would not have survived so long.

At Woolwich Faber was joined by a mass of other cyclists, many of them women, as the workers came streaming out of the munitions factory at the end of the day shift. Their cheerful weariness reminded Faber of his personal reason for disobedience: he thought his side was losing the war.

They certainly were not winning. The Russians and the Americans had joined in, Africa was lost, the Italians had collapsed; the Allies must invade France this year, 1944.

Faber did not want to risk his life to no purpose.

He arrived home and put his bicycle away. While he was washing his face it dawned on him that, against all logic, he *wanted* to make the rendezvous.

It was a foolish risk, taken in a lost cause, but he was itching to get to it. And the simple reason was that he was unspeakably bored. The routine transmissions, the bird-watching, the bicycle, the boarding-house teas: it was four years since he had experienced anything remotely like action. He seemed to be in no danger whatsoever, and that made him jumpy, because he imagined invisible perils. He was happiest when every so often he could identify a threat and take steps to neutralize it.

Yes, he would make the rendezvous. But not in the way they expected.

There were still crowds in the West End of London, despite the war; Faber wondered whether it was the same in Berlin. He bought a Bible at Hatchard's bookshop in Piccadilly, and stuffed it into his inside coat pocket, out of sight. It was a mild, damp day, with intermittent drizzle, and Faber was carrying an umbrella.

This rendezvous was timed for either between nine and ten o'clock in the morning or between five and six in the afternoon, and the arrangement was that one went there every day until the other party turned up. If no contact was made for five successive days one went there on alternate days for a fortnight. After that one gave up.

Faber got to Leicester Square at ten past nine. The contact was there, in the tobacconist's doorway, with a blackbound Bible under his arm, pretending to shelter from the rain. Faber spotted him out of the corner of his eye and hurried past, head down. The man was youngish, with a blond moustache and a well-fed look. He wore a black double-breasted showerproof coat, and he was reading the *Daily Express* and chewing gum. He was not familiar.

When Faber walked by the second time on the opposite side of the street, he spotted the tail. A short, stocky man wearing the trench coat and trilby hat beloved of English plain-clothes policemen was standing just inside the foyer of an office building, looking through the glass doors across the street to the spy in the doorway.

There were two possibilities. If the agent did not know he had been rumbled, Faber had only to get him away from the rendezvous and lose the tail. However, the alternative was that the agent had been captured and the man in the doorway was a substitute, in which case neither he nor the tail must be allowed to see Faber's face.

Faber assumed the worst, then thought of a way to deal with it.

There was a telephone kiosk in the Square. Faber went inside and memorized the number. Then he found I Kings 13 in the Bible, tore out the page, and scribbled in the margin: 'Go to the phone box in the Square.'

He walked around the back streets behind the National Gallery until he found a small boy, aged about ten or eleven, sitting on a doorstep throwing stones at puddles.

Faber said: 'Do you know the tobacconist in the Square?'

The boy said: 'Yerst.'

'Do you like chewing-gum?'

'Yerst.'

Faber gave him the page torn from the Bible. 'There's a man in the doorway of the tobacconist's. If you give him this he'll give you some gum.'

'All right,' the boy said. He stood up. 'Is this geezer a Yank?'

Faber said: 'Yerst.'

The boy ran off. Faber followed him. As the boy approached the agent, Faber ducked into the doorway of the building opposite. The tail was still there, peering through the glass. Faber stood just outside the door, blocking the tail's view of the scene across the street, and opened his umbrella. He pretended to be struggling with it. He saw the agent give something to the boy and walk off. He ended his charade with the umbrella, and walked in the direction opposite to the way the agent had gone. He looked back over his shoulder to see the tail run into the street, looking for the vanished agent.

Faber stopped at the nearest call box and dialled the number of the kiosk in the Square. It took a few minutes to get through. At last a deep voice said: 'Hello?'

Faber said: 'What is today's chapter?'

'One Kings thirteen.'

'Most inspiring.'

'Yes, isn't it.'

The fool has no idea of the trouble he's in, Faber thought. Aloud he said: 'Well?'

'I must see you.'

'That is impossible.'

'But I must!' There was a note in the voice which Faber thought close to despair. 'The message comes from the very top – do you understand?'

Faber pretended to waver. 'All right, then. I will meet you in one week's time under the arch at Euston Station at nine a.m.'

'Can't you make it sooner?'

Faber hung up and stepped outside. Walking quickly, he rounded two corners and came within sight of the phone box in the Square. He saw the agent walking in the direction of Piccadilly. There was no sign of the tail. Faber followed the agent.

The man went into Piccadilly Circus underground station and bought a ticket to Stockwell. Faber immediately realized he could get there by a more direct route. He came out of the station, walked quickly to Leicester

Square, and got on a Northern Line train. The agent would have to change trains at Waterloo, whereas Faber's train was direct; so Faber would reach Stockwell first, or at the worst they would arrive on the same train.

In fact Faber had to wait outside the station at Stockwell for twenty-five minutes before the agent emerged. Faber followed him again. He went into a café.

There was absolutely nowhere nearby where a man could plausibly stand still for any length of time: no shop windows to gaze into, no benches to sit on or parks to walk around, no bus stops or taxi ranks or public buildings. It was a dreary, blank suburb. Faber had to walk up and down the street, always looking as if he were going somewhere, carrying on until he was just out of sight of the café then returning on the opposite side, while the agent sat in the warm, steamy café drinking tea and eating hot toast.

He came out after half an hour. Faber tailed him through a succession of residential streets. The agent knew where he was going, but was in no hurry: he walked like a man who is going home with nothing to do for the rest of the day. He did not look back, and Faber thought: Another amateur.

At last he went into a house – one of the poor, anonymous, inconspicuous lodging-houses used by spies everywhere. It had a dormer window in the roof: that would be the agent's room, high up for better wireless reception.

Faber walked past, scanning the opposite side of the

street. Yes – there. A movement behind an upstairs window, a glimpse of a jacket and tie, a watching face withdrawn: the opposition was here too. The agent must have gone to the rendezvous yesterday and allowed himself to be followed home by MI5 – unless, of course, he *was* MI5.

Faber turned the corner and walked down the next parallel street, counting the houses. Almost directly behind the place the agent had entered there was the bomb-damaged shell of what had been a pair of semi-detached houses. Good.

As he walked back to the station he felt a buzz of excitement. His step was springier, his heart beat a shade faster, and he looked around him with bright-eyed interest. It was good. The game was on.

He dressed in black that night: a woollen hat, a roll-neck sweater under a short leather flying jacket, trousers tucked into socks, rubber-soled shoes; all black. He would be almost invisible, for London, too, was blacked out.

He cycled through the quiet streets with dimmed lights, keeping off main roads. It was after midnight, and he saw no one. He left the bike a quarter of a mile away from his destination, padlocking it to the fence in a pub yard.

He went, not to the agent's house, but to the bombed-out shell in the next street. He picked his way carefully across the rubble in the front garden, entered the gaping doorway, and went through the house to the back. It was very dark. A thick screen of low cloud hid the moon and stars. Faber had to walk slowly with his hands in front of him.

He reached the end of the garden, jumped over the fence, and crossed the next two gardens. In one of the houses a dog barked for a minute.

The garden of the lodging-house was unkempt. Faber walked into a blackberry bush and stumbled. The thorns scratched his face. He ducked under a line of washing – there was enough light for him to see that.

He found the kitchen window and took from his pocket a small tool with a scoop-shaped blade. The putty around the glass was old and brittle, and already flaking away in places. After twenty minutes' silent work he took the pane out of the frame and laid it gently on the grass. He shone a torch through the empty hole to make sure there were no noisy obstacles in his way, then climbed in.

The darkened house smelled of boiled fish and disinfectant. Faber unlocked the back door – a precaution for fast escape – before entering the hall. He flashed his pencil torch on and off quickly, once. In that instant of light he took in a tiled hallway, a kidney table he must circumvent, a row of coats on hooks and a staircase, to the right, carpeted.

He climbed the stairs silently.

He was halfway across the landing to the second flight when he saw the light under the door. A split-second later there was an asthmatic cough and the sound of a toilet flushing. Faber reached the door in two strides and froze against the wall.

Light flooded the landing as the door opened. Faber slipped his stiletto out of his sleeve. The old man came out of the toilet and crossed the landing, leaving the light on. At his bedroom door he grunted, turned, and came back.

He must see me, Faber thought. He tightened his grip on the handle of his knife. The old man's half-open eyes were directed to the floor. He looked up as he reached for the light cord, and Faber almost killed him then – but the man fumbled for the switch, and Faber realized he was so sleepy he was practically sleepwalking.

The light died, the old man shuffled back to bed, and Faber breathed again.

There was only one door at the top of the second flight of stairs. Faber tried it gently. It was locked.

He took another tool from the pocket of his jacket. The noise of the cistern filling covered the sound of Faber picking the lock. He opened the door and listened.

He could hear deep, regular breathing. He stepped inside. The sound came from the opposite corner of the room. He could see nothing. He crossed the pitch-black room very slowly, feeling the air in front of him at each step, until he was beside the bed.

He had the torch in his left hand, the stiletto loose in his sleeve, and his right hand free. He switched on the torch and grabbed the sleeping man's throat in a strangling grip.

The agent's eyes snapped open, full of fear, but he could make no sound. Faber straddled the bed and sat on him. Then he whispered: 'One Kings thirteen,' and relaxed his grip.

'You!' the agent said. He peered into the torchlight, trying to see Faber's face. He rubbed his neck where Faber's hand had squeezed.

Faber hissed: 'Be still!' He shone the torch into the agent's eyes, and with his right hand drew the stiletto.

'Aren't you going to let me get up?'

'I prefer you in bed where you can do no more damage.'

'Damage? More damage?'

'You were watched in Leicester Square, you let me follow you here, and they are observing this house. Should I trust you to do anything?'

'My God, I'm sorry.'

'Why did they send you?'

'The message had to be delivered personally. The orders come from the Führer himself.' The agent stopped.

'Well? What orders?'

'I . . . have to be sure it is you.'

'How can you be sure?'

'I must see your face.'

Faber hesitated, then shone the torch at himself briefly. 'Satisfied?'

'Die Nadel,' the man breathed.

'And who are you?'

'Major Friedrich Kaldor, at your service, sir.'

'Then I should call you "Sir".'

'Oh, no, sir. You've been promoted twice in your absence. You are now a lieutenant-colonel.'

'Have they nothing better to do in Hamburg?'

'Aren't you pleased?'

'I should be pleased to go back and put Major von Braun on latrine duty.'

'May I get up, sir?'

'Certainly not. What if Major Kaldor is languishing in Wandsworth gaol, and you are a substitute, just waiting to give some kind of signal to your watching friends in the house opposite?'

'Very well.'

'So – what are these orders from Hitler himself?'

'Well, sir, the Reich believes there will be an invasion of France this year.'

'Brilliant, brilliant. Go on.'

'They believe that General Patton is massing the First United States Army Group in the part of England known as East Anglia. If that army is the invasion force, then it follows that they will attack via the Pas de Calais.'

'That makes sense. But I have seen no sign of this army of Patton's.'

'There is some doubt in the highest circles in Berlin. The Führer's astrologer—'

'What?'

'Yes, sir, he has an astrologer, who tells him to defend Normandy.'

'My God. Are things that bad there?'

'He gets plenty of earthbound advice, too. I personally believe he uses the astrologer as an excuse when he thinks the generals are wrong but he cannot fault their arguments.'

Faber sighed. He had been afraid of news like this. 'Go on.'

'Your assignment is to assess the strength of FUSAG: numbers of troops, artillery, air support—'

'I know how to measure armies, thank you.'

'Of course.' He paused. 'I am instructed to emphasize the importance of the mission, sir.'

'And you have done so. Tell me: are things that bad in Berlin?'

The agent hesitated, and said: 'No, sir. Morale is high, output of munitions increases every month, the people spit at the bombers of the RAF—'

'Never mind,' Faber interrupted him. 'I can get the propaganda from my radio.'

The younger man was silent.

Faber said: 'Do you have anything else to tell me? Officially, I mean.'

'Yes. For the duration of the assignment you have a special bolthole.'

'They *do* think it's important,' Faber said.

'You rendezvous with a U-boat in the North Sea, ten miles due east of a town called Aberdeen. Just call them in on your normal radio frequency and they will surface. As soon as you or I have told Hamburg that the orders have been passed from me to you, the route will be open. The boat will be there every Friday and Monday at six p.m. and will wait until six a.m.'

'Aberdeen is a big town. Do you have an exact map reference?'

'Yes.' The agent recited the numbers, and Faber memorized them.

'Is that everything, Major?'

'Yes, sir.'

'What do you plan to do about the gentlemen from MI5 in the house across the road?'

The agent shrugged. 'I shall have to give them the slip.'

Faber thought: It's no good. 'What are your orders for action after you have seen me? Do you have a bolthole?'

'No. I am to go to a place called Weymouth and steal a boat in which to return to France.'

That was no plan at all. So, Faber thought: Canaris knew how it would be. Very well.

He said: 'And if you are caught by the British, and tortured?'

'I have a suicide pill.'

'And you will use it?'

'Most certainly.'

Faber looked at him. 'I think you might,' he said. He placed his left hand on the agent's chest and put his weight on it, as if he were about to get off the bed. That way he was able to feel exactly where the rib cage ended and the soft belly began. He thrust the point of the stiletto in just under the ribs and stabbed upward to the heart.

The agent's eyes widened for a terror-stricken instant. A cry came to his throat but did not escape. His body convulsed. Faber pushed the stiletto an inch farther in. The eyes closed and the body went limp.

Faber said: 'You saw my face.'

EIGHT

'I think we've lost control of it,' said Percival Godliman.

Frederick Bloggs nodded agreement, and added: 'It's my fault.'

The boy looked weary, Godliman thought. He had had that look for almost a year, ever since the night they dragged the crushed remains of his wife from underneath the rubble of their bombed house in Hoxton.

'I'm not interested in apportioning blame,' Godliman said briskly. 'The fact is that something happened in Leicester Square those few seconds when you lost sight of Blondie.'

'Do you think the contact was made?'

'Possibly.'

'When we picked him up again back in Stockwell, I thought he had simply given up for the day.'

'If that were the case he would have made the rendezvous again yesterday and today.' Godliman was making patterns with matchsticks on his desk, an aid to thinking he had developed into a habit. 'Still no movement at the house?'

'Nothing. He's been in there for forty-eight hours.' Bloggs repeated: 'It's my fault.'

'Don't be a bore, old chap,' Godliman said. 'It was my decision to let him run, so that he would lead us to someone else; and I still think it was the right move.'

Bloggs sat motionless, his expression blank, his hands in the pockets of his raincoat. 'If the contact has been made, we shouldn't delay picking Blondie up and finding out what his mission was.'

'That way we lose whatever chance we have of following Blondie to somebody really dangerous.'

'Your decision.'

Godliman had made a church with his matches. He stared at it for a moment, then took a halfpenny from his pocket and tossed it. 'Tails,' he observed. 'Give him another twenty-four hours.'

The landlord was a middle-aged Irish Republican from Lisdoonvarna, County Clare, who harboured a secret hope that the Germans would win the war and thus free the Emerald Isle from English oppression forever. He limped arthritically around the old house, collecting his weekly rents, thinking how much he would be worth if those rents were allowed to rise to their true market value. He was not a rich man – he owned only two houses, this and the smaller one in which he lived. He was permanently bad-tempered.

On the first floor he tapped on the door of the old man. This tenant was always pleased to see him. He was probably pleased to see anybody. He said: 'Hello, Mr Riley, would you like a cup of tea?'

'No time today.'

'Oh, well.' The old man handed over the money. 'I expect you've seen the kitchen window.'

'No, I didn't go in there.'

'Oh! Well, there's a pane of glass out. I patched it over with blackout curtain, but of course there is a draught.'

'Who smashed it?' the landlord asked.

'Funny thing, it ain't broke. Just lying there on the grass. I expect the old putty just gave way. I'll mend it myself, if you can get hold of a bit of putty.'

You old fool, the landlord thought. Aloud he said: 'I don't suppose it occurred to you that you might have been burgled?'

The old man looked astonished. 'I never thought of that.'

'Nobody's missing any valuables?'

'Nobody's said so to me.'

The landlord went to the door. 'All right, I'll have a look when I go down.'

The old man followed him out. 'I don't think the new bloke is in, upstairs,' he said. 'I haven't heard a sound for a couple of days.'

The landlord was sniffing. 'Has he been cooking in his room?'

'I wouldn't know, Mr Riley.'

The two of them went up the stairs. The old man said: 'He's very quiet, if he is in there.'

'Whatever he's cooking, he'll have to stop. It smells bloody awful.'

The landlord knocked on the door. There was no answer. He opened it and went in, and the old man followed him.

'Well, well, well,' the old sergeant said heartily. 'I think you've got a dead one.'

He stood in the doorway, surveying the room. 'You touched anything, Paddy?'

'No,' the landlord replied. 'And the name's Mr Riley.'

The policeman ignored this. 'Not long dead, though. I've smelled worse.' His survey took in the old chest of drawers, the suitcase on the low table, the faded square of carpet, the dirty curtains on the dormer window, and the rumpled bed in the corner. There were no signs of a struggle.

He went over to the bed. The young man's face was peaceful, his hands clasped over his chest. 'I'd say heart attack, if he wasn't so young.' There was no empty sleeping-pill bottle to indicate suicide. He picked up the leather wallet on top of the chest and looked through its contents. There was an identity card and a ration book, and a fairly thick wad of notes. 'Papers in order and he ain't been robbed.'

'He's only been here a week or so,' the landlord ventured. 'I don't know much about him at all. He came from North Wales to work in a factory.'

The sergeant observed: 'If he was as healthy as he looked he'd be in the Army.' He opened the suitcase on the table. 'Bloody hell, what's this lot?'

The landlord and the old man had edged their way into the room now. The landlord said: 'It's a radio' at the same time as the old man said: 'He's bleeding.'

'Don't touch that body!' the sergeant said.

'He's had a knife in the guts,' the old man persisted.

The sergeant gingerly lifted one of the dead hands from the chest to reveal a small patch of dried blood. 'He *was* bleeding,' he said. 'Where's the nearest phone?'

'Five doors down,' the landlord told him.

'Lock this room and stay out until I get back.'

The sergeant left the house and knocked at the door of the neighbour with the phone. A woman opened it. 'Good morning, madam. May I use your telephone?'

'Come in.' She showed him the phone, on a stand in the hall. 'What's happened – anything exciting?'

'A tenant died in a lodging-house just up the road,' he told her as he dialled.

'Murdered?' she asked, wide-eyed.

'I leave that to the experts. Hello? Superintendent Jones, please. This is Canter.' He looked at the woman. 'Might I ask you just to pop in the kitchen while I talk to my governor?'

She went, disappointed.

'Hello, Super. This body's got a knife wound and a suitcase radio.'

'What's the address again, Sarge?'

Sergeant Canter told him.

'Yes, that's the one they've been watching. This is an MI5 job, Sarge. Go to number forty-two and tell the surveillance team what you've found. I'll get on to their chief. Off you go.'

Canter thanked the woman and crossed the road. He was quite thrilled: this was only his second murder in 31 years as a Metropolitan Policeman, and it turned out to involve espionage! He might make Inspector yet.

He knocked on the door of number forty-two. It opened, and two men stood there.

Sergeant Canter said: 'Are you the secret agents from MI5?'

Bloggs arrived at the same time as a Special Branch man, Detective-Inspector Harris, whom he had known in his Scotland Yard days. Canter showed them the body.

They stood still for a moment, looking at the peaceful young face with its blond moustache.

Harris said: 'Who is he?'

'Codename Blondie,' Bloggs told him. 'We think he came in by parachute a couple of weeks ago. We picked up a radio message to another agent arranging a rendezvous. We knew the code, so we were able to watch the rendezvous. We hoped Blondie would lead us to the resident agent, who would be a much more dangerous specimen.'

'So what happened here?'

'Buggered if I know.'

Harris looked at the wound in the agent's chest. 'Stiletto?'

'Something like that. A very neat job. Under the ribs and straight up into the heart. Quick.'

'There are worse ways to die.'

Sergeant Canter said: 'Would you like to see the method of entry?'

He led them downstairs to the kitchen. They looked at the window-frame and the unbroken pane of glass lying on the lawn.

Canter said: 'Also, the lock on the bedroom door had been picked.'

They sat down at the kitchen table, and Canter made tea. Bloggs said: 'It happened the night after I lost him in Leicester Square. I fouled it all up.'

Harris said: 'Nobody's perfect.'

They drank their tea in silence for a while. Harris said: 'How are things with you, anyway? You don't drop in at the Yard.'

'Busy.'

'How's Christine?'

'Killed in the bombing.'

Harris's eyes widened. 'You poor bastard.'

'You all right?'

'Lost my brother in North Africa. Did you ever meet Johnny?'

'No.'

'He was a lad. Drink? You've never seen anything like it. Spent so much on booze, he could never afford to get married – which is just as well, the way things turned out.'

'Most people have lost somebody.'

'If you're on your own, come round our place for dinner on Sunday.'

'Thanks, I work Sundays now.'

Harris nodded. 'Well, whenever you feel like it.'

A detective-constable poked his head around the door and addressed Harris. 'Can we start bagging-up the evidence, guv?'

Harris looked at Bloggs.

'I've finished,' Bloggs said.

'All right, son, carry on,' Harris told him.

Bloggs said: 'Suppose he made contact after I lost him, and arranged for the resident agent to come here. The resident may have suspected a trap – that would explain why he came in through the window and picked the lock.'

'It makes him a devilish suspicious bastard,' Harris observed.

'That might be why we've never caught him. Anyway, he gets into Blondie's room and wakes him up. Now he knows it isn't a trap, right?'

'Right.'

'So why does he kill Blondie?'

'Maybe they quarrelled.'

'There were no signs of a struggle.'

Harris frowned into his empty cup. 'Perhaps he twigged that Blondie was being watched, and he was afraid we'd pick the boy up and make him spill the beans.'

Bloggs said: 'That makes him a ruthless bastard.'

'That might be why we've never caught him.'

'Come in. Sit down. I've just had a call from MI6. Canaris has been fired.'

Bloggs went in, sat down, and said: 'Is that good news or bad?'

'Very bad,' said Godliman. 'It's happened at the worst possible moment.'

'Do I get told why?'

Godliman looked at him through narrow eyes, then said: 'I think you need to know. At this moment we have forty double-agents broadcasting to Hamburg false information about Allied plans for the invasion of France.'

Bloggs whistled. 'I didn't know it was quite that big. I suppose the doubles say we're going in at Cherbourg, but really it will be Calais, or vice versa.'

'Something like that. Apparently I don't need to know the details. Anyway they haven't told me. However, the whole thing is in danger. We knew Canaris; we knew we had him fooled; we could have gone on fooling him. A new broom may mistrust his predecessor's agents. There's more: we've had some defections from the other side, people who could have betrayed the Abwehr's people over here if they hadn't been betrayed already. It's another reason for the Germans to begin to suspect our doubles.

'Then there's the possibility of a leak. Literally thousands of people now know about the double-cross system. There are doubles in Iceland, Canada, and Ceylon. We ran a double-cross in the Middle East.

'And we made a bad mistake last year by repatriating a German called Erich Carl. We later learned he was an Abwehr agent – a real one – and that while he was in internment on the Isle of Man he may have learned about two doubles called Mutt and Jeff, and possibly a third called Tate.

'So we're skating on thin ice. If one decent Abwehr agent in Britain gets to know about Fortitude – that's the codename for the deception plan – the whole strategy will be endangered. Not to mince words, we could lose the fucking war.'

Bloggs suppressed a smile: he could remember a time when Professor Godliman did not know the meaning of such words.

The professor went on: 'The Twenty Committee has made it quite clear that they expect me to make sure there aren't any decent Abwehr agents in Britain.'

'Last week we would have been quite confident that there weren't,' Bloggs said.

'Now we know there's at least one.'

'And we let him slip through our fingers.'

'So now we have to find him again.'

'I don't know,' Bloggs said gloomily. 'We don't know what part of the country he's operating from, we haven't the faintest idea what he looks like. He's too crafty to be pinpointed by triangulation while he's transmitting – otherwise we would have nabbed him long ago. We don't even know his codename. So where do we start?'

'Unsolved crimes,' said Godliman. 'Look: a spy is bound to break the law. He forges papers, he steals petrol and ammunition, he evades checkpoints, he enters restricted areas, he takes photographs, and when people rumble him he kills them. The police are bound to get to know of some of these crimes, if the spy has been operating for any length of time. If we go through the unsolved crimes files since the war, we'll find traces.'

'Don't you realize that *most* crimes are unsolved?' Bloggs said incredulously. 'The files would fill the Albert Hall!'

Godliman shrugged. 'So, we narrow it down to London, and we start with murders.'

They found what they were looking for on the very first day of their search.

It happened to be Godliman who came across it, and at first he did not realize its significance.

It was the file on the murder of a Mrs Una Garden in Highgate in 1940. Her throat had been cut and she had been sexually molested, although not raped. She had been found in the bedroom of her lodger, with a considerable amount of alcohol in her bloodstream. The picture was fairly clear: she had had a tryst with the lodger, he had wanted to go farther than she was prepared to let him, they had quarrelled, he had killed her, and the murder had neutralized his libido. But the police had never found the lodger.

Godliman had been about to pass over the file: spies did not get involved in sexual assaults. But he was a meticulous man with records, so he read every word, and consequently discovered that the unfortunate Mrs Garden had received stiletto wounds in her back, as well as the fatal wound to her throat.

Godliman and Bloggs were on opposite sides of a wooden table in the records room at Old Scotland Yard. Godliman tossed the file across the table and said: 'I think this is it.'

Bloggs glanced through it and said: 'The stiletto.'

They signed for the file and walked the short distance to the War Office. When they returned to Godliman's room, there was a decoded signal on his desk. He read it casually, then thumped the table in excitement. 'It's him!'

Bloggs read: 'Orders received. Regards to Willi.'

'Remember him?' Godliman said. 'Die Nadel?'

'Yes,' Bloggs said hesitantly. 'The Needle. But there's not much information here.'

'Think, think! A stilletto is like a needle. It's the same man: the murder of Mrs Garden, all those signals in 1940 that we couldn't trace, the rendezvous with Blondie . . .'

'Possibly.' Bloggs looked thoughtful.

'I can prove it,' Godliman said. 'Remember the transmission about Finland that you showed me the first day I came here? The one which was interrupted?'

'Yes.' Bloggs went to the file to find it.

'If my memory serves me well, the date of that transmission is the same as the date of this murder . . . and I'll bet the time of death coincides with the interruption.'

Bloggs looked at the signal in the file. 'Right both times.'

'There!'

'He's been operating in London for at least five

years, and it's taken us until now to get on to him,' Bloggs reflected. 'He won't be easy to catch.'

Godliman suddenly looked wolfish. 'He may be clever, but he's not as clever as me,' he said tightly. 'I'm going to nail him to the fucking wall.'

Bloggs laughed out loud. 'My God, you've changed, Professor.'

Godliman said: 'Do you realize that's the first time you've laughed for a year?'

NINE

The supply boat rounded the headland and chugged into the bay at Storm Island under a blue sky. There were two women in it: one was the skipper's wife – he had been called up and now she ran the business – and the other was Lucy's mother.

Mother got out of the boat, wearing a utility suit – a mannish jacket and an above-the-knee skirt. Lucy hugged her mightily.

'Mother! What a surprise!'

'But I wrote to you.'

The letter was with the mail on the boat – Mother had forgotten that the post only came once a fortnight on Storm Island.

'Is this my grandson? Isn't he a big boy?'

Little Jo, almost three years old, turned bashful and hid behind Lucy's skirt. He was dark-haired, pretty, and tall for his age.

Mother said: 'Isn't he like his father!'

'Yes,' Lucy said. Her assent held a note of disapproval. 'You must be freezing – come up to the house. Where *did* you get that skirt?'

They picked up the groceries and began to walk up the ramp to the cliff top. Mother chattered as they went. 'It's the fashion, dear. It saves on material. But it isn't as cold as this on the mainland. Such a wind! I suppose it's all right to leave my case on the jetty – nobody to steal it! Jane is engaged to an American soldier – a white one, thank God. He comes from a place called Milwaukee, and he doesn't chew gum. Isn't that nice? I've only got four more daughters to marry off now. Your father is a Captain in the Home Guard, did I tell you? He's up half the night patrolling the common waiting for German parachutists. Uncle Stephen's warehouse was bombed – I don't know *what* he'll do, it's an Act of War or something—'

'Don't rush, Mother, you've got fourteen days to tell me the news.' Lucy laughed.

They reached the cottage. Mother said: 'Isn't this *lovely*?' They went in. 'I think this is just lovely.'

Lucy parked Mother at the kitchen table and made tea. 'Tom will get your case up. He'll be here for his lunch shortly.'

'The shepherd?'

'Yes.'

'Does he find things for David to do, then?'

Lucy laughed. 'It's the other way around. I'm sure he'll tell you all about it himself. You haven't told me why you're here.'

'My dear, it's about time I saw you. I know we're not supposed to make unnecessary journeys, but once in four years isn't extravagant, is it?'

They heard the jeep outside, and a moment later David wheeled himself in. He kissed his mother-in-law and introduced Tom.

Lucy said: 'Tom, you can earn your lunch today by bringing Mother's case up, as she carried your groceries.'

David was warming his hands at the stove. 'It's raw today.'

Mother said: 'You're really taking sheep-farming seriously, then?'

'The flock is double what it was three years ago,' David told her. 'My father never farmed this island seriously. I've fenced six miles of the cliff top, improved the grazing, and introduced modern breeding methods. Not only do we have more sheep, but each animal gives us more meat and wool.'

Mother said tentatively: 'I suppose Tom does the physical work and you give the orders.'

David laughed. 'Equal partners, Mother.'

They had hearts for lunch, and both men ate mountains of potatoes. Mother commented favourably on Jo's table manners. Afterwards David lit a cigarette and Tom stuffed his pipe.

Mother said: 'What I really want to know is when you're going to give me more grandchildren.' She smiled brightly.

There was a long silence.

'Well, I think it's wonderful, the way David copes,' said Mother.

Lucy said: 'Yes,' and again there was that note of disapproval.

They were walking along the cliff top. The wind had

dropped on the third day of Mother's visit, and it was mild enough to go out. They took Jo, dressed in a fisherman's sweater and a fur coat. They had stopped at the top of a rise to watch David, Tom and the dog herding sheep. Lucy could see in Mother's face an internal struggle as concern vied with discretion. She decided to save her mother the effort of asking.

'He doesn't love me,' she said.

Mother looked quickly to make sure Jo was out of earshot. 'I'm sure it's not that bad, dear. Different men show their love in diff—'

'Mother, we haven't been man and wife – properly – since we were married.'

'But . . .?' She indicated Jo with a nod.

'That was a week before the wedding.'

'Oh! Oh, dear.' She was shocked. 'Is it, you know, the accident?'

'Yes, but not in the way you mean. It's nothing physical. He just . . . won't.' Lucy was crying quietly, the tears trickling down her wind-browned cheeks.

'Have you talked about it?'

'I've tried. Mother, what shall I do?'

'Perhaps with time—'

'It's been almost four years!'

There was a pause. They began to walk on across the heather, into the weak afternoon sun. Jo chased gulls. Mother said: 'I almost left your father, once.'

It was Lucy's turn to be shocked. 'When?'

'It was soon after Jane was born. We weren't so well-off in those days, you know – Father was still working for his father, and there was a slump. I was expecting for the third time in three years, and it seemed that a life of having babies and making ends meet stretched out in front of me with nothing to relieve the monotony. Then I discovered he was seeing an old flame of his – Brenda Simmonds, you never knew her, she went to Basingstoke. Suddenly I asked myself what I was doing it for, and I couldn't think of a sensible answer.'

Lucy had dim, patchy memories of those days: her grandfather with a white moustache; her father, a more slender edition; extended-family meals in the great farmhouse kitchen; a lot of laughter and sunshine and animals. Even then her parents' marriage had seemed to represent solid contentment, happy permanence. She said: 'Why didn't you? Leave, I mean.'

'Oh, people just didn't, in those days. There wasn't all this divorce, and a woman couldn't get a job.'

'Women work at all sorts of things now.'

'They did in the last war, but everything changed afterwards with a bit of unemployment. I expect it will be the same this time. Men get their way, you know, generally speaking.'

'And you're glad you stayed.' It was not a question.

'People my age shouldn't make pronouncements about Life. But *my* life has been a matter of making-do, and the same goes for most of the women I know. Steadfastness always looks like a sacrifice, but usually it isn't. Anyway, I'm not going to give you advice. You wouldn't take it, and if you did you'd blame your problems on me, I expect.'

'Oh, Mother.' Lucy smiled.

Mother said: 'Shall we turn round? I think we've gone far enough for one day.'

In the kitchen one evening Lucy said to David: 'I'd like Mother to stay another two weeks, if she will.'

Mother was upstairs putting Jo to bed, telling him a story.

David said: 'Isn't a fortnight long enough for you to dissect my personality?'

'Don't be silly, David.'

He wheeled himself over to her chair. 'Are you telling me you don't talk about me?'

'Of course we talk about you – you're my husband.'

'What do you say to her, then?'

'Why are you so worried?' Lucy said, not without malice. 'What are you so ashamed of?'

'Damn you, I've nothing to be ashamed of. No one wants his personal life talked about by a pair of gossiping women.'

'We don't gossip about you.'

'What do you say?'

'Aren't you touchy!'

'Answer my question.'

'I say I want to leave you, and she tries to talk me out of it.'

He spun around and wheeled away. 'Tell her not to bother for my sake.'

She called: 'Do you mean that?'

He stopped. 'I don't need anybody, do you understand? I can manage alone. I'm self-sufficient.'

'And what about me?' she said quietly. 'Perhaps I need somebody.'

'What for?'

'To love me.'

Mother came in, and sensed the atmosphere. 'He's fast asleep,' she said. 'Dropped off before Cinderella got to the ball. I think I'll pack a few things, not to leave it all until tomorrow.' She went out again.

'Do you think it will ever change, David?' Lucy asked.

'I don't know what you mean.'

'Will we ever be . . . the way we were, before the wedding?'

'My legs won't grow back, if that's what you mean.'

'Oh, God, don't you know that doesn't bother me? I just want to be loved.'

David shrugged. 'That's your problem.' He went out before she started to cry.

Mother did not stay the second fortnight. Lucy walked with her down to the jetty the next day. It was raining hard, and they both wore mackintoshes. They stood in silence waiting for the boat, watching the rain pit the sea with tiny craters. Mother held Jo in her arms.

'Things will change, in time, you know,' she said. 'Four years is nothing in a marriage.'

Lucy said: 'I don't think he'll change, but there's not much I can do other than give it a chance. There's Jo, and the war, and David's disability – how can I leave?'

The boat arrived, and Lucy exchanged her mother for three boxes of groceries and five letters. The water was choppy. Mother sat in the boat's tiny cabin. They waved her around the headland. Lucy felt very lonely.

Jo began to cry. 'I don't want Gran to go away!'

'Nor do I,' said Lucy.

TEN

Godliman and Bloggs walked side by side along the pavement of a bomb-damaged London shopping street. They were a mismatched pair: the stooped, bird-like professor, with pebble-lensed spectacles and a pipe, not looking where he was going, taking short, scurrying steps; and the flatfooted youngster, blond and purposeful, in his detective's raincoat and melodramatic hat: a cartoon looking for a caption.

Godliman was saying: 'I think Die Nadel is well-connected.'

'Why?'

'The only way he could be so insubordinate with impunity. It's this "Regards to Willi" line. It must refer to Canaris.'

'You think he was pals with Canaris.'

'He's pals with somebody – perhaps someone more powerful than Canaris was.'

'I have the feeling this is leading somewhere.'

'People who are well-connected generally make those connections at school, or university, or staff college. Look at that.'

They were outside a shop which had a huge empty space where once there had been a plate-glass window. A rough sign, hand-painted and nailed to the window-frame, said: 'Even more open than usual.'

Bloggs laughed, and said: 'I saw one outside a bombed police station: "Be good. We are still open."'

'It's become a minor art form.'

They walked on. Bloggs said: 'So, what if Die Nadel did go to school with someone high in the Wermacht?'

'People always have their pictures taken at school. Midwinter down in the basement at Kensington – that house where MI6 used to be before the war – he's got a collection of thousands of photographs of German officers: school photos, binges in the Mess, passing-out parades, shaking hands with Adolf, newspaper pictures – everything.'

'I see,' Bloggs said. 'So if you're right, and Die Nadel has been through Germany's equivalent of Eton and Sandhurst, we've probably got a picture of him.'

'Almost certainly. Spies are notoriously camera-shy, but they don't become spies until they're well into adulthood. It will be a youthful Die Nadel that we find in Midwinter's files.'

They skirted a huge crater outside a barber's. The shop was intact, but the traditional red-and-white striped pole lay in shards on the pavement. The sign in the window said: 'We've had a close shave – come and get one yourself.'

Bloggs said: 'How will we recognize him? No one has ever seen him.'

'Yes, they have. At Mrs Garden's boarding-house in Highgate they know him quite well.'

The Victorian house stood on a hill overlooking London. It was built of red brick, and Bloggs thought it looked angry at the damage Hitler was doing to its city. It was high up; a good place from which to broadcast. Die Nadel would have lived on the top floor. Bloggs wondered what secrets the spy had transmitted to Hamburg from this place in the dark days of 1940. Map references for aircraft factories and steelworks, details of coastal defences, political gossip, gas masks and Anderson shelters and sandbags, British morale, bomb damage reports, 'Well done, boys, you got Christine Bloggs at last – ' Shut up.

The door was opened by an elderly man in a black jacket and striped trousers.

'Good morning. I'm Inspector Bloggs, from Scotland Yard. I'd like a word with the householder, please.'

Bloggs saw fear leap to the man's eyes, then a young woman appeared in the doorway and said: 'Come in, please.'

The tiled hall smelled of wax polish. Bloggs hung his hat and coat on a stand. The old man disappeared into the depths of the house, and the woman led Bloggs into a lounge. It was expensively furnished in a rich, old-fashioned way. There were bottles of whisky, gin and sherry on a trolley: all the bottles were unopened. The woman sat down on a floral armchair and crossed her legs.

Bloggs said: 'Why is the old man frightened of the police?'

'My father-in-law is a German Jew. He came here in 1935 to escape Hitler, and in 1940 you put him in a concentration camp. His wife killed herself at the prospect. He has just been released from the Isle of Man. He had a letter from the King, apologizing for the inconvenience to which he had been put.'

Bloggs said: 'We don't have concentration camps.'

'We invented them. In South Africa. Didn't you know? We go on about our history, but we forget bits. We're so good at blinding ourselves to unpleasant facts.'

'Perhaps it's just as well.'

'What?'

'In 1939 we blinded ourselves to the unpleasant fact that we couldn't win a war with Germany – and look what happened.'

'That's what my father-in-law says. He's not as cynical as I. What can we do to assist Scotland Yard?'

Bloggs had been enjoying the exchange, and now it was with reluctance that he turned his attention to work. 'It's about a murder that took place here four years ago.'

'So long!'

'Some new evidence may have come to light.'

'I know about it, of course. The previous owner was killed by a tenant. My husband bought the house from her executor – she had no heirs.'

'I want to trace the other people who were tenants at that time.'

'Yes.' The woman's hostility had gone, now, and her intelligent face showed the effort of recollection. 'When we arrived there were three who had been here before the murder: a retired naval officer, a salesman, and a young boy from Yorkshire. The boy joined the Army – he still writes to us. The salesman was called up, and he died at sea. I know because two of his five wives got in touch with us! And the Commander is still here.'

'Still here!' That was a piece of luck. 'I'd like to see him, please.'

'Surely.' She stood up. 'He's aged a lot. I'll take you to his room.'

They went up the carpeted stairs to the first floor. She said: 'While you're talking to him, I'll look up the last letter from the boy in the Army.' She knocked on the door. It was more than Bloggs's landlady would have done, he thought wryly.

A voice called: 'It's open,' and Bloggs went in.

The Commander sat in a chair by the window with a blanket over his knees. He wore a blazer, a collar and a tie, and spectacles. His hair was thin, his moustache grey, his skin loose and wrinkled over a face that might once have been strong. The room was the home of a man living on memories: there were paintings of sailing ships, a sextant and a telescope, and a photograph of himself as a boy aboard HMS *Winchester*.

'Look at this,' he said without turning around. 'Tell me why that chap isn't in the Navy.'

Bloggs crossed to the window. A horse-drawn baker's van was at the kerb outside the house, the elderly horse dipping into its nosebag while the deliveries were made. That 'chap' was a woman with short blonde hair in trousers. She had a magnificent bust. Bloggs laughed. 'It's a woman in trousers,' he said.

'Bless my soul, so it is!' The Commander turned around. 'Can't tell, these days, you know. Women in trousers!'

Bloggs introduced himself. 'We've reopened the case of a murder committed here in 1940. I believe you lived here at the same time as the main suspect, one Henry Faber.'

'Indeed! What can I do to help?'

'How well do you remember Faber?'

'Perfectly. Tall chap, dark hair, well-spoken, quiet. Rather shabby clothes – if you were the kind who judges by appearances, you might well mistake him. I didn't dislike him – wouldn't have minded getting to know him better, but he didn't want that. I suppose he was about your age.'

Bloggs suppressed a smile: he was used to people assuming he must be older simply because he was a detective.

The Commander added: 'I'm sure he didn't do it, you know. I know a bit about character – you can't command a ship without learning – and if that man was a sex maniac, I'm Hermann Goering.'

Bloggs suddenly connected the blonde in trousers with the mistake about his age, and the conclusion depressed him. He said: 'You know, you should always ask to see a policeman's warrant card.'

The Commander was slightly taken aback. 'All right, then, let's have it.'

Bloggs opened his wallet and folded it to display the picture of Christine. 'Here.'

The Commander studied it for a moment, then said: 'A very good likeness.'

Bloggs sighed. The old man was very nearly blind.

He stood up. 'That's all, for now,' he said. 'Thank you.'

'Any time. Whatever I can do to help. I'm not much value to England these days – you've got to be pretty useless to get invalided out of the Home Guard, you know.'

'Goodbye.' Bloggs went out.

The woman was in the hall downstairs. She handed Bloggs a letter. 'The address is a Forces box number,' she said. 'No doubt you'll be able to find out where he is.'

'You knew the Commander would be no use,' Bloggs said.

'I guessed not. But a visitor makes his day.' She opened the door.

On impulse, Bloggs said: 'Will you have dinner with me?'

A shadow crossed her face. 'My husband is still on the Isle of Man.'

'I'm sorry – I thought—'

'It's all right. I'm flattered.'

'I wanted to convince you we're not the Gestapo.'

'I know you're not. A woman alone just gets bitter.'

Bloggs said: 'I lost my wife in the bombing.'

'Then you know how it makes you hate.'

'Yes,' said Bloggs. 'It makes you hate.' He went down the steps. The door closed behind him. It had started to rain.

It had been raining then. Bloggs was late. He had been going over some new material with Godliman. Now he was hurrying, so that he would have half an hour with Christine before she went out to drive her ambulance. It was dark, and the raid had already started. The things Christine saw at night were so awful she had stopped talking about them.

Bloggs was proud of her, proud. The people she worked with said she was better than two men: she hurtled through blacked-out London, driving like a veteran, taking corners on two wheels, whistling and cracking jokes as the city turned to flame around her. Fearless, they called her. Bloggs knew better: she was terrified, but she would not let it show. He knew because he saw her eyes in the morning, when he got up and she went to bed; when her guard was down and it was over for a few hours. He knew it was not fearlessness but courage, and he was proud.

It was raining harder when he got off the bus. He pulled down his hat and put up his collar. At a kiosk he bought cigarettes for Christine: she had started smoking recently, like a lot of women. The shopkeeper would let him have only five, because of the shortage. He put them in a Woolworth's bakelite cigarette case.

A policeman stopped him and asked for his identity

card: another two minutes wasted. An ambulance passed him, similar to the one Christine drove; a requisitioned fruit lorry, painted grey.

He began to get nervous as he approached home. The explosions were sounding closer, and he could hear the aircraft clearly. The East End was in for another bruising tonight: he would sleep in the Morrison shelter. There was a big one, terribly close, and he quickened his step. He would eat his supper in the shelter, too.

He turned into his own street, saw the ambulances and the fire engines, and broke into a run.

The bomb had landed on his side of the street, around the middle. It must be close to his own home. Jesus in heaven, not us, no—

There had been a direct hit on the roof, and the house was literally flattened. He raced up to the crowd of people, neighbours and firemen and volunteers. 'Is my wife all right? Is she out? IS SHE IN THERE?'

A fireman looked at him with compassion. 'Nobody's come out of there, mate.'

Rescuers were picking over the rubble. Suddenly one of them shouted: 'Over here!' Then he said: 'Bugger me, it's Fearless Bloggs!'

Frederick dashed to where the man stood. Christine was underneath a huge chunk of brickwork. Her face was visible: the eyes were closed.

The rescuer called: 'Lifting gear, boys, sharp's the word.'

Christine moaned and stirred.

Bloggs said: 'She's alive!' He knelt down beside her

and got his hands under the edge of the lump of rubble.

The rescuer said: 'You won't shift that, son.'

The brickwork lifted.

The rescuer said: 'Strewth, you'll kill yourself,' and bent down to help.

When it was two feet off the ground they got their shoulders under it. The weight was off Christine now. A third man joined in, and a fourth. They all straightened up together.

Bloggs said: 'I'll lift her out.'

He crawled under the sloping roof of brick and cradled his wife in his arms.

Someone shouted: 'Fuck me it's slipping!'

Bloggs scurried out from under with Christine held tightly to his chest. As soon as he was clear the rescuers let go of the rubble and jumped away. It fell back to earth with a sickening thud; and when Bloggs realized that *that* had landed on Christine, he knew she was going to die.

He carried her to the ambulance, and it took off immediately. She opened her eyes again once, before she died, and said: 'You'll have to win the war without me, kiddo.'

More than a year later, as he walked downhill from Highgate into the bowl of London, with the rain on his face mingling with the tears again, he thought the woman in the spy's house had said a mighty truth: it makes you hate.

*

In war boys become men, and men become soldiers, and soldiers get promoted; and this is why Billy Parkin, aged 18, who should have been an apprentice in his father's tannery at Scarborough, was believed by the Army to be twenty-one, made up to sergeant, and given the job of leading his advance squad through a hot, dry forest toward a dusty whitewashed Italian village.

The Italians had surrendered but the Germans had not, and it was the Germans who were defending Italy against the combined British-American invasion. The Allies were going to Rome, and for Sergeant Parkin's squad it was a long walk.

They came out of the forest at the top of a hill, and lay flat on their bellies to look down on the village. Parkin got out his binoculars and said: 'What wouldn't I fookin give for a fookin cup of fookin tea.' He had taken to drinking, and cigarettes, and women, and his language was like that of soldiers everywhere. He no longer went to prayer meetings.

Some of these villages were defended and some were not. Parkin recognized that as sound tactics: you didn't know which were undefended, so you approached them all cautiously, and caution cost time.

The downside of the hill held little cover – just a few bushes – and the village began at its foot. There were a few white houses, a river with a wooden bridge, then more houses around a little piazza with a town hall and a clock tower. There was a clear line-of-sight from the tower to the bridge: if the enemy were here at all, he would be in the town hall. A few figures worked in the surrounding fields: God knew who they were. They might be genuine peasants, or any one of a host of factions: fascisti, mafia, corsos, partigianos, communisti . . . or even Germans. You didn't know whose side they would be on until the shooting started.

Parkin said: 'All right, Corporal.'

Corporal Watkins disappeared back into the forest and emerged, five minutes later, on the dirt road into the village, wearing a civilian hat and a filthy old blanket over his uniform. He stumbled, rather than walked, and over his shoulder was a bundle that could have been anything from a bag of onions to a dead rabbit. He reached the near edge of the village and vanished into the darkness of a low cottage.

After a moment he came out. Standing close to the wall, where he could not be seen from the village, he looked toward the soldiers on the hilltop and waved: one, two, three.

The squad scrambled down the hillside into the village.

Watkins said: 'All the houses empty, Sarge.'

Parkin nodded. It meant nothing.

They moved through the houses to the edge of the river. Parkin said: 'Your turn, Smiler. Swim the Mississippi here.'

Private 'Smiler' Hudson put his equipment in a neat pile, took off his helmet, boots and tunic, and slid into the narrow stream. He emerged on the far side, climbed the bank, and disappeared among the houses. This time there was a longer wait: more area to check. Finally Hudson walked back across the wooden bridge. 'If they're 'ere, they're 'iding,' he said.

He retrieved his gear and the squad crossed the bridge into the village. They kept to the sides of the street as they walked toward the piazza. A bird flew off a roof and startled Parkin. Some of the men kicked open a few doors as they passed. There was nobody.

They stood at the edge of the piazza. Parkin nodded at the town hall. 'Did you go inside the place, Smiler?'

'Yes, sir.'

'Looks like the village is ours, then.'

'Yes, sir.'

Parkin stepped forward to cross the piazza, and then the storm broke. There was a crash of rifles, and bullets hailed all around them. Someone screamed. Parkin was running, dodging, ducking. Watkins, in front of him, shouted with pain and clutched his leg: Parkin picked him up bodily. A bullet clanged off his tin hat. He raced for the nearest house, charged the door, and fell inside.

The shooting stopped. Parkin risked a peep outside. One man lay wounded in the piazza: Hudson. Rough justice. Hudson moved, and a solitary shot rang out. Then he was still. Parkin said: 'Fookin bastards.'

Watkins was doing something to his leg, cursing. Parkin said: 'Bullet still in there?'

Watkins yelled: 'Ouch!' then grinned and held something up. 'Not any more.'

Parkin looked outside again. 'They're in the clock tower,' he said. 'You wouldn't think there was room. Can't be many of them.'

'They can shoot, though.'

'Yes. They've got us pinned.' Parkin frowned. 'Got any fireworks?'

'Aye.'

'Let's have a look.' Parkin opened Watkins's pack and took out the dynamite. 'Here. Fix me a ten-second fuse.'

The others were in the house across the street. Parkin called out: 'Hey!'

A face appeared at the door. 'Sarge?'

'I'm going to throw a tomato. When I shout, give me covering fire.'

'Right.'

Parkin lit a cigarette. Watkins handed him a bundle of dynamite. Parkin shouted: 'Fire!' He lit the fuse with the cigarette, stepped into the street, drew back his arm, and threw the bomb at the clock tower. He ducked back into the house, the fire of his own men ringing in his ears. A bullet shaved the woodwork, and he caught a splinter under his chin. He heard the dynamite explode.

Before he could look, someone across the street shouted: 'Bull's-eye!'

Parkin stepped outside. The ancient clock tower had crumbled. A chime sounded incongruously as dust settled over the ruins.

Watkins said: 'You ever play cricket? That was a bloody good shot.'

Parkin walked to the centre of the piazza. There seemed to be enough human spare parts to make about three Germans. He said: 'The tower was pretty unsteady anyway. It would probably have fallen down if we'd all sneezed at it in unison.' He turned away. 'Another day, another dollar.' It was a phrase the Yanks used.

'Sarge? Radio.' It was the R/T operator.

Parkin walked back and took the handset from him. 'Sergeant Parkin.'

'Major Roberts. You're discharged from active duty as of now, Sergeant.'

'Why?' Parkin's first thought was that they had discovered his true age.

'The brass want you in London. Don't ask me why because I don't know. Leave your corporal in charge and make your way back to base. A car will meet you on the road.'

'Yes, sir.'

'The orders also say that on no account are you to risk your life. Got that?'

Parkin grinned, thinking of the clock tower and the dynamite. 'Got it.'

'All right. On your way. You lucky sod.'

Everyone had called him a boy, but they had known him before he joined the Army, Bloggs thought. There was no doubt he was a man now. He walked with confidence and grace, looked about him sharply, and was respectful without being ill-at-ease in the company of superior officers. Bloggs knew that he was lying about his age, not because of his looks or manner, but because of the small signs that appeared whenever age was mentioned – signs which Bloggs, an experienced interrogator, picked up out of habit.

He had been amused when they told him they wanted him to look at pictures. Now, in his third day in

Mr Midwinter's dusty Kensington vault, the amusement had gone and tedium had set in. What irritated him most was the no-smoking rule.

It was even more boring for Bloggs, who had to sit and watch him.

At one point Parkin said: 'You wouldn't call me back from Italy to help in a four-year-old murder case that could wait until after the war. Also, these pictures are mostly of German officers. If this case is something I should keep mum about, you'd better tell me.'

'It's something you should keep mum about,' said Bloggs.

Parkin went back to his pictures.

They were all old, mostly browned and fading. Many were out of books, magazines and newspapers. Sometimes Parkin picked up a magnifying glass Mr Midwinter had thoughtfully provided, to peer more closely at a tiny face in a group; and each time this happened Bloggs's heart raced, only to slow down when Parkin put the glass to one side and picked up the next photograph.

They went to a nearby pub for lunch. The ale was weak, like most wartime beer, but Bloggs still thought it wise to restrict young Parkin to two pints – on his own he would have sunk a gallon.

'Mr Faber was the quiet sort,' Parkin said. 'You wouldn't think he had it in him. Mind you, the landlady wasn't bad looking. And she wanted it. Looking back, I think I could have had her myself if I'd known how to go about it. There, I was, only – eighteen.'

They ate bread and cheese, and Parkin swallowed a

dozen pickled onions. When they went back, they stopped outside the house while Parkin smoked another cigarette.

'Mind you,' he said, 'he was a biggish chap, good-looking, well-spoken. We all thought he was nothing much because his clothes were poor, and he rode a bike, and he'd no money. I suppose it could have been a subtle kind of disguise.' His eyebrows were raised in a question.

'It could have been,' Bloggs said.

That afternoon Parkin found not one but three pictures of Faber.

One of them was only nine years old.

And Mr Midwinter had the negative.

Henrik Rudolph Hans von Muller-Guder ('Let's just call him Faber,' said Godliman with a laugh) was born on 26 May 1900 at a village called Oln in West Prussia. His father's family had been substantial landowners in the area for generations. His father was the second son; so was Henrik. All the second sons were Army officers. His mother, the daughter of a senior official of the Second Reich, was born and raised to be an aristocrat's wife, and that was what she was.

At the age of thirteen he went to the Karlsruhe cadet school in Baden; two years later he was transferred to the more prestigious Gross-Lichterfelde, near Berlin. Both places were hard, disciplinarian institutions where the minds of the pupils were improved with canes and cold baths and bad food. However, Henrik learned to speak English and French and studied history, and passed the Reifeprüfung with the highest mark recorded since the turn of the century. There were only three other points of note in his school career: one bitter winter he rebelled against authority to the extent of sneaking out of the school at night and walking 150 miles to his aunt's house; he broke the arm of his wrestling instructor during a practice bout; and he was flogged for insurbordination.

He served briefly as an ensign-cadet in the neutral zone of Friedrichsfeld, near Wesel, in 1920; did token officer training at the War School at Metz in 1921, and was commissioned Second Lieutenant in 1922.

('What was the phrase you used?' Godliman asked Bloggs. 'The German equivalent of Eton and Sandhurst.')

Over the next few years he did short tours of duty in half a dozen places, in the manner of one who is being groomed for the general staff. He continued to distinguish himself as an athlete, specializing in longer-distance running. He made no close friendships, never married, and refused to join the National Socialist party. His promotion to lieutenant was somewhat delayed by a vague incident involving the pregnancy of the daughter of a lieutenant-colonel in the Defence Ministry, but eventually came about in 1928. His habit of talking to superior officers as if they were equals came to be accepted as pardonable in one who was both a rising young officer and a Prussian aristocrat.

In the late twenties Admiral Wilhelm Canaris became friendly with Henrik's Uncle Otto, his father's elder brother, and spent several holidays at the family estate at Oln. In 1931 Adolf Hitler, not yet Chancellor of Germany, was a guest there.

In 1933 Henrik was promoted Captain, and went to Berlin for unspecified duties. This is the date of the last photograph.

About then, according to published information, he seems to have ceased to exist.

'We can conjecture the rest,' said Percival Godliman. 'The Abwehr trains him in wireless transmission, codes, map-making, burglary, blackmail, sabotage and silent killing. He comes to London in about 1937 with plenty of time to set himself up with a solid cover – perhaps two. His loner instincts are honed sharp by the spying game. When war breaks out, he considers himself licensed to kill.' He looked at the photograph on his desk. 'He's a handsome fellow.'

It was a picture of the running team of the 10th Hanoverian Jaeger Battalion. Faber was in the middle, holding a cup. He had a high forehead, with cropped hair; a long chin; and a small mouth decorated with a narrow moustache.

Godliman passed the picture to Billy Parkin. 'Has he changed much?'

'He looks a lot older, but that might be his . . . bearing.' He studied the photograph thoughtfully. 'His hair is longer now, and the moustache has gone.' He passed the picture back across the desk. 'But it's him, all right.'

'There are two more items in the file, both of them conjectural,' Godliman said. 'First, they say he may have gone into Intelligence in 1933 – that's the routine assumption when an officer's record just stops for no apparent reason. The second item is a rumour, unconfirmed by any reliable source, that he spent some years as a confidential advisor to Stalin, using the name Vasily Zankov.'

'That's incredible,' Bloggs said. 'I don't believe that.'

Godliman shrugged. '*Somebody* persuaded Stalin to execute the cream of his officer corps during the years Hitler rose to power.'

Bloggs shook his head, and changed the subject. 'Where do we go from here?'

Godliman considered. 'Let's have Sergeant Parkin transferred to us. He's the only man we know who has actually seen Die Nadel. Besides, he knows too much for us to risk him in the front line: he could get captured and interrogated, and give the game away. Next, make a first-class print of this photo, and have the hair thickened and the moustache obliterated by a re-touch artist. Then we can distribute copies.'

'Do we want to start a hue and cry?' Bloggs said doubtfully.

'No. For now, let's tread softly. If we put the thing in the newspapers he'll get to hear of it, and vanish. Just send the photo to police forces for the time being.'

'Is that all?'

'I think so. Unless you've got other ideas.'

Parkin cleared his throat. 'Sir?'

'Yes.'

'I really would prefer to go back to my unit. I'm not really the administrative type, if you know what I mean.'

'You're not being offered a choice, Sergeant. At this stage of the conflict, one Italian village more or less makes no difference – but this man Faber could lose us the war. As the Americans say, I'm not kidding.'

ELEVEN

Faber had gone fishing.

He was stretched out on the deck of a thirty-foot boat, enjoying the spring sunshine, moving along the canal at about three knots. One lazy hand held the tiller, the other rested on a rod which trailed its line in the water behind the boat.

He hadn't caught a thing all day.

As well as fishing, he was bird-watching – both out of interest (he was actually getting to know quite a lot about the damn birds) and as an excuse for carrying binoculars. Earlier today he had seen a kingfisher's nest.

The people at the boatyard in Norwich had been delighted to rent him the vessel for a fortnight. Business was bad: they had only two boats nowadays, and one of them had not been used since Dunkirk. Faber had haggled over the price, just for the sake of form. In the end they had thrown in a locker of tinned food.

He had bought bait in a shop nearby; the fishing tackle he had brought from London. They had observed that he had nice weather for it, and wished him good fishing. Nobody even asked to see his identity card.

So far, so good.

The difficult bit was to come. For assessing the strength of an army was difficult. First you had to find it.

In peacetime the Army would put up its own road signs to help you. Now they had taken down, not only their own but everyone else's road signs.

The simple solution would be to get in a car and follow the first military vehicle you saw until it stopped. However, Faber had no car; it was nearly impossible for a civilian to hire one; and even if you got one you couldn't get petrol for it. Besides, a civilian driving around the countryside following Army lorries and looking at Army camps was liable to be arrested.

Hence the boat.

Some years ago, before it had become illegal to sell maps, Faber had discovered that Britain had thousands of miles of inland waterways. The original network of rivers had been augmented during the nineteenth century by a spider-web of canals. In some areas there was almost as much waterway as there was road. Norfolk was one of these areas.

The boat had many advantages. On a road, a man was going somewhere: on a river he was just sailing. Sleeping in a parked car was conspicuous: sleeping in a moored boat was natural. The waterway was lonely. And who ever heard of a canal-block?

There were disadvantages. Airfields and barracks had to be near roads, but they were located without reference to access by water. Faber had to explore the countryside at night, leaving his moored boat and tramping the hillsides by moonlight, exhausting forty-mile round trips during which he could easily miss what he was looking for because of the darkness or because he simply did not have enough time to check every square mile of land.

When he returned, a couple of hours after dawn, he would sleep until midday then move on, stopping occasionally to climb a nearby hill and check the outlook. At locks, isolated farmhouses and riverside pubs he would talk to people, hoping for hints of a military presence. So far there had been none.

He was beginning to wonder whether he was in the right area. He had tried to put himself in General Patton's place, thinking: If I were planning to invade France east of the Seine from a base in eastern England, where would I locate that base? Norfolk was obvious: a vast expanse of lonely countryside, plenty of flat ground for aircraft, close to the sea for rapid departure. And the Wash was a natural place to gather a fleet of ships. However, his guesswork might be wrong for reasons unknown to him. Soon he would have to consider a rapid move across country to a new area: perhaps the Fens.

A lock appeared ahead of him, and he trimmed his sails to slow his pace. He glided gently into the lock and bumped softly against the gates. The lock-keeper's house was on the bank. Faber cupped his hands around his mouth and hallooed. Then he settled down to wait. He had learned that lock-keepers were a breed that could not be hurried. Moreover, it was tea-time, and at tea-time they could hardly be moved at all.

A woman came to the door of the house and beckoned. Faber waved back, then jumped on to the bank, tied up the boat, and went into the house. The lock-keeper was in his shirt-sleeves at the kitchen table. He said: 'Not in a hurry, are you?'

Faber smiled. 'Not at all.'

'Pour him a cup of tea, Mavis.'

'No, really,' Faber said politely.

'It's all right, we've just made a pot.'

'Thank you.' Faber sat down. The little kitchen was airy and clean, and his tea came in a pretty china cup.

'Fishing holiday?' the lock-keeper asked.

'Fishing and bird-watching,' Faber answered. 'I'm thinking of tying-up quite soon and spending a couple of days on land.'

'Oh, aye. Well, best keep to the far side of the canal, then. Restricted area this side.'

'Really? I didn't know there was Army land hereabouts.'

'Aye, it starts about half a mile from here. As to whether it's Army, I wouldn't know. They don't tell me.'

'Well, I suppose we don't need to know,' Faber said.

'Aye. Drink up, then, and I'll see you through the lock. Thanks for letting me finish my tea.'

They left the house, and Faber got into the boat and untied it. The gates behind him closed slowly, and then the keeper opened the sluices. The boat gradually sank with the level of the water in the lock, then the keeper opened the front gates.

Faber made sail and moved out. The lock-keeper waved.

He stopped again about four miles away and moored the boat to a stout tree on the bank. While he waited for night to fall he made a meal of tinned sausage-meat, dry biscuits, and bottled water. He dressed in his black clothes, put into a shoulder-bag his binoculars, camera, and copy of *Rare Birds of East Anglia,* pocketed his compass and picked up his torch. He was ready.

He doused the hurricane lamp, locked the cabin door, and jumped on to the bank. Consulting his compass by torchlight, he entered the belt of woodland alongside the canal.

He walked due south from his boat for about half a mile until he hit the fence. It was six feet high, chicken-wire, with coiled barbed wire on top. He backtracked into the wood and climbed a tall tree.

There was scattered cloud above. The moon showed through fitfully. Beyond the fence was open land, a gentle rise. Faber had done this sort of thing before, at Biggin Hill, Aldershot, and a host of military areas all over Southern England. There were two levels of security: a mobile patrol around the perimeter fence, and stationary sentries at the installations.

Both could be evaded by patience and caution.

Faber came down the tree and returned to the fence. He concealed himself behind a bush and settled down to wait.

He had to know when the mobile patrol passed this point. If they did not come until dawn, he would simply return the following night. If he was lucky, they would pass shortly. From the apparent size of the area under guard he guessed they would only make one complete tour of the fence each night.

He was lucky. Soon after ten o'clock he heard the tramp of feet, and three men marched by on the inside of the fence.

Five minutes later Faber crossed the fence.

He walked due south: when all directions are equal, a straight line is best. He did not use his flashlight. He kept close to hedges and trees when he could, and avoided high ground where he might be silhouetted against a sudden flash of moonlight. The sparse countryside was an abstract in black, grey and silver. The ground underfoot was a little soggy, as if there might be marshes nearby. A fox ran across a field in front of him, as fast as a greyhound, as graceful as a cat.

It was 11.30 p.m. when he came across the first indications of military activity – and very odd indications they were.

The moon came out and he saw, perhaps a quarter of a mile ahead, several rows of one-storey buildings laid out with the unmistakable precision of an Army barracks. He dropped to the ground immediately, but he was already doubting the reality of what he apparently saw; for there were no lights and no noise.

He lay still for ten minutes, to give explanations a chance to emerge, but nothing happened except that a badger lumbered into view, saw him, and made off.

Faber crawled forward.

As he got closer he realized that the barracks were

not just unoccupied, but unfinished. Most of them were little more than a roof supported by cornerposts. Some had one wall.

A sudden sound stopped him: a man's laugh. He lay still and watched. A match flared briefly and died, leaving two glowing red spots in one of the unfinished huts: guards.

Faber touched the stiletto in his sleeve, then began to crawl again, making for the side of the camp away from the sentries.

The half-built huts had no floors and no foundations. There were no construction vehicles around, no wheelbarrows, concrete mixers, shovels or piles of bricks. A mud track led away from the camp across the fields, but spring grass was growing in the ruts: it had not been used much lately.

It was as if someone had decided to billet ten thousand men here, then changed his mind a few weeks after building started.

Yet there was something about the place that did not quite fit that explanation.

Faber walked around softly, alert lest the sentries should take it into their heads to make a patrol. There was a group of military vehicles in the centre of the camp. They were old and rusting, and had been degutted – none had an engine or any interior components. But if one was going to cannibalize obsolete vehicles, why not take the shells for scrap?

Those huts which did have a wall were on the outermost rows, and their walls faced out. It was like a movie set, not a building site.

Faber decided he had learned all he could from this place. He walked to the east edge of the camp, then dropped to his hands and knees and crawled away until he was out of sight behind a hedge. Half a mile farther on, near the top of a rise, he looked back. Now it looked exactly like a barracks again.

The glimmer of an idea formed in his mind. He gave it time.

The land was still relatively flat, relieved only by gentle folds. There were patches of woodland and marshy scrub which Faber took advantage of. Once he had to detour around a lake, its surface a silver mirror under the moon. He heard the hoot of an owl, and looked in that direction to see a tumbledown barn in the distance.

Five miles on, he saw the airfield.

There were more planes here than he thought were possessed by the entire Royal Air Force. There were Pathfinders to drop flares, Lancasters and American B-17S for softening-up bombing, Hurricanes and Spitfires and Mosquitoes for reconnaissance and strafing: enough planes for an invasion.

Without exception their undercarriages had sunk into the soft earth, and they were up to their bellies in mud.

Once again there were no lights and no noise.

Faber followed the same procedure, crawling flat toward the planes until he located the guards. In the middle of the airfield was a small tent. The faint glow of a lamp shone through the canvas. Two men, perhaps three.

As Faber approached the planes they seemed to become flatter, as if they had all been squashed.

He reached the nearest and touched it in amazement. It was a piece of half-inch plywood, cut out in the outline of a Spitfire, painted with camouflage, and roped to the ground.

Every other plane was the same.

There were more than a thousand of them.

Faber got to his feet, watching the tent from the corner of his eye, ready to drop to the ground at the slightest sign of movement. He walked all around the phoney airfield, looking at the phoney fighters and bombers, connecting them with the movie-set barracks, reeling at the implications of what he had found.

He knew that if he continued to explore he would find more airfields like this, more half-built barracks. If he went to the Wash he would find a fleet of plywood destroyers and troop ships.

It was a vast, meticulous, costly, outrageous trick.

Of course, it could not possibly fool an onlooker for very long. But it was not designed to deceive observers on the ground.

It was meant to be seen from the air.

Even a low-flying reconnaissance plane equipped with the latest cameras and fast film would come back with pictures which indisputably showed an enormous concentration of men and machines.

No wonder the general staff were anticipating an invasion east of the Seine.

There would be other elements to the deception, he guessed. The British would refer to FUSAG in signals, using codes they knew to be broken. There would be phoney espionage reports channelled through the Spanish diplomatic bag to Hamburg. The possibilities were endless.

The British had had four years to arm themselves for this invasion. Most of the German army was fighting Russia. Once the Allies got a toehold on French soil, they would be unstoppable. The Germans' only chance was to catch them on the beaches and annihilate them as they came off the troop ships.

If they were waiting in the wrong place, they would lose that one chance.

The whole strategy was immediately clear. It was simple, and it was devastating.

Faber had to tell Hamburg.

He wondered whether they would believe him.

War strategy was rarely altered on the word of one man. His own standing was particularly high, but was it that high?

He needed to get proof, and then take it to Berlin.

He needed photographs.

He would take pictures of this gigantic dummy army, then he would go to Scotland and meet the U-boat, and he would deliver the pictures personally to the Führer. He could do no more.

For photography he needed light. He would have to wait until dawn. There had been a ruined barn a little way back: he could spend the rest of the night there.

He checked his compass and set off. The barn was farther than he thought, and the walk took him an hour. It was an old wooden building with holes in the roof. The rats had long ago deserted it for lack of food, but there were bats in the hayloft.

Faber lay down on some planks, but he could not sleep for the knowledge that he was now personally capable of altering the course of the greatest war in history.

Dawn was due at 05.21. At 04.20 Faber left the barn.

Although he had not slept, the two hours of immobility had rested his body and calmed his mind, and he was now in fine spirits. The cloud was clearing with a west wind, so although the moon had set there was starlight.

His timing was good. The sky was growing perceptibly brighter as he came in sight of the 'airfield'.

The sentries were still in their tent. With luck, they would be sleeping: Faber knew from his own experience of such duties that it was hardest to stay awake during the last few hours.

And if they did come out, he would just have to kill them.

He selected his position and loaded the Leica with a 36-frame roll of 35mm fast Agfa film. He hoped the film's light-sensitive chemicals had not spoiled, for it had been stored in his suitcase since before the war: you couldn't buy film in Britain nowadays. It should be all right, for he had kept it in a light-proof bag away from any heat.

When the red rim of the sun edged over the horizon he began shooting. He took a series of shots from different vantage points and various distances, finishing with a close-up of one dummy plane: the pictures would show both the illusion and the reality.

As he took the last he saw movement from the corner of his eye. He dropped flat and crawled under a plywood Mosquito. A soldier emerged from the tent, walked a few paces, and urinated on the ground. The man stretched and yawned, then lit a cigarette. He looked around the airfield, shivered, and returned to the tent.

Faber got up and ran.

A quarter of a mile away he looked back. The airfield was out of sight. He headed west, toward the barracks.

This would be more than an ordinary espionage coup. Hitler had had a life of being the only one in step. The man who brought the proof that, yet again, the Führer was right and all the experts were wrong, could look for more than a pat on the back. Faber knew that already Hitler rated him the Abwehr's best agent: this triumph would probably get him Canaris's job.

If he made it.

He increased his pace, jogging twenty yards, walking the next twenty, and jogging again, so that he reached the barracks by 06.30. It was bright daylight now, and he could not approach close, because these sentries were not in a tent, but in one of the wall-less huts, with a clear view all around them. He lay down by the hedge and took his pictures from a distance. Ordinary prints would just show a barracks, but big enlargements ought to reveal the details of the deception.

When he headed back toward the boat he had exposed thirty frames. Again he hurried, for he was now terribly conspicuous, a black-clad man carrying a canvas bag of equipment, jogging across the open fields of a restricted area.

He reached the fence an hour later, having seen nothing but wild geese. As he climbed over the wire, he felt a great release of tension. Inside the fence the balance of suspicion had been against him; outside it was in his favour. He could revert to his bird-watching, fishing, sailing role. The period of greatest risk was over.

He strolled through the belt of woodland, catching his breath and letting the strain of the night's work seep away. He would sail a few miles on, he decided, before mooring again to catch a few hours' sleep.

He reached the canal. It was over. The boat looked pretty in the morning sunshine. As soon as he was under way he would make some tea, then—

A man in uniform stepped out of the cabin of the boat and said: 'Well, well. And who might you be?'

Faber stood stock still, letting the icy calm and the old instincts come into play. The intruder wore the uniform of a captain in the Home Guard. He had some kind of handgun in a holster with a buttoned flap. He was tall and rangy, but he looked to be in his late fifties. White hair showed under his cap. He made no move to draw his gun. Faber took all this in as he said: 'You are on my boat, so I think it is I who should ask who you are.'

'Captain Stephen Langham, Home Guard.'

'James Baker.' Faber stayed on the bank. A captain did not patrol alone.

'And what are you doing?'

'I'm on holiday.'

'Where have you been?'

'Bird-watching.'

'Since before dawn? Cover him, Watson.'

A youngish man in denim uniform appeared on Faber's left, carrying a shotgun. Faber looked around. There was another man to his right and a fourth behind him.

The captain called: 'Which direction did he come from, Corporal?'

The reply came from the top of an oak tree. 'From the restricted area, sir.'

Faber was calculating odds. Four to one – until the corporal came down from the tree. They had only two guns: the shotgun and the captain's pistol. And they were amateurs. The boat would help, too.

He said: 'Restricted area? All I saw was a bit of fence. Look, do you mind pointing that blunderbuss away? It might go off.'

The captain said: 'Nobody goes bird-watching in the dark.'

'If you set up your hide under cover of darkness, you're concealed by the time the birds wake up. It's the accepted way to do it. Now look, the Home Guard is jolly patriotic and keen and all that, but let's not take it too far, what? Don't you just have to check my papers and file a report?'

The captain was looking a shade doubtful. 'What's in that canvas bag?'

'Binoculars, a camera, and a reference book.' Faber's hands went to the bag.

'No, you don't,' the captain said. 'Look inside it, Watson.'

There it was: the amateur's error.

Watson said: 'Hands up.'

Faber raised his hands above his head, his right hand close to the left sleeve of his jacket. Faber choreographed the next few seconds: there must be no gunfire.

Watson came up on Faber's left side, pointing the shotgun at him, and opened the flap of Faber's canvas bag. Faber drew the stiletto from his sleeve, moved inside Watson's guard, and plunged the knife downward into Watson's neck up to the hilt. Faber's other hand twisted the shotgun out of the young man's grasp.

The other two soldiers on the bank moved toward him, and the corporal began to crash down through the branches of the oak.

Faber tugged the stiletto out of Watson's neck as the man collapsed to the ground. The captain was fumbling at the flap of his holster. Faber leaped into the well of the boat. It rocked, sending the captain staggering. Faber struck at him with the knife, but the man was too far away for an accurate thrust. The point caught in the lapel of his uniform jacket, then jerked up, slashing his chin. His hand came away from the holster to clutch the wound.

Faber whipped around to face the bank. One of the soldiers jumped. Faber stepped forward and held his right arm out rigidly. The leaping soldier impaled himself on the eight-inch needle.

The impact knocked Faber off his feet, and he lost his grip on the stiletto. The soldier fell on top of the weapon. Faber got to his knees: there was no time to retrieve the stiletto, for the captain was opening his holster. Faber jumped at him, his hands going for the officer's face. The gun came out. Faber's thumbs gouged at the captain's eyes, and he screamed in pain and tried to push Faber's arms aside.

There was a thud as the fourth guardsman landed in the well of the boat. Faber turned from the captain, who would now be unable to see to fire his pistol even if he could get the safety off. The fourth man held a policeman's truncheon. He brought it down hard. Faber shifted to the right, so that the blow missed his head and caught his left shoulder. His left arm momentarily became paralysed. He chopped the man's neck with the side of his right hand, a powerful, accurate blow. Amazingly, the man survived it, and brought his truncheon up for a second swipe. Faber closed in. The feeling returned to his left arm, and it began to hurt mightily. He took the soldier's face in both his hands, pushed, twisted, and pushed again. There was a sharp crack as the man's neck broke. At the same instant the truncheon landed again, this time on Faber's head. He reeled away, dazed.

The captain bumped into him, still staggering. Faber pushed him. His cap went flying as he stumbled backward over the gunwale and fell into the canal with a huge splash.

The corporal jumped the last six feet from the oak tree on to the ground. Faber retrieved his stiletto from the impaled guard and leaped to the bank. Watson was still alive, but it would not be for long: blood was pumping out of the wound in his neck.

Faber and the corporal faced each other. The corporal had a gun.

He was utterly terrified. In the few seconds it had taken him to climb down the oak tree, this stranger had killed three of his mates and thrown the fourth into the canal. Horror shone from his eyes like torchlight.

Faber looked at the gun. It was *old* – it looked like a museum piece. If the corporal had any confidence in it, he would have fired it already.

The corporal took a step forward, and Faber noticed that he favoured his right leg – perhaps he had hurt it coming out of the tree. Faber stepped sideways, forcing the corporal to put his weight on the weak leg as he swung to keep his gun on target. Faber got the toe of his shoe under a stone and kicked upward. The corporal's eyes flicked to the stone, and Faber moved.

The corporal pulled the trigger, and nothing happened. The old gun had jammed. Even if it had fired, he would have missed Faber: his eyes were on the stone, he stumbled on the weak leg, and Faber had moved.

Faber killed him with the neck stab.

Only the captain was left.

Faber looked, to see the man clambering out of the water on the far bank. He found a stone and threw it.

It hit the captain's head, but the man heaved himself on to dry land and began to run.

Faber ran to the bank, dived in, swam a few strokes, and came up on the far side. The captain was a hundred yards away and running; but he was old. Faber gave chase. He gained steadily until he could hear the man's agonized, ragged breathing. The captain slowed, then collapsed into a bush.

Faber came up to him and turned him over.

The captain said: 'You're a . . . devil.'

'You saw my face,' Faber said, and killed him.

TWELVE

The Ju-52 trimotor transport plane with swastikas on the wings bumped to a halt on the rain-wet runway at Rastenburg in the East Prussian forest. A small man with big features – a large nose, a wide mouth, big ears – disembarked and walked quickly across the tarmac to a waiting Mercedes car.

As the car drove through the gloomy, damp forest, Field Marshal Erwin Rommel took off his cap and rubbed a nervous hand along his receding hairline. In a few weeks' time, he knew, another man would travel this route with a bomb in his briefcase – a bomb destined for the Führer himself. Meanwhile the fight must go on, so that the new leader of Germany – who might even be Rommel himself – could negotiate with the Allies from a strong position.

At the end of a ten-mile drive the car arrived at the Wolfsschanze, the Wolves' Lair, headquarters now for Hitler and the increasingly tight, neurotic circle of generals who surrounded him.

There was a steady drizzle, and raindrops dripped from the tall conifers in the compound. At the gate to Hitler's personal quarters, Rommel put on his cap and got out of the car. Oberführer Rattenhuber, the chief of the SS bodyguard, wordlessly held out his hand to receive Rommel's pistol.

The conference was to be held in the underground bunker, a cold, damp, airless shelter lined with concrete. Rommel went down the steps and entered. There were a dozen or so there already, waiting for the noon meeting: Himmler, Goering, von Ribbentrop, Keitel. Rommel nodded greetings and sat on a hard chair to wait.

They all stood when Hitler entered. He wore a grey tunic and black trousers, and he was becoming more and more stooped, Rommel observed. He walked straight to the far end of the bunker, where a large wall map of north-western Europe was tacked to the concrete. He looked tired and irritable. He spoke without preamble.

'There will be an Allied invasion of Europe. It will come this year. It will be launched from Britain, with English and American troops. They will land in France. We will destroy them at the high-water mark. On this there is no room for discussion.'

He looked around, as if daring his staff to contradict him. There was silence. Rommel shivered: the bunker was as cold as death.

'The question is: where will they land? Von Roenne – your report.'

Colonel Alexis von Roenne, who had taken over, effectively, from Canaris, got to his feet. A mere captain at the outbreak of war, he had distinguished himself with a superb report on the weaknesses of the French army – a report which had been called a decisive factor in the German victory. He had become chief of the army intelligence bureau in 1942, and that bureau had absorbed the Abwehr on the fall of Canaris. Rommel had heard that he was proud and outspoken, but able.

Roenne said: 'Our information is extensive, but by no means complete. The Allies' codename for the invasion is Overlord. Troop concentrations in Britain are as follows.' He picked up a pointer and crossed the room to the wall map. 'First: along the south coast. Second: here in the district known as East Anglia. Third: in Scotland. The East Anglian concentration is *by far* the greatest. We conclude that the invasion will be three-pronged. First: a diversionary attack on Normandy. Second: the main thrust, across the Straits of Dover to the Calais coast. Third: a flanking invasion from Scotland across the North Sea to Norway. All intelligence sources support this prognosis.' He sat down.

Hitler said: 'Comments?'

Rommel, who was Commander of Army Group B, which controlled the north coast of France, said: 'I can report one confirming sign: the Pas de Calais has received by far the greatest tonnage of bombs.'

Goering said: 'What intelligence sources support your prognosis, von Roenne?'

Roenne stood up again. 'There are three: air reconnaissance, monitoring of enemy wireless signals, and the reports of agents.' He sat down.

Hitler crossed his hands protectively in front of his genitals, a nervous habit which was a sign that he was about to make a speech. 'I shall now tell you,' he began, 'how I would be thinking if I were Winston Churchill. Two choices confront me: east of the Seine, or west of the Seine. East has one advantage: it is nearer. But in modern warfare there are only two distances – *within* fighter range and *outside* fighter range. *Both* of these choices are within fighter range. Therefore distance is not a consideration.

'West has a great port – Cherbourg – but east has none. And most important – east is more heavily fortified than west. The enemy too has air reconnaissance.

'So, I would choose west. And what would I do then? I would try to make the Germans think the opposite! I would send two bombers to the Pas de Calais for every one to Normandy. I would try to knock out every bridge over the Seine. I would put out misleading wireless signals, send false intelligence reports, dispose my troops in a misleading fashion. I would deceive fools like Rommel and von Roenne. I would hope to deceive the Führer himself!'

Goering spoke first after a lengthy silence. 'My Führer, I believe you flatter Churchill by crediting him with ingenuity equal to your own.'

There was a noticeable easing of tension in the uncomfortable bunker. Goering had said exactly the right thing, managing to voice his disagreement in the form of a compliment. The others followed him, each stating the case a little more strongly: the Allies would choose the shorter sea crossing for speed; the closer coast would allow the covering fighter aircraft to refuel and return in shorter time; the south-east was a better launch pad, with more estuaries and harbours; it was unlikely that all the intelligence reports would be unanimously wrong.

Hitler listened for half an hour, then held up his hand for silence. He picked up a yellowing sheaf of papers from the table and waved them. 'In 1941,' he said, 'I issued my directive *Construction of Coastal Defences*, in which I forecast that the decisive landing of the Allies would come at the protruding parts of Normandy and Brittany, where the excellent harbours would make ideal beachheads. That was what my intuition told me then, and that is what it tells me now!' A fleck of foam appeared on the Führer's lower lip.

Von Roenne spoke up. (He has more courage than I, Rommel thought.) 'My Führer, our investigations continue, quite naturally, and there is one particular line of inquiry which you should know about. I have in recent weeks sent an emissary to England to contact the agent known as Die Nadel.'

Hitler's eyes gleamed. 'Ah! I know the man. Carry on.'

'Die Nadel's orders are to assess the strength of the First United States Army Group under General Patton in East Anglia. If he finds that this has been exaggerated, we must surely reconsider our prognosis. If, however, he reports that the army is as strong as we presently believe, there can be little doubt that Calais is the target.'

Goering looked at von Roenne. 'Who is this Nadel?'

Hitler answered the question. 'The only decent agent Canaris ever recruited – because he recruited him at my behest,' he said. 'I know his family – a pillar of the Reich. Strong, loyal, upright Germans. And Die Nadel – a brilliant man, brilliant! I see all his reports. He has been in London since before the English started the war. Earlier than that, in Russia—'

Von Roenne interrupted: 'My Führer—'

Hitler glared at him, but he seemed to realize that the spy chief had been right to stop him. 'Well?'

Von Roenne said tentatively: 'Then you will accept Die Nadel's report?'

Hitler nodded. 'That man will discover the truth.'

PART THREE

THIRTEEN

Faber leaned against a tree, shivering, and threw up.

Then he considered whether he should bury the five dead men.

It would take between thirty and sixty minutes, he estimated, depending on how well he concealed the bodies. During that time he might be caught.

He had to weigh that risk against the precious hours he might gain by delaying the discovery of the deaths. The five men would be missed very soon: there would be a search under way by around nine o'clock. Assuming they were on a regular patrol, their route would be known. The searchers' first move would be to send a runner to cover the route. If the bodies were left as they were, he would see them and raise the alarm. Otherwise, he would report back and a full-scale search would be mounted, with bloodhounds and policemen beating the bushes. It might take them all day to discover the corpses. By that time Faber could be in London. It was important for him to be out of the area before they knew they were looking for a murderer. He decided to risk the additional hour.

He swam back across the canal with the elderly captain across his shoulder. He dumped him unceremoniously behind a bush. He retrieved the two bodies from the well of the boat and piled them on top of the captain. Then he added Watson and the corporal to the heap.

He had no spade, and he needed a big grave. He found a patch of loose earth a few yards into the wood. The ground there was slightly hollowed, to give him an advantage. He got a saucepan from the boat's tiny galley and began to dig.

For a couple of feet there was just leaf-mould, and the going was easy. Then he got down to clay, and digging became extremely difficult. In half an hour he had added only another eighteen inches of depth to the hole. It would have to do.

He carried the bodies to the hole one by one and threw them in. Then he took off his muddy, blood-stained clothes and dropped them on top. He covered the grave with loose earth and a layer of foliage ripped from nearby bushes and trees. It should be good enough to pass that first, superficial inspection.

He kicked earth over the patch of ground near the bank where the life-blood of Watson had poured out. There was blood in the boat, too, where the impaled soldier had lain. Faber found a rag and swabbed-down the deck.

Then he put on clean clothes, made sail, and moved off.

He did not fish or watch birds: this was no time for pleasant embellishments to his cover. Instead he piled-on the sail, putting as much distance as possible between himself and the grave. He had to get off the water and into some faster transport as soon as possible. He reflected, as he sailed, on the relative merits of catching a train or stealing a car. A car was faster, if one could be found to steal; but the search for it might start quite soon, regardless of whether the theft was connected with the missing Home Guard patrol. Finding a railway station might take a long time, but it seemed safer: if he were careful he could escape suspicion for most of the day.

He wondered what to do about the boat. Ideally he would scuttle it, but he might be seen doing so. If he left it in a harbour somewhere, or simply moored at the canalside, the police would connect it with the murders that much sooner; and that would tell them in which direction he was moving. He postponed the decision.

Unfortunately, he was not sure where he was. His map of England's waterways gave every bridge, harbour and lock; but it did not show railway lines. He calculated he was within an hour or two's walk of half a dozen villages, but a village did not necessarily mean a station.

In the end luck solved two problems at once: the canal went under a railway bridge.

He took his compass, the film from the camera, his wallet and his stiletto. All his other possessions would go down with the boat.

The towpath on both sides was shaded with trees, and there were no roads nearby. He furled the sails, dismantled the base of the mast, and laid the pole on the deck. Then he removed the bung-hole stopper from the keel and stepped on to the bank, holding the rope.

Gradually filling with water, the boat drifted under the bridge. Faber hauled on the rope to hold the vessel in position directly under the brick arch as it sank. The after-deck went under first, the prow followed, and finally the water of the canal closed over the roof of the cabin. There were a few bubbles, then nothing. The outline of the boat was hidden from a casual glance by the shadow of the bridge. Faber threw the rope in.

The railway line ran north-east to south-west. Faber climbed the embankment and walked south-west, which was the direction in which London lay. It was a two-line track, probably a rural branch line. There would be few trains, but they would stop at all stations.

The sun grew stronger as he walked, and the exertion made him hot. When he had buried his blood-stained black clothes he had put on a double-breasted blazer and heavy flannel trousers. Now he took off the blazer and slung it over his shoulder.

After forty minutes he heard a distant chuff-chuff-chuff, and hid in a bush beside the line. An old steam engine went slowly by, heading north-west, puffing great clouds of smoke and hauling a train of coal trucks. If one came by in the opposite direction, he could jump it. Should he? It would save him a long walk. On the other hand, he would get conspicuously dirty, and he might have trouble disembarking without being seen. No, it was safer to walk.

The line ran straight as an arrow across the flat countryside. Faber passed a farmer, ploughing a field with a tractor. There was no way to avoid being seen.

The farmer waved to him without stopping in his work. He was too far away to get a good sight of Faber's face.

He had walked about ten miles when he saw a station ahead. It was half a mile away, and all he could see was the rise of the platforms and a cluster of signals. He left the line and cut across the fields, keeping close to borders of trees, until he met a road.

Within a few minutes he entered the village. There was nothing to tell him its name. Now that the threat of invasion was a memory, signposts and place-names were being re-erected, but this village had not got around to it.

There was a Post Office, a Corn Store, and a pub called The Bull. A woman with a pram gave him a friendly 'Good morning!' as he passed the War Memorial. The little station basked sleepily in the spring sunshine. Faber went in.

A timetable was pasted to a notice-board. Faber stood in front of it. From behind the little ticket window a voice said: 'I shouldn't take any notice of that, if I were you. It's the biggest work of fiction since *The Forsyte Saga.*'

Faber had known the timetable would be out-of-date, but he had needed to establish whether the trains went to London. They did. He said: 'Any idea what time the next train leaves for Liverpool Street?'

The clerk laughed sarcastically. 'Some time today, if you're lucky.'

'I'll buy a ticket anyway. Single, please.'

'Five-and-fourpence. They say the Italian trains run on time,' the clerk said.

'Not any more,' Faber remarked. 'Anyway, I'd rather have bad trains and our politics.'

The man shot him a nervous look. 'You're right, of course. Do you want to wait in The Bull? You'll hear the train – or, if not, I'll send for you.'

Faber did not want more people to see his face. 'No, thanks, I'd only spend money.' He took his ticket and went on to the platform.

The clerk followed him a few minutes later, and sat on the bench beside him in the sunshine. He said: 'You in a hurry?'

Faber shook his head. 'I've written today off. I got up late, I quarrelled with the boss, and the lorry that gave me a lift broke down.'

'One of those days. Ah, well.' The clerk looked at his watch. 'She went up on time this morning, and what goes up must come down, they say. You might be lucky.' He went back into his office.

Faber was lucky. The train came twenty minutes later. It was crowded with farmers, families, businessmen and soldiers. Faber found a space on the floor close to a window. As the train lumbered away, he picked up a discarded two-day-old newspaper, borrowed a pencil, and started to do the crossword. He was proud of his ability to do crosswords in English: it was the acid test of fluency in a foreign language. After a while the motion of the train lulled him into a shallow sleep, and he dreamed.

*

It was a familiar dream, the dream of his arrival in London.

He had crossed from France, carrying a Belgian passport which said he was Jan van Gelder, a representative for Philips (which would explain his suitcase radio if the Customs opened it). His English then was fluent but not colloquial. The Customs had not bothered him: he was an ally. He had caught the train to London. In those days there had been plenty of empty seats in the carriages, and you could get a meal. Faber had dined on roast beef and Yorkshire pudding. It amused him. He had talked with a history student from Cardiff about the European political situation. The dream was like the reality until the train stopped at Waterloo. Then it turned into a nightmare.

The trouble started at the ticket barrier. Like all dreams it had its own weird illogicality. The document they queried was not his forged passport but his perfectly legitimate railway ticket. The collector said: 'This is an Abwehr ticket.'

'No, it is not,' said Faber, speaking with a ludicrously thick German accent. What had happened to his dainty English consonants? They would not come. 'I have it in Dover gekauft.' Damn, that did it.

But the ticket collector, who had turned into a London policeman complete with helmet, seemed to ignore the sudden lapse into German. He smiled politely and said: 'I'd better just check your Klamotte, sir.'

The station was crowded with people. Faber thought that if he could get into the crowd he might escape. He dropped the suitcase radio and fled, pushing his way through the crowd. Suddenly he realized he had left his trousers on the train, and there were swastikas on his socks. He would have to buy trousers at the very first shop, before people noticed the trouserless running man with Nazi hose – then someone in the crowd said: 'I've seen your face before,' and tripped him, and he fell with a bump and landed on the floor of the railway carriage where he had gone to sleep.

He blinked, yawned, and looked around him. He had a headache. For a moment he was filled with relief that it was all a dream, then he was amused by the ridiculousness of the symbolism – swastika socks, for God's sake!

A man in overalls beside him said: 'You had a good sleep.'

Faber looked up sharply. He was always afraid of talking in his sleep and giving himself away. He said: 'I had an unpleasant dream.' The man made no comment.

It was getting dark. He *had* slept for a long time. The carriage light came on suddenly, a single blue bulb, and someone drew the blinds. People's faces turned into pale, featureless ovals. The workman became talkative again. 'You missed the excitement,' he told Faber.

Faber frowned. 'What happened?' It was impossible he should have slept through some kind of police check.

'One of them Yank trains passed us. It was going about ten miles an hour, nigger driving it, ringing its bell, with a bloody great cow-catcher on the front! Talk about the Wild West.'

Faber smiled and thought back to the dream. In fact his arrival in London had been without incident. He had checked into an hotel at first, still using his Belgian cover. Within a week he had visited several country churchyards, taken the names of men his age from the gravestones, and applied for three duplicate birth certificates. Then he took lodgings and found humble work, using forged references from a non-existent Manchester firm. He had even got on to the electoral register in Highgate before the war. He voted Conservative. When rationing came in, the ration books were issued via householders to every person who had slept in the house on a particular night. Faber contrived to spend part of that night in each of three different houses, and so obtained papers for each of his personae. He burned the Belgian passport – in the unlikely event he should need a passport, he could get three British ones.

The train stopped, and from the noise outside the passengers guessed they had arrived. When Faber got out he realized how hungry and thirsty he was. His last meal had been sausage-meat, dry biscuits and bottled water, the day before. He went through the ticket barrier and found the station buffet. It was full of people, mostly soldiers, sleeping or trying to sleep at the tables. Faber asked for a cheese sandwich and a cup of tea.

'The food is reserved for servicemen,' said the woman behind the counter.

'Just the tea, then.'

'Got a cup?'

Faber was surprised. 'No, I haven't.'

'Neither have we, chum.'

Faber left in disgust. He contemplated going into the Great Eastern Hotel for dinner, but that would take time. He found a pub and drank two pints of weak beer, then bought a bag of chips at a fish-and-chip shop and ate them from the newspaper wrapping, standing on the pavement. They made him feel surprisingly full.

Now he had to find a chemist's shop and break in.

He wanted to develop his film, to make sure the pictures came out. He was not going to risk returning to Germany with a roll of spoiled, useless film. If the pictures were no good he would have to steal more film and go back. The thought was unbearable.

It would have to be a small independent shop, not a branch of a chain which would process film centrally. It must be in an area where the local people could afford cameras (or could have afforded them before the war). The part of East London in which Liverpool Street Station stood was no good. He decided to head toward Bloomsbury.

The moonlit streets were quiet. There had been no sirens so far tonight. Two Military Policemen stopped him in Chancery Lane and asked for his identity card. Faber pretended to be slightly drunk, and the MPs did not ask what he was doing out of doors.

He found the shop he was looking for at the north end of Southampton Row. There was a Kodak sign in the window. Surprisingly, the shop was open. He went in.

A stooped, irritable man with thinning hair and glasses stood behind the counter, wearing a white coat. He said: 'We're only open for doctors' prescriptions.'

'That's all right. I just want to ask whether you develop photographs.'

'Yes, if you come back tomorrow—'

'Do you do them on the premises?' Faber asked. 'I need them quickly, you see.'

'Yes, if you come back tomorrow—'

'Could I have the prints the same day? My brother's on leave, and he wants to take some back—'

'Twenty-four hours is the best we can do. Come back tomorrow.'

'Thank you, I will,' Faber lied. On his way out he noticed that the shop was due to close in ten minutes. He crossed the road and stood in the shadows, waiting.

Promptly at nine o'clock the pharmacist came out, locking the shop behind him, and walked off down the road. Faber went in the opposite direction and turned two corners.

There seemed to be no access to the back of the shop. That was something of a blow: Faber did not want to break in the front way, in case the unlocked door was noticed by a patrolling policeman while he was in there. He walked along the parallel street, looking for a way through. Apparently there was none. Yet there had to be a well of some kind at the back, for the two streets were too far apart for the buildings to be joined back-to-back.

Finally he came across a large old house with a nameplate marking it as a Hall of Residence for a nearby college. The front door was unlocked. Faber went in and walked quickly through to a communal kitchen. A lone girl sat at a table, drinking coffee and reading a book. Faber muttered: 'College blackout check.' She nodded and returned to her text. Faber went out of the back door.

He crossed a yard, bumping into a cluster of garbage cans on the way, and found a door to a lane. In seconds he was at the rear of the chemist's shop. This entrance was obviously never used. He clambered over some tyres and a discarded mattress, and threw his shoulder at the door. The rotten wood gave easily, and Faber was inside.

He found the darkroom and shut himself in. The light switch operated a dim red lamp in the ceiling. The place was quite well-equipped, with neatly labelled bottles of developing fluid, an enlarger, and even a dryer for prints.

Faber worked quickly but carefully, getting the temperature of the tanks exactly right, agitating the fluids to develop the film evenly, timing the processes by the hands of a large electric clock on the wall.

The negatives were perfect.

He let them dry, then fed them through the enlarger and made one complete set of ten-by-eight prints. He felt a sense of elation as he saw the images gradually appear in the bath of developer – God, he had done a good job!

There was now a major decision to be made.

The problem had been in his mind all day, and now that the pictures had come out he was forced to confront it.

What if he did not make it home?

The journey ahead of him was, to say the least, hazardous. He was confident of his own ability to make the rendezvous in spite of travel restrictions and coastal security; but he could not guarantee that the U-boat would be there; or that it would get back across the North Sea. Indeed, he might walk out of here and get run over by a bus.

The possibility that, having discovered the greatest secret of the war, he might die and his secret die with him, was too awful to contemplate.

He had to have a fall-back stratagem; a second method of ensuring that the evidence of the Allied deception reached the Abwehr. And that meant writing to Hamburg.

There was, of course, no postal service between England and Germany. Mail had to go via a neutral country. All such mail was sure to be censored. He could write in code, but there was no point: he had to send the pictures, for it was the evidence that counted.

There was a route, but it was an old one. At the Portuguese Embassy in London there was an official, sympathetic to Germany for political reasons and because he was well bribed, who would pass messages via the diplomatic bag to the German Embassy in Lisbon. The route had been opened early in 1939, and Faber had never used it except for one routine test communication Canaris had asked for.

It would have to do.

Faber felt irrationally angry. He *hated* to place his faith in others. This route might no longer be open, or it might be insecure; in which case the British could discover that he had found out their secret.

It was a fundamental rule of espionage that the opposition must not know which of their secrets you have found out; for if they do, the value of your discoveries is nullified. However, in this case that was not so; for what could the British do with their knowledge? They still had the problem of conquering France.

Faber's mind was clear. The balance of argument indisputably favoured entrusting his secret to the Portuguese Embassy contact.

Against all his instincts, he sat down to write a letter.

FOURTEEN

Frederick Bloggs had spent an unpleasant afternoon in the countryside.

When five worried wives had contacted their local police station to say their husbands had not come home, a rural constable had exercised his limited powers of deduction and concluded that a whole patrol of the Home Guard had gone missing. He was fairly sure they had simply got lost – they were all deaf, daft or senile, otherwise they would have been in the Army – but all the same he notified his Constabulary headquarters, just to cover himself. The operations-room sergeant who took the message realized at once that the missing men had been patrolling a particularly sensitive military area, and he notified his inspector, who notified Scotland Yard, who sent a Special Branch man down there and notified M15, who sent Bloggs.

The Special Branch man was Harris, who had been on the Stockwell murder. He and Bloggs met on the train, which was one of the Wild West locomotives lent to Britain by the Americans because of the shortage of trains. Harris repeated his invitation to Sunday dinner, and Bloggs told him again that he worked most Sundays.

When they got off the train they borrowed bicycles to ride along the canal towpath until they met up with the search party. Harris, ten years older than Bloggs and four stone heavier, found the ride a strain.

They met a section of the search party under a railway bridge. Harris welcomed the opportunity to get off the bicycle. 'What have you found?' he said. 'Bodies?'

'No, a boat,' said a policeman. 'Who are you?'

They introduced themselves. A constable stripped to his underwear was diving down to examine the vessel. He came up with a bung in his hand.

Bloggs looked at Harris. 'Deliberately scuttled?'

'Looks like it.' Harris turned to the diver. 'Notice anything else?'

'She hasn't been down there for long, she's in good condition, and the mast has been taken down, not broken.'

Harris said: 'That's a lot of information from a minute under water.'

'I'm a weekend sailor,' the diver said.

Harris and Bloggs mounted their cycles and moved on.

When they met up with the main party, the bodies had been found.

'Murdered, all five,' said the uniformed inspector in charge. 'Captain Langham, Corporal Lee, and Privates Watson, Dayton and Forbes. Dayton's neck was broken, the rest were killed with some kind of knife. Langham's body had been in the canal. All found together in a shallow grave. Bloody murder.' He was quite shaken.

Harris looked closely at the five bodies, laid out in a line. 'I've seen wounds like this before, Fred,' he said.

Bloggs looked closely. 'Jesus Christ, it's him.'

Harris nodded. 'Stiletto.'

The inspector said in astonishment: 'You know who did it?'

'We can guess,' Harris said. 'We think he's killed twice before. If it's the same man, we know *who* he is but not *where* he is.'

The inspector's eyes narrowed. 'What with the restricted area so close, and Special Branch and MI5 arriving on the scene so quick, is there anything else I need to know about this case?'

Harris answered: 'Just that you keep very quiet until your Chief Constable has talked to our people.'

''Nuff said.'

Bloggs asked. 'Anything else found, Inspector?'

'We're still combing the area, in ever-widening circles; but nothing so far. There were some clothes in the grave.' He pointed.

Bloggs touched them gingerly: black trousers, a black sweater, a short black leather jacket, RAF-style.

Harris said: 'Clothes for night work.'

'To fit a big man,' Bloggs added.

'How tall is your man?'

'Over six foot.'

The inspector said: 'Did you pass the men who found the sunken boat?'

'Yes.' Bloggs frowned. 'Where's the nearest lock?'

'Four miles upstream.'

'If our man was in a boat, the lock-keeper must have seen him, mustn't he?'

'Must have,' the inspector agreed.

Bloggs said: 'We'd better talk to him.' He returned to his cycle.

'Not another four miles,' Harris complained.

Bloggs said: 'Work off some of those Sunday dinners.'

The four-mile ride took them most of an hour, because the towpath was made for horses, not wheels, and it was uneven, muddy, and mined with loose boulders and tree roots. Harris was sweating and cursing by the time they reached the lock.

The lock-keeper was sitting outside his little house, smoking a pipe and enjoying the mild air of afternoon. He was a middle-aged man of slow speech and slower movements. He regarded the two cyclists with faint amusement.

Bloggs spoke, because Harris was out of breath. 'We're police officers,' he said.

'Is that so?' said the lock-keeper. 'What's the excitement?' He looked as excited as a cat in front of a fire.

Bloggs took the photograph of Die Nadel out of his wallet and gave it to the man. 'Have you ever seen him?'

The lock-keeper put the picture on his lap while he held a fresh match to his pipe. Then he studied the photograph for a while, and handed it back.

'Well?' Harris said.

'Aye.' The lock-keeper nodded slowly. 'He was here about this time yesterday. Came in for a cup of tea.

Nice enough chap. What's he done, shown a light after blackout?'

Bloggs sat down heavily. 'That clinches it,' he said.

Harris thought aloud. 'He moors the boat downstream from here, and goes into the restricted area after dark.' He spoke quietly, so that the lock-keeper should not hear. 'When he comes back, the Home Guard has his boat staked out. He deals with them, sails a bit farther to the railway, scuttles his boat and . . . hops a train?'

Bloggs said to the lock-keeper: 'The railway line that crosses the canal a few miles downstream – where does it go?'

'London.'

Bloggs said: 'Oh, shit.'

Bloggs got back to the War Office in Whitehall at midnight. Godliman and Parkin were there, waiting for him. Bloggs said: 'It's him, all right,' and told them the story.

Parkin was excited, Godliman just looked tense. When Bloggs had finished, Godliman said: 'So now he's back in London, and we're looking for a needle in a haystack again.' He was playing with matches, forming a picture with them on his desk. 'Do you know, every time I look at that photograph I get the feeling I've actually *met* the damn fellow.'

'Well, think! 'Bloggs said. 'Where?'

Godliman shook his head in frustration. 'It must have been only once, and somewhere strange. It's like a face I've seen in a lecture audience, or in the background at a cocktail party. A fleeting glimpse, a casual encounter – when I remember it probably won't do us any good.'

Parkin said: 'What's in that area?'

'I don't know, which means it's probably highly important,' Godliman said.

There was a silence. Parkin lit a cigarette with one of Godliman's matches. Bloggs looked up. 'We could print a million copies of his picture – give one to every policeman, ARP warden, member of the Home Guard, serviceman, railway porter; paste them up on hoardings and publish them in the papers . . .'

Godliman shook his head. 'Too risky. What if he's already talked to Hamburg about whatever he's seen? If we make a public fuss about the man they'll know that his information is good. We'd only be lending credence to him.'

'We've got to do something.'

'Surely. We will circulate his picture to police officers. We'll give his description to the press, and say he's just a straightforward murderer. We can give the details of the Highgate and Stockwell murders, without saying that security is involved.'

Parkin said: 'What you're saying is, we can fight with one hand tied behind our back.'

'For now, anyway.'

'I'll start the ball rolling with the Yard,' Bloggs said. He picked up the phone.

Godliman looked at his watch. 'There's not much

more we can do tonight, but I don't feel like going home. I shan't sleep.'

Parkin stood up. 'In that case I'm going to find a kettle and make some tea.' He went out.

The matches on Godliman's desk made a picture of a horse and carriage. He took away one of the horse's legs and lit his pipe with it. 'Have you got a girl, Fred?' he asked conversationally.

'No.'

'Not since—?'

'No.'

Godliman puffed at his pipe. 'There has to be an end to grief, you know.'

Bloggs made no reply.

Godliman said: 'Look, perhaps I shouldn't talk to you like a Dutch uncle. But I know how you feel – I've been through it myself. The only difference was that I didn't have anyone to blame.'

'You didn't remarry,' Bloggs said, not looking at Godliman.

'No. And I don't want you to make the same mistake. When you reach middle age, living alone can be very depressing.'

'Did I ever tell you, they called her Fearless Bloggs.'

'Yes, you did.'

Bloggs looked at Godliman at last. 'Tell me, where in the world will I find another girl like that?'

'Does she have to be a hero?'

'After Christine – yes.'

'England is full of heroes, Fred.'

At that moment Colonel Terry walked in.

Godliman said: 'Ah, Uncle Andrew—'

Terry interrupted: 'Don't get up. This is important. Listen carefully, because I have to give it to you fast. Bloggs, you need to know this, too. Whoever killed those five Home Guard has learned our most vital secret.

'Number one: our invasion force for Europe will land at Normandy. Number two: the Germans believe it will land at Calais. Number three: one of the most vital aspects of the deception is a very large phoney army, called the First United States Army Group, located in the restricted area those men were patrolling. That area contains dummy barracks, cardboard aircraft, rubber tanks – a huge toy army which looks real to the observers in the reconnaissance planes we've been letting through.'

Bloggs said: 'How come you're so sure the spy found out?'

Terry went to the door. 'Come in, Rodriguez.'

A tall, handsome man with jet-black hair and a long nose entered the room and nodded politely to Godliman and Bloggs. Terry said: 'Senhor Rodriguez is our man at the Portuguese Embassy. Tell them what happened, Rodriguez.'

The man stood by the door, holding his hat. 'A taxi came to the Embassy at about eleven o'clock. The passenger did not get out, but the driver came to the door with an envelope addressed to Francisco. The doorman called me, as he has been instructed to do, and I took possession of the envelope. I was in time to take the number of the cab.'

'I'm having the cabbie traced,' Terry said. 'All right, Rodriguez, you'd better get back. And thank you.'

The tall Portuguese left the room. Terry handed to Godliman a large yellow envelope, addressed to Manuel Francisco. Godliman opened it – it had already been unsealed – and withdrew a second envelope marked with a meaningless series of letters: presumably a code.

Within the inner envelope were several sheets of paper covered with handwriting and a set of ten-by-eight photographs. Godliman examined the letter. 'It looks like a very basic code,' he said.

'You don't need to read it,' Terry said impatiently. 'Look at the photographs.'

Godliman did so. There were about thirty of them, and he looked at each one before speaking. He handed them to Bloggs and said: 'This is a catastrophe.'

Bloggs glanced through the pictures then put them down.

Godliman said: 'This is only his back-up. He's still got the negatives, *and he's going somewhere with them.*'

The three men sat still in the little office, like a tableau. The only illumination came from a spotlight on Godliman's desk. With the cream walls, the blacked-out window, the spare furniture and the worn Civil Service carpet, they might have been anywhere in the world.

Terry said: 'I'm going to have to tell Churchill.'

The phone rang, and the Colonel picked it up. 'Yes. Good. Bring him here right away, please – but before you do, ask him where he dropped the passenger. What? Really? Thank you, get here fast.' He hung up. 'The taxi dropped our man at University College Hospital.'

Bloggs said: 'Perhaps he was injured in the fight with the Home Guard.'

Terry said: 'Where is that hospital?'

'About five minutes' walk from Euston Station,' Godliman said. 'Trains from Euston go to Holyhead, Liverpool, Glasgow . . . all places from which you can catch a ferry to Ireland.'

'Liverpool to Belfast,' Bloggs said. 'Then a car to the border and across into Eire, and a U-boat on the Atlantic coast. He wouldn't risk Holyhead-to-Dublin because of the passport control, and there would be no point in going beyond Liverpool to Glasgow.'

Godliman said: 'Fred, you'd better go to the station and show the picture of Faber around, see if anyone noticed him getting on a train. I'll phone the station and warn them you're coming, and at the same time find out which trains have left since about ten-thirty.'

Bloggs picked up his hat and coat. 'I'm on my way.'

Godliman lifted the phone. 'Yes, we're on our way.'

There were still plenty of people at Euston Station. Although in normal times the station closed around midnight, wartime delays were such that the last train often had not left before the earliest milk train of the morning arrived. The station concourse was a mass of kitbags and sleeping bodies.

Bloggs showed the picture to three railway policemen. None of them recognized the face. He tried ten women porters: nothing. He went to every ticket barrier. One of the guards said: 'We look at tickets, not faces.' He tried half a dozen passengers without result. Finally he went into the ticket office and showed the picture to each of the clerks.

A very fat, bald clerk with ill-fitting false teeth recognized the face. 'I play a game,' he told Bloggs. 'I try to spot something about a passenger that tells me why he's catching a train. Like, he might have a black tie for a funeral, or muddy boots means he's a farmer going home, or there might be a college scarf, or a white mark on a woman's finger where she's took off her wedding ring . . . know what I mean? This is a dull job – not that I'm complaining—'

'What did you notice about this chap?' Bloggs interrupted him.

'Nothing. That was it, see – I couldn't make him out at all. Almost like he was trying to be inconspicuous, know what I mean?'

'I know what you mean.' Bloggs paused. 'Now, I want you to think very carefully. Where was he going – can you remember?'

'Yes,' said the fat clerk. 'Inverness.'

'That doesn't mean he's going there,' said Godliman. 'He's a professional – he knows we can ask questions at railway stations. I expect he automatically buys a ticket for the wrong destination.' He looked at his watch. 'He must have caught the eleven forty-five. That train is now pulling into Stafford. I checked with the railway, they checked with the signalman,' he added by way of explanation. 'They're going to stop the train this side of Crewe. I've got a plane standing by to fly you two to Stoke-on-Trent.

'Parkin, you'll board the train where it's stopped, outside Crewe. You'll be dressed as a ticket inspector, and you'll look at every ticket – and every face – on that train. When you've spotted Faber, just stay close to him.

'Bloggs, you'll be waiting at the ticket barrier at Crewe, just in case Faber decides to hop off there. But he won't. You'll get on the train, and be first off at Liverpool, and waiting at the ticket barrier for Parkin and Faber to come off. Half the local constabulary will be there to back you up.'

'That's all very well if he doesn't recognize me,' Parkin said. 'What if he remembers my face from Highgate?'

Godliman opened a desk drawer, took out a pistol, and gave it to Parkin. 'If he recognizes you, shoot the bastard.'

Parkin pocketed the weapon without comment.

Godliman said: 'I want both of you to be quite clear on the importance of all this. If we don't catch this man, the invasion of Europe will have to be postponed – possibly for a year. In that year the balance of war could turn against us. The time may never be this right again.'

Bloggs said: 'Do we get told how long it is to D-Day?'

'All I know is that it's a matter of weeks.'

Parkin was thinking. 'It'll be June, then.'

Bloggs said: 'Shit.'

Godliman said: 'No comment.'

The phone rang and Godliman picked it up. After a moment he looked up. 'Your car's here.'

Bloggs and Parkin stood up.

Godliman said: 'Wait a minute.'

They stood by the door, looking at the professor. He was saying: 'Yes, sir. Certainly. I will. Goodbye, sir.'

Bloggs could not think of anyone Godliman called Sir. He said: 'Who was that?'

Godliman said: 'Churchill.'

'What did he have to say?' Parkin asked, awestruck.

Godliman said: 'He wishes you both good luck and Godspeed.'

FIFTEEN

The carriage was pitch dark. Faber thought of the jokes people made: 'Take your hand off my knee. No, not you, you.' The British would make jokes out of anything. Their railways were now worse than ever, but nobody complained any more because it was in a good cause. Faber preferred the dark: it was anonymous.

There had been singing, earlier on. Three sailors in the corridor had started it, and the whole carriage had joined in. They had been through *Be Like The Kettle And Sing, There'll Always Be An England* (followed by *Glasgow Belongs To Me* and *Land Of My Fathers* for ethnic balance), and appropriately, *Don't Get Around Much Any More.*

There had been an air-raid warning, and the train slowed to thirty miles an hour. They were all supposed to lie on the floor, but of course there was no room. An anonymous female voice had said: 'Oh, God, I'm frightened,' and a male voice, equally anonymous except that it was Cockney, had said: 'You're in the safest place, girl – they can't 'it a movin' target.' Then everyone laughed and nobody was scared any more. Someone opened a suitcase and passed around a packet of dried-egg sandwiches.

One of the sailors wanted to play cards.

'How can we play cards in the dark?'

'Feel the edges. All Harry's cards are marked.'

The train stopped unaccountably at about 4 a.m. A cultured voice – the dried-egg sandwich supplier, Faber thought – said: 'My guess is we're outside Crewe.'

'Knowing the railways, we could be anywhere from Bolton to Bournemouth,' said the Cockney.

The train jerked and moved off, and everyone cheered. Where, Faber wondered, was the caricature Englishman, with his icy reserve and his stiff upper lip? Not here.

A few minutes later a voice in the corridor said: 'Tickets, please.' Faber noted the Yorkshire accent: they were in the north now. He fumbled in his pockets for his ticket.

He had the corner seat, near the door, so he could see into the corridor. The inspector was shining a torch on to the tickets. Faber saw the man's silhouette in the reflected light. It looked vaguely familiar.

He settled back in his seat to wait. He remembered the nightmare: 'This is an Abwehr ticket' – and smiled in the dark.

Then he frowned. The train stops unaccountably; shortly afterwards a ticket inspection begins; the inspector's face is vaguely familiar . . . It might be nothing, but Faber stayed alive by worrying about things that *might* be nothing. He looked in the corridor again, but the man had entered a compartment.

The train stopped briefly – the station was Crewe, according to informed opinion in Faber's compartment – and moved off again.

Faber got another look at the inspector's face, and now he remembered. The boarding house in Highgate! The boy from Yorkshire who wanted to get into the Army!

Faber watched him carefully. His torch flashed across the face of every passenger. He was not just looking at the tickets.

No, Faber told himself, don't jump to conclusions. How could they possibly have got on to him? They could not have found out which train he was on, got hold of one of the few people in the world who knew what he looked like, and got the man on the train dressed as a ticket inspector in so short a time. It was unbelievable.

Parkin, that was his name. Billy Parkin. Somehow he looked a lot older now. He was coming closer.

It must be a look-alike – perhaps an elder brother. This had to be a coincidence.

Parkin entered the compartment next to Faber's. There was no time left.

Faber assumed the worst and prepared to deal with it.

He got up, left the compartment, and went along the corridor, picking his way over suitcases and kitbags and bodies, to the lavatory. It was vacant. He went in and locked the door.

He was only buying time – ticket inspectors did not fail to check the toilets. He sat on the seat and wondered how to get out of this. The train had speeded up, and was travelling too fast for him to jump off.

Besides, someone would see him go, and if they were really searching for him they would stop the train.

'All tickets, please.'

Parkin was getting close again.

Faber had an idea. The coupling between the carriages was a tiny space like an air-lock, enclosed by a bellows-like cover between the cars of the train, shut off at both ends by doors because of the noise and draughts. He left the lavatory, fought his way to the end of the carriage, opened the door, and stepped into the connecting passage. He closed the door behind him.

It was freezing cold, and the noise was terrific. Faber sat on the floor and curled up, pretending to sleep. Only a dead man could sleep here, but people did strange things on trains these days. He tried not to shiver.

The door opened behind him. 'Tickets, please.'

He ignored it. He heard the door close.

'Wake up, Sleeping Beauty.' The voice was unmistakable.

Faber pretended to stir, then got to his feet, keeping his back to Parkin. When he turned the stiletto was in his hand. He pushed Parkin up against the door, held the point of the knife at his throat, and said: 'Be still or I'll kill you.'

With his left hand he took Parkin's torch, and shone it into the young man's face. Parkin did not look as frightened as he ought to be.

Faber said: 'Well, well. Billy Parkin, who wanted to

join the Army, and ended up on the railways. Still, it's a uniform.'

Parkin said: 'You.'

'You know damn well it's me, little Billy Parkin. You were looking for me. Why?' He was doing his best to sound vicious.

'I don't know why I should be looking for you – I'm not a policeman.'

Faber jerked the knife melodramatically. 'Stop lying to me.'

'Honest, Mr Faber. Let me go – I promise I won't tell anyone I've seen you.'

Faber began to have doubts. Either Parkin was telling the truth, or he was overacting as much as Faber himself.

Parkin's body shifted, his right arm moving in the darkness. Faber grabbed the wrist in an iron grip. Parkin struggled for an instant, but Faber let the needle point of the stiletto sink a fraction of an inch into Parkin's throat, and the man was still. Faber found the pocket Parkin had been reaching for, and pulled out a gun.

'Ticket inspectors do not go armed,' he said. 'Who are you with, Parkin?'

'We all carry guns now – there's a lot of crime on trains because of the dark.'

Parkin was lying courageously and persistently. Faber decided that threats were not enough to loosen his tongue.

His movement was sudden, swift and accurate. The blade of the stiletto leaped in his fist. Its point entered a measured half-inch into Parkin's left eye and came out again.

Faber's hand covered Parkin's mouth. The muffled scream of agony was drowned by the noise of the train. Parkin's hands went to his ruined eye.

Faber pressed his advantage. 'Save yourself the other eye, Parkin. Who are you with?'

'Military Intelligence, oh God, please don't do it again.'

'Who? Menzies? Masterman?'

'Oh, God, it's Godliman, Percy Godliman.'

'Godliman!' Faber knew the name, but this was no time to search his memory for details. 'What have they got?'

'A picture – I picked you out from the files.'

'What picture? *What picture*?'

'A racing team – running – with a cup – the Army—'

Faber remembered. Christ, where had they got hold of that? It was his nightmare: *they had a picture.* People would know his face. His *face.*

He moved the knife closer to Parkin's right eye. 'How did you know where I was?'

'Don't do it, please – agent in the Portuguese Embassy intercepted your letter – took the cab's number – inquiries at Euston – please, not the other eye—' He covered both his eyes with his hands.

'What's the plan? Where is the trap?'

'Glasgow. They're waiting for you at Glasgow. The train will be emptied there.'

Faber lowered the knife to the level of Parkin's belly.

To distract him, he said: 'How many men?' Then he pushed hard, inward and upward to the heart.

Parkin's one eye stared in horror, and he did not die. It was the drawback to Faber's favoured method of killing. Normally the shock of the knife was enough to stop the heart. But if the heart was strong it did not always work – after all, surgeons sometimes stuck a hypodermic needle directly into the heart to inject adrenalin. If the heart continued to pump, the motion would work a hole around the blade, from which the blood would leak. It was just as fatal, but longer.

At last Parkin's body went limp. Faber held him against the wall for a moment, thinking. There had been something – a flicker of courage, the ghost of a smile – before the man died. It meant something. Such things always did.

He let the body fall to the floor, then arranged it in a sleeping position, with the wounds hidden from view. He kicked the railway cap into a corner. He cleaned his stiletto on Parkin's trousers, and wiped the ocular liquid from his hands. It had been a messy business.

He put the knife away in his sleeve and opened the door to the carriage. He made his way back to his compartment in the dark.

As he sat down the Cockney said: 'You took your time – is there a queue?'

Faber said: 'It must have been something I ate.'

'Probably a dried-egg sandwich.' The Cockney laughed.

Faber was thinking about Godliman. He knew the name – he could even put a vague face to it: a middle-aged, bespectacled face, with a pipe and an absent, professorial air. That was it – he was a professor.

It was coming back. In his first couple of years in London Faber had had little to do. The war had not yet started, and most people believed it would not come. (Faber was not among the optimists.) He had been able to do a little useful work – mostly checking and revising the Abwehr's out-of-date maps, plus general reports based on his own observations and his reading of the newspapers – but not much. To fill in time, to improve his English, and to flesh out his cover, he had gone sightseeing.

His purpose in visiting Canterbury Cathedral had been innocent, although he did buy an aerial view of the town and the cathedral which he sent back for the Luftwaffe – not that it did much good: they spent most of 1942 missing it. Faber had taken a whole day to see the building: reading the ancient initials carved in walls, distinguishing the different architectural styles, reading the guidebook line by line as he walked slowly around.

He had been in the south ambulatory of the choir, looking at the blind arcading, when he became conscious of another absorbed figure by his side; an older man. 'Fascinating, isn't it?' the man said; and Faber asked him what he meant.

'The one pointed arch in an arcade of round ones. No reason for it – that section obviously hasn't been rebuilt. For some reason, somebody just altered that one. I wonder why.'

Faber saw what he meant. The choir was Romanesque, the nave Gothic; yet here in the choir was a solitary Gothic arch. 'Perhaps,' he said, 'the monks demanded to see what the pointed arches would look like, and the architect did this to show them.'

The older man stared at him. 'What a splendid conjecture! Of course that's the reason. Are you an historian?'

Faber laughed. 'No, just a clerk and an occasional reader of history books.'

'People get doctorates for inspired guesses like that!'

'Are you? An historian, I mean.'

'Yes, for my sins.' He stuck out his hand. 'Percy Godliman.'

Was it possible, Faber thought as the train rattled on through Lancashire, that that unimpressive figure in a tweed suit could be the man who had discovered his identity? Spies generally claimed they were civil servants, or something equally vague; not historians – that lie could be too easily found out. Yet it was rumoured that Military Intelligence had been bolstered by a number of academics. Faber had imagined them to be young, fit, aggressive and bellicose as well as clever. Godliman was clever, but none of the rest. Unless he had changed.

Faber had seen him once again, although he had not spoken to him on the second occasion. After the brief encounter in the cathedral Faber had seen a notice advertising a public lecture on Henry II to be given by Professor Godliman at his college. He had gone along, out of curiosity. The talk had been erudite, lively and convincing. Godliman was still a faintly comic figure, prancing about behind the lectern, getting enthusiastic about his subject; but it was clear his mind was as sharp as a knife.

So that was the man who had discovered what Die Nadel looked like.

Jesus Christ, an *amateur.*

Well, he would make amateur mistakes. Sending Billy Parkin had been one: Faber had recognized the boy. Godliman should have sent someone Faber did not know. Parkin had a better chance of recognizing Faber, but no chance at all of surviving the encounter. A professional would have known that.

The train shuddered to a halt, and a muffled voice outside announced that this was Liverpool. Faber cursed under his breath: he should have been spending the time working out his next move, not remembering Percival Godliman.

They were waiting at Glasgow, Parkin had said before he died. Why Glasgow? Their inquiries at Euston would have told them he was going to Inverness. And if they suspected Inverness to be a red herring, they would have speculated that he was coming here, to Liverpool, for this was the nearest link point for an Irish ferry.

Faber hated snap decisions.

He had to get off the train, whatever.

He stood up, opened the door, stepped out, and headed for the ticket barrier.

He thought of something else. What was it that had flashed in Billy Parkin's eyes before he died? Not hatred, not fear, not pain – although all those had been present. It was more like . . . triumph.

Faber looked up, past the ticket collector, and understood.

Waiting on the other side, dressed in a hat and raincoat, was the blond young tail from Leicester Square.

Parkin, dying in agony and humiliation and betrayal, had deceived Faber at the last. The trap was here.

The man in the raincoat had not yet noticed Faber in the crowd. Faber turned and stepped back on to the train. Once inside, he pulled aside the blind and looked out. The tail was searching the faces in the crowd. He had not noticed the man who got back on the train.

Faber watched while the passengers filtered through the gate until the platform was empty. The blond man spoke urgently to the ticket collector, who shook his head in negation. The man seemed to insist. After a moment he waved to someone out of sight. A police officer emerged from the shadows and spoke to the collector. The platform guard joined the group, followed by a man in a civilian suit who was presumably a more senior railway official.

The engine driver and his fireman left the locomotive and went over to the barrier. There was more waving of arms and shaking of heads.

Finally the railwaymen shrugged, turned away, or rolled their eyes upward, all telegraphing surrender. The blond and the police officer summoned other policemen, and they moved determinedly on to the platform.

They were going to search the train.

All the railway officials, including the engine crew,

had disappeared in the opposite direction, no doubt to seek tea and sandwiches while the lunatics tried to search a jampacked train. That gave Faber an idea.

He opened the door and jumped out of the wrong side of the train, the side opposite the platform. Concealed from the police by the carriages, he ran along the tracks, stumbling on the sleepers and slipping on the gravel, toward the engine.

It had to be bad news, of course. From the moment he realized Billy Parkin was not going to saunter off that train, Frederick Bloggs knew that Die Nadel had slipped through their fingers again. As the uniformed police moved on to the train in pairs, two men to search each carriage, Bloggs thought of several possible explanations of Parkin's non-appearance; and all the explanations were depressing.

He turned up his coat collar and paced the draughty platform. He wanted very badly to catch Die Nadel: not just for the sake of the invasion – although that was reason enough, God knew – but for Percy Godliman, and for the five Home Guard, and for Christine.

He looked at his watch: four o'clock. Soon it would be day. Bloggs had been up all night, and he had not eaten since breakfast yesterday, but until now he had kept going on adrenalin. The failure of the trap – he was quite sure it *had* failed – drained him of energy. Hunger and fatigue caught up with him. He had to make a conscious effort not to daydream about hot food and a warm bed.

'Sir!' A policeman was leaning out of a carriage and waving at him. 'Sir!'

Bloggs walked toward him, then broke into a run. 'What have you found?'

'It might be your man Parkin.'

Bloggs climbed into the carriage. 'What do you mean, might be?'

'You'd better have a look.' The policeman opened the communicating door between the carriages and shone his torch inside.

It was Parkin; Bloggs could tell by the ticket-inspector's uniform. He was curled up on the floor. Bloggs took the policeman's torch, knelt down beside Parkin, and turned him over.

He saw Parkin's face, looked quickly away, and said: 'Oh, dear God.'

'I take it this is Parkin?' the policeman said.

Bloggs nodded. He got up, very slowly, without looking again at the body. 'We'll interview everybody in this carriage and the next,' he said. 'Anyone who saw or heard anything unusual will be detained for further questioning. Not that it will do us any good: the murderer must have jumped off the train before it got here.'

Bloggs went back out on to the platform. All the searchers had completed their tasks and were gathered in a group. He detailed six of them to help with the interviewing.

The police inspector said: 'Your villain's hopped it, then.'

'Almost certainly,' Bloggs agreed. 'You've looked in every toilet, and the guard's van?'

'Yes, and on top of the train and under it, and in the engine and the coal tender.'

A passenger got off the train and approached Bloggs and the inspector. He was a small man with a bad chest, and he wheezed badly. He said: 'Excuse me.'

'Yes, sir,' the inspector said.

The passenger said: 'I was wondering, are you looking for somebody?'

'Why do you ask?'

'Well, if you are, I was wondering, would he be a tall chap?'

The inspector said: 'Why do you ask?'

Bloggs interrupted impatiently. 'Yes, a tall man. Come on, spit it out.'

'Well, it's just that a tall chap got out the wrong side of the train.'

'When?'

'A minute or two after the train pulled into the station. He got on, like, then he got off, on the wrong side. Jumped down on to the track. Only he had no luggage, you see, which was another odd thing, and I just thought—'

The inspector said: 'Balls.'

'He must have spotted the trap,' Bloggs said. 'But how? He doesn't know my face, and your men were out of sight.'

'Something made him suspicious.'

'So he crossed the line to the next platform and went out that way. Wouldn't he have been seen?'

The inspector shrugged. 'Not too many people about, this late. And if he was seen he could just say he was too impatient to queue at the ticket barrier.'

'Didn't you have the other ticket barriers covered?'

'I didn't think of it.'

'Nor did I.'

'Well, we can search the surrounding area, and later on we can check various places in the city, and of course we'll watch the ferry—'

'Yes, please do,' Bloggs said.

But somehow he knew Faber would not be found.

It was more than an hour before the train started to move. Faber had cramp in his left calf and dust in his nose. He heard the footplatemen climb back into their cab, and caught snatches of conversation about a body being found on the train. There was a metallic rattle as the fireman shovelled coal, then the hiss of steam, a clanking of pistons, a jerk and a sigh of smoke as the train moved off. Gratefully, Faber shifted his position and indulged in a smothered sneeze. Then he felt better.

He was at the back of the coal tender, buried deep in the coal, where it would take a man with a shovel ten minutes' hard work to expose him. As he had hoped, the police search of the tender had consisted of one good long look and no more.

He wondered whether he could risk emerging now. It must be getting light: would he be visible from a bridge over the line? He thought not. His skin was now quite black, and in a moving train in the pale light of dawn he would just be a dark blur on a dark background. Yes, he would chance it. Slowly and carefully, he dug his way out of his grave of coal.

He breathed the cool air deeply. The coal was shovelled out of the tender via a small hole in the front end. Later, perhaps, the fireman would have to enter the tender, when the pile of fuel got lower. Faber was safe for now.

As the light strengthened he looked himself over. He was covered from head to toe in coal dust, like a miner coming up from the pit. Somehow he had to wash and change his clothes.

He chanced a peep over the side of the tender. The train was still in the suburbs, passing factories and warehouses and rows of grimy little houses. He had to think about his next move.

His original plan had been to get off the train at Glasgow and there catch another train to Dundee and up the east coast to Aberdeen. It was still possible for him to disembark at Glasgow. He could not get off at the station, of course, but he might jump off either just before or just after. However, there were risks in that. The train was sure to stop at intermediate stations between Liverpool and Glasgow, and at those stops Faber might be spotted. No, he had to get off the train soon and find other means of transport.

The ideal spot would be a lonely stretch of track just outside a city or village. It had to be lonely, for he must not be seen leaping from the coal tender; but it had to be fairly near houses so that he could steal clothes and a car. And it needed to be an uphill stretch of track, so that the train would be travelling slowly enough for him to jump.

Right now its speed was about forty miles an hour. Faber lay back on the coal to wait. He could not keep a permanent watch on the country through which he was passing, for fear of being seen. He decided he would look out whenever the train slowed down. Otherwise he would lie still.

After a few minutes he caught himself dropping off to sleep, despite the discomfort of his bed. He shifted his position and reclined on his elbows, so that if he did sleep he would fall and be wakened by the impact.

The train was gathering speed. Between London and Liverpool it had seemed to be stationary more than moving; now it steamed through the country at a fine pace. To complete his discomfort, it started to rain; a cold, steady drizzle that soaked right through his clothes and seemed to turn to ice on his skin. There was another reason for getting off the train: he could die of exposure before they reached Glasgow!

After half an hour at high speed he was contemplating killing the footplate crew and stopping the train himself. A signal box saved their lives. The train slowed suddenly as brakes were applied. It decelerated in stages: Faber guessed the track was marked with descending speed limits. He looked out. They were in the countryside again. He could see the reason for the slowdown – they were approaching a track junction, and the signals were against them.

Faber stayed in the tender while the train stood still. After five minutes it started up again. Faber scrambled up the side of the tender, perched on the edge for a moment, and jumped.

He landed on the embankment and lay, face down, in the overgrown weeds. When the train was out of earshot he got to his feet. The only sign of civilization nearby was the signal box, a two-storey wooden structure with large windows in the control room at the top, an outside staircase, and a door at ground-floor level. On the far side was a cinder track leading away.

Faber walked in a wide circle to approach the place from the back, where there were no windows. He entered a ground-floor door and found what he had been expecting: a toilet, a washbasin and a coat hanging on a peg.

He took off his soaking wet clothes, washed his hands and face, and rubbed himself vigorously all over with a grubby towel. The little cylindrical film can containing the negatives was still taped securely to his chest. He put his clothes back on, but substituted the signalman's overcoat for his own sopping wet jacket.

Now all he needed was transport. The signalman must have got here somehow. Faber went outside and found a bicycle padlocked to a rail on the other side of the little building. He snapped the little lock with the blade of his stiletto. Moving in a straight line away from the blank rear wall of the signal box, he wheeled the cycle until he was out of sight of the building. Then he cut across until he reached the cinder track, climbed on the cycle, and rode away.

SIXTEEN

Percival Godliman had brought a little camp bed from his home. He lay on it in his office, dressed in trousers and shirt, trying in vain to sleep. He had not suffered insomnia for almost forty years, since he took his final exams at university. He would gladly swap the anxieties of those days for the worries which kept him awake now.

He had been a different man then, he knew; not just younger, but also a lot less . . . abstracted. He had been outgoing, aggressive, ambitious: he planned to go into politics. He was not studious then – he had reason to be anxious about the exams.

His two mismatched enthusiasms in those days had been debating and ballroom dancing. He had spoken with distinction at the Oxford Union and had been pictured in *The Tatler* waltzing with debutantes. He was no great womanizer: he wanted sex with a woman he loved, not because he believed in any high-minded principle to that effect, but because that was the way he felt about it.

And so he had been a virgin until he met Eleanor, who was not one of the debutantes, but a brilliant graduate mathematician with grace and warmth and a father dying of lung disease after forty years as a collier. The young Percival had taken her to meet his people. His father was Lord Lieutenant of the county, and the house had seemed a mansion to Eleanor, but she had been natural and charming and not in the least awestruck; and when Percy's mother had been disgracefully condescending to her at one point she had reacted with merciless wit, for which he loved her all the more.

He had taken his master's degree, then after the Great War he taught in a public school and stood in three by-elections. They were both disappointed when they discovered they could not have children; but they loved each other totally, and they were happy, and her death was the most appalling tragedy Godliman ever knew. It had ended his interest in the real world, and he had retreated into the Middle Ages.

It had drawn him and Bloggs together, this common bereavement. The war had brought Godliman back to life; revived in him those characteristics of dash and aggression and fervour which had made him a great speaker and teacher and the hope of the Liberal Party. He wished for something in Bloggs's life to rescue him from an existence of bitterness and introversion.

While he was in Godliman's thoughts, Bloggs phoned from Liverpool to say that Die Nadel had slipped through the net, and Parkin had been killed.

Godliman, sitting on the edge of the camp bed to speak on the phone, closed his eyes in despair. 'I should have put you on the train,' he murmured.

'Thanks!' Bloggs said.

'Only because he doesn't know your face.'

'I think he may,' Bloggs argued. 'We suspect he spotted the trap, and mine was the only face visible to him as he got off the train.'

'But where could he have seen you? Oh! No, surely . . . not Leicester Square?'

'I don't see how, but then . . . we always seem to underestimate him.'

'I wish he were on our side,' Godliman muttered. 'Have you got the ferry covered?'

'Yes.'

'He won't use it, of course – too obvious. He's more likely to steal a boat. On the other hand, he may still be heading for Inverness.'

'I've alerted the police up there.'

'Good. But look, I don't think we can make any assumptions about his destination. Let's keep an open mind.'

'Agreed.'

Godliman stood, picked up the phone, and began to pace the carpet. 'Also, don't assume it was he who got off the train on the wrong side. Work on the premise that he got off before, at, or after Liverpool.' Godliman's brain was in gear again, sorting permutations and possibilities. 'Let me talk to the Chief Superintendent.'

'He's here.'

There was a pause, then a new voice said: 'Chief Superintendent Anthony speaking.'

Godliman said: 'Do you agree with me that our man has got off this train somewhere in your area?'

'That seems likely, yes.'

'Good. Now the first thing he needs is transport – so I want you to get details of every car, boat, bicycle or donkey stolen within a hundred miles of Liverpool during the next twenty-four hours. Keep me informed, but give the information to Bloggs and work closely with him in following-up the leads.'

'Yes, sir.'

'Keep an eye on other crimes that might be committed by a fugitive – theft of food or clothing, unexplained assaults, identity card irregularities, and so on.'

'Right.'

'Now, Mr Anthony, you realize this man is more than just a mass murderer?'

'I assume so, sir, from the fact of your involvement. However, I don't know the details.'

'Nor shall you. Suffice it to say that this is a matter of national security so grave that the Prime Minister is in hourly contact with this office.'

'I understand. Uh, Mr Bloggs would like a word, sir.'

Bloggs came back on. 'Have you remembered how you know his face?'

'Oh, yes – but it's of no value, as I forecast. I met him by chance at Canterbury Cathedral, and we had a conversation about the architecture. All it tells us is that he's clever – he made some rather perceptive remarks, as I recall.'

'We knew he was clever.'

'Only too well.'

*

Chief Superintendent Anthony was a burly member of the middle class with a carefully softened Liverpool accent. He did not know whether to be peeved at the way MI5 ordered him about or thrilled at the chance to save England on his own manor.

Bloggs knew of the man's inner struggle – he met this sort of thing all the time when working with local police forces – and he knew how to tip the balance in his own favour. He said: 'I'm grateful for your helpfulness, Chief Superintendent. These things don't go unnoticed in Whitehall.'

'Only doing our duty,' Anthony said. He was not sure whether he was supposed to call Bloggs 'Sir'.

'Still, there's a big difference between reluctant assistance and willing help.'

'Yes. Well, it'll likely be a few hours before we pick up this man's scent again. Do you want to catch forty winks?'

'Yes,' Bloggs said gratefully. 'If you've got a chair in a corner somewhere . . .'

'Stay here,' Anthony said, indicating his office. 'I'll be down in the operations room. I'll wake you as soon as we've got something. Make yourself comfortable.'

Anthony went out, and Bloggs moved to an easy chair and sat back with his eyes closed. Immediately, he saw Godliman's face, as if projected on to the backs of his eyelids like a film, saying: 'There has to be an end to bereavement . . . I don't want you to make the same mistake.' Bloggs realized suddenly that he did not want the war to end, for that would make him face issues like the one Godliman had raised. The war made life simple, for he knew why he hated the enemy and he knew what he was supposed to do about it. Afterwards . . . the thought of another woman seemed disloyal, not just to Christine but, in some obscure way, to England.

He yawned and slumped farther into his seat, his thinking becoming woolly as sleep crept up on him. If Christine had died before the war, he would have felt very differently about remarrying. He had always been fond of her and respected her, of course; but after she took that ambulance job respect had turned to awe-struck admiration, and fondness turned to love. Then they had something special, something they knew other lovers did not share. Now, more than a year later, it would be easy for Bloggs to find another woman he could respect and be fond of, but he knew that would never be enough for him. An ordinary marriage, an ordinary woman, would always remind him that once he had possessed the ideal.

He stirred in his chair, trying to shake off imponderables so that he could sleep. England was full of heroes, Godliman had said. If Die Nadel got away England would be full of slaves. First things first . . .

Someone shook him. He was in a very deep sleep, dreaming that he was in a room with Die Nadel but could not pick him out because Die Nadel had blinded him with the stiletto. When he awoke he still thought he was blind because he could not see who was shaking him, until he realized he simply had his eyes closed. He opened them to see the large uniformed figure of Superintendent Anthony above him.

Bloggs raised himself to a more upright position and rubbed his eyes. 'Got something?' he asked.

'Lots of things,' Anthony said. 'Question is, which of 'em counts? Here's your breakfast.' He put a cup of tea and a biscuit on the desk and went to sit on the other side of it.

Bloggs left his easy chair and pulled a hard chair up to the desk. He sipped the tea. It was weak and very sweet. 'Let's get to it,' he said.

Anthony handed him a sheaf of five or six slips of paper.

Bloggs said: 'Don't tell me these are the only crimes in your area—'

'Of course not,' Anthony said. 'We're not interested in drunkenness, domestic disputes, blackout violations, traffic offences, or crimes for which arrests have already been made.'

'Sorry,' Bloggs said. 'I'm still waking up. Give me a chance to read these.'

There were three house burglaries. In two of them, valuables had been taken – jewellery in one case, furs in another. Bloggs said: 'He might steal valuables just to throw us off the scent. Mark these on the map, will you? They may show some pattern.' He handed the two slips back to Anthony. The third burglary had only just been reported, and no details were available. Anthony marked the location on the map.

A Food Office in Manchester had been robbed of

hundreds of ration books. Bloggs said: 'He doesn't need ration books – he needs food.' He set that one aside. There was a bicycle theft just outside Preston and a rape in Birkenhead. 'I don't think he's a rapist, but mark it anyway,' Bloggs told Anthony.

The bicycle theft and the third of the house burglaries were close together. Bloggs said: 'The signal box that the bike was stolen from – is that on the main line?'

'Yes, I think so,' Anthony said.

'Suppose Faber was hiding on that train and somehow we missed him. Would the signal box be the first place at which the train stopped after it left Liverpool?'

'It might be.'

Bloggs looked at the sheet of paper. 'An overcoat was stolen and a wet jacket left in its place.'

Anthony shrugged. 'Could mean anything.'

'No cars stolen?' Bloggs said sceptically.

'Nor boats, nor donkeys,' Anthony replied. 'We don't get many car thefts these days. Cars are easy to come by – it's petrol people steal.'

'I felt sure he'd steal a car in Liverpool,' Bloggs said. He thumped his knee in frustration. 'A bicycle isn't much use to him, surely.'

'I think we should follow it up, anyway,' Anthony pressed. 'It's our best lead.'

'All right. But meanwhile, double-check the burglaries to see whether food or clothing was pinched – the losers might not have noticed at first. Show Faber's picture to the rape victim, too. And keep checking all crimes. Can you fix me transport to Preston?'

'I'll get you a car,' Anthony said.

'How long will it take to get details of this third burglary?'

'They're probably interviewing at this minute,' Anthony said. 'By the time you reach the signal box I should have the complete picture.'

'Don't let them drag their feet.' Bloggs reached for his coat. 'I'll check with you the minute I get there.'

'Anthony? This is Bloggs. I'm at the signal box.'

'Don't waste any time there. The third burglary was your man.'

'Sure?'

'Unless there are two buggers running around threatening people with stiletto knives.'

'Who?'

'Two old ladies living alone in a little cottage.'

'Oh, God. Dead?'

'Not unless they died of excitement.'

'Eh?'

'Get over there. You'll see what I mean.'

'I'm on my way.'

It was the kind of cottage which is always inhabited by two elderly ladies living alone. It was small and square and old, and around the door grew a wild rose bush fertilized by thousands of pots of used tea leaves. Rows of vegetables sprouted tidily in a little front garden with a trimmed hedge. There were pink-and-white curtains at the leaded windows, and the gate creaked. The front door had been painted painstakingly by an amateur, and its knocker was made from a horse brass.

Bloggs's knock was answered by an octogenarian with a shotgun.

He said: 'Good morning. I'm from the police.'

'No, you're not,' she said. 'They've been already. Now get going before I blow your head off.'

Bloggs regarded her. She was less than five feet tall, with thick white hair in a bun and a pale, wrinkled face. Her hands were matchstick-thin, but her grasp on the shotgun was firm. The pocket of her apron was full of clothes-pegs. Bloggs looked down at her feet, and saw that she was wearing a man's working boots. He said: 'The police you saw this morning were local. I'm from Scotland Yard.'

'How do I know that?' she said.

Bloggs turned and called to his police driver. The constable got out of the car and came to the gate. Bloggs said to the old lady: 'Is the uniform enough to convince you?'

'All right,' she said, and stood aside for him to enter.

He stepped down into a low-ceilinged room with a tiled floor. The room was crammed with heavy, old furniture, and every surface was decorated with ornaments of china and glass. A small coal fire burned in the grate. The place smelled of lavender and cats.

A second old lady got out of a chair. She was like the first, but about twice as wide. Two cats spilled from her lap as she rose. She said: 'Hello, I'm Emma Parton, my sister is Jessie. Don't take any notice of that shotgun

– it's not loaded, thank God. Jessie loves drama. Will you sit down? You look so young to be a policeman. I'm surprised Scotland Yard is interested in our little robbery. Have you come from London this morning? Make the boy a cup of tea, Jessie.'

Bloggs sat down. 'If we're right about the identity of the burglar, he's a fugitive from justice,' he said.

'I told you! 'Jessie said. 'We might have been done in – slaughtered, in cold blood!'

'Don't be silly,' Emma said. She turned to Bloggs. 'He was such a nice man.'

'Tell me what happened,' Bloggs said.

'Well, I'd gone out the back,' Emma began. 'I was in the hen coop, hoping for some eggs. Jessie was in the kitchen—'

'He surprised me,' Jessie interrupted. 'I didn't have time to go for me gun.'

'You see too many cowboy films,' Emma admonished her.

'They're better than your love films – all tears and kisses—'

Bloggs took the picture of Faber from his wallet. 'Is this the man?'

Jessie scrutinized it. 'That's him.'

'Aren't you clever?' Emma marvelled.

'If we were clever we'd have caught him by now,' Bloggs said. 'What did he do?'

Jessie said: 'He held a knife to my throat and said: "One false move and I'll slit your gizzard." And he meant it.'

'Oh, Jessie, you told me he said: "I won't harm you if you do as I say." '

'Words to that effect, Emma!'

Bloggs said: 'What did he want?'

'Food, a bath, dry clothes and a car. Well, we gave him the eggs, of course. We found some clothes that belonged to Jessie's late husband Norman—'

'Would you describe them?'

'Yes. A blue donkey jacket, blue overalls, a check shirt. And he took poor Norman's car. I don't know how we'll be able to go to the pictures without it. That's our only vice, you know – the pictures.'

'What sort of car?'

'A Morris. Norman bought it in 1924. It's served us well, that little car.'

Jessie said: 'He didn't get his hot bath, though!'

'Well,' Emma said, 'I had to explain to him that two ladies living alone can hardly have a man taking a bath in their kitchen . . .' She blushed.

Jessie said: 'You'd rather have your throat slit than see a man in his combinations, wouldn't you, you silly fool.'

Bloggs said: 'What did he say when you refused?'

'He laughed,' Emma said. 'But I think he understood our position.'

Bloggs could not help but smile. 'I think you're very brave,' he said.

'I don't know about that, I'm sure.'

'So he left here in a 1924 Morris, wearing overalls and a blue jacket. What time was that?'

'About half-past nine.'

Bloggs absently stroked a marmalade cat. It blinked and purred. 'Was there much petrol in the car?'

'A couple of gallons – but he took our coupons.'

A thought struck Bloggs. 'How do you ladies qualify for a petrol ration?'

'Agricultural purposes,' Emma said defensively. She blushed.

Jessie snorted. 'And we're isolated, and we're elderly. Of course we qualify.'

'We always go to the corn stores at the same time as the pictures,' Emma added. 'We don't waste petrol.'

Bloggs smiled and held up a hand. 'All right, don't worry – rationing isn't my department anyway. How fast does the car go?'

Emma said: 'We never exceed thirty miles per hour.'

Bloggs looked at his watch. 'Even at that speed he could be seventy-five miles away by now.' He stood up. 'I must phone the details to Liverpool. You don't have a telephone, do you?'

'No.'

'What kind of Morris is it?'

'A Cowley. Norman used to call it a Bullnose.'

'Colour?'

'Grey.'

'Registration number?'

'MLN 29.'

Bloggs wrote it all down.

Emma said: 'Will we ever get our car back, do you think?'

'I expect so – but it may not be in very good

condition. When someone is driving a stolen car he generally doesn't take good care of it.' He walked to the door.

'I hope you catch him,' Emma called.

Jessie saw him out. She was still clutching the shotgun. At the door she caught Bloggs's sleeve and said in a stage whisper: 'Tell me – what is he? Escaped convict? Murderer? Rapist?'

Bloggs looked down at her. Her small green eyes were bright with excitement. She would believe anything he chose to tell her. He bent his head to speak quietly in her ear. 'Don't tell a soul,' he murmured, 'but he's a German spy.'

SEVENTEEN

Faber crossed the Sark Bridge and entered Scotland shortly after midday. He passed the Sark Toll Bar House, a low building with a signboard announcing that it was the first house in Scotland and a tablet above the door bearing some legend about marriages which he could not read. A quarter of a mile farther on he understood, when he entered the village of Gretna: he knew this was a place runaways came to get married.

The roads were still damp from the early rain, but the sun was drying them rapidly. Signposts and name-boards had been re-erected since the relaxation of invasion precautions, and Faber sped through a series of small lowland villages: Kirkpatrick, Kirtlebridge, Ecclefechan. The open countryside was pleasant, the green moors sparkling in the sunshine.

He had stopped for petrol in Carlisle. The pump attendant, a middle-aged woman in an oily apron, had not asked any awkward questions. Faber had filled the tank and the spare can fixed to the offside running-board.

He was very pleased with the little two-seater. It would still do fifty miles an hour, despite its age. The four-cylinder, 1548cc side-valve engine worked smoothly and tirelessly as he climbed and descended the Scottish hills. The leather-upholstered bench seat was comfortable. He squeezed the bulb horn to warn a straying sheep of his approach.

He went through the little market town of Lockerbie, crossed the River Annan by the picturesque Johnstone Bridge, and began the ascent to Beattock Summit. He found himself using the three-speed gearbox more and more.

He had decided not to take the most direct route to Aberdeen, via Edinburgh and the coast road. Much of Scotland's east coast, either side of the Firth of Forth, was a restricted area. Visitors were prohibited from a ten-mile-wide strip of land. Of course, the authorities could not seriously police such a long border. Nevertheless, Faber was less likely to be stopped and questioned while he stayed outside the security zone.

He would have to enter it eventually – later rather than sooner – and he turned his mind to the story he would tell if he were interrogated. Private motoring for pleasure had virtually ceased in the last couple of years because of the ever-stricter petrol rationing, and people who had cars for essential journeys were liable to be prosecuted for going a few yards off their necessary route for personal reasons. Faber had read of a famous impresario gaoled for using petrol supplied for agricultural purposes to take several actors from a theatre to the Savoy Hotel. Endless propaganda told people that a Lancaster bomber needed 2,000 gallons to get to the Ruhr. Nothing would please Faber more than to waste petrol which might otherwise be used to bomb his homeland, in normal circumstances; but to be stopped now, with the information he had taped to his chest, and arrested for a rationing violation would be an unbearable irony.

It was difficult. Most traffic was military, but he had no military papers. He could not claim to be delivering essential supplies because he had nothing in the car to deliver. He frowned. Who travelled, these days? Sailors on leave, officials, rare holidaymakers, skilled workmen . . . That was it. He would be an engineer, a specialist in some esoteric field like high-temperature gearbox oils, going to solve a manufacturing problem in a factory at Inverness. If he were asked which factory, he would say it was classified. (His fictitious destination had to be a long way from the real one so that he would never be questioned by someone who knew for certain there were no such factory.) He doubted whether consulting engineers ever wore overalls like the ones he had stolen from the elderly sisters – but anything was possible in wartime.

Having figured all that out, he felt he was reasonably safe from any random spot checks. The danger of being stopped by someone who was looking specifically for Henry Faber, fugitive spy, was another problem. They had that picture—

They knew his face. His face!

—and before long they would have a description of the car in which he was travelling. He did not think they would set up roadblocks, as they had no way of guessing where he was headed; but he was sure that every policeman in the land would be on the lookout for the grey Morris Cowley Bullnose, registration number MLN 29.

If he were spotted in the open country, he would not be captured immediately, for country policemen had bicycles, not cars. But the policeman would telephone his headquarters, and cars would be after Faber within minutes. If he saw a policeman, he decided, he would have to ditch this car, steal another, and divert from his planned route. However, in the sparsely populated Scottish lowlands there was a good chance he could get all the way to Aberdeen without passing a country policeman. The towns would be different. There, the danger of being chased by a police car was very great. He would be unlikely to escape: his car was old and relatively slow, and the police were generally good drivers. His best chance would be to get out of the vehicle and hope to lose himself in crowds or back streets. He contemplated ditching the car and stealing another each time he was forced to enter a major town. The problem there was that he would be leaving a trail a mile wide for MI5 to follow. Perhaps the best solution was a compromise: he would drive into the towns but try to use only the back streets. He looked at his watch. He would reach Glasgow around dusk, and thereafter he would benefit from the darkness.

Well, it was not satisfactory, but the only way to be totally safe was not to be a spy.

As he topped the one-thousand-feet-high Beattock Summit, it began to rain. Faber stopped the car and got out to raise the canvas roof. The air was oppressively warm. Faber looked up. The sky had clouded over very quickly. Thunder and lightning were promised.

As he drove on he discovered some of the little car's shortcomings. Wind and rain leaked in through several flaws in the canvas roof, and the small wiper sweeping the top half of the horizontally divided windscreen provided only a tunnel-like view of the road ahead. As the terrain became progressively more hilly, the engine note began to sound faintly ragged. It was hardly surprising: the twenty-year-old car was being pushed hard.

The shower ended. The threatened storm had not arrived, but the sky remained dark and the atmosphere forbidding.

Faber passed through Crawford, nestling in green hills; Abington, a church and a Post Office on the west bank of the River Clyde; and Lesmahagow, on the edge of a heathery moor.

Half an hour later he reached the outskirts of Glasgow. As soon as he entered the built-up area, he turned north off the main road, hoping to circumvent the city. He followed a succession of minor roads, crossing the major arteries into the city's east side, until he reached Cumbernauld Road, where he turned east again and sped out of the city.

It had been quicker than he expected. His luck was holding.

He was on the A80 road, passing factories, mines and farms. More Scots place-names drifted in and out of his consciousness: Millerston, Stepps, Muirhead, Mollinsburn, Condorrat.

His luck ran out between Cumbernauld and Stirling.

He was accelerating along a straight stretch of road, slightly downhill, with open fields on either side. As the speedometer needle touched forty-five there was a sudden, very loud noise from the engine; a heavy rattle, like the sound of a large chain pulling over a cog. He slowed to thirty, but the noise did not get perceptively quieter. Clearly some large and important piece of the mechanism had failed. Faber listened carefully. It was either a cracked ball-bearing in the transmission, or a hole in a big end. Certainly it was nothing so simple as a blocked carburettor or a dirty sparking-plug; nothing that could be repaired outside a workshop.

He pulled up and looked under the bonnet. There seemed to be a lot of oil everywhere, but otherwise he could see no clues. He got back behind the wheel and drove off. There was a definite loss of power, but the car would still go.

Three miles farther on, steam began to billow out of the radiator. Faber realized that the car would soon stop altogether. He looked for a place to dump it.

He found a mud track leading off the main road, presumably to a farm. One hundred yards from the road, the track curved behind a blackberry bush. Faber parked the car close to the bush and killed the engine. The hiss of escaping steam gradually subsided. He got out and locked the door. He felt a twinge of regret for Emma and Jessie, who would find it very difficult to get their car repaired before the end of the war.

He walked back to the main road. From there, the car could not be seen. It might be a day or even two before the abandoned vehicle aroused suspicion. By then, Faber thought, I may be in Berlin.

He began to walk. Sooner or later he would hit a town where he could steal another vehicle. He was doing well enough: it was less than twenty-four hours since he had left London, and he still had a whole day before the U-boat arrived at the rendezvous at six p.m. tomorrow.

The sun had set long ago, and now darkness fell suddenly. Faber could hardly see. Fortunately there was a painted white line down the middle of the road – a safety innovation made necessary by the blackout – and he was just about able to follow it. Because of the night silence he would hear an oncoming car in plenty of time.

In fact only one car passed him. He heard its deep-throated engine in the distance, and went off the road a few yards to lie out of sight until it had gone. It was a large car, a Vauxhall Ten, Faber guessed, and it was travelling at speed. He let it go by, then got up and resumed walking. Twenty minutes later he saw it again, parked by the roadside. He would have taken a detour across the field if he had noticed the car in time, but its light were off and its engine silent, and he almost bumped into it in the darkness.

Before he could consider what to do, a torch shone up toward him from under the car's bonnet, and a voice said: 'I say, is anybody there?'

Faber moved into the beam and said: 'Having trouble?'

'I'll say.'

The torch was pointed down, and as Faber moved closer he could see, by the reflected light, the moustached face of a middle-aged man in a double-breasted coat. In his other hand the man held, rather uncertainly, a large spanner; seeming unsure of what to do with it.

Faber looked at the engine. 'What's wrong?'

'Loss of power,' the man said, pronouncing it 'Lorse of par'. 'One moment she was going like a top, the next she started to hobble. I'm afraid I'm not much of a mechanic.' He shone the torch at Faber again. 'Are you?' he finished hopefully.

'Not exactly,' Faber said, 'but I know a disconnected lead when I see one.' He took the torch from the man, reached down into the engine, and plugged the stray lead back on to the cylinder head. 'Try her now.'

The man got into the car and started the engine. 'Perfect!' he shouted over the noise. 'You're a genius! Hop in.'

It crossed Faber's mind that this might be an elaborate MI5 trap, but he dismissed the thought: in the unlikely event they knew where he was, why should they tread softly? They could as easily send twenty policemen and a couple of armoured cars to pick him up.

He got in.

The driver pulled away and moved rapidly up through the gears until the car was travelling at a good speed. Faber made himself comfortable. The driver said: 'By the way, I'm Richard Porter.'

Faber thought quickly of the identity card in his wallet. 'James Baker.'

'How do you do. I must have passed you on the road back there – didn't see you.'

Faber realized the man was apologizing for not picking him up – everyone picked up hitch-hikers since the petrol shortage. 'It's okay,' Faber said. 'I was probably off the road, behind a bush, answering a call of nature. I did hear a car.'

'Have you come far?' Porter offered a cigar.

'It's good of you, but I don't smoke,' Faber said. 'Yes, I've come from London.'

'Hitch-hiked all the way?'

'No, my car broke down in Edinburgh. Apparently it requires a spare part which isn't in stock, so I had to leave it at the garage.'

'Hard luck. Well, I'm going to Aberdeen, so I can drop you anywhere along the way.'

Faber thought fast. This was a piece of good fortune. He closed his eyes and pictured the map of Scotland. 'That's marvellous,' he said. 'I'm going to Banff, so Aberdeen would be a great help. But I was planning to take the high road, because I didn't get myself a pass – is Aberdeen a Restricted Area?'

'Only the harbour,' Porter said. 'Anyway, you neen't worry about that sort of thing while you're in my car – I'm a JP and a member of the Watch Committee. How's that?'

Faber smiled in the darkness. It was his lucky day. 'Thank you,' he said. He decided to change the subject of the conversation. 'Is that a full-time job? Being a magistrate, I mean.'

Porter put a match to his cigar and puffed smoke.

'Not really. I'm semi-retired, y'know. Used to be a solicitor, until they discovered my weak heart.'

'Ah.' Faber tried to put some sympathy into his voice.

'Hope you don't mind the smoke?' Porter waved the fat cigar.

'Not a bit.'

'What takes you to Banff?'

'I'm an engineer. There's a problem in a factory . . . actually, the job is sort of classified.'

Porter held up his hand. 'Don't say another word. I understand.'

There was silence for a while. The car flashed through several towns. Porter obviously knew the road very well, to drive so fast in the blackout. The big car gobbled up the miles. Its smooth progress was soporific. Faber smothered a yawn.

'Damn, you must be tired,' Porter said. 'Silly of me. Don't be too polite to have a nap.'

'Thank you,' said Faber. 'I will.' He closed his eyes.

The motion of the car was like the rocking of a train, and Faber had his arrival nightmare again, only this time it was slightly different. Instead of dining on the train and talking politics with a fellow passenger, he was obliged for some unknown reason to travel in the coal tender, sitting on his suitcase radio with his back against the hard iron side of the truck. When the train arrived at Waterloo, everyone – including the disembarking passengers – was carrying a little duplicated photograph of Faber in the running team; and they were all looking at each other and comparing the faces they saw with the face in the picture. At the ticket barrier the collector took his shoulder and said: 'You're the man in the photo, aren't you?' Faber found himself dumb. All he could do was stare at the photograph and remember the way he had run to win that cup. God, how he had run: he had peaked a shade too early, started his final burst a quarter of a mile sooner than he had planned, and for the last 500 metres he wanted to die – and now perhaps he would die, because of that photograph in the ticket collector's hand . . . The collector was saying: 'Wake up! Wake up!' and suddenly Faber was back in Richard Porter's Vauxhall Ten, and it was Porter who was telling him to wake up.

His right hand was half way to his left sleeve, where the stiletto was sheathed, in the split-second before he remembered that as far as Porter was concerned James Baker was an innocent hitch-hiker. Then his hand dropped and he relaxed.

'You wake up like a soldier,' Porter said with amusement. 'This is Aberdeen.'

Faber noted that 'soldier' had been pronounced 'sol-juh', and recalled that Porter was a magistrate and a member of the police authority. He looked at the man in the dull light of early day: Porter had a red face and a waxed moustache, and his camel-coloured overcoat looked expensive. He was wealthy and powerful in this town, Faber guessed. If he were to disappear he would be missed almost immediately. Faber decided not to kill him.

Faber said: 'Good morning.'

He looked out of the window at the granite city.

They were moving slowly along the main street with shops on either side. There were several early workers about, all moving purposefully in the same direction: fishermen, Faber reckoned. It seemed a cold, windy place.

Porter said: 'Would you like to have a shave and a bit of breakfast before you continue your journey? You're welcome to come to my place.'

'You're very kind—'

'Not at all. If it weren't for you I should still be on the A80 at Stirling, waiting for a garage to open.'

'—but I won't, thank you. I want to get on with the journey.'

Porter did not insist, and Faber suspected that he was relieved not to have his offer taken up. The man said: 'In that case, I'll drop you at George Street – that's the start of the A96, and it's a straight road to Banff.' A moment later he stopped the car at a corner. 'Here you are.'

Faber opened the door. 'Thanks for the lift.'

'A pleasure.' Porter offered a handshake. 'Good luck!'

Faber got out and closed the door, and the car pulled away. He had nothing to fear from Porter, he thought; the man would go home and sleep all day, and by the time he realized he had helped a fugitive, it would be too late to do anything about it.

He watched the Vauxhall out of sight, then crossed the road and entered the promisingly named Market Street. Shortly he found himself in the docks and, following his nose, arrived at the fish market. He felt safely anonymous in the bustling, noisy, smelly market, where everyone was dressed in working clothes as he was. Wet fish and cheerful profanities flew through the air. Faber found it hard to understand the clipped, guttural accents. At a stall he bought hot, strong tea in a chipped half-pint mug and a large bread roll with a doorstep of white cheese.

He sat on a barrel to eat and drink. This evening would be the time to steal a boat. It was galling, to have to wait all day; and it left him with the problem of concealing himself for the next twelve hours; but he was too close now to take risks, and stealing a boat in broad daylight was much more risky than at the twilit end of the day.

He finished his breakfast and stood up. It would be a couple of hours before the rest of the city came to life. He would use the time to pick out a good hiding-place.

He made a circuit of the docks and the tidal harbour. The security was perfunctory, and he spotted several places where he could slip past the checkpoints. He worked his way around to the sandy beach, and set off along the two-mile esplanade. At its far end, a couple of pleasure yachts were moored at the mouth of the River Don. They would have suited Faber's purpose very well, but they would have no fuel.

A thick ceiling of cloud hid the sunrise. The air became very warm and thundery again. A few determined holidaymakers emerged from the seafront hotels and sat stubbornly on the beach, waiting for sunshine. Faber doubted they would get it today.

The beach might be the place to hide. The police would check the railway station and the bus depot, but they would not mount a full-scale search of the city. They might check a few hotels and guest-houses. It was unlikely they would approach everyone on the beach. He decided to spend the day in a deck-chair.

He bought a newspaper from a stall and hired a chair. He removed his shirt and put it back on over his overalls. He left his jacket off.

He would see a policeman, if one came, well before he reached the spot where Faber sat. There would be plenty of time to leave the beach and vanish into the streets.

He began to read the paper. There was a new Allied offensive in Italy, the newspaper rejoiced. Faber was sceptical. Anzio had been a shambles. The paper was badly printed and there were no photographs. He read that the police were searching for one Henry Faber, who had murdered two people in London with a stiletto . . .

A woman in a bathing suit walked by, looking hard at Faber. His heart missed a beat. Then he realized she was being flirtatious. For an instant he was tempted to speak to her. It had been so long . . . He shook himself mentally. Patience, patience. Tomorrow he would be home.

She was a small fishing boat, fifty or sixty feet long and broad in the beam, with an inboard motor. The aerial told of a powerful radio. Most of the deck was taken up with hatches to the small hold below. The cabin was aft, and only large enough to hold two men, standing, plus the dashboard and controls. The hull was clinker-built and newly caulked, and the paintwork looked fresh.

Two other boats in the harbour would have done as well, but Faber had stood on the quay and watched the crew of this one tie her up and refuel before they left for their homes.

He gave them a few minutes to get well away, then walked around the edge of the harbour and jumped on to the boat. She was called *Marie II.*

He found the wheel chained up. He sat on the floor of the little cabin, out of sight, and spent ten minutes picking the lock. Darkness was coming early because of the cloud layer which still blanketed the sky.

When he had freed the wheel he raised the small anchor, then sprang back on to the quay and untied the ropes. He returned to the cabin, primed the diesel engine, and pulled the starter. The motor coughed and died. He tried again. This time it roared to life. He began to manoeuvre out of the mooring.

He got clear of the other craft at the quayside and found the main channel out of the harbour, marked by buoys. He guessed that only boats of much deeper draught really needed to stick to the channel, but he saw no harm in being overcautious.

Once outside the harbour, he felt a stiff breeze, and hoped it was not a sign that the weather was about to break. The sea was surprisingly rough, and the stout little boat lifted high on the waves. Faber opened the throttle wide, consulted the dashboard compass, and set a course. He found some charts in a locker below the wheel. They looked old and little-used: no doubt the boat's skipper knew the local waters too well to need charts. Faber checked the map reference he had memorized that night in Stockwell, set a more exact course, and engaged the wheel-clamp.

The cabin windows were obscured by water. Faber could not tell whether it was rain or spray. The wind was slicing off the tops of the waves now. He poked his head out of the cabin door for a moment, and got his face thoroughly wet.

He switched on the radio. It hummed for a moment, then crackled. He moved the frequency control, wandering the airwaves, and picked up a few garbled messages. The set was working perfectly. He tuned to the U-boat's frequency, then switched off – it was too soon to make contact.

The waves increased in size as he progressed into deeper waters. Now the boat reared up like a bucking horse with each wave, then teetered momentarily at the top before plunging sickeningly down into the next trough. Faber stared blindly out of the cabin windows. Night had fallen, and he could see nothing at all. He felt faintly seasick.

Each time he convinced himself that the waves could not possibly get bigger, a new monster taller than the rest lifted the vessel toward the sky. They started to come closer together, so that the boat was always lying with its stern pointed either up at the sky or down at the sea bed. In a particularly deep trough the little boat was suddenly illuminated, as clearly as if it were day, by a flash of lightning. Faber saw a grey-green mountain of water descend on the prow and wash over the deck and the cabin where he stood. He could not tell whether the terrible crack which sounded a second afterwards was the thunderclap or the noise of the timbers of the boat breaking up. Frantically he searched the little cabin for a life jacket. There was none.

The lightning came repeatedly then. Faber held the locked wheel and braced his back against the cabin wall to stay upright. There was no point in operating the controls now – the boat would go where the sea threw it.

He kept telling himself that the boat must be built to withstand such sudden summer gales. He could not convince himself. Experienced fishermen probably would have seen the signs of such a storm, and refrained from leaving shore, knowing their vessel could not survive such weather.

He had no idea where he was, now. He might be almost back in Aberdeen, or he might be at his rendezvous. He sat on the cabin floor and switched on the radio. The wild rocking and shuddering made it difficult to operate the set. When it warmed up he experimented with the dials, and could pick up nothing. He turned the volume to maximum: still no sound.

The aerial must have been broken off its fixing on the cabin roof.

He switched to Transmit and repeated the simple message 'Come in, please,' several times; then left the set on Receive. He had little hope of his signal getting through.

He killed the engine to conserve fuel. He was going to have to ride out the storm – if he could – then find a way to repair or replace the aerial. He might need his fuel.

The boat slid terrifyingly sideways down the next big wave, and Faber realized he needed the engine power to ensure the vessel met waves head-on. He pulled the starter, but nothing happened. He tried several times, then gave up, cursing his foolishness for switching off.

The boat rolled so far on to its side that Faber fell and cracked his head on the wheel. He lay dazed on the cabin floor, expecting the vessel to turn turtle at any minute. Another wave crashed on the cabin, and this time the glass in the windows shattered. Suddenly Faber was under water. Certain the boat was sinking, he struggled to his feet, and broke surface. All the windows were out, but the vessel was still floating. He kicked open the cabin door, and the water gushed out. He clutched the wheel to prevent himself being washed into the sea.

Incredibly, the storm continued to get worse. One of Faber's last coherent thoughts was that these waters probably did not see such a storm more than once in a century. Then all his concentration and will were focused on the problem of keeping hold of the wheel. He should have tied himself to it, but now he did not dare to let go long enough to find a piece of rope. He lost all sense of up and down as the boat pitched and rolled on waves like cliffs. Gale force winds and thousands of gallons of water strained to pull him from his place. His feet slipped continually on the wet floor and walls, and the muscles of his arms burned with pain. He sucked air when he found his head above water, but otherwise held his breath. Many times he came close to blacking out. He vaguely realized that the flat roof of the cabin had disappeared.

He got brief, nightmarish glimpses of the sea whenever the lightning flashed. He was always surprised to see where the wave was: ahead, below, rearing up beside him, or completely out of sight. He discovered with a shock that he could not feel his hands, and looked down to see that they were still locked to the wheel, frozen in a grip like rigor mortis. There was a continuous roar in his ears, the wind indistinguishable from the thunder and the sea.

The power of intelligent thought slipped slowly away from him. In something that was less than a hallucination but more than a daydream, he saw the girl who had stared at him on the beach. She walked endlessly toward him over the bucking deck of the fishing boat, her swimsuit clinging to her body, always getting closer but never reaching him. He knew that, when she came within touching distance, he would take his dead hands from the wheel and reach for her, but he kept saying 'Not yet, not yet,' as she walked and smiled and swayed her hips. He was tempted to leave the wheel and close the gap himself, but something at the back of his mind told him that if he moved he would never reach her, so he waited and watched and smiled back at her from time to time, and even when he closed his eyes he could see her still.

He was slipping in and out of consciousness now.

His mind would drift away, the sea and the boat disappearing first, then the girl fading, until he would jerk awake to find that, incredibly, he was still standing, still holding the wheel, still alive; then for a while he would will himself to stay conscious, but eventually exhaustion would take over again.

In one of his last clear moments he noticed that the waves were moving in one direction, carrying the boat with them. Lightning flashed again, and he saw to one side a huge dark mass, an impossibly high wave – no, it was not a wave, it was a cliff . . . The realization that he was close to land was swamped by the fear of being hurled against the cliff and smashed. Stupidly, he pulled the starter, then hastily returned his hand to the wheel; but it would no longer grip.

A new wave lifted the boat and threw it down like a discarded toy. As he fell through the air, still clutching the wheel with one hand, Faber saw a pointed rock like a stiletto sticking up out of the trough of the wave. It seemed certain to impale the boat. But the hull of the little craft scraped the edge of the rock and was carried past.

The mountainous waves were breaking now. The next one was too much for the vessel's timbers. The boat hit the trough with a solid impact, and the sound of the hull splitting cracked the night like an explosion. Faber knew the boat was finished.

The water retreated, and Faber realized that the hull had broken because it had hit land. He stared in dumb astonishment as a new flash of lightning revealed a beach. The sea lifted the ruined boat off the sand as water crashed over the deck again, knocking Faber to the floor. But he had seen everything with daylight clarity in that moment. The beach was narrow, and the waves were breaking right up to the cliff. But there was a jetty, over to his right, and a bridge of some kind leading from the jetty to the cliff top. He knew that if he left the boat for the beach, the next wave would kill him with tons of water or break his head like an egg against the cliff. But if he could reach the jetty in between waves, he might scramble far enough up the bridge to be out of reach of the water.

He might survive yet.

The next wave split the deck open as if the seasoned wood were no stronger than a banana skin. The boat collapsed under Faber, and he found himself sucked backward by the receding surf. He scrambled upright, his legs like jelly beneath him, and broke into a run, splashing through the shallows toward the jetty. Running those few yards was the hardest thing he had ever done. He *wanted* to stumble, so that he could rest in the water and die; but he stayed upright, just as he had when he won the 5,000 metres race, until he crashed into one of the pillars of the jetty. He reached up and grabbed the boards with his hands, willing them to come back to life for a few seconds; and lifted himself until his chin was over the edge; then he swung his legs up and rolled over.

The wave came as he got to his knees. He threw himself forward. The wave carried him a few yards then flung him brutally against the wooden planking. He swallowed water and saw stars. When the weight lifted from his back he summoned the will to move. It would not come. He felt himself being dragged inexorably back. A sudden rage possessed him. He would not be beaten, not now! He screamed his hatred of the storm and the sea and the British and Percival Godliman, and suddenly he was on his feet and running, running, away from the sea and up the ramp, running with his eyes shut and his mouth open and madness in his heart, daring his lungs to burst and his bones to break; remembering, dimly, that he had called on this madness once before and almost died; running with no sense of destination, but knowing he would not stop until he lost his mind.

The ramp was long and steep. A strong man might have run all the way to the top, if he were in training and rested. An Olympic athlete, if he were tired, might have got half way. The average forty-year-old man would have managed a yard or two.

Faber made it to the top.

A yard from the end of the ramp he had a slight heart attack and lost consciousness, but his legs pumped twice more before he hit the sodden turf.

He never knew how long he lay there. When he opened his eyes the storm still raged, but day had broken, and he could see, a few yards away from him, a small cottage which looked inhabited.

He got to his knees and began the long crawl to the front door.

EIGHTEEN

The *U-505* wheeled in a tedious circle, her powerful diesels chugging slowly as she nosed through the depths like a grey, toothless shark. Lieutenant-Commander Werner Heer, her master, was drinking ersatz coffee and trying not to smoke any more cigarettes. It had been a long day and a long night. He disliked his assignment, for he was a fighting man and there was no fighting to be done; and he disliked the quiet Abwehr officer with sly blue eyes who was an unwelcome guest aboard the submarine.

The Intelligence man, Major Wohl, sat opposite the captain. The man never looked tired, damn him. Those blue eyes looked around, taking things in, but the expression in them never changed. His uniform never got rumpled, despite the rigours of underwater life; and he lit a new cigarette every twenty minutes, on the dot, and smoked it to a quarter-inch stub. Heer would have stopped smoking, just so that he could enforce regulations and prevent Wohl from enjoying tobacco, but Heer himself was too much of an addict.

Heer never liked Intelligence people, because he always had the feeling they were gathering intelligence on him. Nor did he like working with Abwehr. His vessel was made for battle, not for skulking around the British coast waiting to pick up secret agents. It seemed to him plain madness to put at risk a costly piece of fighting machinery, not to mention its skilled crew, for the sake of one man who might even fail to appear.

He emptied his cup and made a face. 'Damn coffee,' he said. 'It tastes vile.'

Wohl's expressionless gaze rested on him for a moment then moved away. He said nothing.

Heer shifted restlessly in his seat. On the bridge of a ship he would have paced up and down, but men on submarines learn to avoid unnecessary movement. He said: 'Your man won't come in this weather, you know.'

Wohl looked at his watch. 'We will wait until six a.m.,' he said calmly.

It was not an order, for Wohl could not give orders to Heer; but the bald statement of fact was still an insult to a superior officer. Heer said: 'Damn you, I'm the master of this vessel!'

'We will both follow our orders,' Wohl said. 'As you know, they originate from a very high authority indeed.'

Heer controlled his anger. The young whipper-snapper was right, of course. Heer would follow his orders. When they returned to port he would report Wohl for insubordination. Not that it would do much good: fifteen years in the Navy had taught Heer that headquarters people were a law unto themselves.

He said: 'If your man is fool enough to venture out tonight, he is certainly not seaman enough to survive.'

Wohl's only reply was the same blank gaze.

Heer called to the radio operator. 'Weissman?'

'Nothing, sir.'

Wohl said: 'I have an unpleasant feeling that the murmurs we heard a few hours ago were from him.'

'If they were, he was a long way from the rendezvous, sir,' the radio operator volunteered. 'To me it sounded more like lightning.'

Heer added: 'If it was not him, it was not him. If it was him, he is now drowned.' His tone was smug.

'You don't know the man,' Wohl said, and this time there was a trace of emotion in his voice.

Heer subsided into silence. The engine note altered slightly, and he thought he could distinguish a faint rattle. If it increased on the journey home he would have it looked at in port. He might do that anyway, just to avoid another voyage with the unspeakable Major Wohl.

A seaman looked in. 'Coffee, sir?'

Heer shook his head. 'If I drink any more I'll be pissing coffee.'

Wohl said: 'I will, please.' He took out a cigarette.

That made Heer look at his watch. It was ten past six. The subtle Major Wohl had delayed his six o'clock cigarette to keep the U-boat there a few extra minutes. Heer said: 'Set a course for home.'

'One moment,' Wohl said. 'I think we should take a look on the surface before we leave.'

'Don't be a fool,' Heer said. He knew he was on safe ground now. 'Do you realize what kind of storm is raging up there? We would not be able to open the hatch, and the periscope will show us nothing that is more than a few yards away.'

'How can you tell what the storm is like from this depth?'

'Experience,' Heer told him.

'Then at least send a signal to base, telling them that our man has not made contact. They may order us to stay here.'

Heer gave an exasperated sigh. 'It's not possible to make radio contact from this depth, not with base,' he said.

Wohl's calm was shattered at last. 'Commander Heer, I strongly recommend you surface and radio home before leaving this rendezvous. The man we are to pick up has information vital to the future of the Reich. The Führer himself is waiting for his report!'

Heer looked at him. 'Thank you for letting me have your opinion, Major,' he said. He turned away. 'Full ahead both!' he barked.

The sound of the twin diesels rose to a roar, and the U-boat began to pick up speed.

PART FOUR

NINETEEN

When Lucy woke up, the storm that had broken the evening before was still raging. She leaned over the edge of the bed, moving cautiously so that she would not disturb David, and picked up her wristwatch from the door. It was just after six. The wind was howling around the roof. David could sleep on: little work would be done today.

She wondered whether they had lost any slates off the roof during the night. She would need to check the loft. The job would have to wait until David was out, otherwise he would be angry that she had not asked him to do it.

She slipped out of bed. It was very cold. The warm weather of the last few days had been a phoney summer, the build-up to the storm. Now it was as cold as November. She pulled the flannel nightdress off over her head and quickly got into her underwear, trousers and sweater. David stirred. She looked at him: he turned over, but did not wake.

She crossed the tiny landing and looked into Jo's room. The three-year-old had graduated from a cot to a bed, and he often fell out during the night without waking. This morning he was on his bed, lying asleep on his back with his mouth wide open. Lucy smiled. He looked adorable when he was asleep.

She went quietly downstairs, wondering briefly why she had woken up so early. Perhaps Jo had made a noise, or maybe it was the storm.

She knelt in front of the fireplace, pushing back the sleeves of her sweater, and began to make the fire. As she swept out the grate she whistled a tune she had heard on the radio, *Is You Is Or Is You Ain't My Baby?* She raked the cold ashes, using the biggest lumps to form the base for today's fire. Dried bracken provided the tinder and wood and then coal went on top. Sometimes she just used wood, but coal was better in this weather. She held a page of newspaper across the fireplace for a few minutes to create an updraught in the chimney. When she removed it the wood was burning and the coal glowing red. She folded the paper and placed it under the coal scuttle for use tomorrow.

The blaze would soon warm the little house, but a hot cup of tea would help meanwhile. Lucy went into the kitchen and put the kettle on the electric cooker. She put two cups on a tray, then found David's cigarettes and an ashtray. She made the tea, filled the cups, and carried the tray through the hall to the stairs.

She had one foot on the lowest stair when she heard the tapping. She stopped, frowned, decided it was the wind rattling something, and took another step. The sound came again. It was like someone knocking on the front door.

That was ridiculous, of course. There was no one to

knock on the front door – only Tom, and he always came to the kitchen door and never knocked.

The tapping came again.

Just to assuage her curiosity, she came down the stairs and, balancing the tea tray on one hand, opened the front door.

She dropped the tray in shock. The man fell into the hall, knocking her over. Lucy screamed.

She was frightened only for a moment. The stranger lay prone beside her on the hall floor, plainly incapable of attacking anyone. His clothes were soaking wet, and his hands and face were stone-white with cold.

Lucy got to her feet. David slid down the stairs on his bottom, saying: 'What is it? What is it?'

'Him,' Lucy said, and pointed.

David arrived at the foot of the stairs, clad in pyjamas, and hauled himself into his wheelchair. 'I don't see what there is to scream about,' he said. He wheeled himself closer and peered at the man on the floor.

'I'm sorry. He startled me.' She bent over and, taking the man by his upper arms, dragged him into the living-room. David followed. Lucy laid the man in front of the fire.

David stared pensively at the unconscious body. 'Where the devil did he come from?' he wondered.

'He must be a shipwrecked sailor.'

'Of course.'

But he was wearing the clothes of a workman, not a sailor, Lucy noticed. She studied him. He was quite a big man, longer than the six-foot hearth-rug, and heavy around the neck and shoulders. His face was strong and fine-boned, with a high forehead and a long jaw. He might be handsome, she thought, if he were not such a ghastly colour.

The stranger stirred and opened his eyes. At first he looked terribly frightened, like a little boy waking in strange surroundings; but, very quickly, his expression became relaxed, and he looked about him sharply, his gaze resting briefly on Lucy, David, the window, the door, and the fire.

Lucy said: 'We must get him out of these clothes. Fetch a pair of pyjamas and a robe, David.'

David wheeled himself out, and Lucy knelt beside the stranger. She took off his boots and socks first. There almost seemed to be a hint of amusement in his eyes as he watched her. But when she reached for his jacket he crossed his arms protectively over his chest.

'You'll die of pneumonia if you keep these clothes on,' she said in her best bedside manner. 'Let me take them off.'

The stranger said: 'I really don't think we know each other well enough – after all, we haven't been introduced.'

It was the first time he had spoken. His voice was so confident, his words so formal, that the contrast with his terrible appearance made Lucy laugh out loud. 'You're shy?' she said.

'I just think a man should preserve an air of mystery.' He was grinning broadly, but his smile collapsed suddenly and his eyes closed in pain.

David came back in with clean nightclothes over his arm. 'You two seem to be getting on remarkably well already,' he said.

'You'll have to undress him,' Lucy said. 'He won't let me.'

David's look was unreadable.

The stranger said: 'I'll manage on my own, thanks – if it's not too awfully ungracious of me.'

'Suit yourself,' David said. He dumped the clothes on a chair and wheeled out.

'I'll make some more tea,' Lucy said as she followed. She closed the living-room door behind her.

In the kitchen, David was already filling the kettle, a lighted cigarette dangling from his lips. Lucy quickly cleared up the broken china in the hall then joined him.

David said: 'Five minutes ago I wasn't at all sure the chap was alive – and now he's dressing himself.'

Lucy busied herself with a teapot. 'Perhaps he was shamming.'

'The prospect of being undressed by you certainly brought about a rapid recovery.'

'I can't believe anyone could be that shy.'

'Your own deficiency in that area may lead you to underestimate its power in others.'

Lucy rattled cups. 'You don't usually get all bitter and twisted until after breakfast. Besides, how can an area be powerful?'

'Semantics is always your last line of defence.' David doused the butt of his cigarette in a pool of water in the sink.

Lucy poured boiling water into the teapot. 'Let's not quarrel today – we've got something more interesting to do, for a change.' She picked up the tray and walked into the living-room.

The stranger was buttoning his pyjama jacket. He turned his back to her as she walked in. She put the tray down and poured tea. When she turned back he was wearing David's robe.

'You're very kind,' he said. His gaze was direct.

He really didn't seem the shy type, Lucy thought. However, he was some years older than she – about forty, she guessed. That might account for it. He was looking less of a castaway every minute.

'Sit close to the fire,' she told him. She handed him a cup of tea.

'I'm not sure I can manage the saucer,' he said. 'My fingers aren't functioning.' He took the cup from her stiff-handed, holding it between both palms, and carried it carefully to his lips.

David came in and offered him a cigarette. He declined.

The stranger emptied the cup. 'Where am I?' he asked.

David said: 'This place is called Storm Island.'

The man showed a trace of relief. 'I thought I might have been blown back to the mainland.'

David spread his hands to the fire to warm his fingers. 'You were probably swept into the bay,' he said. 'Things usually are. That's how the beach was formed.'

Jo came in, bleary-eyed, trailing a one-armed panda

as big as himself. When he saw the stranger he ran to Lucy and hid his face.

'I've frightened your little girl,' the man smiled.

'He's a boy. I must cut his hair.' Lucy lifted Jo on to her lap.

'I'm sorry.' The stranger's eyes closed again, and he swayed in his seat.

Lucy stood up, dumping Jo on the sofa. 'We must put the poor man to bed, David.'

'Just a minute,' David said. He wheeled himself closer to the man. 'Might there be any other survivors?' he asked.

The man's face looked up. 'I was alone,' he muttered. He was very nearly all in.

'David—' Lucy began.

'One more question: Did you notify the coastguard of your route?'

'What does it matter?' Lucy said.

'It matters because, if he did, there may be men out there risking their lives looking for him, and we can let them know he's safe.'

The man said slowly: 'I . . . did . . . not.'

'That's enough,' Lucy told David. She knelt in front of the man. 'Can you make it upstairs?'

He nodded and got slowly to his feet.

Lucy looped his arm over her shoulders and began to walk him out. 'I'll put him in Jo's bed,' she said.

They took the stairs one at a time, pausing on each. When they reached the top, the little colour that the fire had restored to the man's face had drained away again. Lucy led him into the smaller bedroom. He collapsed on to the bed.

Lucy arranged the blankets over him, tucked him in, and left the room, closing the door quietly.

Relief washed over Faber in a tidal wave. For the last few minutes, the effort of self-control had been superhuman. He felt limp, defeated and ill.

After the front door had opened, he had allowed himself to collapse for a while. The danger had come when the beautiful girl had started to undress him, and he had remembered the can of film taped to his chest. Dealing with that had restored his alertness for a while. He had also been afraid they might call for an ambulance, but that had not been mentioned: perhaps the island was too small to have a hospital. At least he was not on the mainland – there, it would have been impossible to prevent the reporting of the shipwreck. However, the trend of the husband's questions had indicated that no report would be made immediately.

Faber had no energy to speculate about perils farther in the future. He seemed to be safe for the time being, and that was as far as he could go. In the meantime he was warm and dry and alive, and the bed was soft.

He turned over, reconnoitring the room: door, window, chimney. The habit of caution survived everything but death itself. The walls were pink, as if the couple had hoped for a baby girl. There was a train set and a great many picture books on the floor. It was a safe, domestic place; a home. He was a wolf in a sheep fold, but a lame wolf.

He closed his eyes. Despite his exhaustion, he had to

force himself to relax, muscle by muscle. Gradually his head emptied of thought, and he slept.

Lucy tasted the porridge, and added another pinch of salt. They had got to like it the way Tom made it, the Scots way, without sugar. She would never go back to making sweet porridge, even when sugar became plentiful and unrationed again. It was funny how you got used to things when you had to: brown bread and margarine and salt porridge.

She ladled it out and the family sat down to breakfast. Jo had lots of milk to cool his. David ate vast quantities these days, without getting fat: it was the outdoor life. She looked at his hands, on the table. They were rough, and permanently brown, the hands of a manual worker. She had noticed the stranger's hands. His fingers were long, the skin white under the blood and the bruising. He was unused to the abrasive work of crewing a boat.

Lucy said: 'You won't get much done today. The storm looks like staying.'

'Makes no difference,' David grunted. 'Sheep still have to be cared for, whatever the weather.'

'Where will you be?'

'Tom's end. I'll go up there in the jeep.'

Jo said: 'Can I come?'

'Not today,' Lucy told him. 'It's too wet and cold.'

'But I don't like the man.'

Lucy smiled. 'Don't be silly. He won't do us any harm. He's almost too ill to move.'

'Who is he?'

'We don't know his name. He's been shipwrecked, and we have to look after him until he's well enough to go back to the mainland. He's a very nice man.'

'Is he my uncle?'

'Just a stranger, Jo. Eat up.'

Jo looked disappointed. He had met an uncle once. In his mind uncles were people who gave out candy, which he liked, and money, which he had no use for.

David finished his breakfast and put on his mackintosh. It was a tent-shaped garment, with sleeves and a hole for his head, and it covered most of his wheelchair as well as him. He put a sou'wester on his head and tied it under his chin. He kissed Jo and said goodbye to Lucy.

A minute or two later she heard the jeep start up. She went to the window to watch David drive off into the rain. The rear wheels of the vehicle slithered about in the mud. He would have to take care.

She turned to Jo. He said: 'This is a dog.' He was making a picture on the tablecloth with porridge and milk.

Lucy slapped his hand, saying: 'What a horrid mess!' The boy's face took on a grim, sulky look, and Lucy thought how much he resembled his father. They had the same dark skin and nearly black hair, and they both had a way of withdrawing when they were cross. But Jo laughed a lot – he had inherited something from Lucy's side of the family, thank God.

Jo mistook her contemplative stare for anger, and said: 'I'm sorry.'

She washed him at the kitchen sink, then cleared away the breakfast things, thinking about the stranger upstairs. Now that the immediate crisis was past, and she knew the man was not going to die, she was consumed with curiosity about him. Who was he? Where was he from? What had he been doing in the storm? Did he have a family? Why did he have workman's clothes, a clerk's hands, and a Home Counties accent? It was rather exciting.

It occurred to her that, if she had lived anywhere else, she would not have accepted his sudden appearance so readily. He might, she supposed, be a deserter, or a criminal, or even an escaped prisoner-of-war. But one forgot, living on the island, that other human beings could be threatening instead of companionable. It was so nice to see a new face that to harbour suspicions seemed ungrateful. Maybe – unpleasant thought – she more than most people was ready to welcome an attractive man . . . She pushed the thought out of her mind.

Silly, silly. He was so tired and ill that he could not possibly threaten anyone. Even on the mainland, who could have refused to take him in, bedraggled and unconscious? When he felt better they could question him, and if his account of how he got here was less than plausible, they could radio the mainland from Tom's cottage.

When she had washed up she crept upstairs to peep at him. He slept facing the door, and when she looked in his eyes opened instantly. Again there was that initial, split-second flash of fear.

'It's all right,' Lucy whispered. 'Just making sure you're okay.'

He closed his eyes without speaking.

She went downstairs again. She dressed herself and Jo in oilskins and wellington boots, and they went out. The rain was still coming down in torrents and the wind was terrific. She glanced up at the roof: they had lost some slates. Leaning into the wind, she headed for the cliff top.

She held Jo's hand tightly – he might quite easily be blown away. Two minutes later she was wishing she had stayed indoors. Rain came in under her raincoat collar and over the tops of her boots, and she was soaked. Jo must be too, but now that they were wet they might as well stay wet for a few minutes more. Lucy wanted to go to the beach.

However, when they reached the top of the ramp she realized it was impossible. The narrow wooden walkway was slippery with rain, and in this wind she might lose her balance and fall off, to plunge sixty feet to the beach below. She had to content herself with looking.

It was quite a sight.

Vast waves, each the size of a small house, were rolling in rapidly, close on each other's heels. Crossing the beach the wave would rise even higher, its crest curling in a question mark, then throw itself against the foot of the cliff in a rage. Spray rose over the cliff top in sheets, causing Lucy to step back hurriedly and Jo to squeal with delight. Lucy could hear her son's laughter only because he had jumped into her arms, and his mouth was now close to her ear: the noise of the wind and the sea drowned more distant sounds.

There was something terribly thrilling in watching the elements spit and sway and roar in fury, in standing fractionally too close to the cliff edge, feeling threatened and safe at the same time, shivering with cold and yet perspiring in fear. It was thrilling, and there were few thrills in Lucy's life.

She was about to go back, mindful of Jo's health, when she saw the boat.

It was not a boat any more, of course; that was what was so shocking about it. All that was left were the huge timbers of the deck and the keel. They were scattered on the rocks below the cliffs like a dropped handful of matches. It had been a *big* boat, Lucy realized. One man might have piloted it alone, but not easily. And the damage the sea had wrought on man's craftsmanship was awesome. It was hard to spot two bits of wood still joined together.

How, in Heaven's name, had the stranger come out of it alive?

She shuddered when she thought of what those waves and those rocks might have done to a human body. Jo caught her sudden change of mood, and said into her ear: 'Go home, now.' She turned quickly away from the sea and hurried back along the muddy path to the cottage.

Back inside, they took off their wet coats, hats and boots, and hung them in the kitchen to dry. Lucy went upstairs and looked in on the stranger again. This time he did not open his eyes. He seemed to be sleeping very peacefully, yet she had a feeling that he had awakened and recognized her tread on the stairs, and closed his eyes again before she opened the door.

She ran a hot bath. She and the boy were soaked to the skin. She undressed Jo and put him in the tub, then – on impulse – took off her own clothes and got in with him. The heat was blissful. She closed her eyes and relaxed. This was good, too: to be in a house, feeling warm, while the storm beat impotently at the strong stone walls.

Life had turned interesting, all of a sudden. In one night there had come a storm, a shipwreck and a mystery man; this after three years of tedium. She hoped the stranger would wake up soon, so that she could find out all about him.

It was time she started cooking lunch for the men. She had some breast of lamb to make a stew. She got out of the bath and towelled herself gently. Jo was playing with his bath toy, a much-chewed rubber cat. Lucy looked at herself in the mirror, examining the stretch-marks on her belly left by pregnancy. They were fading, slowly, but they would never completely disappear. An all-over suntan would help, though. She smiled to herself, thinking: Fat chance of that! Besides, who was interested in her tummy? Nobody but herself.

Jo said: 'Can I stay in a minute more?' It was a phrase he used, 'a minute more', and it could mean anything up to half a day.

Lucy said: 'Just while I get dressed.' She hung the towel on a rail and moved toward the door.

The stranger stood in the doorway, looking at her.

They stared at each other. It was odd – Lucy thought later – that she felt not a bit afraid. It was the way he looked at her: there was no threat in his expression, no lewdness, no smirk, no lust. He was not looking at her pubis, or even her breasts, but at her face – into her eyes. She gazed back, a little shocked but not embarrassed, with just a tiny part of her mind wondering why she did not squeal, cover herself with her hands, and slam the door on him.

Something did come into his eyes, at last – perhaps she was imagining it, but she saw admiration, and a faint twinkle of honest humour, and a trace of sadness – and then the spell was broken, and he turned away and went back into his bedroom, closing the door. A moment later Lucy heard the springs creak as his weight settled on the bed.

And for no good reason at all she felt dreadfully guilty.

TWENTY

By this time Percival Godliman had pulled out all the stops.

Every policeman in the UK had a copy of the photograph of Faber, and about half of them were engaged full-time in the search. In the cities they were checking hotels and guest-houses, railway stations and bus terminals, cafés and shopping centres; and the bridges, arches, and bombed lots where the derelict hang out. In the country they were looking in barns and silos, empty cottages and ruined castles, thickets and clearings and cornfields. They were showing the photograph to ticket clerks, petrol station staff, ferry hands and toll collectors. All the passenger ports and airfields were covered, with the picture pinned behind a board at every Passport Control desk.

The police thought they were looking for a straightforward murderer.

The cop on the street knew that the man in the picture had killed two people with a knife in London. Senior officers knew a bit more: that one of the murders had been a sexual assault, another apparently motiveless, and a third – which their men were not to know of – was an unexplained but bloody attack on a soldier on the Euston-to-Liverpool train. Only chief constables, and a few officers at Scotland Yard, realized that the soldier had been on temporary attachment to MI5 and that all the murders were connected with Security.

The newspapers, too, thought it was just an ordinary murder hunt. The day after Godliman had released details, most of the papers had carried the story in their later editions – the first editions, bound for Scotland, Ulster and North Wales, had missed it, so they had carried a shortened version a day later. The Stockwell victim had been identified as a labourer, and given a false name and a vague London background. Godliman's press release had connected that murder with the death of Mrs Una Garden in 1940, but had been vague about the nature of the link. The murder weapon was said to be a stiletto.

The two Liverpool newspapers heard very quickly of the body on the train, and both wondered whether the London knife murderer was responsible. Both made enquiries with the Liverpool police. The editors of both papers received phone calls from the Chief Constable. Neither paper carried the story.

A total of one hundred and fifty-seven tall dark men were arrested on suspicion of being Faber. All but twenty-nine of them were able to prove that they could not possibly have committed the murders. Interviewers from MI5 talked to the twenty-nine. Twenty-seven called in parents, relatives and neighbours who affirmed that they had been born in Britain and had been living there during the twenties, when Faber had been in Germany.

The last two were brought to London and interviewed again, this time by Godliman. Both were bachelors, living alone, with no surviving relatives, leading a transient existence.

The first was a well-dressed, confident man who claimed implausibly that his way of life was to travel the country taking odd jobs as a manual labourer. Godliman explained that he was looking for a German spy, and that he – unlike the police – had the power to incarcerate anyone for the duration of the war, and no questions asked. Furthermore, he went on, he was not in the least interested in capturing ordinary criminals, and any information given him here at the War Office was strictly confidential, and would go no further.

The prisoner promptly confessed to being a confidence trickster and gave the addresses of nineteen elderly ladies whom he had cheated out of their old jewellery during the past three weeks. Godliman turned him over to the police.

He felt no obligation to be honest with a professional liar.

The last suspect also cracked under Godliman's treatment. His secret was that he was not a bachelor at all, not by a long way. He had a wife in Brighton. And in Solihull, Birmingham. And in Colchester, Newbury and Exeter. All five were able to produce marriage certificates later that day. The bigamist went to gaol to await trial.

Godliman slept in his office while the hunt went on.

*

Bristol, Temple Meads, railway station:

'Good morning, Miss. Would you look at this, please?'

'Hey, girls – the bobby's going to show us his snaps!'

'Now, don't muck about, just tell me if you've seen him.'

'Ooh, ain't he handsome! I wish I had!'

'You wouldn't if you knew what he'd done. Would you all take a look, please?'

'Never seen him.'

'Me neither.'

'Not me.'

'No.'

'When you catch him, ask him if he wants to meet a nice young Bristol girl.'

'You girls – I don't know . . . Just because they give you a pair of trousers and a porter's job, you think you're supposed to act like men . . .'

The Woolwich Ferry:

'Filthy day, Constable.'

'Morning, Captain. I expect it's worse on the high seas.'

'Can I help you? Or are you just crossing the river?'

'I want you to look at a face, Captain.'

'Let me put my specs on. Oh, don't worry, I can see to guide the ship. It's close things I need the glasses for, Now then . . .'

'Ring any bells?'

'Sorry, Constable. Means nothing to me.'

'Well, let me know if you see him.'

'Certainly.'

'Bon voyage.'

Number thirty-five Leak Street, London E1:

'Sergeant Riley – what a nice surprise!'

'Never mind the lip, Mabel. Who've you got here?'

'All respectable guests, Sergeant; you know me.'

'I know you, all right. That's why I'm here. Would any of your nice respectable guests happen to be on the trot?'

'Since when have you been recruiting for the Army?'

'I'm not, Mabel, I'm looking for a villain, and if he's here, he's probably told you he's on the trot.'

'Look, Jack – if I tell you there's nobody here I don't know, will you go away and stop pestering me?'

'Why should I trust you?'

'Because of 1936.'

'You were better looking then, Mabel.'

'So were you, Jack.'

'You win . . . Take a butcher's at this. If chummy comes in here, send word, okay?'

'Promise.'

'Don't waste any time about it, either.'

'All right!'

'Mabel . . . he knifed a woman your age. I'm just marking your cards.'

'I know. Thanks.'

'Ta-ta.'

'Take care, Jacko.'

Bill's Café, on the A30 near Bagshot:

'Tea, please, Bill. Two sugars.'

'Good morning, Constable Pearson. Filthy day.'

'What's on that plate, Bill – pebbles from Portsmouth?'

'Buttered buns, as well you know.'

'Oh! I'll have two, then. Thanks . . . Now then, lads! Anyone who wants his lorry checked from top to bottom can leave right away . . . That's better. Take a look at this picture, please.'

'What are you after him for, Constable – cycling without lights?'

'Never mind the jokes, Harry – pass the picture round. Anybody given a lift to that bloke?'

'Not me.'

'No.'

'Sorry, Constable.'

'Never clapped eyes on him.'

'Thank you, lads. If you see him, report it. Cheerio.'

'Constable?'

'Yes, Bill?'

'You haven't paid for the buns.'

'I'm confiscating them as evidence. Cheerio.'

Smethwick's Garage, Carlisle:

'Morning, Missus. When you've got a minute . . .'

'Be right with you, officer. Just let me attend to this

gentleman . . . Twelve and sixpence, please, sir. Thank you. Goodbye . . .'

'How's business?'

'Terrible, as usual. What can I do for you?'

'Can we go in the office for a minute?'

'Aye, come on . . . Now, then.'

'Take a look at this picture and tell me whether you've served that man with petrol recently.'

'Well, it shouldn't be too difficult. It's not as if we get hordes of customers passing through . . . ooh! D'you know, I think I have served him!'

'When?'

'Day before yesterday, in the morning.'

'How sure are you?'

'Well . . . he was older than the picture, but I'm pretty sure.'

'What was he driving?'

'A grey car. I'm no good on makes, this is my husband's business really, but he's in the Navy now.'

'Well, what did it look like? Sports car? Limousine?'

'It was the old sort, with a canvas roof that comes up. A two-seater. Sporty. It had a spare petrol tank bolted to the running-board, and I filled that, too.'

'Do you remember what he was wearing?'

'Not really. Working clothes, I think.'

'A tall man?'

'Yes, taller than you.'

'By the heck, I think it's him! Have you got a telephone . . .?'

*

William Duncan was twenty-five years old, five-feet-ten, weighed a trim 150 pounds, and was in first-class health. His open-air life and total lack of interest in tobacco, drink, late nights and loose living kept him that way. Yet he was not in the Armed Services.

He had seemed to be a normal child, if a little backward, until the age of eight, when his mind simply stopped developing. There had been no trauma that anyone knew about, no physical damage to account for sudden breakdown. Indeed, it was some years before anyone noticed that there was anything wrong, for at the age of ten he was no more than a little backward, and at twelve he was just dim-witted; but by fifteen he was obviously simple, and by eighteen he was known as Daft Willie.

His parents both belonged to an obscure Fundamentalist religious group whose members were not allowed to marry outside the Church (which may or may not have had something to do with Willie's daftness). They prayed for him, of course; but they also took him to a specialist in Stirling. The doctor, an elderly man, did several tests and then told them, over the tops of his gold-rimmed half-glasses, that the boy had a mental age of eight and his mind would grow no older, ever. They continued to pray for him, but they suspected that the Lord had sent this to try them, so they made sure that Willie was Saved and looked forward to the day when they would meet him again in the Glory and he would be healed. Meanwhile, he needed a job.

An eight-year-old can herd cows, but herding cows is nevertheless a job, so Daft Willie became a cowherd.

And it was while herding cows that he saw the car for the first time.

He assumed there were lovers in it.

Willie knew about lovers. That is to say, he knew that lovers existed, and that they did unmentionable things to one another in dark places like copses and cinemas and cars; and that one did not speak of them. So he hurried the cows quickly past the bush beside which was parked the 1924 Morris Cowley Bullnose two-seater (he knew about cars, too, like any eight-year-old) and tried very hard not to look inside it in case he should behold sin.

He took his little herd into the cowshed for milking, went by a roundabout route to his home, ate supper, read a chapter from Leviticus to his father – aloud, painstakingly – then went to bed to dream about lovers.

The car was still there on the evening of the next day.

For all his innocence, Willie knew that lovers did not do whatever it was that they did to one another for twenty-four hours at a stretch.

This time he went right up to the car and looked inside. It was empty. The ground beneath the engine was black and sticky with oil. Willie devised a new explanation: the car had broken down and had been abandoned by its driver. It did not occur to him to wonder why it had been semi-concealed in a bush.

When he arrived at the cowshed he told the farmer what he had seen. 'There's a broken-down car on the path up by the main road.'

The farmer was a big man with heavy sand-coloured eyebrows which drew together when he was thinking. 'Was there nobody about?'

'No – and it was there yesterday.'

'Why did you not tell me yesterday, then?'

Willie blushed. 'I thought it was maybe . . . lovers.'

'Och! 'The farmer realized that Willie was not being coy, but was genuinely embarrassed. He patted the boy's shoulder. 'Well, away home and leave it to me to deal with.'

After the milking the farmer went to look for himself. It did occur to him to wonder why the car was semi-concealed. He had heard about the London stiletto murderer; and while he did not jump to the conclusion that the car had been abandoned by the killer, all the same he thought there might be a connection between the car and some crime or other. So after supper he sent his eldest son into the village on horseback to telephone the police in Stirling.

The police arrived before his son got back from the phone. There were at least a dozen of them, every one apparently a non-stop tea drinker. The farmer and his wife were up half the night looking after them.

Daft Willie was summoned to tell his story again, repeating that he had first seen the car the previous evening, blushing again when he explained that he had assumed it contained lovers.

All in all, it was the most exciting night of the war.

*

That evening Percival Godliman, facing his fourth consecutive night in the office, went home to bathe, change, and pack a suitcase.

He had a service flat in a block in Chelsea. It was small, though plenty big enough for a single man, and it was clean and tidy except for the study, which the cleaner was not allowed to enter and in consequence was littered with books and papers. The furniture was all pre-war, of course, but it was rather well-chosen, and the flat had a comfortable air. There were leather club chairs and a gramophone in the living-room, and the kitchen was full of hardly used labour-saving devices.

While his bath was filling he smoked a cigarette – he had taken to them lately, a pipe was so much fuss – and looked at his most valuable possession, a grimly fantastic medieval scene which was probably by Hieronymous Bosch. It was a family heirloom and Godliman had never sold it, even when he needed the money, because he liked it.

In the bath he thought about Barbara Dickens and her son, Peter. He had not told anyone about her, not even Bloggs, although he had been about to mention her during their conversation about remarrying, but Colonel Terry had interrupted. She was a widow: her husband had been killed in action at the very beginning of the war. Godliman did not know how old she was, but she looked about forty, which was young for the mother of a twenty-two-year-old boy. She worked on translations of intercepted enemy signals, and she was bright, amusing, and very attractive. She was also rich. Godliman had taken her to dinner, three times, before the present crisis blew up. He thought she was in love with him.

She had contrived a meeting between Godliman and her son Peter, who was a captain. Godliman liked the boy. But he knew something which neither Barbara nor her son was aware of: Peter was going to Normandy.

Which was all the more reason to catch Die Nadel.

He got out of the bath and took a long, careful shave, thinking: Am I in love with her? He was not sure what love ought to feel like in middle age. Not, surely, the burning passion of youth. Affection, admiration, tenderness, and a trace of uncertain lust? If they amounted to love, he loved her.

And he needed to share his life, now. For years he had wanted only solitude and his research. Now the camaraderie of Military Intelligence was sucking him in: the parties, the all-night sessions when something big broke, the spirit of dedicated amateurism, the frantic pleasure-seeking of people to whom death is always close and never predictable – all these had infected him. It would vanish after the war, he knew; but other things would remain: the need to talk to someone close about his disappointment and his triumphs, the need to touch someone else at night, the need to say: 'There! Look at that! Isn't it fine?'

War was gruelling and oppressive and frustrating and uncomfortable, but one had friends. If peace brought back loneliness, Godliman thought he would be unhappy.

Right now the feel of clean underwear and a crisply ironed shirt was the height of luxury. He put more fresh clothes in a case, then sat down to enjoy a glass of whisky before returning to the office. The military chauffeur in the commandeered Daimler outside could wait a little longer.

He was filling a pipe when the phone rang. He put down the pipe and lit a cigarette instead.

His phone was connected to the War Office switchboard. The telephonist told him that a Chief Superintendent Dalkeith was calling from Stirling.

He waited for the click of the connection, and said: 'Godliman speaking.'

'We've found your Morris Cowley,' Dalkeith said without preamble.

'Where?'

'On the A80 just south of Stirling.'

'Empty?'

'Aye, broken down. It's been there at least twenty-four hours. It was driven a few yards off the main road and hidden in a bush. A half-witted farm boy found it.'

'Is there a bus stop or railway station within walking distance of the spot?'

'No.'

Godliman grunted. 'So it's likely our man had to walk or hitch-hike after leaving the car.'

'Aye.'

'In that case, will you ask around—'

'We're already trying to find out whether anyone local saw him or gave him a lift.'

'Good. Let me know . . . Meanwhile, I'll pass the news to the Yard. Thank you, Dalkeith.'

'We'll keep in touch. Goodbye, sir.'

Godliman put the phone on the hook and went into his study. He sat down with an atlas open to the road map of northern Britain. London, Liverpool, Carlisle, Stirling . . . Faber was heading for north-east Scotland.

Godliman wondered whether he should reconsider the theory that Faber was trying to get out. The best way out was west, via neutral Eire. Scotland's east coast, however, was the scene of military activity of various kinds. Was it possible that Faber had the nerve to continue his reconnaissance, knowing that MI5 was on his tail? It was possible, Godliman decided – he knew Faber had a lot of guts – but nevertheless unlikely. Nothing the man might discover in Scotland could be as important as the information he already had.

Therefore Faber was getting out via the east coast. Godliman ran over the methods of escape which were open to the spy: a light plane, landing on a lonely moor; a one-man voyage across the North Sea in a stolen vessel; a rendezvous with a U-boat off the coast; a passage in a merchant ship via a neutral country to the Baltic, disembarking in Sweden and crossing the border to occupied Norway . . . there were many ways.

The Yard must be told of the latest development. They would ask all Scots police forces to try to find someone who had picked up a hitch-hiker outside Stirling. Godliman returned to the living-room to phone, but the instrument rang before he got there. He picked it up.

'Godliman speaking.'

'A Mr Richard Porter is calling from Aberdeen.'

'Oh!' Godliman had been expecting Bloggs to check in from Carlisle. 'Put him on, please. Hello? Godliman speaking.'

'Ah, Richard Porter here. I'm on the local Watch Committee up here.'

'Yes, what can I do for you?'

'Well, actually, old boy, it's terribly embarrassing.'

Godliman controlled his impatience. 'Go on.'

'This chappie you're looking for – knife murders and so on. Well, I'm pretty sure I gave the bally fellow a lift in my own car.'

Godliman gripped the receiver more tightly. 'When?'

'Night before last. My car broke down on the A80 just outside Stirling. Middle of the bally night. Along comes this chappie, on foot, and mends it, just like that. So naturally—'

'Where did you drop him?'

'Right here in Aberdeen. Said he was going on to Banff. Thing is, I slept most of yesterday, so it wasn't until this afternoon—'

'Don't reproach yourself, Mr Porter. Thank you for calling.'

'Well, goodbye.'

Godliman jiggled the receiver and the War Office telephonist came back on the line.

Godliman said: 'Get Mr Bloggs for me, would you? He's in Carlisle.'

'He's holding on for you right now, sir.'

'Good!'

'Hello, Percy. What news?'

'We're on his trail again, Fred. He abandoned the Morris just outside Stirling and hitched a lift to Aberdeen.'

'Aberdeen!'

'He must be trying to get out through the east door.'

'When did he reach Aberdeen?'

'Probably early yesterday morning.'

'In that case he won't have had time to get out, unless he was very quick indeed. They're having the worst storm in living memory up here. It started last night and it's still going on. No ships are going out and it's certainly too rough to land a plane.'

'Good! Get up there as fast as you can. I'll start the local police moving in the meantime. Call me when you reach Aberdeen.'

'I'm on my way.'

'Fred?'

'Yes?'

'We'll catch the bastard yet.'

Fred was still laughing as Godliman hung up.

TWENTY-ONE

When Faber woke up it was almost dark. Through the bedroom window he could see the last streaks of grey being inked out of the sky by the encroaching night. The storm had not eased: rain drummed on the roof and overflowed from a gutter, and the wind howled and gusted tirelessly.

He switched on the little lamp beside the bed. The effort tired him, and he slumped back on to the pillow. It frightened him, to be this weak. Those who believe that Might is Right must always be mighty, and Faber was sufficiently self-aware to know the implications of his own ethics. Fear was never far from the surface of his emotions: perhaps that was why he had survived so long. He was chronically incapable of feeling safe. He understood, in that vague way in which we understand the most fundamental things about ourselves, that his insecurity was the reason he chose the profession of spy: it was the only walk of life which permitted him instantly to kill anyone who posed him the slightest threat. The fear of being weak was part of the syndrome which included his obsessive independence, his insecurity, and his contempt for his military superiors.

He lay on the child's bed in the pink-walled bedroom

and inventoried his body. He seemed to be bruised just about everywhere, but apparently nothing was broken. He did not feel feverish: his constitution had withstood bronchial infection despite the night on the boat. There was just the weakness. He suspected it was more than exhaustion. He remembered a moment, as he had reached the top of the ramp, when he had thought he was going to die; and he wondered whether he had inflicted upon himself some permanent damage with that last mindbending uphill dash.

He checked his possessions, too. The can of photographic negatives was still taped to his chest, the stiletto was strapped to his left arm, and his papers and money were in the jacket pocket of his borrowed pyjamas.

He pushed the blankets aside and swung himself into a sitting position with his feet on the floor. A moment of dizziness came and went. He stood up. It was important not to permit oneself the psychological attitudes of the invalid. He put on the dressing-gown and went into the bathroom.

When he returned his own clothes were at the foot of the bed, clean and pressed: underwear, overalls, and shirt. Suddenly he remembered getting up some time during the morning and seeing the woman naked in the bathroom: it had been an odd scene, and he was not sure what it meant. She was very beautiful, he recalled.

He dressed slowly. He would have liked a shave, but he decided to ask his host's permission before borrowing the blade on the bathroom shelf: some men were as possessive of their razors as they were of their wives.

However, he did take the liberty of using the child's plastic comb he found in the top drawer of the chest.

He looked into the mirror without pride. He had no conceit. He knew that some women found him attractive, and others did not; and he assumed this was so for most men. Of course, he had had more women than most men, but he attributed this to his appetite, not to his looks. His reflection told him he was presentable, and that was all he needed to know.

Satisfied, he left the bedroom and went slowly down the stairs. Again he felt a wave of weakness; again he willed himself to overcome it, gripping the banister rail and placing one foot deliberately before the other until he reached the ground floor.

He paused outside the living-room door and, hearing no noise, went on to the kitchen. He knocked and went in. The young couple were at the table, finishing supper.

The woman stood up when he entered. 'You got up!' she said. 'Are you sure you should?'

Faber permitted himself to be led to a chair. 'Thank you,' he said. 'You really mustn't encourage me to pretend to be ill.'

'I don't think you realize what a terrible experience you've been through,' she said. 'Do you feel like food?'

'I'm imposing on you—'

'Not at all. Don't be silly. I kept some soup hot for you.'

Faber said: 'You're so kind, and I don't even know your names.'

'David and Lucy Rose.' She ladled soup into a bowl

and placed it on the table in front of him. 'Cut some bread, David, would you?'

'I'm Henry Baker.' Faber did not know why he had said that: he had no papers in that name. Henry Faber was the man the police were hunting, so he should have used his James Baker identity; but somehow he wanted this woman to call him Henry, the nearest English equivalent of his real name, Henrik. Perhaps it did not matter – he could always say his name was James but he had always been called Henry.

He took a sip of the soup, and suddenly he was ravenously hungry. He ate it all quickly, then the bread. When he had finished, Lucy laughed. She looked lovely when she laughed: her mouth opened wide, showing lots of even white teeth, and her eyes crinkled merrily at the corners.

'More?' she offered.

'Thank you very much.'

'I can see it doing you good. The colour is coming back to your cheeks.'

Faber realized he felt physically better. He ate his second helping more slowly, out of courtesy rather than repletion.

David said: 'How did you happen to be out in this storm?' It was the first time he had spoken.

Lucy said: 'Don't badger him, David.'

'It's all right,' Faber said. 'I was foolish, that's all. This is the first fishing holiday I've been able to have since before the war, and I just refused to let the weather spoil it. Are you a fisherman?'

David shook his head. 'Sheep farmer.'

'Do you have many employees?'

'Just one, old Tom.'

'I suppose there are other sheep farms on the island.'

'No. We live at this end, Tom lives at the other end, and in between there's nothing but sheep.'

Faber nodded slowly. This was good – very good. A woman, a cripple, a child and an old man could not constitute an obstacle. And he was feeling much stronger already.

Faber said: 'How do you contact the mainland?'

'There's a boat once a fortnight. It's due this Monday, but it won't come if the storm keeps up. There's a radio transmitter in Tom's cottage, but we can only use that in emergencies. If I thought people might be searching for you, or if you needed urgent medical help, I should use it. But as things are I don't feel it's necessary. There's little point: nobody can come to fetch you off the island until the storm clears, and when that happens the boat will come anyway.'

'Of course.' Faber concealed his delight. The problem of how to contact the U-boat on Monday had been nagging at the back of his mind. He had seen an ordinary wireless set in the Roses' living-room, and he would, in a pinch, have been able to rig up a transmitter from that. But the fact that Tom had a proper radio made everything so much easier.

Faber said: 'What does Tom need a transmitter for?'

'He's a member of the Royal Observer Corps. Aberdeen was bombed in July 1940. There was no air-raid warning. Consequently there were fifty casualties. That was when they recruited Tom. It's a good thing his hearing is better than his eyesight.'

'I suppose the bombers come from Norway.'

'I suppose so.'

Lucy stood up. 'Let's go into the other room.'

The two men followed her. Faber felt no weakness, no dizziness. He held the living-room door for David, who wheeled himself close to the fire. Lucy offered Faber brandy. He declined. She poured for her husband and herself.

Faber sat back and studied the couple. Lucy's looks were really quite striking: she had an oval face, wide-set eyes of an unusual, cat-like amber colour, and a lot of rich, dark-red hair. Under the mannish fisherman's sweater and baggy trousers there was the suggestion of a very fine, fullish figure. If she were to curl her hair and put on silk stockings and a cocktail dress she might be very glamorous. David was also good-looking – almost pretty, except for the shadow of a very dark beard. His hair was nearly black and his skin looked Mediterranean. He would have been tall, if he had had legs in proportion to his arms. Faber suspected that those arms might be powerful, muscled from years of pushing the wheels of the chair to get from A to B.

Yes, they were an attractive couple – but there was something badly wrong between them. Faber was no expert on marriage, but his training in interrogation techniques had taught him to read the silent language of the body – to know, from small gestures, when someone was frightened, confident, hiding something, or lying. Lucy and David rarely looked at one another, and never touched. They spoke to him more than to each other. They circled one another, like turkeys trying to keep in front of them a few square feet of vacant portable territory. The tension between them was enormous. They were like Churchill and Stalin, obliged temporarily to fight side by side, fiercely suppressing a deeper enmity. Faber wondered what awful trauma lay at the back of their hatred.

This cosy little house must be an emotional pressure-cooker, despite its rugs and its bright paintwork, its floral armchairs and blazing fires and framed water-colours. To live alone, with only an old man and a child for company, with this thing between them . . . it reminded him of a play he had seen in London, by an American called Tennessee something.

Abruptly, David swallowed his drink and said: 'I must turn in. My back's playing up.'

Faber got to his feet and said: 'I'm sorry – I've been keeping you up.'

David waved him down. 'Not at all. You've been asleep all day – you won't want to go back to bed right away. Besides, Lucy would like to chat, I'm sure. It's just that I mistreat my back – backs were designed to share the load with the legs, you know.'

Lucy said: 'You'd better take two pills tonight, then.' She took a bottle from the top shelf of the bookcase, shook out two tablets, and gave them to her husband.

He swallowed them dry. 'I'll say goodnight.' He wheeled himself out.

'Goodnight, David.'

'Goodnight, Mr Rose.'

After a moment Faber heard David dragging himself up the stairs, and wondered just how he did it.

Lucy spoke, as if to cover the sound of David. 'Where do you live, Mr Baker?'

'Please call me Henry. I live in London.'

'I haven't been to London for years. There's probably not much of it left.'

'It's changed, but not as much as you might think. When were you last there?'

'Nineteen-forty.' She poured herself another brandy. 'Since we came here, I've only been off the island once, and that was to have the baby. One can't travel much these days, can one?'

'What made you come here?'

'Um.' She sat down, sipped her drink, and looked into the fire.

'Perhaps I shouldn't—'

'It's all right. We had an accident the day we got married. That's how David lost his legs. He'd been training as a fighter pilot . . . we both wanted to run away, I think. I believe it was a mistake, but it seemed like a good idea at the time.'

'It has allowed his resentment to incubate.'

She shot him a sharp look. 'You're a perceptive man.'

'It's obvious.' He spoke very quietly. 'You don't deserve such unhappiness.'

She blinked several times. 'You see too much.'

'It's not difficult. Why do you continue, if it's not working?'

'I don't know what to tell you. Do you want clichés? The vows of marriage, the child, the war . . . If there's another answer, I can't find words for it.'

'Guilt,' Faber said. 'But you're thinking of leaving him, aren't you?'

She stared at him, slowly shaking her head with incredulity. 'How do you know so much?'

'You've lost the art of dissembling in four years on this island. Besides, these things are so much simpler from the outside.'

'Have you ever been married?'

'No. That's what I mean.'

'Why not? I think you ought to be.'

It was Faber's turn to look pensively into the fire. Why not, indeed? His stock answer – to himself – was his profession. But he could not tell her that, and anyway it was too glib. He said suddenly: 'I don't trust myself to love anyone that much.' The words had come out without forethought, and he wondered whether they were true. A moment later he wondered how Lucy had got past his guard, when he had thought he was disarming her.

Neither of them spoke for a while. The fire was dying. A few stray raindrops found their way down the chimney and hissed in the cooling coals. The storm showed no sign of letting up. Faber found himself thinking of the last woman he had had. What was her name? Gertrude. It was seven years ago, but he could picture her now, in the flickering fire: a round German face, fair hair, green eyes, beautiful breasts, much-too-wide hips, fat legs, bad feet; the conversational style of an express train, a wild, inexhaustible enthusiasm for sex . . . She had flattered him, admiring his mind (she said) and adoring his body (she had no need to tell him). She wrote lyrics for popular songs, and read them to him in a poor basement flat in Berlin: it was not a lucrative profession. He visualized her in that untidy bedroom, lying naked, urging him to do more bizarre and erotic things with her: to hurt her, to touch himself, to lie completely still while she made love to him . . . He shook his head slightly to brush away the memories. He had not thought like that in all the years he had been celibate. Such visions were disturbing. He looked at Lucy.

'You were far away,' she said with a smile.

'Memories,' he said. 'This talk of love . . .'

'I shouldn't burden you.'

'You're not.'

'Good memories?'

'Very good. And yours? You were thinking, too.'

She smiled again. 'I was in the future, not the past.'

'What do you see there?'

She seemed about to answer, then changed her mind. It happened twice. There were signs of tension about her eyes.

'I see you finding another man,' Faber said. As he spoke he was thinking: Why am I doing this? 'He is a weaker man than David, and less handsome; but it is for his weakness that you love him. He is clever, but not rich; compassionate without being sentimental; tender, caring, loving. He—'

The brandy glass in her hand shattered under the

pressure of her grip. The fragments fell into her lap and on to the carpet, and she ignored them. Faber crossed to her chair and knelt in front of her. Her thumb was bleeding. He took her hand.

'You've hurt yourself.'

She looked at him. She was crying.

'I'm sorry,' he said.

The cut was superficial. She took a handkerchief from her trousers pocket and staunched the blood. Faber released her hand and began to pick up the pieces of broken glass, wishing he had kissed her when he had the chance. He put the shards on the chimney-breast.

'I didn't mean to upset you,' he said.

She took away the handkerchief and looked at her thumb. It was still bleeding.

'A little bandage,' he suggested.

'In the kitchen.'

He found a roll of bandage, a pair of scissors, and a safety pin. He filled a small bowl with hot water and returned to the living-room.

In his absence she had somehow obliterated the evidence of tears on her face. She sat passively, limp, while he bathed her thumb in the hot water, dried it, and fixed a small strip of bandage over the cut. She looked all the time at his face, not at his hands; but her expression was unreadable.

He finished the job and stood back abruptly. This was silly: he had taken the thing too far. It was time to disengage. He said: 'I think I'd better go to bed.'

She nodded.

'I'm sorry—'

'Stop apologizing,' she told him. 'It doesn't suit you.'

Her tone was harsh. He guessed that she, too, felt the thing had got out of hand.

'Are you staying up?' he asked.

She shook her head.

'Well . . .' He walked to the door and held it for her.

She avoided his eyes as she passed him. He followed her through the hall and up the stairs. As he watched her climb, he could not help imagining her in other clothes, her hips swaying gently underneath some silky material, long legs clad in stockings instead of worsted grey trousers, high-heeled dress shoes instead of worn felt slippers.

At the top of the stairs, on the tiny landing, she turned and whispered: 'Goodnight.'

He said: 'Goodnight, Lucy.'

She looked at him for a moment. He reached for her hand, but she foresaw his intention and turned quickly away, entering her bedroom and closing the door without a backward look, leaving him standing there with his hand out and his mouth open, wondering what was in her mind and – more to the point – what was in his.

TWENTY-TWO

Bloggs drove dangerously fast through the night in a commandeered Sunbeam Talbot with a souped-up engine. The hilly, winding Scottish roads were slick with rain and, in a few low places, two or three inches deep in water. The rain drove across the windscreen in sheets. On the more exposed hilltops the gale-force winds threatened to blow the car off the road and into the soggy turf alongside. For mile after mile, Bloggs sat forward in the seat, peering through the small area of glass that was cleared by the wiper, straining his eyes to make out the shape of the road in front as the headlights battled with the obscuring rain. Just north of Edinburgh he ran over three rabbits, feeling the sickening bump as the tyres squashed their small furry bodies. He did not slow the car, but for a while afterwards he wondered whether rabbits normally came out at night.

The strain gave him a headache, and his sitting position made his back hurt. He also felt hungry. He opened the window for a cold breeze to keep him awake, but so much water came in that he was forced to close it again immediately. He thought about Die Nadel, or Faber or whatever he was calling himself now:

a smiling young man in running-shorts holding a trophy. Well, Faber was winning this race. He was forty-eight hours ahead and he had the advantage that only he knew the route that had to be followed. Bloggs would have enjoyed a contest with that man, if the stakes had not been so high, so bloody high.

He wondered what he would do if he ever came face to face with the man. I'd shoot the bugger out of hand, he thought, before he killed me. Faber was a pro, and you couldn't mess with that type. Most spies were amateurs: frustrated revolutionaries of the left or right, people who wanted the imaginary glamour of espionage, greedy men or lovesick women, or blackmail victims. The few professionals were very dangerous indeed, because they knew that the professionals they were up against were not merciful men.

Dawn was still an hour or two away when Bloggs drove into Aberdeen. Never in his life had he been so grateful for street lights, dimmed and masked though they were. He had no idea where the police station was, and there was no one on the streets to give him directions, so he drove around the town until he saw the familiar blue lamp (also dimmed).

He parked the car and dashed through the rain into the building. He was expected. Godliman had been on the phone, and Godliman was now very senior indeed. Bloggs was shown into the office of Alan Kincaid, a Detective-Chief-Inspector in his middle fifties. There were three other officers in the room: Bloggs shook their hands and instantly forgot their names.

Kincaid said: 'You made bloody good time from Carlisle.'

'Nearly killed myself doing it,' Bloggs replied. He sat down. 'If you can rustle up a sandwich . . .'

'Of course.' Kincaid leaned his head out of the door and shouted something. 'It'll be here in two shakes,' he told Bloggs.

The office had off-white walls, a plank floor, and plain hard furniture: a desk, a few chairs and a filing cabinet. It was totally unrelieved: no pictures, no ornaments, no personal touches of any kind. There was a tray of dirty cups on the floor, and the air was thick with smoke. It smelled like somewhere men had been working all night.

Kincaid had a small moustache, thin grey hair, and spectacles. A big, intelligent-looking man in shirtsleeves and braces, he was the kind of policeman that – Bloggs thought – made up the backbone of the British police force. He spoke with a local accent, a sign that, like Bloggs, he had come up through the ranks – though from his age it was clear that his rise had been slower than Bloggs's.

Bloggs said: 'How much do you know of what this is all about?'

'Not much,' Kincaid said. 'But your governor, Godliman, did say that the London murders are the least of this man's crimes. We also know which department you're with, so we can put two and two together and conclude that Faber is a very dangerous spy.'

'That's about it,' Bloggs said.

Kincaid nodded.

'What have you done so far?' Bloggs asked.

Kincaid put his feet on his desk. 'He arrived here two days ago, yes?'

'Yes.'

'That was when we started looking for him. We had the pictures – I assume every force in the country got them.'

'Yes.'

'We checked the hotels and lodging houses, the station and the bus depot. We did it quite thoroughly, although at the time we didn't know he had come here. Needless to say, we had no results. We're checking again, of course; but my opinion is that he probably left Aberdeen immediately.'

A woman police constable came in with a cup of tea and a very thick cheese sandwich. Bloggs thanked her and set about the sandwich greedily.

Kincaid went on: 'We had a man at the railway station before the first train left in the morning. Ditto for the bus depot. So, if he left the town, either he stole a car or he hitched a ride. We've had no stolen cars reported.'

'Damn,' Bloggs said through a mouthful of whole-meal bread. He swallowed. 'That makes it about as difficult as it can be to trace him.'

'No doubt that's why he chose to hitch-hike.'

'He might have gone by sea.'

'Of the boats that left the harbour that day, none was big enough to stow away on. Since then, of course, nothing's gone out because of the storm.'

'Stolen boats?'

'None reported.'

Bloggs shrugged. 'If there's no prospect of going out, the owners might not come to the harbour – in which case the theft of a boat might go unnoticed until the storm ends.'

One of the officers in the room said: 'We missed that one, Chief.'

'We did,' Kincaid said.

Bloggs said: 'Perhaps the harbourmaster could look around all the regular moorings—'

'I'm with you,' Kincaid said. He was already dialling. After a moment he spoke into the phone. 'Captain Douglas? Kincaid. Aye, I know civilized people sleep at this hour. You haven't heard the worst – I want you to take a walk in the rain. Aye, you heard me right . . .'

The other policemen started to laugh.

Kincaid put his hand over the mouthpiece and said: 'You know what they say about seamen's language? It's true.' He spoke into the phone again. 'Go round all the regular moorings and make a note of any vessels not in their usual spot. Ignoring those you know to be legitimately out of port, give me the names and addresses – and phone numbers if you have them – of the owners. Aye. Aye, I know . . . I'll make it a double. All right, a bottle. And a good morning to you too, old friend.' He hung up.

Bloggs smiled. 'Salty?'

'If I did what he suggested I do with my truncheon, I'd never be able to sit down again.' Kincaid became serious. 'It'll take him about half an hour, then we'll need a couple of hours to check all the addresses.

It's worth doing, although I still think he hitched a ride.'

'So do I,' Bloggs said.

The door opened, and a middle-aged man in civilian clothes walked in. Kincaid and his officers stood up, and Bloggs followed suit.

Kincaid said: 'Good morning, sir. This is Mr Bloggs. Mr Bloggs, Richard Porter.'

They shook hands. Porter had a red face and a carefully cultivated moustache. He wore a double-breasted, camel-coloured overcoat. He said: 'How do you do. I'm the blighter that gave your chappie a lift to Aberdeen. Most embarrassing.' He had no local accent.

Bloggs said: 'How do you do.' On first acquaintance Porter seemed to be exactly the kind of silly ass who would give a spy a lift half across the country. However, Bloggs knew the type: the air of empty-headed heartiness might well mask a shrewd mind. He asked: 'What made you realize that the man you'd picked up was the . . . the stiletto murderer?'

'I heard about the abandoned Morris. I picked him up at that very spot.'

'You've seen the picture?'

'Yes. Of course, I didn't get a good look at the chappie, because it was dark for most of the journey. But I saw enough of him, in the light of the torch when we were under the bonnet, and afterwards when we entered Aberdeen – it was dawn by then. If I'd only seen the picture, I'd say it *could* have been him. Given the spot at which I picked him up, so near to where the Morris was found, I say it *was* him.'

'I agree,' Bloggs said. He thought for a moment, wondering what useful information he could get out of this man. 'How did Faber impress you?' he asked eventually.

Porter said promptly: 'He struck me as exhausted, nervous and determined, in that order. Also, he was no Scotsman.'

'How would you describe his accent?'

'Neutral. No trace of the Hun in his voice . . . except perhaps in retrospect, and that might be my imagination. The accent – minor public school, Home Counties. Jarred with his clothes, if you know what I mean. He was wearing overalls. Another thing I didn't remark until afterwards.'

Kincaid interrupted to offer tea. Everyone accepted. The policeman went to the door.

Bloggs had decided that Porter was less foolish than he looked. 'What did you talk about?'

'Oh, nothing much.'

'But you were together for hours—'

'He slept most of the way. He mended the car – it was only a disconnected lead, but I'm afraid I'm hopeless with machines – then he told me his own car had broken down in Edinburgh, and he was going to Banff. Said he didn't really want to go through Aberdeen, as he didn't have a Restricted Area Pass. I'm afraid I . . . I told him not to worry about that. Said I'd vouch for him if we were stopped. Makes one feel such a bloody fool, you know – but I felt I owed him a favour. He had got me out of a bit of a hole, y'know.'

Kincaid said: 'Nobody's blaming you, sir.'

Bloggs was, but he did not say so. Instead he said: 'There are very few people who have met Faber and can tell us what he's like. Can you think hard and tell me what kind of a man you took him to be?'

'He woke up like a soldier,' Porter said. 'He was courteous, and seemed intelligent. Firm handshake. I take notice of handshakes.'

'Anything else? Think very hard.'

'Something else about when he woke up . . .' Porter's florid face creased up in a frown. 'His right hand went to his left forearm, like this.' He demonstrated.

'That's something,' Bloggs said. 'That'll be where he keeps the knife. A sleeve-sheath.'

'Nothing else, I'm afraid.'

'And he said he was going to Banff. That means he's not.'

'Really?'

'Spies always lie, on principle. I'll bet you told him where you were going before he told you where he was going.'

'I believe I did.' Porter nodded thoughtfully. 'Well, well.'

'Either Aberdeen was his destination, or he went south after you dropped him. Since he said he was going north, he probably didn't go north.'

Kincaid said: 'That kind of second-guessing could get out of hand.'

'Sometimes it does,' Bloggs grinned. 'Did you tell him that you're a magistrate?'

'Yes.'

'That's why he didn't kill you.'

'What? Good Lord! What do you mean?'

'He knew you'd be missed.'

'Good Lord!' Porter repeated. He had gone slightly pale. The idea that he might actually have been killed clearly had not occurred to him.

The door opened again. The man who walked in said: 'I've got your information, and I hope it was fucken worth it.'

Bloggs grinned. This was, undoubtedly, the harbour-master: a short man with cropped white hair, smoking a large pipe and wearing a blazer with brass buttons.

Kincaid said: 'Come in, Captain. How did you get so wet? You shouldn't go out in the rain.'

'Fuck off,' the Captain said. Bloggs was not sure how much of his anger was real: very little of it, to judge by the delighted expressions on the other faces in the room.

Porter said: 'Morning, Captain.'

'Good morning, Your Worship,' the Captain said.

Kincaid said: 'What have you got?'

The Captain took off his cap and shook drops of rain from its crown. 'The *Marie II* has gone missing,' he said. 'I saw her come in on the afternoon the storm began. I didn't see her go out, but I know she shouldn't have sailed again that day. However, it seems she did.'

'Who owns her?'

'Tam Halfpenny. I telephoned him. He left her in her mooring that day and hasn't seen her since.'

Bloggs said: 'What kind of vessel is she?'

'A small fishing boat, sixty feet and broad in the beam. Stout little craft. Inboard motor. No particular style – the fishermen round here don't follow the pattern book when they build boats.'

'Let me ask you a very important question,' Bloggs said. 'Could that boat have survived the storm?'

The Captain paused in the act of putting a match to his pipe. After a moment he said: 'With a very skilful sailor at the helm – maybe. Maybe not.'

'How far might he have got before the storm broke?'

'Not far – a few miles. The *Marie II* was not tied up until evening.'

Bloggs stood up, walked around his chair, and sat down again. 'So where is he now?'

'At the bottom of the sea, in all probability, the bloody fool.' The Captain's statement was not without relish.

Bloggs could take no satisfaction in the likelihood that Faber was dead. It was too inconclusive. The discontent spread to his body, and he felt restless, itchy, and frustrated. He scratched his chin: he needed a shave. 'I'll believe it when I see it,' he said.

'You won't.'

'Save your lugubrious guesswork,' Bloggs said sharply. 'I want information, not pessimism.' The other men in the room suddenly remembered that, despite his youth, he was the senior officer there. 'Let's rehearse the possibilities. One: he left Aberdeen by land and someone else stole the *Marie II.* In that case he has probably reached his destination by now, but he won't have left the country because of the storm. We already have all the other police forces looking for him, and that's all we can do about number one.

'Two: he's still in Aberdeen. Again, we have this possibility covered: we're still looking for him.

'Three: he left Aberdeen by sea. I think we're agreed this is the strongest option. Let's break it down. Three A: he transferred to another vessel – probably a U-boat – before the storm broke. We don't think he had time, but he might've. Three B: he found shelter somewhere, or was shipwrecked somewhere – mainland or island. Three C: he died.

'If he caught a U-boat, we've had it. We've lost. There's nothing more we can do. So let's forget that one. If he found shelter, or was shipwrecked, we'll find evidence sooner or later – either the *Marie II*, or bits of it. We can search the coastline right away and survey the sea as soon as the weather clears sufficiently for us to get a plane up. If he's gone to the bottom of the ocean we may still find bits of the boat floating.

'So we have three courses of action to take. We continue the searches already going on; we mount a new search of the coastline, working north and south from Aberdeen; and we prepare for an air-sea search the minute the weather improves.'

Bloggs had begun to pace up and down as he spoke, thinking on his feet. He stopped now, and looked around. 'Comments, queries and suggestions?'

The late hour had got to all of them. Bloggs's sudden access of energy jerked them out of a creeping lethargy. One leaned forward, rubbing his hands; another tied his shoelaces; a third put his jacket on. They wanted to go to work. There were no questions.

'All right,' said Bloggs. 'Let's win the war.'

TWENTY-THREE

Faber was awake. His body probably needed sleep, despite the fact that he had spent the day in bed; but his mind was hyperactive, turning over possibilities, sketching scenarios, thinking about women and about home.

Now that he was so close to getting out, his memories of home became quite painfully sweet. He thought of quite silly things, like sausages fat enough to eat in slices, and motor cars on the right-hand side of the road, and *really* tall trees, and most of all his own language – words with guts and precision, hard consonants and pure vowels and the verb at the end of the sentence where it ought to be, finality and meaning in the same climactic terminal.

Thoughts of climaxes brought Gertrude to mind again: her face beneath his, make-up washed away by his kisses, eyes closing tight in pleasure then opening again to look with delight into his, mouth stretched wide in a permanent gasp, saying '*Ja, Liebling, ja . . .*'

It was silly. He had led the life of a monk for seven years, but she had no reason to do the same. She would have had a dozen men since Faber. She might even be dead, bombed by the RAF or murdered by the maniacs because her nose was half an inch too long or run over by a motor car in the blackout. Anyway, she would hardly remember him. He would probably never see her again. But she was a symbol.

He did not normally permit himself the indulgence of sentiment. There was in his nature a very cold streak, and he cultivated it because it protected him. Now, however, he was within an inch of success, and he felt free, not to relax his vigilance, but to fantasize a little.

The storm was his safeguard while it continued. He would simply contact the U-boat with Tom's radio on Monday, and its captain would send a dinghy into the bay as soon as the weather cleared. However, if the storm ended before Monday, there was a slight complication: the supply boat. David and Lucy would naturally expect him to take the boat back to the mainland.

Lucy came into his thoughts in vivid, full-colour visions which he could not quite control. He saw her striking amber eyes watching him as he made a bandage for her thumb; her outline walking up the stairs in front of him clad in shapeless man's clothing; her heavy breasts, perfectly round, as she stood naked in the bathroom: and as the visions developed from memory into fantasy she leaned over the bandage and kissed his mouth, turned back on the stairs and took him in her arms, stepped out of the bathroom and placed his hands on her breasts.

He turned restessly in the little bed, cursing the imagination which sent him dreams the like of which he had not suffered since his schooldays. At that time, before he had experienced the reality of sex, he had constructed elaborate sexual scenarios featuring the older women with whom he came into daily contact: the starchy Matron; Professor Nagel's dark, thin, intellectual wife; the shopkeeper in the village who wore red lipstick and talked to her husband with contempt. Sometimes he put all three of them into one orgiastic fantasy. When at the age of fifteen he had seduced a housemaid's daughter in the twilight of a West Prussian forest, he abandoned the imaginary orgies because they were so much better than the disappointing real thing. Young Henrik had been greatly puzzled by this: where was the blinding ecstasy, the sensation of soaring through the air like a bird, the mystical fusion of two bodies into one? The fantasies became painful, reminding him of his failure to make them real. Later, of course, the reality improved, and Henrik formed the view that ecstasy comes not from a man's pleasure in a woman, but from their pleasure in each other. He had voiced that opinion to his elder brother, who seemed to think it banal, a truism rather than a discovery; and before long Henrik saw it that way too.

He became a good lover, eventually. He found sex interesting, as well as physically pleasant. He was never a great seducer, for the thrill of conquest was not what he wanted. But he was expert at giving and receiving sexual gratification, without the expert's illusion that technique is all. For some women he was a highly desirable man, and the fact that he did not know this only served to make him even more attractive.

He tried to remember how many women he had had: Anna, Gretchen, Ingrid, the American girl, those two whores in Stuttgart . . . he could not recall them all, but there could not have been more than about twenty.

None of them, he thought, had been quite as beautiful as Lucy. He gave an exasperated sigh: he had let this woman get to him, just because he was close to home and had been so careful for so long. He was annoyed with himself. It was undisciplined: one should not relax until the assignment was over, and this was not over, not quite.

There was the problem of the supply boat. Several solutions came to mind: perhaps the most promising was to incapacitate the island's inhabitants, meet the boat himself, and send the boatman away with a cock-and-bull story. He could say he was visiting them, had come out on another boat; that he was a relative, or a bird-watcher . . . anything. It was too small a problem to engage his full attention at present. Later, when and if the weather improved, he would work something out.

He had no serious problems. A lonely island, miles off the coast, with four inhabitants – it was an ideal hideout. From now on, leaving Britain was going to be as easy as breaking out of a baby's playpen. When he thought of the situations he had already come through, the people he had killed – the five Home Guard men, the Yorkshire lad on the train, the Abwehr messenger – he considered himself now to be sitting pretty.

An old man, a cripple, a woman and a child . . . Killing them would be so simple.

*

Lucy, too, lay awake. She was listening. There was a lot to hear. The weather was an orchestra, rain drumming on the roof, wind fluting in the eaves of the cottage, sea performing glissandi with the beach. The old house talked, too, creaking in its joints as it suffered the buffeting of the storm. Within the room there were more sounds: David's slow, regular breathing, threatening but never quite achieving a snore as he slept deeply under the influence of the double dose of soporific; and the quicker, shallow breaths of Jo, sprawled comfortably across a camp bed beside the far wall.

The noise is keeping me awake, Lucy thought; then immediately: Who am I trying to fool? Her wakefulness was caused by Henry, who had looked at her naked body, and had touched her hands gently as he bandaged her thumb, and who now lay in bed in the next room, probably fast asleep.

He had not told her much about himself, she realized: only that he was unmarried. She did not know where he had been born – his accent gave no clue. He had not even hinted at what he did for a living, though she imagined he must be a professional man, perhaps a dentist or a soldier. He was not dull enough to be a solicitor, too intelligent to be a journalist, and doctors could never keep their profession secret for longer than five minutes. He was not rich enough to be a barrister, too self-effacing to be an actor. She would bet on the Army.

Did he live alone, she wondered? Or with his mother? Or a woman? What did he wear when he wasn't fishing? She would like to see him in a dark blue suit, double-breasted, with a white handkerchief in the top pocket. Did he have a motor car? Yes, he would; something rather unusual, and quite new. He probably drove very fast.

That thought brought back memories of David's two-seater, and she closed her eyes tightly to shut out the nightmare images. Think of something else, think of something *else.*

She thought of Henry again, and realized an odd thing: she wanted to make love to him.

It was a peculiar wish; the kind of wish that, in her scheme of things, afflicted men but not women. A woman might meet a man briefly and find him attractive, want to get to know him better, even begin to fall in love with him; but she did not feel an immediate physical desire, not unless she was . . . abnormal.

She told herself that this was ridiculous; that what she needed was to make love with her husband, not to copulate with the first eligible man who came along. She told herself she was not that kind.

All the same, it was pleasant to speculate. David and Jo were fast asleep: there was nothing to stop her getting out of bed, crossing the landing, entering his room, sliding into bed next to him . . .

Nothing to stop her, except character, good breeding, and a respectable upbringing.

If she were going to do it with anybody, she would do it with someone like Henry. He would be kind, and gentle, and considerate; he would not despise her for offering herself like a Soho streetwalker.

She turned over in the bed, smiling at her own foolishness: for how could she possibly know whether he would despise her? She had known him only for a day, and he had spent most of that day asleep.

Still, it would be nice to have him look at her again, his expression of admiration tinged with some kind of amusement. It would be nice to feel his hands, to touch his body, to squeeze against the warmth of his skin.

She realized that her body was responding to the images in her mind. She felt the urge to touch herself, and resisted it, as she had done for four years. At least I haven't dried up, like an old crone, she thought.

She moved her legs, and sighed as a warm sensation spread through her loins. This was getting unreasonable. It was time to go to sleep. There was just no way she would make love to Henry, or to anyone else, tonight.

With that thought she got out of bed and went to the door.

Faber heard a footfall on the landing, and he reacted automatically.

His mind cleared instantly of the idle, lascivious thoughts with which it had been occupied. He swung his legs to the floor and slid out from under the bedclothes in a single, fluid movement; then silently crossed the room to stand beside the window in the darkest corner, the stiletto knife in his hand.

He heard the door open, heard the intruder step inside, heard the door close again. At that point he started to think, for an assassin would have left the door open for a quick getaway, and it occurred to him that there were a hundred reasons why it was impossible that an assassin should have found him here.

He ignored the thought, for he had survived this long by catering for the one-in-a-thousand chance. The wind dropped momentarily, and he heard an indrawn breath, a faint gasp, from beside his bed, enabling him to locate the intruder's exact position. He sprang.

He had her on the bed, face down, with his knife at her throat and his knee in the small of her back, before he realized that the intruder was a woman. A split-second later he guessed her identity. He eased his grip, reached out to the bedside table, and switched on the light.

Her face was pale in the dim glow of the lamp.

Faber sheathed the knife before she could see it. He took his weight off her body. 'I'm awfully sorry,' he said.

She turned on to her back and looked up at him as he straddled her. She began to giggle.

Faber added: 'I thought you were a burglar.'

'And where would a burglar come from?' she laughed. The colour rushed back to her cheeks in a blush.

She was wearing a very loose, old-fashioned flannel nightgown which covered her from her throat to her ankles. Her dark-red hair spread across Faber's pillow in disarray. Her eyes seemed very large, and her lips were moist.

'You are remarkably beautiful,' Faber said quietly.

She closed her eyes.

Faber bent over her and kissed her mouth. Her lips parted immediately, and she returned his kiss hungrily. With his fingertips he stroked her shoulders, her neck and her ears. She moved beneath him.

He wanted to kiss her for a long time, to explore her mouth and savour the intimacy; but he realized that she had no time for tenderness. She reached inside his pyjama trousers and squeezed. She moaned softly and began to breathe hard.

Still kissing her, Faber reached for the light and killed it. He pulled away from her and took off his pyjama jacket. Quickly, so that she would not wonder what he was doing, he tugged at the can stuck to his chest, ignoring the sting as the sticky tape was jerked away from his skin. He slid the photographs under the bed. He also unbuttoned the sheath on his left forearm and dropped that.

He pushed the skirt of her nightdress up to her waist. She wore nothing underneath.

'Quickly,' she said. 'Quickly.'

Faber lowered his body to hers.

Lucy did not feel the least bit guilty afterwards. She just felt content, satisfied, replete. She had had what she wanted, and she was glad. She lay still, eyes closed, stroking the bristly hair at the back of Henry's neck, enjoying the rough tickling sensation on her hands.

After a while she said: 'I was in such a rush . . .'

'It's not over yet,' he murmured.

She frowned in the dark. 'Didn't you . . . ?'

'No, I didn't. You hardly did.'

She smiled. 'I beg to differ.'

He turned on the light and looked at her. 'We'll see.'

He slipped down the bed, his torso between her thighs, and kissed her belly. His tongue flicked in and out of her navel. It was quite nice. Then his head went lower. Surely, she thought, he doesn't want to kiss me *there.* He did. And he did more than kiss. His lips pulled at the soft folds of her skin. She was paralysed by shock as his tongue began to probe in the crevices and then, as he parted her lips with his fingers, to thrust deep inside her.

Finally his restless tongue found a tiny, sensitive place, so small she had not known it existed, so sensitive that his touch was almost painful at first. She forgot her shock as she was overwhelmed by the most piercing sensation she had ever experienced. Unable to restrain herself, she moved her hips up and down, faster and faster, rubbing her slippery flesh over his mouth, his chin, his nose, his forehead; totally absorbed in her own pleasure. The thrill built and built, like feedback in a microphone, feeding upon itself, until she felt utterly possessed by joy and opened her mouth to scream, whereupon Henry clapped his hand over her face to quiet her; but she screamed in her throat as the climax went on and on, ending in something that felt like an explosion and left her so drained that she thought she would never get up.

Her mind seemed to go blank for a while. She knew

vaguely that Henry still lay between her legs, his bristly cheek against the soft inside of her thigh, his lips moving gently, affectionately.

Eventually she said: 'Now I *know* what Lawrence means.'

He lifted his head. 'I don't understand.'

She sighed. 'I didn't realize it could be like that. It was lovely.'

'*Was*?'

'Oh, God, I've no more energy . . .'

He changed position, kneeling astride her chest, and she realized what he wanted her to do, and for the second time she was frozen by shock: it was just too *big* . . . but suddenly she *wanted* to do it, she *needed* to take him into her mouth; so she lifted her head, and her lips closed around him, and he gave a soft groan.

He held her head in his hands, moving it to and fro, moaning quietly. She looked at his face. He was staring wild-eyed at her, drinking in the sight of what she was doing. She wondered what she would do when he . . . *came* . . . and she decided she didn't care, because everything else had been so good with him that she knew she would enjoy even that.

But it was not to be. When she thought he was on the point of losing control he stopped, moved away, lay on top of her, and entered her again. This time it was very slow and relaxed, like the rhythm of the sea on the beach; until he put his hands under her hips and grasped the globes of her bottom, and she looked at his face and knew that now, now he was ready to shed his self-control and lose himself in her. That excited her more than anything, so that when at last he arched his back, his face screwed up into a mask of pain, and groaned deep in his chest, she wrapped her legs around his waist and abandoned herself to ecstasy; and then, after so long, she heard the trumpets and thunder-storms and the clash of cymbals that Lawrence had promised.

They were quiet for a long time. Lucy felt warm, as if she were glowing; she had never felt so warm in all her time on the island. When their breathing subsided she could hear the storm outside. Henry was heavy on top of her, but she did not want him to move: she liked his weight, and the faint tang of perspiration from his white skin. From time to time he moved his head to brush his lips against her cheek.

He was the perfect man to have an affair with. He knew more about her body than she did. His own body was very beautiful: broad and muscular at the shoulders, narrow at the waist and hips, with long, strong, hairy legs. She thought he had some scars: she was not sure. Strong, gentle and handsome: perfect. Yet she knew she would never fall in love with him, never want to run away with him and marry him. Deep inside him, she sensed, there was something very cold and hard, some part of him that was committed elsewhere, a readiness to abandon commonplace emotions for some higher duty. He would never belong to any woman, for he had some other ultimate loyalty – like a painter's art, a businessman's greed, a patriot's country, a socialist's revolution. She would have to hold him at arm's length, and use him cautiously, like an addictive drug.

Not that she would have time to get hooked: he would be gone in little more than a day.

She stirred at last, and immediately he rolled off her and on to his back. She lifted herself on one elbow and looked at his naked body. Yes, he did have scars: a long one on his chest, and a small mark like a star – it might have been a burn – on his hip. She rubbed his chest with the palm of her hand.

'It's not very ladylike,' she said, 'but I want to say thank you.'

He reached out to touch her cheek, and smiled. 'You're very ladylike.'

'You don't know what you've done. You've—'

He put a finger over her lips. 'I know what I've done.'

She bit his finger, then put his hand on her breast. He felt for her nipple. She said: 'Please do it again.'

'I don't think I can,' he said.

But he did.

She left him a couple of hours after dawn. There was a small noise from the other bedroom, and she seemed suddenly to remember that she had a husband and a son in the house. Faber wanted to tell her that it didn't matter, that neither he nor she had the least reason to care what the husband knew or thought; but he held his tongue and let her go. She kissed him once more, very wetly; then she stood up, smoothed her rumpled nightgown over her body, and tiptoed out. He watched her fondly.

She's quite something, he thought. He lay on his back and looked at the ceiling. She was quite naive, and very inexperienced, but all the same she had been very good. I could fall in love with her, he thought.

He got up and retrieved the film can and the knife in its sheath from under the bed. He wondered whether to keep them on his person. He might want to make love to her in the day . . . He decided to wear the knife – he would feel undressed without it – and leave the can somewhere. He put it on top of the chest-of-drawers and covered it with his papers and his wallet. He knew that he was breaking all the rules; but this was sure to be his last assignment, and he felt entitled to enjoy a woman. It would hardly matter if someone saw the pictures – what could they do?

He lay down on the bed, then got up again. Years of training would not let him take risks. He put the can and his papers into the pocket of his jacket. Now he could relax.

He heard the child's voice, then Lucy's tread as she went down the stairs, and then David dragging himself to the bathroom. He would have to get up and have breakfast with the household. He did not want to sleep now, anyway.

He stood at the rain-streaked window, watching the weather rage, until he heard the bathroom door open. Then he put on his pyjama jacket and went in to shave. He used David's razor, without permission.

It did not seem to matter now.

TWENTY-FOUR

Erwin Rommel knew from the start that he was going to quarrel with Heinz Guderian.

General Guderian was exactly the kind of aristocratic Prussian officer Rommel hated. He had known him for some time. They had both, in their early days, commanded the Goslar Jaeger Battalion, and they had met again during the Polish campaign. When Rommel left Africa he had recommended Guderian to succeed him, knowing the battle was lost: the manoeuvre was a failure because at that time Guderian had been out of favour with Hitler and the recommendation was rejected out of hand.

The General was, Rommel felt, the kind of man who put a silk handkerchief on his knee to protect the crease in his trousers as he sat drinking in the Herrenklub. He was an officer because his father had been an officer and his grandfather had been rich. Rommel, the schoolteacher's son who had risen from Lieutenant-Colonel to Field Marshal in only four years, despised the military caste of which he had never been a member.

Now he stared across the table at the General, who was sipping brandy appropriated from the French

Rothschilds. Guderian and his sidekick, General von Geyr, had come to Rommel's headquarters at La Roche Guyon in Northern France to tell him how to deploy his troops. Rommel's reactions to such visits ranged from impatience to fury. In his view the General Staff were there to provide reliable intelligence and regular supplies, and he knew from his experience in Africa that they were incompetent at both tasks.

Guderian had a cropped, fair moustache, and the corners of his eyes were heavily wrinkled so that he always appeared to be grinning at you. He was tall and handsome, which did nothing to endear him to the short, ugly, balding Rommel. He seemed relaxed, and any German general who could relax at this stage of the war was surely a fool. The meal they had just finished – local veal and wine from farther south – was no excuse.

Rommel looked out of the window and watched the rain dripping from the lime trees into the courtyard while he waited for Guderian to begin the discussion. When eventually he spoke, it was clear the General had been thinking about the best way to make his point, and had decided to approach it sideways.

'In Turkey,' he began, 'the British 9th and 10th armies, with the Turkish army, are grouping at the border with Greece. In Yugoslavia, the partisans are also concentrating. The French in Algeria are preparing to invade the Riviera. The Russians appear to be mounting an amphibious invasion of Sweden. In Italy, the Allies are ready to march on Rome.

'There are smaller signals: a general kidnapped in

Crete; an Intelligence officer murdered at Lyon; a radar post attacked at Rhodes; an aircraft sabotaged with abrasive grease and destroyed at Athens; a commando raid on Sagvaag; an explosion in the oxygen factory at Boulogne-sur-Seine; a train derailed in the Ardennes; a petrol dump fired at Boussens . . . I could go on.

'The picture is clear. In occupied territories, there is ever-increasing sabotage and treachery; on our borders, everywhere we see preparations for invasion. None of us doubts that there will be a major Allied offensive this summer; and we can be equally sure that all this skirmishing is intended to confuse us about where the attack will come.'

The General paused. The lecture, delivered in schoolmaster style, was irritating Rommel, and he took the opportunity to interrupt. 'This is why we have a General Staff: to digest such information, produce appreciations of enemy activity, and forecast his future moves.'

Guderian smiled indulgently. 'We must also be aware of the limitations of such crystal-gazing. You have your ideas about where the attack will come, I'm sure: we all do. Our strategy must take into account the possibility that our guesses are wrong.'

Rommel now saw where the General's roundabout argument was leading, and he suppressed the urge to shout his disagreement before the conclusion was stated.

'You have four armoured divisions under your command,' Guderian continued. 'The 2nd Panzers at Amiens; the 116th at Rouen; the 21st at Caen; and the

2nd SS at Toulouse. General von Geyr has already proposed to you that these should be grouped well back from the coast, all together, ready for fast retaliation at any point. Indeed, this stratagem is a principle of OKW policy. Nevertheless, you have not only resisted von Geyr's suggestion, but have in fact moved the 21st right up to the Atlantic coast.'

'And the other three must be moved to the coast as soon as possible,' Rommel burst out. 'When will you people learn? *The Allies rule the air.* Once the invasion is launched there will be no further major movements of armour. Mobile operations are no longer possible. If your precious panzers are in Paris when the Allies land on the coast, they will *stay* in Paris – pinned down by the RAF – until the Allies march along the Boulevard St Michel. I *know* – they've done it to me. Twice!' He paused to draw breath. 'To group our armour as a mobile reserve is to render it useless. There will be no counter-attack. The invasion must be met on the beaches, when it is most vulnerable, and pushed back into the sea.'

The flush receded from his face as he began to expound his own defensive strategy. 'I have created underwater obstacles, strengthened the Atlantic Wall, laid minefields, and driven stakes into every meadow that might be used to land airplanes behind our lines. All my troops are engaged in digging defences whenever they're not actually training.

'My armoured divisions must be moved to the coast. The OKW reserve should be redeployed in France. The 9th and 10th SS divisions have to be brought back from the Eastern Front. Our whole strategy must be to prevent the Allies from securing a beachhead, for once they achieve that, the battle is lost . . . perhaps even the war.'

Guderian leaned forward, his eyes narrowing in that infuriating half-grin. 'You want us to defend the European coastline from Tromso in Norway all around the Iberian Peninsula to Rome. From where shall we get the armies?'

'That question should have been asked in 1938,' Rommel muttered.

There was an embarrassed silence after this remark, which was all the more shocking coming from the notoriously apolitical Rommel.

Von Geyr broke the spell. 'Where do *you* believe the attack will come, Field-Marshal?'

Rommel considered. 'Until recently I was convinced of the Pas de Calais theory. However, last time I was with the Führer I was impressed by his arguments in favour of Normandy. I am also impressed by his instinct, and its record of accuracy. Therefore I believe our panzers should be deployed primarily along the Normandy coast, with perhaps one division at the mouth of the Somme – this last supported by forces outside my group.'

Guderian shook his head solemnly. 'No, no, no. It's far too risky.'

'I'm prepared to take this argument to Hitler himself,' Rommel threatened.

'Then that's what you must do,' Guderian said resignedly, 'for I shan't assent to your plan, unless . . .'

'Well?' Rommel was surprised that the General's position might be qualified.

Guderian shifted in his seat, reluctant to give a concession to so obdurate an antagonist as Rommel. 'You may know that the Führer is waiting for a report from an unusually effective agent in England.'

'I remember,' Rommel nodded. 'Die Nadel.'

'Yes. He has been assigned to assess the strength of the First United States Army Group under Patton's command in the eastern part of England. If he finds – as I am certain he will – that that army is large, strong, and ready to move, then I shall continue to oppose you. However, if he finds that FUSAG is a bluff – a small army masquerading as an invasion force – then I shall concede that you are right, and you shall have your panzers. Will you accept that compromise?'

Rommel bowed his large head in assent. 'It all depends on Die Nadel, then.'

'It all depends on Die Nadel.'

PART FIVE

TWENTY-FIVE

The cottage was terribly small, Lucy realized quite suddenly. As she went about her morning chores – lighting the stove, making porridge, tidying up, dressing Jo – the walls seemed to press in on her claustrophobically. After all, it was only four rooms, linked by a little passage with a staircase; you couldn't move without bumping into someone else. If you stood still and listened you could hear what everyone was doing: Henry running water into the wash-basin, David sliding down the stairs, Jo chastising his teddy-bear in the living-room. Lucy would have liked some time on her own before meeting people: time to let the events of the night settle into her memory, recede from the forefront of her thoughts, so that she could act normally without a conscious effort.

She guessed she was not going to be good at deception. It did not come naturally to her. She had no experience of it. She tried to think of another occasion in her life when she had deceived someone close to her, and she could not. It was not that she lived by very high principles – the *thought* of lying did not trouble her. It was just that she had never had reason for dishonesty. Does that mean, she wondered, that I've led a sheltered life?

David and Jo sat down at the kitchen table and began to eat. David was silent, Jo talked non-stop just for the pleasure of making words. Lucy did not want food.

'Aren't you eating?' David said casually.

'I've had some.' There – her first lie. It wasn't so bad.

The storm made the claustrophobia worse. The rain was so heavy that Lucy could hardly see the barn from the kitchen window. One felt even more shut-in when to open a door or window was a major operation. The low, steel-grey sky and the wisps of mist created a permanent twilight. In the garden, the rain ran in rivers between the rows of potato plants, and the herb patch was a shallow pond. The sparrow's nest under the outhouse roof had been washed away, and the birds flitted in and out of the eaves, panicking.

Lucy heard Henry coming down the stairs, and she felt better. For some reason, she was quite sure that he was very good at deception.

'Good morning!' Faber said heartily. David, sitting at the table in his wheelchair, looked up and smiled. Lucy busied herself at the stove. There was guilt written all over her face. Faber groaned inwardly, but David did not seem to notice her expression. Faber began to think that David was an oaf.

Lucy said: 'Sit down and have some breakfast, Henry.'

'Thank you very much.'

David said: 'Can't offer to take you to church, I'm

afraid. Hymn-singing on the wireless is the best we can do.'

Faber realized it was Sunday. 'Are you churchgoing people?'

'No,' David said. 'You?'

'No.'

'Sunday is much the same as any other day for farmers,' David continued. 'I'll be driving over to the other end of the island to see my shepherd. You could come, if you feel up to it.'

'I'd like to,' Faber told him. It would give him a chance to reconnoitre. He would need to know the way to the cottage with the transmitter. 'Would you like me to drive you?'

David looked at him sharply. 'I can manage quite well.' There was a strained moment of silence. 'In this weather, the road is just a memory. We'll be a lot safer with me at the wheel.'

'Of course.' Faber began to eat.

'It makes no difference to me,' David persisted. 'I don't want you to come if you think it would be too much—'

'Really, I'd be glad to.'

'Did you sleep all right? It didn't occur to me you might still be tired. I hope Lucy didn't keep you up late.'

Faber willed himself not to look at Lucy. Out of the corner of his eye he could see that she was blushing to the roots of her hair. 'I slept all day yesterday,' he said, trying to fix David's eyes with his own.

It was no use. David was looking at his wife. She

turned her back. The trace of a frown creased his forehead, and then just for a moment, his jaw dropped open in a classic expression of surprise.

Faber was mildly annoyed. David would be hostile now, and antagonism was half way to suspicion. It was not dangerous, but it might be tiresome.

The husband recovered his composure quickly. He pushed his chair away from the table and wheeled himself to the back door. 'I'll get the jeep out of the barn,' he muttered. He took an oilskin off a hook and put it over his head, then opened the door and rolled out.

In the few moments the door was open, the storm blew into the little kitchen, leaving the floor wet and the people cold. When it shut, Lucy shivered and began to mop the water from the tiles.

Faber reached out and touched her arm.

'Don't,' she said, jerking her head toward Jo in warning.

'You're being silly,' Faber told her.

'I think he knows,' she said.

'But, if you reflect for a minute, you don't really care whether he knows or not, do you?'

She considered. 'I'm not supposed to.'

Faber shrugged. The jeep's horn sounded impatiently outside. Lucy handed him an oilskin and a pair of wellington boots.

'Don't talk about me,' she said.

Faber put on the waterproof clothes and went to the front door. Lucy followed him, closing the kitchen door on Jo.

With his hand on the latch, Faber turned and kissed her.

She kissed him back, forcefully, then turned and went into the kitchen.

Faber dashed through the rain, across a sea of mud, and jumped into the jeep beside David. He pulled away immediately.

The vehicle had been specially adapted for the legless man to drive. It had a hand throttle, automatic gearshift, and a handle on the rim of the wheel to enable the driver to steer one-handed. The folded-up wheelchair slid into a special compartment behind the driver's seat. There was a shotgun in a rack above the windscreen.

David drove competently. He had been right about the road: it was no more than a strip of heath worn bare by the jeep's tyres. The rain pooled in the deep ruts. The car slithered about in the mud. David seemed to enjoy it. There was a cigarette between his lips, and he wore an incongruous air of bravado. Perhaps this was his substitute for flying.

'What do you do when you're not fishing?' he said around the cigarette.

'Civil servant,' Faber told him.

'What sort of work?'

'Finance. I'm just a cog in the machine.'

'Treasury, eh?'

'Mainly.'

Even that asinine answer did not stop David's questioning. 'Interesting work?' he persisted.

'Fairly.' Faber summoned up the energy to invent a

story. 'I know a bit about how much a given piece of engineering ought to cost, and I spend most of my time making sure the taxpayer isn't being overcharged.'

'Any particular sort of engineering?'

'Everything from paper clips to aircraft engines.'

'Ah, well. We all contribute to the war effort in our own way.'

It was a snide remark, and David would naturally have no idea why Faber did not resent it. 'I'm too old to fight,' Faber said mildly.

'Were you in the first lot?'

'Too young.'

'A lucky escape.'

'Doubtless.'

The track ran quite close to the cliff edge, but David did not slow down. It crossed Faber's mind that he might want to kill them both. He reached for a grab handle.

'Am I going too fast for you?' David asked.

'You seem to know the road,' Faber replied.

'You looked frightened,' David said.

Faber ignored that, and David slowed down a little, apparently satisfied that he had made some kind of point.

The island was fairly flat, and bare, Faber observed. The ground rose and fell slightly, but as yet he had seen no hills. The vegetation was mostly grass, with some ferns and bushes, but few trees: there was little protection from the weather. David Rose's sheep must be hardy, he thought.

'Are you married?' David asked suddenly.

'No.'

'Wise man.'

'Oh, I don't know.'

'I'll bet you put yourself about a bit up in London,' David leered.

Faber had never liked the nudging, contemptuous way some men talked about women. He said sharply: 'I should think you're extremely fortunate to have Lucy.'

'Oh, would you.'

'Yes.'

'Nothing like variety, though, eh?'

Faber thought: What the devil is he getting at? He said: 'I haven't had the chance to discover the merits of monogamy.'

'Quite.'

Faber thought: *He* doesn't know what he's getting at, either. He decided to say no more, since everything he said was fuel to the fire.

'I must say, you don't *look* like a Government accountant. Where's the rolled umbrella and the bowler hat?'

Faber tried a thin smile.

'And you seem quite fit for a pen-pusher.'

'I ride a bicycle.'

'You must be quite tough, to have survived that wreck.'

'Thank you.'

'You don't *look* too old to be in the Army, either.'

Faber turned his gaze on David. 'What are you driving at, David?' he asked calmly.

'We're there,' David said.

Faber looked out of the windscreen and saw a

cottage very similar to Lucy's, with stone walls, a slate roof, and small windows. It stood at the top of a hill, the only hill Faber had seen on the island, and not much of a hill at that. The house had a squat, resilient look about it. Climbing up to it, the jeep skirted a small stand of pine and fir trees. Faber wondered why the cottage had not been built in the shelter of the trees.

Beside the house was a hawthorn tree in bedraggled blossom. David stopped the car. Faber watched him unfold the wheelchair and ease himself out of the driving seat into the chair: he would have resented an offer of help.

They entered the house by a plank door with no lock. They were greeted in the hall by a black-and-white collie, a small, broad-headed dog who wagged his tail but did not bark. The layout of the cottage was identical with that of Lucy's, but the atmosphere was different: this place was bare, cheerless, and none too clean.

David led the way into the kitchen. The shepherd sat by an old-fashioned wood-burning kitchen range, warming his hands. He stood up.

David said: 'Henry, this is Tom McAvity.'

'Pleased to meet you,' Tom said formally.

Faber shook his hand. He was a short man, and broad, with a face like an old tan suitcase. He was wearing a cloth cap and smoking a very large briar pipe with a lid. His grip was firm, and the skin of his hand felt like sandpaper. He had a very big nose. Faber had to concentrate hard to understand what he was saying: his Scots accent was very broad.

'I hope I'm not going to be in the way,' Faber said. 'I only came along for the ride.'

David wheeled himself up to the table. 'I don't suppose we'll do much this morning, Tom – just take a look around.'

'Aye. We'll have some tay before we go, though.'

Tom poured strong tea into three mugs, and added a shot of whisky to each. The three men sat and sipped it in silence, David smoking a cigarette and Tom drawing gently at his pipe, and Faber felt certain that the other two spent a great deal of time together in this way, smoking and warming their hands and saying nothing.

When they had finished their tea Tom put the mugs in the shallow stone sink and they went out in the jeep. Faber sat in the back. David drove slowly this time, and the dog, which was called Bob, loped alongside, keeping pace without apparent effort. It was obvious that David knew the terrain very well, for he steered confidently across the open grassland without once getting bogged down in swampy ground. The sheep looked very sorry for themselves. With their fleeces sopping wet, they huddled in hollows, or close to bramble bushes, or on the leeward slopes, too dispirited to graze. Even the lambs were subdued, hiding beneath their mothers.

Faber was watching the dog when it stopped, listened for a moment, and then raced off at a tangent.

Tom had been watching, too. 'Bob's found something,' he said.

The jeep followed the dog for a quarter of a mile. When they stopped Faber could hear the sea: they were close to the island's northern edge. The dog was standing at the brink of a small gully. When the men got out of the car they could hear what the dog had heard: the bleating of a sheep in distress. They went to the edge of the gully and looked down.

The animal lay on its side about twenty feet down, balanced precariously on the steeply sloping bank. It held one foreleg at an awkward angle. Tom went down to it, treading cautiously, and examined the leg.

'Mutton tonight,' he called.

David got the gun from the jeep and slid it down to him. Tom put the sheep out of its misery.

'Do you want to rope it up?' David called.

'Aye – unless Henry wants to come and give me a hand.'

'Surely,' Faber said. He picked his way down to where Tom stood. They took a leg each and dragged the dead animal back up the slope. Faber's oilskin caught on a thorny bush, and he almost fell before he tugged the material free with a loud ripping sound.

They threw the sheep into the jeep and drove on. Faber felt very wet, and he realized he had torn away most of the back of the oilskin. 'I'm afraid I've ruined this garment,' he said.

'All in a good cause,' Tom told him.

Soon they returned to Tom's cottage. Faber took off

the oilskin and his wet donkey jacket, and Tom put the jacket over the stove to dry. Then each went to the outhouse – Tom's cottage did not have the modern plumbing that had been added to Lucy's – and Tom made more tea.

'She's the first we've lost this year,' David said.

'Aye.'

'We'll fence the gully this summer.'

'Aye.'

Faber sensed a change in the atmosphere: it was not the same as it had been two or three hours earlier. They sat, drinking and smoking as before, but David seemed restless. Twice Faber caught the man staring at him, deep in thought.

Eventually David said: 'We'll leave you to butcher the ewe, Tom.'

'Aye.'

David and Faber left. Tom did not get up, but the dog saw them to the door.

Before starting the jeep David took the shotgun from its rack above the windscreen, reloaded it, and put it back.

On the way home he underwent another change of mood and became chatty. 'I used to fly Spitfires, you know. Lovely kites. Four guns in each wing – American Brownings, they were, firing one thousand two hundred and sixty rounds a minute. The Jerries prefer cannon, of course – their Me 109s only have two machine guns. A cannon does more damage, but our Brownings are faster, and more accurate.'

'Really?' Faber said politely.

'They put cannon in the Hurricanes later, but it was the Spitfire that won the Battle of Britain.'

Faber found his boastfulness irritating. He said: 'How many enemy aircraft did you shoot down?'

'I lost my legs while I was training,' David said.

Faber stole a glance at his face: it was a mask of repressed fury.

David said: 'No, I haven't killed a single German, yet.'

It was an unmistakable signal. Faber suddenly became very alert. He had no idea what David might have deduced or discovered, but there could be no doubt that the man knew something was up. Faber turned slightly sideways to face David, braced himself with his foot against the transmission tunnel on the floor, and rested his right hand lightly on his left forearm. He waited for David's next move.

'Are you interested in aircraft?' David asked.

'No.' Faber's voice was flat.

'It's become a national pastime, I gather – aircraft spotting. Like bird-watching. People buy books on aircraft identification. Spend whole afternoons on their backs, looking at the sky through telescopes. I thought you might be an enthusiast.'

'Why?'

'Pardon?'

'What made you think I might be an enthusiast?'

'Oh, I don't know.' David stopped the jeep to light a cigarette. They were at the island's mid-point, five miles from Tom's cottage with another five miles to go to

Lucy's. David dropped the match on the floor. 'Perhaps it was the photographs that fell out of your jacket pocket—'

As he spoke, he tossed the lighted cigarette at Faber's face, and reached for the gun above the windscreen.

TWENTY-SIX

Sid Cripps looked out of the window and cursed under his breath. The meadow was full of American tanks – at least eighty of them. He realized there was a war on, and all that, but if only they'd asked him he would have offered them another field, where the grass was not so lush. By now the caterpillar tracks would have chewed up his best grazing.

He pulled on his boots and went out. There were some Yank soldiers in the field, and he wondered whether they had noticed the bull. When he got to the stile he stopped and scratched his head. There was something very funny going on.

The tanks had *not* chewed up his grass. They had left no tracks. But the American soldiers were *making* tank tracks with a tool something like a harrow.

While Sid was trying to figure it all out, the bull noticed the tanks. It stared at them for a while, then pawed the ground and lumbered into a run. It was going to charge a tank.

'Daft bugger, you'll break your head,' Sid muttered.

The soldiers were watching the bull, too. They seemed to think it was funny.

The bull ran full-tilt into the tank, its horns piercing the armour-plated side of the vehicle. Sid hoped fervently that British tanks were stronger than the American ones.

There was a loud hissing noise as the bull worked its horns free. The tank collapsed like a deflated balloon. The American soldiers fell about laughing.

Sid Cripps scratched his head again. It was all very strange.

Percival Godliman walked quickly across Parliament Square, carrying an umbrella. He wore a dark striped suit under his raincoat, and his black shoes were highly polished – at least, they had been until he stepped out into the rain – for it was not every day, come to that it was not every year, that he had a private audience with Churchill.

A career soldier would have been nervous at going with such bad news to see the supreme commander of the nation's armed forces. Godliman was not nervous, for a distinguished historian has nothing to fear from soldiers and politicians, not unless his view of history is a good deal more radical than Godliman's was. Not nervous, then; but he was worried.

He was thinking about the effort, the forethought, the care, the money and the manpower that had gone into the creation of the totally phoney First United States Army Group stationed in East Anglia: the four hundred landing ships, made of canvas and scaffolding floated on oil drums, which thronged the harbours and estuaries; the carefully manufactured inflatable dummies of tanks, artillery, trucks, half-tracks and even ammunition dumps; the complaints planted in the correspondence columns of the local newspapers about the decline in moral standards since the arrival of thousands of American troops in the area; the phoney oil dock at Dover, designed by Britain's most distinguished architect and built – out of cardboard and old sewage pipes – by craftsmen borrowed from film studios; the carefully faked reports transmitted to Hamburg by German agents who had been 'turned' by the XX Committee; and the incessant radio chatter, broadcast solely for the benefit of the German listening posts, consisting of messages compiled by professional writers of fiction, and including such gems as 'I/5th Queen's Royal Regiment report a number of civilian women, presumably unauthorized, in the baggage train. What are we going to do with them – take them to Calais?'

A lot had been achieved. The signs were that the Germans had fallen for it. And now the whole elaborate deception had been placed in jeopardy because of one spy – a spy Godliman had failed to catch.

His short, birdlike paces measured the Westminster pavement to the small doorway at No 2, Great George Street. The armed guard standing beside the wall of sandbags examined his pass and waved him in. He crossed the lobby and went down the stairs to Churchill's underground headquarters.

It was like going below decks on a battleship. Protected from bombs by a four-foot-thick ceiling of reinforced concrete, the command post featured steel bulkhead doors and roof props of ancient timber. As

Godliman entered the map room a cluster of youngish people with solemn faces emerged from the conference room beyond. An aide followed them a moment later, and spotted Godliman.

'You're very punctual, sir,' the aide said. 'He's ready for you.'

Godliman stepped into the small, comfortable conference room. There were rugs on the floor and a portrait of the King on the wall. An electric fan stirred the tobacco smoke in the air. Churchill sat at the head of an old, mirror-smooth table in the centre of which was a statuette of a faun – the emblem of Churchill's own deception outfit, the London Controlling Section.

Godliman decided not to salute.

Churchill said: 'Sit down, Professor.'

Godliman suddenly realized that Churchill was not a big man – but he *sat* like a big man: shoulders hunched, elbows on the arms of his chair, chin lowered, legs apart. Instead of the famous siren suit he was wearing a solicitor's black-and-stripes – short black jacket and striped grey trousers – with a spotted blue bow tie and a brilliant-white shirt. Despite his stocky frame and his paunch, the hand holding the fountain pen was delicate, thin-fingered. His complexion was baby-pink. The other hand held a cigar, and on the table beside the papers stood a glass containing what looked like whisky.

He was making notes in the margin of a typewritten report, and as he scribbled he muttered occasionally. Godliman was not in the least awed by the great man. As a peacetime statesman Churchill had been, in Godliman's view, a disaster. However, the man had the qualities of a great warrior chieftain, and Godliman respected him for that. (Years later, Churchill modestly denied having been the British lion, saying that he had merely been privileged to give the roar: Godliman thought that assessment was just about right.)

He looked up abruptly and said: 'I suppose there's no doubt this damned spy has discovered what we're up to?'

'None whatsoever, sir,' Godliman said.

'You think he's got away?'

'We chased him to Aberdeen. It's almost certain that he left there two nights ago in a stolen boat – presumably for a rendezvous in the North Sea. However, he can't have been far out of port when the storm blew up. He may have met the U-boat before the storm hit, but it's unlikely. In all probability he drowned. I'm sorry we can't offer more definite information.'

'So am I,' Churchill said. Suddenly he seemed angry, though not with Godliman. He got out of his chair and went over to the clock on the wall, staring as if mesmerized at the inscription *Victoria RI, Ministry of Works, 1889.* Then, as if he had forgotten that Godliman was there, he began to pace up and down alongside the table, muttering to himself. Godliman was able to make out the words, and what he heard astonished him. The great man was mumbling: 'This stocky figure, with a slight stoop, striding up and down, suddenly unconscious of any presence beyond his own thoughts . . .' It was as if Churchill were acting out a Hollywood screenplay which he wrote as he went along.

The performance ended as abruptly as it had begun,

and if the man knew he had been behaving eccentrically, he gave no sign of it. He sat down, handed Godliman a sheet of paper, and said: 'This is the German order of battle as of last week.'

Godliman read:

Russian front:	*122*	*infantry divisions*
	25	*panzer divisions*
	17	*miscellaneous divisions*
Italy & Balkans:	*37*	*infantry divisions*
	9	*panzer divisions*
	4	*miscellaneous divisions*
Western front:	*64*	*infantry divisions*
	12	*panzer divisions*
	12	*miscellaneous divisions*
Germany:	*3*	*infantry divisions*
	1	*panzer division*
	4	*miscellaneous divisions*

Churchill said: 'Of those twelve panzer divisions in the west, only *one* is actually on the Normandy coast. The great SS divisions, *Das Reich* and *Adolf Hitler*, are at Toulouse and Brussels respectively and show no signs of moving. What does all this tell you, Professor?'

'Our deception and cover plans seem to have been successful,' Godliman answered.

'Totally!' Churchill barked. 'They are confused and uncertain, and their best guesses about our intentions are wildly wrong. And yet!' He paused for effect. 'And yet, despite all that, General Walter Bedell Smith – Ike's Chief of Staff – tells me that . . .' He picked up another piece of paper from the table and read it aloud. 'Our chances of holding the beachhead, particularly after the Germans get their buildup, are only fifty-fifty.'

He put his cigar down, and his voice became quite soft. 'It will be June the fifth – possibly the sixth or the seventh. The tides are right . . . it has been decided. The build-up of troops in the West Country has already begun. The convoys are even now making their way along the country roads of England. It has taken the total military and industrial might of the whole English-speaking world – the greatest civilization since the Roman Empire – four years to win this fifty-fifty chance. If this spy gets out, we lose even that.'

He stared at Godliman for a moment, then he picked up his pen with a frail white hand. 'Don't bring me probabilities, Professor,' he said. 'Bring me the body of Die Nadel.'

He looked down and began to write. After a moment Percival Godliman got up and quietly left the room.

TWENTY-SEVEN

Cigarette tobacco burns at eight hundred degrees centigrade. However, the coal at the end of the cigarette is normally surrounded by a thin layer of ash. To cause a burn, the cigarette has to be pressed against the skin for the better part of a second: a glancing touch will hardly be felt. This applies even to the eyes, for blinking is the fastest involuntary reaction of the human body. Only amateurs throw cigarettes. Professionals – there are just a few people in the world for whom hand-to-hand fighting is a professional skill – ignore them.

Faber ignored the lighted cigarette that David Rose threw at him. He did right, for the cigarette glanced off his forehead and fell to the metal floor of the jeep. Then he made a grab for David's gun, and this was an error. He should have drawn his stiletto and stabbed David: for although David *might* have shot him first, he had never before pointed a gun at a human being, let alone killed somebody; so he would almost certainly have hesitated, and in that moment Faber could have killed him.

The mistake cost dear.

David had both hands on the midsection of the gun

– left hand on the barrel, right hand around the breech – and had pulled the weapon about six inches from its rack when Faber got a one-handed grip on the muzzle. David tugged the gun toward himself, but for a moment Faber's grasp held, and the gun pointed at the windscreen.

Faber was a strong man, but David was exceptionally strong. His shoulders, arms and wrists had moved his body and his wheelchair for four years, and the muscles had become abnormally developed. Furthermore, he had both hands on the gun in front of him, and Faber was holding on with one hand at an awkward angle. David tugged again, more determinedly this time, and the muzzle slipped from Faber's grasp.

At that instant, with the shotgun pointed at his belly and David's finger curling around the trigger, Faber felt very close to death.

He jerked upwards, catapulting himself out of his seat. His head hit the canvas roof of the jeep as the gun exploded with a crash that numbed the ears and produced a physical pain behind the eyes. The window by the passenger seat shattered into innumerable small pieces and the rain blew in through the empty frame. Faber twisted his body and fell back, not on to his own seat, but across David. He got both hands to David's throat and squeezed with his thumbs.

David tried to bring the gun around between their bodies to fire the other barrel, but the weapon was too big. Faber looked into his eyes, and saw . . . what was it? Exhilaration! Of course – at last the man had a chance to fight for his country. Then his expression changed as his body felt the lack of oxygen and he began to fight for breath.

David released his grip on the gun and brought both elbows back as far as he could, then punched Faber's lower ribs with a powerful double jab.

The pain was excruciating, and Faber screwed up his face in anguish, but he held his grip on David's throat. He knew he could withstand David's punches longer than David could hold his breath.

David must have had the same thought. He crossed his forearms between their bodies and pushed Faber away; then, when the gap was a few inches wide, he brought his hands up in an upward-and-outward blow against Faber's arms, breaking the stranglehold. He bunched his right fist and swung downwards with a mighty but unscientific punch which landed on Faber's cheekbone and brought water to his eyes.

Faber replied with a series of body jabs; David continued to bruise his face. They were too close together to do real damage to each other in a short time, but David's greater strength began to tell.

Grimly, Faber realized that David had shrewdly picked the time and place for the fight: he had had the advantages of surprise, the gun, and the confined space in which his muscle counted for much and Faber's better balance and greater manoeuvrability counted for little.

Faber shifted his weight slightly and his hip came into contact with the gearshift, throwing the transmission into forward. The engine was still running, and the car jerked, putting him off balance. David took the opportunity to release a long straight left which – more by luck than judgement – caught Faber full on the chin and threw him clear across the cab of the jeep. His head cracked against the A-post, he slumped with his shoulder on the door handle, the door opened, and he fell out of the car in a backward somersault to land on his face in the mud.

For a moment he was too dazed to move. When he opened his eyes he could see nothing but flashes of blue lightning against a misty red background. He heard the engine of the jeep racing. He shook his head, desperately trying to clear the fireworks from his vision, and struggled on to his hands and knees. The sound of the jeep receded and came closer again. He turned his head toward the noise, and as the colours in front of his eyes dissolved and disappeared, he saw the vehicle bearing down on him at high speed.

David was going to run him over.

With the front bumper less than a yard from his face he hurled himself sideways. He felt a blast of wind. A fender struck his outflung foot as the jeep roared past, its heavy-gauge tyres tearing up the spongy turf and spitting mud. He rolled over twice in the wet grass, then got to one knee. His foot hurt. He watched the jeep turn in a tight circle and come for him again.

He could see David's face through the windscreen. The young man was leaning forward, hunched over the steering wheel, his lips drawn back over his teeth in a savage, almost maniacal grin. He seemed to be imagining himself in the cockpit of a Spitfire, coming down out of the sun at an enemy plane with all eight Browning machine-guns blazing 1,260 rounds per minute.

Faber moved toward the cliff edge. The jeep gathered speed. Faber knew that, for a moment, he was incapable of running. He looked over the cliff: it was a rocky, almost vertical slope to the angry sea a hundred feet below. The jeep was coming straight down the cliff's edge toward him. Frantically, Faber looked up and down for a ledge, or even a foothold. There was none.

The jeep was four or five yards away, travelling at something like forty miles per hour. Its wheels were less than two feet from the cliff's edge. Faber dropped flat and swung his legs out into space, supporting his weight on his forearms as he hung on the brink.

The wheels passed him within inches. A few yards farther on, one tyre actually slipped over the edge. For a moment Faber thought the whole vehicle would slide over and fall into the sea below, but the other three wheels dragged the jeep to safety.

The ground under Faber's arms shifted. The vibration of the jeep's passing had loosened the earth. He felt himself slip a fraction. One hundred feet below, a raging sea boiled among the rocks. Faber stretched one arm to its farthest extent and dug his fingers deep into the soft ground. He felt a nail tear, and ignored it. He repeated the process with his other arm. With two hands anchored in the earth he pulled himself upward. It was agonizingly slow, but eventually his head drew level with his hands, his hips reached firm ground, and he was able to swivel around and roll away from the edge.

The jeep was turning again. Faber ran toward it. His foot was painful, but not broken. David accelerated for another pass. Faber turned and ran at right angles to the jeep's direction, forcing David to turn the wheel and consequently slow down.

Faber could not keep this up much longer. He was certain to tire before David. This had to be the last pass.

He ran faster. David steered an interception course, headed for a point in front of Faber. Faber doubled back, and the jeep zigzagged. It was now quite close. Faber broke into a sprint, his course compelling David to drive in a tight circle. The jeep was getting slower and Faber was getting closer. There were only a few yards between them when David realized what Faber was up to. He steered away, but it was too late. Faber raced to the jeep's side and threw himself upwards, landing face down on top of the canvas roof.

He lay there for a few seconds, catching his breath. His injured foot felt as if it was being held in a fire, and his lungs ached painfully.

The jeep was still moving. Faber drew the stiletto from its sheath under his sleeve and cut a long, jagged tear in the canvas roof. The material flapped downwards and Faber found himself staring at the back of David's head.

David looked up and back. A look of utter astonishment crossed his face. Faber drew back his arm for a knife thrust.

David jammed the throttle open and heaved the wheel around. The jeep leaped forward and lifted on two wheels as it screeched around in a tight curve. Faber struggled to stay on. The jeep, gathering speed still, crashed down on to four wheels then lifted again. It teetered precariously for a few yards, then the wheels slipped on the sodden ground and the vehicle toppled on to its side with a grinding crash.

Faber was thrown several yards and landed awkwardly. The breath was knocked out of him by the impact. It was several seconds before he could move.

The jeep's crazy course had taken it perilously close to the cliff once more.

Faber saw his knife in the grass a few yards away. He picked it up, then turned to the jeep.

Somehow, David had got himself and his wheelchair out through the ripped roof, and he was now sitting in the chair and pushing himself away along the cliff edge. Faber had to acknowledge his courage.

All the same, he had to die.

Faber ran after him. David must have heard the footsteps, for just before Faber caught up the chair stopped dead and spun around; and Faber glimpsed a heavy spanner in David's hand.

Faber crashed into the wheelchair, overturning it. His last thought was that both men and the chair might end up in the sea below – then the spanner hit the back of his head and he blacked out.

When he came to, the wheelchair lay beside him, but David was nowhere to be seen. He stood up and looked around in dazed puzzlement.

'Here! '

The voice came from over the cliff. David must have been flung from the chair and slid over the edge. Faber crawled to the cliff and looked over.

David had one hand around the stem of a bush which grew just under the lip of the cliff. The other hand was jammed into a small crevice in the rock. He hung suspended, just as Faber had a few minutes earlier. His bravado had gone, and there was naked terror in his eyes.

'Pull me up, for God's sake,' he shouted hoarsely.

Faber leaned closer. 'How did you know about the pictures?' he said.

'Help me, please!'

'Tell me about the pictures.'

'Oh, God.' David made a mighty effort to concentrate. 'When you went to Tom's outhouse you left your jacket drying in the kitchen. Tom went upstairs for more whisky, and I went through your pockets. I found the negatives.'

'And that was evidence enough for you to try to kill me?' Faber said wonderingly.

'That, and what you did with my wife in my house. No Englishman would behave like that.'

Faber could not help laughing. 'Where are the negatives now?'

'In my pocket.'

'Give them to me, and I'll pull you up.'

'You'll have to take them – I can't let go.'

Faber lay flat on his stomach and reached down, under David's oilskin, to the breast pocket of his jacket. He gave a sigh of satisfaction as his fingers touched the film can and withdrew it. He looked at the films: they all seemed to be there. He put the can in the pocket of his jacket, buttoned the flap, and reached down to David again.

He took hold of the bush David was clinging to and uprooted it with a savage jerk.

David screamed: 'No!' He scrabbled desperately for grip as his other hand slipped inexorably out of the crack in the rock.

'It's not fair!' he screamed. Then his hand came away from the crevice.

He seemed to hang in mid-air: then he dropped, faster and faster, bouncing twice against the cliff on his way down, until he hit the water with a huge splash.

Faber watched for a while to make sure he did not come up again. 'Not fair?' he murmured to himself. 'Not fair? Don't you know there's a war on?'

He looked down at the sea for some minutes. Once he thought he saw a flash of yellow oilskin on the surface, but it was gone before he could focus on it. There was just the sea and the rocks.

Suddenly he felt terribly tired. His injuries penetrated his consciousness one by one: the damaged foot, the bump on his head, the bruises all over his face. David Rose had been a fool, a braggart and a poor husband, and he had died screaming for mercy; but he had been a brave man too, and he had died for his country – he had got his wish.

Faber wondered whether his own death would be as good.

At last he turned away from the cliff edge and walked back toward the overturned jeep.

TWENTY-EIGHT

Percival Godliman felt refreshed, determined, even inspired.

When he reflected on it, this made him uncomfortable. Pep-talks are for the rank-and-file, and intellectuals believe themselves immune from inspirational speeches. Yet, although he knew that the great man's performance had been carefully scripted, the crescendos and diminuendos of the speech predetermined like a symphony, nevertheless it had worked on him, as effectively as if he had been the captain of the school cricket team hearing last-minute exhortations from the games master.

He got back to his office itching to do *something*.

He dropped his brolly in the umbrella-stand, hung up his wet raincoat, and looked at himself in the mirror on the inside of the cupboard door. Without doubt something had happened to his face since he became one of England's spycatchers. The other day he had come across a photograph of himself taken in 1937, with a group of students at a seminar in Oxford. In those days he actually looked older than he did now: pale skin, wispy hair, the patchy shave and ill-fitting clothes of a retired man. The wispy hair had gone: he was now bald except for a monkish fringe. His clothes were those of a business executive, not a teacher. It seemed to him – he might, he supposed, have been imagining it – that the set of his jaw was firmer, his eyes were brighter, and he took more care shaving.

He sat down behind his desk and lit a cigarette. *That* innovation was not welcome: he had developed a cough, tried to give it up, and discovered that he had become addicted. But almost everybody smoked in wartime Britain, even some of the women. Well, they were doing men's jobs – they were entitled to masculine vices. The smoke caught in Godliman's throat, making him cough. He put the cigarette out in the tin-lid he used for an ashtray (crockery was scarce).

The trouble with being inspired to perform the impossible, he reflected, was that the inspiration gave you no clues to the practical means. He recalled his college thesis, about the travels of an obscure medieval monk called Thomas of the Tree. Godliman had set himself the minor but difficult task of plotting the monk's itinerary over a five-year period. There had been a baffling gap of eight months when he had been either in Paris or Canterbury, but Godliman had been unable to determine which, and this had threatened the value of the whole project. The records he was using simply did not contain the information. If the monk's stay had gone unrecorded, then there was no way to find out where he had been, and that was that. With the optimism of youth, young Godliman had refused to believe that the information was just not there, and he had worked on the assumption that *somewhere* there had to be a record of how Thomas had spent those months – despite the well-known fact that almost everything that happened in the Middle Ages went unrecorded. If Thomas was not in Paris or Canterbury he must have been in transit between the two, Godliman had argued; and then he had found shipping records in an Amsterdam museum which showed that Thomas had boarded a vessel bound for Dover which got blown off course and was eventually wrecked on the Irish coast. This model piece of historical research had got Godliman his professorship.

He might try applying that kind of thinking to the problem of what had happened to Faber.

It was most likely that Faber had drowned. If he had not, then he was probably in Germany by now. Neither of those possibilities presented any course of action that Godliman could follow, so they should be discounted. He must assume that Faber was alive and had reached land somewhere.

He left his office and went down one flight of stairs to the map room. His uncle, Colonel Terry, was there, standing in front of the map of Europe with a cigarette between his lips, thinking. Godliman realized that this was a familiar sight in the War Office these days: senior men gazing entranced at maps, silently making their own computations of whether the war would be won or lost. He guessed it was because all the plans had been made, the vast machine had been set in motion, and for those who made the big decisions there was nothing to do but wait and see if they had been right.

Terry saw him come in, and said: 'How did you get on with the great man?'

'He was drinking whisky,' Godliman said.

'He drinks all day, but it never seems to make any difference to him,' Terry said. 'What did he say?'

'He wants Die Nadel's head on a platter.' Godliman crossed the room to the wall map of Great Britain and put a finger on Aberdeen. 'If you were sending a U-boat in to pick up a fugitive spy, what would you think was the nearest the sub could safely come to the coast?'

Terry stood beside him and looked at the map. 'I wouldn't want to come closer than the three-mile limit. But for preference, I'd stop ten miles out.'

'Right.' Godliman drew two pencil lines parallel to the coast, three miles and ten miles out respectively. 'Now, if you were an amateur sailor setting out from Aberdeen in a smallish fishing boat, how far would you go before you began to get nervous?'

'You mean, what's a reasonable distance to travel in such a boat?'

'Indeed.'

Terry shrugged. 'Ask the Navy. I'd say fifteen or twenty miles.'

'I agree.' Godliman drew an arc of twenty miles radius with its centre on Aberdeen. 'Now: if Faber is alive, he's either back on the mainland or somewhere within this space.' He indicated the area bounded by the parallel lines and the arc.

'There's no land in that area.'

'Have we got a bigger map?'

Terry pulled open a drawer and got out a large-scale

map of Scotland. He spread it on top of the chest. Godliman copied the pencil marks from the smaller map on to the larger.

There was still no land within the area.

'But look,' Godliman said. Just to the east of the ten-mile limit was a long, narrow island.

Terry peered closer. 'Storm Island,' he read. 'How apt.'

Godliman snapped his fingers. 'I'll bet that's where he is.'

'Can you send someone there?'

'When the storm clears. Bloggs is up there: I'll get a plane laid on for him. He can take off the minute the weather improves.' He went to the door.

'Good luck!' Terry called after him.

Godliman ran up the stairs to the next floor and entered his office. He picked up the phone. 'Get Mr Bloggs in Aberdeen, please.'

While he waited he doodled on his blotter, drawing the island. It was shaped like the top half of a walking-stick, with the crook at the western end. It must have been about ten miles long, and perhaps a mile wide. He wondered what sort of place it was: was it a barren lump of rock, or a thriving community of crofters? If Faber was there he might still be able to contact his U-boat: Bloggs would have to get to the island before the submarine. It would be difficult.

'I have Mr Bloggs,' the switchboard girl said.

'Fred?'

'Hello, Percy.'

'I think he's on an island called Storm Island.'

'No, he's not,' Bloggs said. 'We've just arrested him.'

The stiletto was nine inches long, with an engraved handle and a stubby little crosspiece. Its needle-like point was extremely sharp. Bloggs thought it looked like a highly efficient killing instrument. It had recently been polished.

Bloggs and Detective-Chief-Inspector Kincaid stood looking at it, neither man wanting to touch it.

'He was trying to catch a bus to Edinburgh,' Kincaid said. 'A PC spotted him at the ticket office and asked for his identification. He dropped his suitcase and ran away. A woman bus-conductor hit him over the head with her ticket machine. He took ten minutes to come around.'

'Let's have a look at him,' Bloggs said.

They went down the corridor to the cells. 'This one,' Kincaid said.

Bloggs looked through the judas. The man sat on a stool in the far corner of the cell with his back against the wall. His legs were crossed, his eyes closed, his hands in his pockets. 'He's been in cells before,' Bloggs remarked. The man was tall, with a long, handsome face and dark hair. It could have been the man in the photograph, but it was hard to be certain.

'Want to go in?' Kincaid asked.

'In a minute. What was in his suitcase, apart from the stiletto?'

'The tools of a burglar's trade. Quite a lot of money

in small notes. A pistol and some ammunition. Black clothes and crepe-soled shoes. Two hundred Lucky Strike cigarettes.'

'No photographs?'

Kincaid shook his head.

'Balls,' Bloggs said feelingly.

'Papers identify him as Peter Fredericks, of Wembley, Middlesex. Says he's an unemployed toolmaker looking for work.'

'Toolmaker?' Bloggs said sceptically. 'There hasn't been an unemployed toolmaker in Britain in the last four years. You'd think a spy would know that. Still . . .'

Kincaid asked: 'Shall I start the questioning, or will you?'

'You.'

Kincaid opened the door and Bloggs followed him in. The man in the corner opened his eyes incuriously. He did not alter his position.

Kincaid sat at a small, plain table. Bloggs leaned against the wall.

Kincaid said: 'What's your real name?'

'Peter Fredericks.'

'What are you doing so far from home?'

'Looking for work.'

'Why aren't you in the Army?'

'Weak heart.'

'Where have you been for the last few days?'

'Here, in Aberdeen. Before that Dundee, before that Perth.'

'When did you arrive in Aberdeen?'

'The day before yesterday.'

Kincaid glanced at Bloggs, who nodded. Kincaid said: 'Your story is silly. Toolmakers don't need to look for work. The country hasn't got enough of them. You'd better tell the truth.'

'I'm telling the truth.'

Bloggs took all the loose change out of his pocket and tied it up in his handkerchief. He stood watching, saying nothing, swinging the little bundle in his right hand.

'Where are the photographs?' Kincaid said.

The man's expression did not change. 'I don't know what you're talking about.'

Kincaid shrugged, and looked at Bloggs.

Bloggs said: 'On your feet.'

'Pardon?' the man said.

'On your FEET!' Bloggs bawled.

The man stood up casually.

'Forward!'

He took two steps up to the table.

'Name?'

'Peter Fredericks.'

Bloggs came off the wall and hit the man with the weighted handkerchief. The blow caught him accurately on the bridge of the nose, and he cried out. His hands went to his face.

'Stand to attention!' Bloggs shouted. 'Name!'

The man stood upright, let his hands fall to his sides, and whispered: 'Peter Fredericks.'

Bloggs hit him again in exactly the same place. This time he went down on one knee, and his eyes watered.

'Where are the photographs?' Bloggs screamed.

The man shook his head dumbly.

Bloggs pulled him to his feet, kneed him in the groin, and punched his stomach. 'What did you do with the negatives?'

The man fell to the floor and threw up. Bloggs kicked his face. There was a sharp crack, as if something had broken. 'What about the U-boat? Where is the rendezvous? What is the signal?'

Kincaid grabbed Bloggs from behind. 'That's enough, Bloggs,' he said. 'This is my station, and I can only turn a blind eye for so long, you know.'

Bloggs rounded on him. 'We're not dealing with a case of petty housebreaking, Kincaid – this man is jeopardizing the whole war effort.' He wagged a finger under the detective's nose. 'Just remember: I'm MI5, and I'll do what I fucking well like in your station. If the prisoner dies, I'll take responsibility.' He turned back to the man on the floor.

The man was staring at Bloggs and Kincaid. His face, covered with blood, showed an expression of incredulity. 'What are you talking about?' he said weakly. 'What is this?'

Bloggs hauled him to his feet again. 'You are Henrik Rudolph Hans von Muller-Guder, born at Oln on 26 May 1900; also known as Henry Faber; a lieutenant-colonel in German Intelligence. Within three months you will be hanged for espionage, unless you turn out to be more useful to us dead than alive. You'd better start making yourself useful, Colonel Muller-Guder.'

'No,' the man said. 'No, no! I'm a thief, not a spy. Please!' He cowered away from Bloggs's upraised fist. 'I can prove it.'

Bloggs hit him again, and Kincaid intervened for the second time. 'Wait,' the detective said. 'All right, Fredericks – if that's your name – prove you're a thief.'

'I done three houses in Jubilee Crescent last week,' the man gasped. 'I took about five hundred quid from one and some jewellery from the next one – diamond rings and some pearls – and I never got nothing from the other one because of the dog . . . you must know I'm telling the truth, they must have reported it, didn't they? Oh, Jesus—'

Kincaid looked at Bloggs. 'All those burglaries took place.'

'He could have read about them in the newspapers.'

'The third one wasn't reported.'

'Perhaps he did them – he could still be a spy. Spies can steal.'

'But this was last week – your man was in London, wasn't he?'

Bloggs was silent for a moment. Then he said: 'Well, fuck it,' and walked out.

Peter Fredericks looked up at Kincaid through a mask of blood. 'Who's he, the bleedin' Gestapo?' he said.

Kincaid stared at him thoughtfully. 'Be glad you're not really the man he's looking for.'

*

'Well?' Godliman said into the phone.

'False alarm.' Bloggs's voice was scratchy and distorted over the long-distance line. 'A small-time house-breaker who happens to carry a stiletto and look like Faber.'

'Back to square one,' Godliman said. 'Damn.'

'You said something about an island.'

'Yes. Storm Island – it's about ten miles off the coast, due east of Aberdeen. You'll find it on a large-scale map.'

'What makes you sure he's there?'

'I'm not sure; not at all. We still have to cover every other possibility – other towns, the coast, everything. But if he did steal that boat, the . . . ?'

'*Marie II.*'

'Yes. If he did steal it, his rendezvous was probably in the area of this island; and if I'm right about *that*, then he's either drowned or shipwrecked on the island.'

'Okay, that makes sense.'

'What's the weather like up there?'

'No change.'

'Could you reach the island in a big ship?'

Bloggs grunted. 'I suppose you can ride any storm if your ship's big enough. But this island won't have much of a dock, will it?'

'You'd better find out. However, I expect you're right. Now listen: there's an RAF fighter base near Edinburgh. By the time you get there, I'll have an amphibious plane standing by. You take off the minute the storm begins to clear. Have the local coastguard ready to move at a moment's notice, too – I'm not sure who'll get there first.'

'Mm.' Bloggs sounded dubious. 'If the U-boat is also waiting for the storm to clear, it will get there first.'

'You're right.' Godliman lit a cigarette, fumbling for inspiration. 'Well, we can get a Navy corvette to circle the island and listen for Faber's radio signal. When the storm clears it can land a boat on the island. Yes, that's a good idea.'

'What about some fighters?'

'Yes. Although like you, they'll have to wait until the weather breaks.'

'It can't go on much longer.'

'What do the Scottish meteorologists say?'

'Another day of it, at least.'

'Damn.'

'It doesn't make much difference,' Bloggs said. 'All the time we're grounded he's bottled up.'

'If he's there at all.'

'Yes.'

'All right,' Godliman said. 'We'll have a corvette, the coastguard, some fighters and an amphibian.'

'And me.'

'You'd better get on your way. Call me from Rosyth. Take care.'

'Cheerio.'

Godliman hung up. His cigarette, neglected in the ashtray, had burned down to a tiny stub. He lit another, then picked up the phone again and began organizing.

TWENTY-NINE

Lying on its side, the jeep looked powerful but helpless, like a wounded elephant. The engine had stalled. Faber gave it a hefty push and it toppled majestically on to all four wheels. It had survived the fight relatively undamaged. The canvas roof was destroyed, of course: the rip Faber's knife had made had become a long tear running from one side to the other. The offside front wing, which had ploughed into the earth and stopped the vehicle, was crumpled. The headlight on that side had smashed. The window on the same side had been broken by the shot from the gun. The windscreen was miraculously intact.

Faber climbed into the driving seat, put the gearshift into neutral, and tried the starter. It kicked over and died. He tried again, and the engine fired. He sighed with relief: he could not have faced a long walk just then.

He sat in the car for a while, inventorying his wounds. He touched his right ankle gingerly: it was swelling massively. Perhaps he had cracked a bone. It was as well that the jeep was designed to be driven by a man with no legs, for Faber could not have pressed a brake pedal. The lump on the back of his head felt huge, the size of a golf ball; and when he touched it his hand came away sticky with blood. He examined his face in the driving mirror. It was a mass of small cuts and big bruises, like the face of the loser at the end of a boxing match.

He had abandoned his oilskin back at the cottage, so his jacket and overalls were soggy with rain and smeared with mud. He needed to get warm and dry very soon.

He gripped the steering wheel, and a burning pain shot through his hand: he had forgotten the torn fingernail. He looked at it. It was the nastiest of his injuries. He would have to drive one-handed.

He pulled away slowly and found what he guessed was the road. There was no danger of getting lost on this island – all he had to do was follow the cliff-edge until he came to Lucy's cottage.

He needed to invent a lie to explain to Lucy what had become of her husband. He might, of course, tell her the truth: there was nothing she could do about it. However, if she became awkward he might have to kill her; and there had grown within him an aversion to killing Lucy. Driving slowly along the cliff-top through the pouring rain and howling wind, he marvelled at this new thing inside him, this scruple. It was the first time he had ever felt reluctance to kill. It was not that he was amoral: quite the contrary. He had made up his mind that the killing he did was on the same moral level as death on the battlefield, and his emotions followed his intellect. He always had the physical reaction, the vomiting, after he killed, but that was something incomprehensible which he ignored.

So why did he not want to kill Lucy?

The feeling was on a par with the affection which drove him to send the Luftwaffe erroneous directions to St Paul's Cathedral: a compulsion to protect a thing of beauty. She was a remarkable creation, as full of loveliness and subtlety as a work of art. Faber could live with himself as a killer, but not as an iconoclast. It was, he recognized as soon as the thought occurred to him, a peculiar way to be. But then, spies were peculiar people.

He thought of some of the spies who had been recruited by the Abwehr at the same time as he: Otto, the Nordic giant who made delicate paper sculptures in the Japanese fashion and hated women; Friedrich, the sly little mathematical genius who jumped at shadows and went into a five-day depression if he lost a game of chess; Helmut, who liked to read books about slavery in America and had soon joined the SS . . . all different, all peculiar. If they had anything more specific in common, he did not know what it was.

He seemed to be driving more and more slowly, and the rain and mist became more impenetrable. He began to worry about the cliff-edge on his left-hand side. He felt very hot, but suffered spasms of shivering. He realized he had been speaking aloud about Otto and Friedrich and Helmut; and he recognized the signs of delirium. He made an effort to think of nothing but the problem of keeping the jeep on a straight course.

The noise of the wind took on some kind of rhythm, becoming hypnotic. Once he found himself stationary, staring out over the sea, and had no idea how long he had stopped.

It seemed hours later that Lucy's cottage came into view. He steered toward it, thinking: I must remember to put the brake on before I hit the wall. There was a figure standing in the doorway, looking at him through the rain. He had to stay in control of himself long enough to tell her the lie. He had to remember, had to remember . . .

It was late afternoon by the time the jeep came back. Lucy was worried about what had happened to the men, and at the same time angry with them for not coming home for the lunch she had prepared. As the day waned she had spent more and more time at the windows, looking out for them.

When the jeep came down the slight slope to the cottage, it was clear something was wrong. It was moving terribly slowly, weaving all over the track, and there was only one person in it. It came closer, and she saw that the front was dented and the headlamp smashed.

'Oh, God,' she murmured.

The vehicle shuddered to a halt in front of the cottage, and she saw that the figure inside was Henry. He made no move to get out. Lucy ran out into the rain and opened the driver's door.

Henry sat there with his head back and his eyes half-closed. His hand was on the brake. His face was bloody and bruised.

Lucy said: 'What happened? *What happened?*'

Henry's hand slipped off the brake, and the jeep moved forward. Lucy leaned across him and slipped the gearshift into neutral.

Henry said: 'Left David at Tom's cottage . . . had crash on way back . . .' The words seemed to cost him a great effort.

Now that she knew what had happened, Lucy's panic subsided. 'Come inside,' she said sharply. The urgency in her voice got through to Henry. He turned toward her, put his foot on the running board to step down, and promptly fell to the ground. Lucy saw that his ankle was swollen like a balloon.

She got her hands under his shoulders and pulled him upright, saying: 'Put your weight on the other foot and lean on me.' She got his right arm around her neck and half-carried him inside.

Jo watched wide-eyed as she helped Henry into the living-room and got him on to the sofa. He lay back with his eyes shut. His clothes were soaked and muddy.

Lucy said: 'Jo, go upstairs and get your pyjamas on, please.'

'But I haven't had my story. Is *he* dead?'

'He's not dead, but he's had a car crash, and you can't have a story tonight. Go on.'

The child made a complaining sound, and Lucy looked threateningly at him. He went.

Lucy got the big scissors out of her sewing basket

and cut Henry's clothes away: first the jacket, then the overalls, then the shirt. She frowned in puzzlement when she saw the knife in its sheath strapped to his left forearm: she guessed it was a special implement for cleaning fish, or something. When she tried to take it off, Henry pushed her hand away. She shrugged, and turned her attention to his boots. The left one came off easily, and its sock; but he cried out in pain when she touched the right.

'It must come off,' she told him. 'You'll have to be brave.'

A funny kind of smile came over his face, then, and he nodded assent. She cut the laces, took the shoe gently but firmly in both hands, and pulled it off. This time he made no sound. She cut the elastic in the sock and pulled that off too.

Jo came in and said: 'He's in his pants!'

'His clothes are all wet.' She kissed the boy goodnight. 'Put yourself to bed, darling. I'll tuck you up later.'

'Kiss teddy, then.'

'Goodnight, teddy.'

Jo went out. Lucy looked back to Henry. His eyes were open, and he was smiling. He said: 'Kiss Henry, then.'

She leaned over him and kissed his battered face. Then, carefully, she cut away his underpants.

The heat from the fire would quickly dry his naked skin. She went into the kitchen and filled a bowl with warm water and a little antiseptic to bathe his wounds.

She found a roll of cotton wool and returned to the living-room.

'This is the second time you've turned up on the doorstep half dead,' she said as she set about her task.

'The usual signal,' Henry said.

'What?'

'Waiting at Calais for a phantom army.'

'Henry, what are you talking about?'

'Every Friday and Monday.'

She realized he was delirious. 'Don't try to talk,' she said. She lifted his head slightly to clean away the dried blood from around the bump.

Suddenly he sat upright, looked fiercely at her, and said: 'What day is it? What day is it?'

'It's Sunday, relax.'

'Okay.'

He was quiet after that, and he let her remove the knife. She bathed his face, bandaged his finger where he had lost the nail, and put a dressing on his ankle. When she had finished she stood looking at him for a while. He seemed to be sleeping. She touched the long scar on his chest, and the star-shaped mark on his hip. The star was a birthmark, she decided.

She went through his pockets before throwing the lacerated clothes away. There wasn't much: some money, his papers, a leather wallet and a film can. She put them all in a little pile on the mantelpiece beside his fish knife. He would have to have some of David's clothes.

She left him and went upstairs to see Jo. The boy was

asleep, lying on his teddy bear, with his arms outflung. She kissed his soft cheek and tucked him in. She went outside and put the jeep in the barn.

She made herself a drink in the kitchen then sat watching Henry, wishing he would wake up and make love to her again.

It was almost midnight when he awoke. He opened his eyes, and his face showed the series of expressions which were now familiar to her: first the fear, then the wary survey of the room, then the relaxation. On impulse, she asked him: 'What are you afraid of, Henry?'

'I don't know what you mean.'

'You always look frightened when you wake up.'

'I don't know.' He shrugged, and the movement seemed to hurt. 'God, I'm battered.'

'Do you want to tell me what happened?'

'Yes, if you'll give me a small amount of brandy.'

She got the brandy out of the cupboard. 'You can have some of David's clothes.'

'In a minute . . . unless you're embarrassed.'

She handed him the glass, smiling. 'I'm afraid I'm enjoying it.'

'What happened to my clothes?'

'I had to cut them off you. I've thrown them away.'

'Not my papers, I hope.' He smiled, but there was some other emotion just below the surface.

'On the mantelpiece.' She pointed. 'I suppose that knife is for cleaning fish, or something.'

His right hand went to his left forearm, where the sheath had been. 'Something like that,' he said. He seemed uneasy for a moment, then relaxed with an effort and sipped his drink. 'That's good.'

After a moment she said: 'Well?'

'What?'

'How did you manage to lose my husband and crash my jeep?'

'David decided to stay over at Tom's for the night. Some of the sheep got into trouble in a place they called the Gully—'

'I know it.'

'—and six or seven of them were injured. They're all in Tom's kitchen, being bandaged up and making a frightful row. Anyway, David suggested I came back to tell you he would be staying. I don't really know how I managed to crash. The car is unfamiliar, there's no real road, I hit something and went into a skid, and the jeep ended up on its side. The details . . .' he shrugged.

'You must have been going quite fast – you were in an awful mess when you got here.'

'I suppose I rattled around inside the jeep a bit. Banged my head, twisted my ankle . . .'

'Lost a fingernail, bashed your face, and almost caught pneumonia. You must be accident-prone.'

He swung his legs to the floor, stood up, and went to the mantelpiece.

Lucy said: 'Your powers of recuperation are incredible.'

He was strapping the knife to his arm. 'We fishermen are very healthy. What about those clothes?'

She got up and stood close to him. 'What do you need clothes for? It's bedtime.'

He drew her to him, pressing her against his naked body, and kissed her hard. She stroked his thighs.

After a while he broke away from her. He picked up his things from the mantelpiece, took her hand, then, hobbling, he led her upstairs to bed.

THIRTY

The wide, white autobahn snaked through the Bavarian valley up into the mountains. In the leather rear seat of the staff Mercedes, Field Marshal Gerd von Rundstedt was still and weary. Aged sixtynine, he knew he was too fond of champagne and not fond enough of Hitler. His thin, lugubrious face reflected a career longer and more erratic than that of any of Hitler's other officers: he had been dismissed in disgrace more times than he could remember, but the Führer always asked him to come back.

As the car passed through the sixteenth-century village of Berchtesgaden, he wondered why he always returned to his command when Hitler forgave him. Money meant nothing to him: he had already achieved the highest possible rank; decorations were valueless in the Third Reich; and he believed that it was not possible to win honour in this war.

It was Rundstedt who had first called Hitler 'the Bohemian corporal'. The little man knew nothing of the German military tradition, nor – despite his flashes of inspiration – of military strategy. If he had, he would not have started this war, for it was unwinnable. Rundstedt was Germany's finest soldier, and he had proved it in Poland, France and Russia; but he had no hope of victory.

All the same, he would have nothing to do with the small group of generals who – he knew – were plotting to overthrow Hitler. He turned a blind eye to them, but the *Fahneneid*, the blood oath of the German warrior, was too strong within him to permit him to join the conspiracy. And that, he supposed, was why he continued to serve the Reich. Right or wrong, his country was in danger, and he had no option but to protect it. I'm like an old cavalry horse, he thought: if I stayed at home I should feel ashamed.

He commanded five armies on the Western front, now. A million and a half men were under him. They were not as strong as they might be – some divisions were little better than rest homes for invalids from the Russian front, there was a shortage of armour, and there were many non-German conscripts among the other ranks – but Rundstedt could still keep the Allies out of France if he deployed his forces shrewdly.

It was that deployment that he must now discuss with Hitler.

The car climbed the Kehlsteinstrasse until the road ended at a vast bronze door in the side of the Kehlstein Mountain. An SS guard touched a button, the door hummed open, and the car entered a long marble tunnel lit by bronze lanterns. At the far end of the tunnel the driver stopped the car, and Rundstedt walked to the elevator and sat in one of its leather seats for the four-hundred-foot ascent to the Adlerhorst, the Eagle's Nest.

In the anteroom Rattenhuber took his pistol and left him to wait. He stared unappreciatively at Hitler's porcelain and went over in his mind the words he would say.

A few moments later the blond bodyguard returned to usher him into the conference room.

The place made him think of an eighteenth-century palace. The walls were covered with oil paintings and tapestries, and there was a bust of Wagner and a huge clock with a bronze eagle on its top. The view from the side window was truly remarkable: one could see the hills of Salzburg and the peak of the Untersberg, the mountain where the body of the Emperor Frederick Barbarossa waited, according to legend, to rise from the grave and save the Fatherland. Inside the room, seated in the peculiarly rustic chairs, were Hitler and just three of his staff: Admiral Theodor Krancke, the naval commander in the west; General Alfred Jodl, chief of staff; and Admiral Karl Jesko von Puttkamer, Hitler's aide-de-camp.

Rundstedt saluted and was motioned to a chair. A footman brought a plate of caviar sandwiches and a glass of champagne. Hitler stood at the large window, looking out, with his hands clasped behind his back. Without turning, he said abruptly: 'Rundstedt has changed his mind. He now agrees with Rommel that the Allies will invade Normandy. This is what my instinct has all along told me. Krancke, however, still favours Calais. Rundstedt, tell Krancke how you arrived at your conclusion.'

Rundstedt swallowed a mouthful and coughed into

his hand. Damn, Hitler had no manners: didn't even give a chap a chance to catch his breath. 'There are two things: one new piece of information and one new line of reasoning,' Rundstedt began. 'First, the information. The latest summaries of Allied bombing in France show without doubt that their principal aim is to destroy every bridge across the River Seine. Now, if they land at Calais the Seine is irrelevant to the battle; but if they land in Normandy all our reserves have to cross the Seine to reach the zone of conflict.

'Second, the reasoning. I have given some thought to how I would invade France if I were commanding the Allied forces. My conclusion is that the first goal must be to establish a bridgehead through which men and supplies can be funnelled at speed. The initial thrust must therefore come in the region of a large and roomy harbour. The natural choice is Cherbourg.

'Both the bombing pattern and the strategic requirements point to Normandy,' he finished. He picked up his glass and emptied it, and the footman came forward to refill it.

Jodl said: 'All our intelligence points to Calais—'

'And we have just executed the head of the Abwehr as a traitor,' Hitler interrupted. 'Krancke, are you convinced?'

'My Führer, I am not,' the Admiral said. 'I, too, have considered how I would conduct the invasion if I were on the other side – but I have brought into the reasoning a number of factors of a nautical nature of which Rundstedt may not have been aware. I believe they will attack under cover of darkness, by moonlight, at full tide to sail over Rommel's underwater obstacles, and away from cliffs, rocky waters and strong currents. Normandy? Never.'

Hitler shook his head in disgusted disagreement. Jodl said: 'There is another small piece of information which I find significant. The Guards Armoured Division has been transferred from the north of England to Hove, on the south-east coast, to join the First United States Army Group under General Patton. We learned this from wireless surveillance – there was a baggage mix-up en route, one unit had another's silver cutlery, and the fools have been quarrelling about it over the radio. This is a crack British division, very blue-blooded, commanded by General Sir Allan Henry Shafto Adair. I feel sure they will not be far from the centre of the battle when it comes.'

Hitler's hands moved nervously, and his face twitched in an agony of indecision. 'Generals!' he barked at them. 'Either I get conflicting advice, or no advice at all! I have to tell you everything – everything!'

With characteristic boldness, Rundstedt plunged on. 'My Führer, you have four superb panzer divisions doing nothing here in Germany. If I am right, they will never get to Normandy in time to repel the invasion. I beg you, order them to France and put them under Rommel's command. If we are wrong, and the invasion begins at Calais, they will still be close enough to enter the battle at an early stage.'

'I don't know – I don't know!' Hitler's eyes widened, and Rundstedt wondered if he had pushed too hard – again.

Puttkamer spoke for the first time. 'My Führer, today is Sunday.'

'Well?'

'Tomorrow night the U-boat may pick up the spy, Die Nadel.'

'Ah, yes! Someone I can trust.'

'Of course, he can report by radio at any time. However, there may be some reason for him to avoid the radio; in which case he would bring his information personally. Given this possibility, you may like to consider postponing your decision for twenty-four hours, in case he does contact us, one way or the other, today or tomorrow.'

Rundstedt said: 'There isn't time to postpone decisions. Both air attacks and sabotage activities have increased dramatically. The invasion may come any day.'

'I disagree,' Krancke said. 'The weather conditions will not be right until early June.'

'That is not very far away!'

'Enough!' Hitler shouted. 'I have made up my mind. My panzers stay in Germany – for now. On Tuesday, when we have heard from Die Nadel, I will reconsider the disposition of these forces. If his information favours Normandy – as I believe it will – I will move the panzers.'

Rundstedt said softly: 'And if he does not report?'

'If he does not report, I shall reconsider just the same.'

Rundstedt bowed assent. 'With your permission, I shall return to my command.'

'Very well.'

Rundstedt got to his feet, saluted and went out. In the copper-lined elevator, falling four hundred feet to the underground garage, he felt his stomach turn over, and wondered whether the sensation was caused by the speed of descent or by the thought that the destiny of his country lay in the hands of a single, lonely spy.

PART SIX

THIRTY-ONE

Lucy woke up slowly. She rose gradually, languidly, from the warm void of deep sleep, up through layers of unconsciousness, perceiving the world piece by isolated piece: first the warm, hard male body beside her; then the strangeness of the little bed; the noise of the storm outside, as angry and tireless as yesterday and the day before; the faint smell of the man's skin; her arm across his chest, her leg thrown across his as if to keep him there, her breasts pressed against his side; the light of day beating against her eyelids; the regular, light breathing that blew softly across her face; and then, all at once like the solution to a puzzle, the realization that she was flagrantly and adulterously lying with a man she had met only forty-eight hours before, and that they were naked in bed in her husband's house.

She opened her eyes and saw Jo.

He was standing beside the bed in his rumpled pyjamas, hair tousled, a battered rag doll under his arm, sucking his thumb and staring wide-eyed at his mummy and the strange man cuddling each other in his, Jo's, bed. Lucy could not read his expression, for at this time of day he stared wide-eyed at most things, as if all the world was new and marvellous every morning. She stared back at him in silence, not knowing what to say.

Then Henry's deep voice said: 'Good morning.'

Jo took his thumb out of his mouth, said: 'Good morning,' turned around and went out of the bedroom.

Lucy said: 'Damn, damn, damn.'

Henry slid down in the bed until his face was level with hers, and kissed her. His hand went between her thighs and held her possessively.

She pushed him away. 'For God's sake, stop.'

'Why?'

'Jo's seen us!'

'So what?'

'He can talk, you know. Sooner or later he'll say something to David. What am I going to do?'

'Do nothing. So David finds out. Does it matter?'

'Of course it matters.'

'I don't see why. He has wronged you, and this is the consequence. You shouldn't feel guilty.'

Lucy suddenly realized that Henry simply had no conception of the complex tangle of loyalties and obligations that constituted a marriage. She said: 'It's not *that* simple.'

She got out of bed and crossed the landing to her own bedroom. She slipped into knickers, trousers and a sweater, then remembered she had destroyed all Henry's clothes and had to lend him some of David's. She found underwear and socks, a knitted shirt and a V-necked pullover, and finally – right at the bottom of a trunk – one pair of trousers that were not cut off at the knee and sewn up. All the while Jo watched her in silence.

She took the clothes into the other bedroom. Henry had gone into the bathroom to shave. She called through the door: 'Your clothes are on the bed.'

She went downstairs, lit the stove in the kitchen, and put a saucepan of water on to heat. She decided to have boiled eggs for breakfast. She washed Jo's face at the kitchen sink, combed his hair, and dressed him quickly. 'You're very quiet this morning,' she said brightly. He made no reply.

Henry came down and sat at the table, as naturally as if he had been doing it every morning for years. Lucy felt very weird, seeing him there in David's clothes, handing him a breakfast egg, putting a rack of toast on the table in front of him.

Jo said suddenly: 'Is my daddy dead?'

Henry gave the boy a queer look and said nothing.

Lucy said: 'Don't be silly. He's at Tom's house.'

Jo ignored her and spoke to Henry. 'You've got my daddy's clothes, *and* you've got my mummy. Are you going to be my daddy now?'

Lucy muttered: 'Out of the mouth of babes and sucklings . . .'

Henry said: 'Didn't you see my clothes last night?'

Jo nodded.

'Well, then, you know why I had to borrow some of your daddy's clothes. I'll give them back to him when I get some more of my own.'

'Will you give my mummy back?'

'Of course.'

Lucy said: 'Eat your egg, Jo.'

The child tucked into his breakfast, apparently satisfied. Lucy was gazing out of the kitchen window. 'The boat won't come today,' she said.

'Are you glad?' Henry asked her.

She looked at him. 'I don't know.'

Lucy did not feel hungry. She drank a cup of tea while Jo and Henry ate. Afterwards, Jo went upstairs to play and Henry cleared the table. As he stacked crockery in the sink he said: 'Are you afraid David will hurt you, physically?'

She shook her head in negation.

'You should forget him,' Henry went on. 'You were planning to leave him anyway. Why should it concern you whether he finds out or not?'

'He's my *husband*,' she said. 'That counts for something. The kind of husband he's been . . . all that . . . doesn't give me the right to humiliate him.'

'I think it gives you the right not to care whether he's humiliated or not.'

'It's not a question that can be settled logically. It's just the way I *feel*.'

He made a giving-up gesture with his arms. 'I'd better drive over to Tom's and find out whether your *husband* wants to come back. Where are my boots?'

'In the living-room. I'll get you a jacket.' She went upstairs and got David's old hacking jacket out of the wardrobe. It was a fine grey-green tweed, very elegant with a nipped-in waist and slanted pocket flaps. Lucy had put leather patches on the elbows to preserve it: you couldn't buy clothes like this any more. She took it down to the living-room, where Henry was putting his boots on. He had laced the left one, and was gingerly inserting his injured right foot into the other. Lucy knelt to help him.

'The swelling has gone down,' she said.

'The damn thing still hurts.'

They got the boot on, but left it untied and took the lace out. Henry stood up experimentally.

'It's okay,' he said.

Lucy helped him into the jacket. It was a little tight across the shoulders. 'We haven't got another oilskin,' she said.

'Then I'll get wet.' He pulled her to him and kissed her roughly. She put her arms around him and held tightly for a moment.

'Drive more carefully today,' she said.

He smiled and nodded, kissed her again – briefly this time – and went out. She watched him limp across to the barn, and stood at the window while he started the jeep and drove away, up the slight rise and out of sight. When he had gone she felt relieved, but somehow empty.

She began to put the house straight, making beds and washing dishes, cleaning and tidying; but she could summon up no enthusiasm for the task. She was restless. She worried at the problem of what to do with her life, following old arguments around in familiar circles, unable to put her mind to anything else. She found the cottage claustrophobic instead of snug. There was a big world out there somewhere, a world of war and heroism, full of colour and passion and people, millions of people; she wanted to be out there in the midst of it, to meet new minds and see cities and hear music. She turned on the radio: a futile gesture, for the news broadcast made her feel more isolated, not less. There was a battle report from Italy, the rationing regulations had been eased a little, the London stiletto murderer was still at large, Roosevelt had made a speech. Sandy Macpherson began to play a theatre organ, and Lucy switched off. None of it touched her, for she did not live in that world.

She wanted to scream.

She had to get out of the house, despite the weather. It would be only a symbolic escape, for the stone walls of the cottage were not what imprisoned her; but the symbol was better than nothing. She collected Jo from upstairs, separating him with some difficulty from a regiment of toy soldiers, and wrapped him up in waterproof clothing.

'Why are we going out?' he asked.

'To see if the boat comes.'

'You said it won't come today.'

'Just in case.'

They put bright yellow sou'westers on their heads, lacing them under their chins, and stepped outside the door.

The wind was like a physical blow, unbalancing Lucy so that she staggered. In seconds her face was as wet as if she had dipped it in a bowl, and the ends of hair protruding from under her hat lay limp and clinging on her cheeks and the shoulders of her oilskin. Jo screamed with delight and jumped in a puddle.

They walked along the cliff-top to the head of the bay, and looked down at the huge North Sea rollers hurling themselves to destruction against the cliffs and on the beach. The storm had uprooted underwater vegetation from God-only-knew what depth and flung it in heaps on the sand and rocks. Mother and son became absorbed in the ceaselessly shifting patterns of the waves. They had done this before: the sea had a hypnotic effect on both of them, and Lucy was never quite sure, afterwards, how long they had spent silently watching.

The spell was broken this time by something she saw. At first there was only a flash of colour in the trough of a wave, so fleeting that she was not certain what colour it had been, so small and far away that she immediately doubted whether she had seen it at all. She looked for it, but did not see it again, and her gaze drifted back to the bay and the little jetty, on which flotsam gathered in drifts only to be swept away by the next big wave. After the storm, on the first fine day, she and Jo would go beachcombing to see what treasures the sea had disgorged, and come back with oddly coloured rocks, bits of wood of mystifying origin, huge seashells and twisted fragments of rusted metal.

She saw the flash of colour again, much nearer, and this time it stayed within sight for a few seconds. It was bright yellow, the colour of all their oilskins. She peered at it through the sheets of rain, but could not identify its shape before it disappeared again. But the current was bringing it closer, as it brought everything to the bay, depositing its rubbish on the sand like a man emptying his trouser pockets on to a table.

It *was* an oilskin: she could see that when the sea lifted it on the crest of a wave and showed it to her for the third and final time. Henry had come back without his, yesterday, but how had it got into the sea? The wave broke over the jetty and flung the object on the wet wooden boards of the ramp, and Lucy realized it was not Henry's oilskin, for the owner was still inside it. Her gasp of horror was whipped away by the wind so that not even she could hear it. Who was he? Where had he come from? Another shipwreck?

It occurred to her that he might still be alive. She must go and see. She bent and shouted in Jo's ear: 'Stay here – keep still – don't move.' Then she ran down the ramp.

Half way down she heard footsteps behind her: Jo was following. The ramp was narrow and slippery, quite dangerous. She stopped, turned, and scooped the child up in her arms, saying: 'You naughty boy, I told you to wait!' She looked from the body below to the safety of the clifftop, dithered for a moment in painful indecision, discerned that the sea would wash the body away at any moment, and proceeded downward, carrying Jo.

A smaller wave covered the body, and when the water receded Lucy was close enough to see that it was a man, and that it had been in the sea long enough for the water to swell and distort the features. That meant he was dead. She could therefore do nothing for him, and she was not going to risk her life and her son's to preserve a corpse. She was about to turn back when something about the bloated face struck her as familiar. She stared at it, uncomprehending, trying to fit the features to something in her memory; and then, quite abruptly, she saw the face for what it was, and sheer, paralysing terror gripped her, and it seemed that her heart stopped, and she whispered: 'No, David, no!'

Oblivious now to the danger she walked forward. Another lesser wave broke around her knees, filling her wellington boots with foamy salt water, but she did not notice. Jo twisted in her arms to face forward, but she screamed 'Don't look!' in his ear and pushed his face into her shoulder. He began to cry.

She knelt beside the body and touched the horrible face with her hand. It was David. There was no doubt. He was dead, and had been for some time. Moved by some deep instinct to make absolutely certain, she lifted the skirt of the oilskin and looked at the stumps of his legs.

It was impossible to take in the fact of the death. She had, in a way, been wishing him dead; but her feelings about him were confused by guilt and the fear of being found out in infidelity. Grief, horror, liberation, relief: they fluttered in her mind like birds, none of them willing to settle.

She would have stayed there, motionless, but the next wave was a big one. Its force knocked her flying, and she took a great gulp of sea water. Somehow she managed to keep Jo in her grasp and stay on the ramp;

and when the surf settled she got to her feet and ran up out of the greedy reach of the ocean.

She walked all the way to the cliff-top without looking back. When she came within sight of the cottage, she saw the jeep standing outside. Henry was back.

Still carrying Jo, she broke into a stumbling run, desperate to share her hurt with Henry, to feel his arms around her and have him comfort her. Her breath came in ragged sobs, and tears mixed invisibly with the rain on her face. She went to the back of the cottage, burst into the kitchen, and dumped Jo urgently on the floor.

Henry said: 'David decided to stay over at Tom's another day.'

She stared at him, her mind an incredulous blank; and then, in a flash of intuition, she understood everything.

Henry had killed David.

The conclusion came first, like a punch in the stomach, winding her; the reasons followed a split-second later. The shipwreck, the odd-shaped knife he was so attached to, the crashed jeep, the news bulletin about the London stiletto murderer: suddenly everything fitted together, a box of jigsaw pieces thrown in the air and landing, improbably, fully assembled.

'Don't look so surprised,' Henry said with a smile. 'They've got a lot of work to do over there, and I didn't encourage him to come back.'

Tom. She had to go to Tom. He would know what to do; he would protect her and Jo until the police came; he had a dog and a gun.

Her fear was interrupted by a shaft of sadness, of sorrow for the Henry she had believed in, had almost loved; for clearly he did not exist – she had imagined him. Instead of a warm, strong, affectionate man, she saw in front of her a monster who sat and smiled and calmly gave her invented messages from the husband he had murdered.

She suppressed a shudder. Taking Jo's hand, she walked out of the kitchen, along the hall, and out of the front door. She got into the jeep, sat Jo beside her, and started the engine.

But Henry was there, resting his foot casually on the running-board, and holding David's shotgun, saying: 'Where are you going?'

Her heart sank. If she drove away now he might shoot – what instinct had warned him to take the gun into the house this time? – and while she herself might chance it, she could not endanger Jo. She said: 'Just putting the jeep away.'

'You need Jo's help for that?'

'He likes the ride. Don't cross-examine me!'

Henry shrugged, and stepped back.

She looked at him for a moment, wearing David's hacking jacket and holding David's gun so casually, and wondered whether he really would shoot her if she simply drove away. Then she recalled the vein of ice she had sensed within him right from the start, and knew that that ultimate commitment, that ruthlessness, would permit him to do anything.

With an awful feeling of weariness, she surrendered. She threw the jeep into reverse and backed into the barn. She switched off, got out, and walked with Jo back into the cottage. She had no idea what she would say to Henry, what she would do in his presence, how she would hide her knowledge – if, indeed she had not already betrayed it.

She had no plans.

But she had left the barn door open.

THIRTY-TWO

'That's the place, Number One,' the captain said, and lowered his telescope.

The first lieutenant peered out through the rain and the spray. 'Not quite the ideal holiday resort, what, sir? Jolly stark, I should say.'

'Indeed.' The captain was an old-fashioned naval officer with a grizzled beard who had been at sea during the first war with Germany. However, he had learned to overlook his first lieutenant's foppish conversational style, for the boy had turned out – against all expectations – to be a perfectly good sailor.

The 'boy', who was past thirty and an old salt by this war's standards, had no idea of the magnanimity from which he benefited. He held on to a rail and braced himself as the corvette mounted the steep side of a wave, righted itself at the crest, and dived into the trough 'Now that we're here, sir, what do we do?'

'Circle the island.'

'Very good, sir.'

'And keep our eyes open for a U-boat.'

'We're not likely to get one anywhere near the surface in this weather – and if we did, we couldn't see it unless it came within spitting distance.'

'The storm will blow itself out tonight – tomorrow at the latest.' The captain began stuffing tobacco into a pipe.

'Do you think so?'

'I'm sure.'

'Nautical instinct, I suppose?'

The captain grunted. 'That, and the weather forecast.'

The corvette rounded a headland, and they saw a small bay with a jetty. Above it, on the cliff top, was a little cottage standing small and square, hunched against the wind.

The captain pointed. 'We'll land a party there as soon as we can.'

The first lieutenant nodded. 'All the same . . .'

'Well?'

'Each circuit of the island will take us about an hour, I should say.'

'So?'

'So, unless we're jolly lucky and happen to be in exactly the right place at exactly the right time . . .'

'The U-boat will surface, take on its passenger, and submerge again without us even seeing the ripples,' the captain finished.

'Yes.'

The captain lit his pipe with an expertise which spoke of long experience of lighting pipes in heavy seas. He puffed a few times, then inhaled a lungful of smoke. 'Ours not to reason why,' he said, and blew smoke through his nostrils.

'A rather unfortunate quotation, sir.'

'Why?'

'It refers to the notorious charge of the Light Brigade.'

'Good God! I never knew that.' The captain puffed contentedly. 'What it must be to be educated.'

There was another little cottage at the eastern end of the island. The captain scrutinized it through his telescope, and observed that it had a large, professional-looking radio aerial. 'Sparks!' he called. 'See if you can raise that cottage. Try the Royal Observer Corps's frequency.'

'Aye, aye, sir.'

When the cottage had passed out of sight, the radio operator called: 'No response, sir.'

'All right, Sparks,' the captain said. 'It wasn't important.'

The crew of the coastguard cutter sat below decks in Aberdeen Harbour, playing pontoon for halfpennies and musing on the feeble-mindedness which seemed invariably to accompany high rank.

'Twist,' said Jack Smith, who was more Scots than his name.

Albert 'Slim' Parish, a fat Londoner far from home, dealt him a jack.

'Bust,' Smith said.

Slim raked in his stake. 'A penny-ha'penny,' he said in mock wonder. 'I only hope I live to spend it.'

Smith rubbed condensation off the inside of a port-hole and peered out at the boats bobbing up and down in the harbour. 'The way the skipper's panicking,' he observed, 'you'd think we were going to bloody Berlin, not Storm Island.'

'Didn't you know? We're the spearhead of the Allied invasion.' Slim turned over a ten, dealt himself a king, and said: 'Pay twenty-ones.'

Smith said: 'What is this guy, anyway – a deserter? If you ask me, it's a job for the military police, not us.'

Slim shuffled the pack. 'I'll tell you what he is: an escaped prisoner-of-war.'

There was a chorus of disbelieving jeers.

'All right, don't listen to me. But when we pick him up, just take note of his accent.' He put the cards down. 'Listen: what boats go to Storm Island?'

'Only the grocer,' someone said.

'So, if he's a deserter, the only way he can get back to the mainland is on the grocer's boat. So, the Military Police just have to wait for Charlie's regular trip to the island, and pick the deserter up when he steps off the boat at this end. There's no reason for us to be sitting here, waiting to weigh anchor and shoot over there at the speed of light the minute the weather clears, unless . . .' He paused melodramatically. 'Unless he's got some other means of getting off the island.'

'Like what?'

'A U-boat.'

'Bollocks,' Smith said contemptuously. The others merely laughed.

Slim dealt another hand. Smith won this time, but everyone else lost. 'I'm a shilling up,' Slim said. 'I think

I'll retire to that nice little cottage in Devon. We won't catch him, of course.'

'The deserter?'

'The prisoner-of-war.'

'Why not?'

Slim tapped his head. 'Use your noddle. When the storm clears, we'll be here and the U-boat will be at the bottom of the bay in the island. So who'll get there first? The Jerries.'

'So why are we doing it?' Smith said.

'Because the people who are giving the orders are not as sharp as yours truly, Albert Parish. You may laugh!' He dealt another hand. 'Place your bets. You'll see I'm right. What's that, Smithie, a penny? Gorblimey, don't go mad. I tell you what, I'll give odds of five to one we come back from Storm Island empty-handed. Any takers? What if I say ten to one? Eh? Ten to one?'

'No takers,' said Smith. 'Deal the cards.'

Slim dealt the cards.

Squadron-Leader Peterkin Blenkinsop (he had tried to shorten Peterkin to Peter, but somehow the men always found out) stood ramrod-straight in front of the map and addressed the room. 'We fly in formations of three,' he began. 'The first three will take off as soon as weather permits. Our target—' he touched the map with a pointer. '—is here. Storm Island. On arrival, we will circle for twenty minutes at low altitudes, looking for U-boats. After twenty minutes, we return to base.'

He paused. 'Those of you with a logical turn of mind will by now have deduced that, to achieve continuous cover, the second formation of three aircraft must take off precisely twenty minutes after the first, and so on. Any questions?'

Flying-Officer Longman said: 'Sir?'

'Longman?'

'What do we do if we see this U-boat?'

'Strafe it, of course. Drop a few grenades. Cause trouble.'

'But we're flying fighters, sir – there's not much we can do to stop a U-boat. That's a job for battleships, isn't it?'

Blenkinsop sighed. 'As usual, those of you who can think of better ways to win the war are invited to write directly to Mr Winston Churchill, number ten Downing Street, London South-West-One. Now, are there any questions, as opposed to fat-headed criticisms?'

There were no questions.

The later years of the war had produced a different kind of RAF officer, Bloggs mused. He sat on a soft chair in the scramble room, close to the fire, listening to the rain drumming on the tin roof, and intermittently dozing. The Battle of Britain pilots had seemed incorrigibly cheerful, with their undergraduate slang, their perpetual drinking, their tirelessness, and their cavalier disregard of the flaming death they faced every day. That schoolboy heroism had not been enough to carry them through subsequent years, as the war dragged on in places far from home, and the emphasis shifted from the dashing individuality of aerial dogfighting to the mechanical drudgery of bombing missions. They still drank and talked in jargon, but they appeared older, harder, more cynical: there was nothing in them now of *Tom Brown's Schooldays.* Bloggs recalled what he had done to that poor common-or-garden housebreaker in the police cells at Aberdeen, and he thought: It's happened to us all.

They were very quiet. They sat all around him: some dozing, like himself; others reading books or playing board games. A bespectacled navigator in a corner was learning Russian.

As Bloggs surveyed the room with half-closed eyes, another pilot came in, and he thought immediately that this one had not been aged by the war. He had a wide grin and a fresh face that looked as if it hardly needed shaving more than once a week. He wore his jacket open and carried his helmet. He made a beeline for Bloggs.

'Detective-Inspector Bloggs?'

'That's me.'

'Jolly good show. I'm your pilot. Charles Calder.'

'Fine.' Bloggs shook hands.

'The kite's all ready, and the engine's as sweet as a bird. She's an amphibian, I suppose you know.'

'Yes.'

'Jolly good show. We'll land on the sea, taxi in to about ten yards from the shore, and put you off in a dinghy.'

'Then you wait for me to come back.'

'Indeed. Well, all we need now is the weather.'

'Yes. Look, Charles, I've been chasing this bloke all over the country for six days and nights, so I'm catching up on my sleep while I've got the chance. You won't mind.'

'Of course not!' The pilot sat down and produced a thick book from under his jacket. 'Catching up on my education,' he said. '*War and Peace.*'

Bloggs said: 'Jolly good show,' and closed his eyes.

Percival Godliman and his uncle, Colonel Terry, sat side by side in the map room, drinking coffee and tapping the ash of their cigarettes into a fire bucket on the floor between them. Godliman was repeating himself.

'I can't think of anything more we can do,' he said.

'So you said.'

'The corvette is already there, and the fighters are only a few minutes away, so the sub will come under fire as soon as she shows herself above the surface.'

'If she's seen.'

'The corvette will land a party as soon as possible. Bloggs will be there soon after that, and the coastguard will bring up the rear.'

'And none of them can be sure to get there in time.'

'I know,' Godliman said wearily. 'We've done all we can, but is it enough?'

Terry lit another cigarette. 'What about the inhabitants of the island?'

'Oh, yes. There are only two houses there. There's a

sheep farmer and his wife in one – they have a young child – and an old shepherd lives in the other. The shepherd's got a radio – Royal Observer Corps – but we can't raise him: he probably keeps the set switched to Transmit. He's old.'

'The farmer sounds promising,' Terry said. 'If he's a bright fellow he might stop your spy.'

Godliman shook his head. 'The poor chap's in a wheelchair.'

'Dear God, we don't get any luck, do we?'

'No,' said Godliman. 'Die Nadel gets all the luck there is.'

THIRTY-THREE

Lucy was becoming quite calm. The feeling crept over her gradually, like the icy spread of an anaesthetic, deadening her emotions and sharpening her wits. The times when she was momentarily paralysed by the thought that she was sharing a house with a murderer became fewer, and she was possessed by a cool-headed watchfulness that surprised her.

As she went about the household chores, sweeping around Henry as he sat in the living-room reading a novel, she wondered how much he had noticed of the change in her feelings. He was very observant: he did not miss much, and there had been a definite wariness, if not outright suspicion, in that confrontation over the jeep. He must have known she was shaken by something. On the other hand, she had been upset before he left, because Jo had discovered them in bed together: he might think that that was all that had been wrong.

She had the strangest feeling that he knew exactly what was in her mind, but he preferred to pretend that everything was all right.

She hung her laundry on a clothes-horse in the kitchen to dry. 'I'm sorry about this,' she said, 'but I can't wait forever for the rain to stop.'

He looked uninterestedly at the clothes and said: 'That's all right.' He went back into the living-room.

Scattered among the wet garments was a complete set of clean, dry clothes for Lucy.

For lunch she made a vegetable pie using an austerity recipe. She called Jo and Henry to the table and served up.

David's gun was propped in a corner of the kitchen. Lucy said: 'I don't like having a loaded gun in the house, Henry.'

'I'll take it outside after lunch,' he said. 'The pie is good.'

'I don't like it,' Jo said.

Lucy picked up the gun and put it on top of the Welsh dresser. 'I suppose it's all right as long as it's out of Jo's reach.'

Jo said: 'When I grow up I'm going to shoot Germans.'

'This afternoon I want you to have a sleep,' Lucy told him. She went into the living-room and took one of David's sleeping pills from the bottle in the cupboard. Two of the pills were a heavy dose for a 160-pound man, she reasoned, therefore one quarter of one pill should be just enough to make a 50-pound boy sleep in the afternoon. She put the pill on her chopping-block and halved it, then halved it again. She put a quarter on a spoon, crushed it with the back of another spoon, and stirred the powder into a small glass of milk. She gave the glass to Jo and said: 'I want you to drink every last drop.'

Henry watched the whole thing without comment.

After lunch she settled Jo on the sofa with a pile of books. He could not read, of course; but he had heard the stories read aloud so many times that he knew them by heart, and he could turn the pages of the books, looking at the pictures and reciting from memory the words on the page.

'Would you like some coffee?' she asked Henry.

'Real coffee?' he said, surprised.

'I've got a little hoard.'

'Yes, please!'

He watched her making it. She wondered if he was afraid she might try to give him sleeping pills, too. She could hear Jo's voice from the next room:

'What I said was, "Is anybody at home?"' called out Pooh very loudly.

'No!' said a voice . . .

– and he laughed heartily, as he always did at that joke. Oh, God, Lucy thought: don't let Jo be hurt.

She poured the coffee and sat opposite Henry. He reached across the table and held her hand. They sat in silence, sipping coffee and listening to the rain and Jo's voice.

'How long does getting thin take?' asked Pooh anxiously.

'About a week, I should think.'

'But I can't stay here for a week!'

He began to sound sleepy, and then he stopped. Lucy went and covered him with a blanket. She picked up the book, which had slipped from his fingers to the floor. It had been hers when she was a child, and she, too, knew the stories by heart. The flyleaf was inscribed in her mother's copperplate: 'To Lucy, aged four, with love from Mother and Father.' She put the book on the sideboard.

She went back into the kitchen. 'He's asleep.'

'And . . . ?'

She held out her hand. Henry took it. She tugged gently. He stood up. She led him upstairs and into the bedroom. She closed the door, then pulled her sweater off over her head.

For a moment he stood still, looking at her breasts. Then he began to undress.

As she got into the bed, she thought: Give me strength. This was the part that she dreaded, the part she was not sure she could manage: pretending to enjoy his body, when really all she could feel was fear, loathing, and guilt.

He got into bed and embraced her.

In a little while she found she did not have to pretend after all.

For a few seconds she lay in the crook of his arm, wondering how it was that a man could kill so coldly and love so warmly.

But what she said was: 'Would you like a cup of tea?'

He grinned. 'No, thank you.'

'Well, I would.' She extricated herself and got up. When he moved, she put her hand on his flat belly and said: 'No, you stay there. I'll bring the tea up. I haven't finished with you.'

He grinned again. 'You're really making up for your four wasted years.'

As soon as she was outside the room the smile dropped from her face like a mask. Her heart pounded in her chest as she went quickly, naked, down the stairs. In the kitchen she banged the kettle on the stove and rattled some china for realism. Then she began to put on the clothes she had left hidden in the wet laundry. Her hands were shaking so much that she could hardly button the trousers.

She heard the bed creak upstairs, and she stood frozen to the spot, listening, thinking: Stay there! Stay there! But he was only shifting his position.

She was ready. She went into the living-room. Jo was in a deep sleep, grinding his teeth. Dear God, don't let him wake up, Lucy prayed. She picked him up. He muttered in his sleep, something about Christopher Robin, and Lucy closed her eyes tightly and *willed* him to be quiet.

She wrapped the blanket around him securely. She went back into the kitchen and reached up to the top of the Welsh dresser for the gun. It slipped from her grasp and fell to the shelf, smashing a plate and two cups. The crash was deafening. She stood rooted to the spot.

'What happened?' Henry called from upstairs.

'I dropped a cup,' she shouted. She could not suppress the tremor in her voice.

The bed creaked again, and there was a footfall on the floor above her. But it was now too late for her to turn back. She picked up the gun, opened the back door, and, clutching Jo to her, ran across to the barn.

On the way she had a moment of panic: had she left the keys in the jeep? Surely she had: she always did.

She slipped in the wet mud and fell to her knees. She burst into tears. For a second she was tempted to stay there, and let him catch her and kill her as he had killed her husband; then she remembered the child in her arms, and she got up and ran on.

She entered the barn and opened the passenger door of the jeep. She put Jo on the seat. He slipped sideways. Lucy sobbed: 'Oh, God!' She pulled Jo upright, and this time he stayed that way. She ran around to the other side of the jeep and got in, dropping the gun on to the floor between her legs.

She turned the starter.

It coughed and died.

'Please, *please*!'

She turned it again.

The engine roared into life.

Henry came out of the back door at a run.

Lucy raced the engine and threw the gearshift into forward. The jeep leaped out of the barn. She rammed the throttle open.

The wheels spun in the mud for a second, then bit again. The jeep gathered speed with agonizing languor. She steered away from Henry. He chased the vehicle, barefoot in the mud.

She realized he was gaining on her.

She pushed the hand-throttle with all her might, almost snapping the thin lever. She wanted to scream with frustration. Henry was only a yard or so away, almost level with her, running like an athlete, his arms going like pistons, his bare feet pounding the turf, his cheeks blowing, his naked chest heaving.

The engine screamed, and there was a jerk as the automatic transmission changed up, then a new surge of power.

Lucy looked sideways again. Henry seemed to see that he had almost lost her. He flung himself forward through the air in a dive. He got a grip on the door handle with his left hand, and brought the right hand across. Pulled by the jeep, he ran alongside for a few paces, his feet hardly touching the ground. Lucy stared at his face, so close to hers: it was red with effort, twisted in pain; the cords of his powerful neck bulged with the strain.

Suddenly she knew what she had to do.

She took her hand off the wheel, reached through the open window, and poked him viciously in the eye with a long-nailed forefinger.

He let go and fell away, his hands covering his face.

The distance between him and the jeep increased rapidly.

Lucy realized she was crying like a baby.

Two miles from her cottage she saw the wheelchair.

It stood on the cliff top like a memorial, its metal frame and big rubber tyres impervious to the incessant rain. Lucy approached it from a slight dip, and saw its black outline framed by the slate-grey sky and the boiling sea. It had a wounded look, like the hole left by an uprooted tree or a house with broken windows; as if its passenger had been wrenched from it.

She recalled the first time she had seen it, in the hospital. It had stood beside David's bed, new and shiny, and he had swung himself into it expertly and swished up and down the ward, showing off. 'She's light as a feather – made of aircraft alloy,' he had said with brittle enthusiasm, and sped off between the rows of beds. He had stopped at the far end of the ward with his back to her, and after a minute she went up behind him and saw that he was weeping. She had knelt in front of him and held his hands, saying nothing.

It was the last time she had been able to comfort him.

There on the cliff-top, the rain and the salt wind would soon blemish the alloy, and eventually it would rust and crumble, its rubber perished, its leather seat rotted away.

Lucy drove past without slowing.

Three miles farther on, when she was half way between the two cottages, she ran out of petrol.

She fought down the panic and tried to think rationally as the jeep shuddered to a halt.

People walked at four miles an hour, she remembered reading somewhere. Henry was athletic, but he had hurt his ankle, and even though it seemed to have healed rapidly, the running he had done after the jeep must have hurt it. Therefore she must be a good hour ahead of him.

(She had no doubt he *would* come after her: he knew as well as she did that there was a wireless transmitter in Tom's cottage.)

She had plenty of time. In the back of the jeep was a half-gallon can of fuel for just such occasions as this. She got out of the car, fumbled the can out of the back, and opened the petrol cap.

Then she thought again, and the inspiration that came to her surprised her by its fiendishness.

She replaced the petrol cap and went to the front of the car. She checked that the ignition was off and opened the bonnet. She was no mechanic, but she could identify the distributor cap and trace the leads to the engine. She lodged the petrol can securely beside the wheel arch and took off its cap.

There was a plug spanner in the tool kit. She took out a plug, checked again that the ignition was off, and put the plug in the mouth of the petrol can, securing it there with tape. Then she closed the bonnet.

When Henry came along he was certain to try to start the jeep. He would switch on, the starter motor would turn, the plug would spark and the half-gallon of petrol would explode.

She was not sure how much damage it would do, but she could be certain it would be no help.

An hour later she was regretting her cleverness.

Trudging through the mud, soaked to the skin, with the sleeping child a dead weight over her shoulder, she wanted nothing more than to lie down and die. The booby-trap seemed, on reflection, dubious and risky: petrol would burn, not explode; if there was not enough air in the mouth of the can it might not even ignite; worst of all, Henry might suspect a trap, look under the bonnet, dismantle the bomb, pour the petrol into the tank and drive after her.

She contemplated stopping for a rest, but decided that if she sat down she might never get up again.

She should have been in sight of Tom's house by now. She could not possibly have got lost – even if she had not walked this path a dozen times before, the whole island just was not big enough to get lost on.

She recognized a thicket where she and Jo had once seen a fox. She must be about a mile from the shepherd's home. She could have seen it, but for the rain.

She shifted Jo to the other shoulder, switched the shotgun from one hand to the other, and forced herself to continue putting one foot in front of the other.

When at last the cottage became visible through the sheeting rain she could have cried with relief. She was nearer than she thought – perhaps a quarter of a mile.

Suddenly Jo seemed lighter, and although the last stretch was uphill – the only hill on the island – she seemed to cover it in no time at all.

'Tom!' she called as she approached the front door, 'Tom, oh, Tom!'

She heard the answering bark of Bob.

She went in by the front door. 'Tom, quickly!' Bob dodged excitedly about her ankles, barking furiously. Tom could not be far away – he was probably in the outhouse. Lucy went upstairs and laid Jo on Tom's bed.

The wireless was in the bedroom, a complex-looking construction of wires and dials and knobs. There was something that looked like a Morse key: she touched it experimentally, and it gave a beep. A thought came to her from the depths of her memory – something from a schoolgirl thriller – the Morse code for SOS. She touched the key again: three short, three long, three short.

Where was Tom?

She heard a noise, and rushed to the window.

The jeep was making its way up the hill to the house.

Henry had found the booby-trap, and used the petrol to fill the tank.

Where was Tom?

She rushed out of the bedroom, intending to go and bang on the outhouse door. At the head of the stairs she paused. Bob was standing in the open doorway of the other bedroom, the empty one.

'Come here, Bob,' she said. The dog stood his ground, barking. She went to him and bent to pick him up.

Then she saw Tom.

He lay on his back, on the bare floorboards of the vacant bedroom, his eyes staring sightlessly at the ceiling, his cap upside-down on the floor behind his head. His jacket was open, and there was a small spot of blood on the shirt underneath. Close to his hand was a crate of whisky, and Lucy found herself thinking wildly, irrelevantly: I didn't know he drank that much.

She felt his pulse.

He was dead.

Think, *think*!

Yesterday Henry had returned to Lucy's cottage

battered, as if he had been in a fight. That must have been when he killed David. Today he had come here, to Tom's cottage, 'to fetch David' he had said. But he had known David was not there. So why had he made the journey?

Obviously, to kill Tom.

What drove him? What purpose burned inside him so fiercely that he would get in a car, drive ten miles, stick a knife into an old man, and drive back as calm and quiet and composed as if he had been out to take the air? Lucy shuddered.

Now she was on her own.

She took hold of the dog by its collar and dragged it away from the body of its master. On impulse, she returned and buttoned the jacket over the small stiletto wound which had killed the shepherd. Then she closed the door on the corpse. She said to the dog: 'He's dead, but I need you.'

She returned to the front bedroom and looked out of the window.

The jeep drew up in front of the house and stopped; and Henry got out.

THIRTY-FOUR

Lucy's distress call was heard by the corvette.

'Captain, sir,' said Sparks, 'I just picked up an SOS from the island.'

The captain frowned. 'Nothing we can do until we can land a boat,' he said. 'Did they say anything else?'

'Not a thing, sir. It wasn't even repeated.'

The captain thought a little more. 'Nothing we can do,' he said again. 'Send a signal to the mainland, reporting it. And keep listening.'

'Aye, aye, sir.'

It was also picked up by an M18 listening post on top of a Scottish mountain. The R/T operator, a young man with abdominal wounds who had been invalided out of the RAF and had only six months to live, was trying to pick up German Navy signals from Norway, and he ignored the SOS. However, he went off duty five minutes later, and he mentioned it casually to his Commanding Officer.

'It was only broadcast once,' he said. 'Probably a

fishing vessel off the Scottish coast – there might well be the odd small ship in trouble, in this weather.'

'Leave it with me,' the CO said. 'I'll give the Navy a buzz. And I suppose I'd better inform Whitehall. Protocol, y'know.'

'Thank you, sir.'

At the Royal Observer Corps station there was something of a panic. Of course, SOS was not the signal an observer was *supposed* to give when he sighted enemy aircraft, but they knew that Tom was old, and who could say what he might send if he got excited? So the air-raid sirens were sounded, and all other posts were alerted, and anti-aircraft guns were rolled out all over the east coast of Scotland, and the radio operator tried frantically to raise Tom.

No German bombers came, of course; and the War Office wanted to know why a full alert had been sounded when there was nothing in the sky but a few bedraggled geese?

So they were told.

The Coastguard heard it, too.

They would have responded to it, if it had been on the correct frequency, and if they had been able to establish the position of the transmitter, and if that position had been within reasonable distance of the coast.

As it was they guessed, from the fact that the signal

came over on the Observer Corps frequency, that it originated from Old Tom; and they were already doing all they could about *that* situation, whatever the hell that situation was.

When the news reached the below-deck card game on the cutter in the harbour at Aberdeen, Slim dealt another hand of pontoon and said: 'I'll tell you what's happened. Old Tom's caught the prisoner-of-war and he's sitting on his head waiting for the Army to arrive and take the bugger away.'

'Bollocks,' said Smith, and there was general agreement with that sentiment.

And the *U-505* heard it.

She was still more than thirty nautical miles away from Storm Island, but Weissman was roaming the dial to see what he could pick up – and hoping, improbably, to hear Glenn Miller records from the American Forces Network in Britain – and his tuner happened to be on the right wavelength at the right time. He passed the information to Lieutenant-Commander Heer, adding: 'It was not on our man's frequency.'

Major Wohl, who was still around and as irritating as ever, said: 'Then it means nothing.'

Heer did not miss the opportunity to correct him. 'It means *something*,' he said. 'It means that there may be some activity on the surface when we go up.'

'But this is unlikely to trouble us.'

'Most unlikely,' Heer agreed.

'Then it is meaningless.'

'It is *probably* meaningless.'

They argued about it all the way to the island.

So it was that within the space of five minutes the Navy, the Royal Observer Corps, M18 and the Coastguard all phoned Godliman to tell him about the SOS. And Godliman phoned Bloggs.

Bloggs had finally fallen into a deep sleep in front of the fire in the scramble room. The shrill ring of the telephone startled him, and he leaped to his feet, thinking that the planes were about to take off.

A pilot picked it up, said 'Yes' into it twice, and handed it to Bloggs. 'A Mr Godliman for you.'

Bloggs said: 'Hello, Percy.'

'Fred, somebody on the island just broadcast an SOS.'

Bloggs shook his head to clear the last remaining clouds of sleep. 'Who?'

'We don't know. There was just the one signal, not repeated, and they don't seem to be receiving at all.'

'Still, there's not much doubt now.'

'No. Everything ready up there?'

'All except the weather.'

'Good luck.'

'Thanks.'

Bloggs hung up and turned to the young pilot who was still reading *War and Peace*. 'Good news,' he told him. 'The bastard's definitely on the island.'

'Jolly good show,' said the pilot.

THIRTY-FIVE

Henry closed the door of the jeep and began walking quite slowly toward the house. He was wearing David's hacking jacket again. There was mud all over his trousers, where he had fallen, and his hair was plastered wetly against his skull. He was limping slightly on his right foot.

Lucy backed away from the window and ran out of the bedroom and down the stairs. The shotgun was on the floor in the hall, where she had dropped it. She picked it up. Suddenly it felt very heavy. She had never actually fired a gun, and she had no idea how to check whether this one was loaded. She could figure it out, given time; but there was no time.

She took a deep breath and flung open the front door. 'Stop!' she shouted. Her voice was pitched higher than she had intended, and it sounded shrill and hysterical.

Henry smiled pleasantly and kept on walking.

Lucy pointed the gun at him, holding the barrel with her left hand and the breech with her right. Her finger was on the trigger. 'I'll kill you!' she yelled.

'Don't be silly, Lucy,' he said mildly. 'How could you hurt me? After all the things we've done together? Haven't we loved each other, a little . . . ?'

It was true. She had told herself she could not fall in love with him, and that was true too; but she *had* felt *something* for him, and if it was not love, it was something very like.

'You knew about me this afternoon,' he said, and now he was thirty yards away, 'but it made no difference to you then, did it?'

That was true. For a moment, she saw in her mind's eye a vivid picture of herself sitting astride him, holding his sensitive hands to her breasts, and then she realized what he was doing—

'We can work something out, Lucy, we can still have each other—'

– and she pulled the trigger.

There was an ear-splitting crash, and the weapon jumped in her hands like a live thing, its butt bruising her hip with the recoil. She almost dropped it in shock. She had never imagined that firing a gun would feel like that. She was quite deaf for a moment.

The shot went high over Henry's head, but all the same he ducked, turned, and ran zig-zagging back to the jeep. Lucy was tempted to fire again, but she stopped herself just in time, realizing that if he knew both barrels had been emptied there would be nothing to stop him turning and coming back.

He flung open the door of the jeep, leaped in, and shot off down the hill.

Lucy knew he would be back.

Suddenly she felt happy, almost gay. She had won the first round – she had driven him off – and she was a woman!

But he would be back.

Still, she had the upper hand. She was indoors, and she had the gun. And she had time to prepare.

Prepare. She must be ready for him. Next time he would be more subtle. He would surely try to creep up on her.

She hoped he would wait until dark, for that would give her time.

First she had to reload the gun.

She went into the kitchen. Tom kept everything in his kitchen – food, coal, tools, stores – and he had a gun like David's. She knew the two firearms were the same, for David had examined Tom's then sent away for one exactly like it. The two men had enjoyed long discussions about weaponry.

She found Tom's gun and a box of ammunition. She put the two guns and the box on the kitchen table.

Machines were simple, she was convinced: it was apprehension, not stupidity, which made women fumble when faced with a piece of engineering.

She fiddled with David's gun, keeping the barrel pointed away from herself, until it came open at the breech. Then she worked out what she had done to open it, and practised doing it again a couple of times.

It was incredibly simple.

She loaded both guns. Then, to make sure she had done everything correctly, she pointed Tom's gun at the kitchen wall and pulled the trigger.

There was a shower of plaster, Bob barked like a maniac, and she bruised her hip and deafened herself again. But she was armed.

She must remember to pull the triggers gently so as not to jerk the gun and spoil her aim. Men probably got taught that kind of thing in the Army.

What to do next? She should make it difficult for Henry to get into the house.

Neither of the doors had locks, of course: if a house was burgled on this island, one would know that the culprit lived in the other house. Lucy rummaged in Tom's tool box and found a shiny, sharp-bladed axe. She stood on the stairs and began to hack away at the bannister.

The work made her arms ache, but in five minutes she had six short lengths of stout, seasoned oak. She found a hammer and some nails, and fixed the oak bars across the front and back doors, three bars to each door, four nails to each bar. When it was done her wrists were agony and the hammer felt as heavy as lead, but she was not finished.

She got another handful of the shiny, four-inch nails, and went around every window in the house, nailing them shut. She realized, with a sense of discovery, why men always put nails in their mouths: it was because you needed both hands for the work and if you put them in your pocket they stuck into your skin.

By the time she had finished it was dark. She left the lights off.

He could still get into the house, of course; but he could not get in quietly. He would have to break something and give himself away – and then she would be ready with the guns.

She went upstairs, carrying both guns, to check on

Jo. He was still asleep, wrapped in his blanket, on Tom's bed. Lucy struck a match to look at his face. The sleeping pill must have really knocked him out, but he was an average sort of colour, his temperature seemed normal, and he was breathing easily. 'Just stay that way, little boy,' Lucy whispered. The sudden access of tenderness left her feeling more savage toward Henry.

She patrolled the house restlessly for a while, peering through the windows into the darkness, the dog following her everywhere. She took to carrying just one of the guns, leaving the other at the head of the stairs; but she hooked the axe into the belt of her trousers.

She remembered the radio, and tapped out her SOS several more times. She had no idea whether anybody was listening, or even whether the radio was working. She knew no more Morse, so she could not broadcast anything else.

It occurred to her that Tom probably did not know Morse code. Surely he must have a book somewhere? If only she could tell someone what was happening here! She searched the house, using dozens of matches, feeling terrified every time she lit one within sight of a downstairs window; but she found nothing.

All right, perhaps he *did* know Morse.

On the other hand, why should he need it? He only had to tell the mainland that there were enemy aircraft approaching, and there was no reason why that information shouldn't go over the air . . . what was the phrase David had used? . . . *en clair*.

She went back to the bedroom and looked again at

the wireless set. To one side of the main cabinet, hidden from her previous cursory glance, was a microphone.

If she could talk to them, they could talk to her.

The sound of another human voice – a normal, sane, mainland voice – suddenly seemed the most desirable thing in the world.

She picked up the microphone and began to experiment with the switches.

Bob growled softly.

She put the mike down and reached out her hand toward the dog in the darkness. 'What is it, Bob?'

He growled again. She could feel his ears standing stiffly upright. She was terribly afraid: the confidence won by confronting Henry with the gun, by learning how to reload, by barricading the doors and nailing down the windows . . . all evaporated at one growl from an alert dog.

'Downstairs,' she whispered. 'Quietly.'

She held his collar and let him lead her down the stairs. In the darkness she felt for the bannister, forgetting that she had chopped it up for barricades, and she almost overbalanced. She regained her equilibrium and sucked at a splinter in her finger.

The dog hesitated in the hall, then growled more loudly and tugged her toward the kitchen. She picked him up and held his muzzle shut to silence him. Then she crept through the doorway.

She looked in the direction of the window, but there was nothing in front of her eyes other than velvet blackness.

She listened. The window creaked: at first almost inaudibly, then louder. He was trying to get in. Bob rumbled threateningly, deep in his throat, but seemed to understand the sudden squeeze she gave his muzzle.

The night became quieter. Lucy realized the storm was easing, almost imperceptibly. Henry seemed to have given up on the kitchen window. She moved to the living-room.

She heard the same creak of old wood resisting pressure. Now Henry seemed more determined: there were three muffled bumps, as if he were tapping the window-frame with the cushioned heel of his hand.

Lucy put the dog down and hefted the shotgun. It might almost have been imagination, but she could just make out the window as a square of grey in the blank darkness. If he got the window open, she would fire immediately.

There was a much harder bang. Bob lost control and gave a loud bark. She heard a scuffling noise outside.

Then came the voice.

'Lucy?'

She bit her lip.

'Lucy?'

He was using the voice he used in bed: deep, soft, and intimate.

'Lucy, can you hear me? Don't be afraid. I don't want to hurt you. Talk to me, please.'

She had to fight the urge to pull both triggers there and then, just to silence that awful sound and repress the memories it brought to her unwilling consciousness.

'Lucy, my darling . . .' She thought she heard a muffled sob. 'Lucy, he attacked me – I had to kill him . . . I killed for my country, you shouldn't hate me for that.'

She could not understand that. It sounded mad. Could he be insane, and have hidden it for two intimate days? He had seemed saner than most people – and yet he had murdered before . . . unless he was a victim of injustice . . . Damn. She was softening up, and that must be exactly what he wanted.

She had an idea.

'Lucy, just speak to me . . .'

His voice faded as she tip-toed into the kitchen. Bob would warn her if Henry did anything more than talk. She fumbled in Tom's tool-box and found a pair of pliers. She went to the kitchen window and found with her fingertips the heads of the three nails she had hammered there. Carefully, as quietly as possible, she drew them out. The job demanded all her strength.

When they were out she went back into the living-room to listen.

' . . . don't obstruct me, and I'll leave you . . .'

As silently as she could she lifted the kitchen window open. She crept into the living-room, picked the dog up, and returned yet again to the kitchen.

' . . . hurt you, last thing in the world . . .'

She stroked the dog once or twice, and murmured: 'I wouldn't do this if I didn't have to, boy.' Then she pushed him out of the window.

She closed it rapidly, found a nail, and hammered it in at a new spot with three sharp blows.

She dropped the hammer, picked up the gun, and ran into the front room to stand close to the window, pressing herself up against the wall.

' . . . give you one last chance – ah!'

There was a rush of small feet; a blood-curdling bark Lucy had never heard from a sheepdog before; a scuffling sound; and the noise of a big man falling. She could hear Henry's breathing, gasping, grunting; then another flurry of canine paws; a shout of pain; a curse in a foreign language; another bark. She wished she could see what was happening.

The noises became muffled and more distant, then suddenly ceased. Lucy waited, pressed against the wall next to the window, straining her ears. She wanted to go and check on Jo, wanted to try the radio again, wanted to cough; but she did not dare to move. Bloodthirsty visions of what Bob might have done to Henry passed in and out of her mind, and she yearned to hear the dog snuffling at the door.

She looked at the window. Then she *realized* she was looking at the window: she could see, not just a square patch of faintly lighter grey, but the wooden crosspiece of the frame. It was still night, but only just: she knew that if she looked outside the sky would be faintly diffused with a just-perceptible light, instead of being impenetrably black. Dawn would come at any minute. Then she would be able to see the furniture in the room, and Henry would no longer be able to surprise her in the darkness—

There was a crash of breaking glass inches away from her face. She jumped. She felt a small sharp pain in her cheek, touched the spot, and knew that she had been cut by a flying shard. She hefted the shotgun, waiting for Henry to come through the window; but nothing happened. It was not until a minute or two had passed that she wondered what had broken the window.

She peered at the floor. Among the pieces of broken glass was a large dark shape. She found she could see it better if she looked to one side of it rather than directly at it. When she did that, she was able to make out the familiar shape of the dog.

She closed her eyes, then looked away. She was unable to feel any emotion at all at the death of the faithful sheepdog. Her heart had been numbed by all the danger and death that had gone before: first David, then Tom, then the endless screaming tension of the all-night siege . . . All she felt was hunger. All day yesterday she had been too nervous to eat, which meant it was thirty-six hours since her last meal. Now, incongruously, ridiculously, she found herself longing for a cheese sandwich.

Something else was coming through the window.

She saw it out of the corner of her eye, then turned her head to look directly at it.

It was Henry's hand.

She stared at it, mesmerized: a long-fingered hand, without rings, white under the dirt, with cared-for nails and a band-aid around the tip of the index finger; a hand that had touched her intimately, had played her body like a harp, and thrust a knife into the heart of an old shepherd.

The hand broke away a piece of glass, then another,

enlarging the hole in the pane. Then it reached right through, up to the elbow, and fumbled along the windowsill, searching for a catch to unfasten.

Trying to be utterly silent, with painful slowness, Lucy shifted the gun to her left hand, and with her right took the axe from her belt, lifted it high above her head, and brought it down with all her might on Henry's hand.

He must have sensed it, or heard the rush of wind, or seen a blur of ghostly movement behind the window; for he moved sharply a split-second before the blow landed.

The axe thudded into the wood of the windowsill, sticking there. For a fraction of an instant Lucy thought she had missed: then, from outside, there came a scream of pain and loss, and she saw beside the axe blade, lying on the varnished wood like caterpillars, two severed fingers.

She heard the sound of feet running away.

Lucy threw up.

The exhaustion hit her then, closely followed by a surge of self-pity. She had suffered enough, surely to God, had she not? There were policemen and soldiers in the world to deal with situations like this – nobody could expect an ordinary housewife and mother to keep a killer at bay indefinitely. Who could blame her if she gave up now? Who could honestly say they would have done better, lasted longer, stayed brave and resolute and resourceful for another minute?

She was finished. *They* would have to take over: the outside world, the policemen and soldiers, whoever was at the other end of that radio link. She could do no more.

She tore her eyes away from the grotesque objects on the windowsill and went wearily up the stairs. She picked up the second gun and took both weapons into the bedroom with her.

Jo was still asleep, bless him. He had hardly moved all night, utterly oblivious to the apocalypse going on around him. She could tell, somehow, that he was not sleeping so deeply now: something about the look on his face and the way he breathed let her know that he would wake soon and want his breakfast.

She longed for that simple life, now: getting up in the morning, making breakfast, dressing Jo, doing simple, tedious, *safe* household chores like washing and cleaning and cutting herbs from the garden and making pots of tea. It seemed incredible that she had been so dissatisfied with David's lovelessness, the long boring evenings, the endless bleak landscape of turf and heather and rain.

It would never come back, that life.

She had wanted excitement, cities, music, people, ideas. Now the desire for those things had left her, and she could not understand how she had ever wanted them. Peace was all a human being ought to ask for, it seemed to her.

She sat in front of the radio and studied its switches and dials. She would do this one thing, then she would rest. She made a tremendous effort and forced herself to think analytically for a little longer. There were not *so* many possible combinations of switch and dial. She found a knob with two settings, turned it, and tapped the Morse key. There was no sound. Perhaps that meant the microphone was now in circuit.

She pulled it to her and spoke into it. 'Hello, hello, is there anybody there? Hello?'

There was a switch which had 'Transmit' above it and 'Receive' below. It was turned to 'Transmit'. If the world was to talk back to her, obviously she had to throw the switch to 'Receive'.

She said: 'Hello, is anybody listening?' and threw the switch to 'Receive'.

Nothing.

Then: 'Come in, Storm Island, receiving you loud and clear.'

It was a man's voice. He sounded young and strong, capable and confident and reassuring and alive and *normal.*

'Come in, Storm Island, we've been trying to raise you all night . . . where the devil have you *been*?'

Lucy switched to 'Transmit', tried to speak, and burst into tears.

THIRTY-SIX

Percival Godliman had a headache from too many cigarettes and too little sleep. He had taken a little whisky to help him through the long, worried night in his office, and that had been a mistake. Everything oppressed him: the weather, his office, his job, the war. For the first time since he had become a spycatcher he found himself longing for dusty libraries, illegible manuscripts, and medieval Latin.

Colonel Terry walked in with two cups of tea on a tray. 'Nobody around here sleeps,' he said cheerfully. He sat down. 'Ship's biscuit?' He offered Godliman a plate.

Godliman refused the biscuit and drank the tea. It gave him a temporary lift.

'I just had a call from the man with the fat cigar,' Terry said. 'He's keeping the night vigil with us.'

'I can't imagine why,' Godliman said sourly.

'He's worried.'

The phone rang.

'Godliman.'

'I have the Royal Observer Corps in Aberdeen for you, sir.'

'Yes.'

A new voice came on, the voice of a young man. 'Royal Observer Corps, Aberdeen, here, sir.'

'Yes.'

'Is that Mr Godliman?'

'*Yes.*' Dear God, these military types took their time.

'We've raised Storm Island at last, sir.'

'Thank God!'

'It's not our regular observer. In fact it's a woman.'

'What did she say?'

'Nothing, yet, sir.'

'What do you *mean*?' Godliman fought down the angry impatience that rose inside him.

'She's just . . . well, crying, sir.'

'Oh.' Godliman hesitated. 'Can you connect me to her?'

'Yes. Hold on.' There was a pause punctuated by several clicks and a hum. Then Godliman heard the sound of a woman weeping.

He said: 'Hello, can you hear me?'

The weeping went on.

The young man came back on the line to say: 'She won't be able to hear you until she switches to "Receive", sir – ah, she's done it. Go ahead.'

Godliman said: 'Hello, young lady. When I've finished speaking I'll say "Over", then you switch to "Transmit" to speak to me and *you* say "Over" when *you* have finished. Do you understand? Over.'

The woman's voice came on. 'Oh, thank God for somebody sane. Yes, I understand. Over.'

'Now, then,' Godliman said gently, 'tell me what's been happening there. Over.'

'A man was shipwrecked here two – no, three days ago. I think he's the stiletto murderer from London. He killed my husband and our shepherd, and now he's outside the house, and I've got my little boy here . . . I've nailed the windows shut, and fired at him with a shotgun, and barred the doors, and set the dog on him but he killed the dog, and I hit him with the axe when he tried to get in through the window and *I can't do it any more so please come and save me* . . . Over.'

Godliman put his hand over the phone. His face was white. 'You poor woman,' he breathed. But when he spoke to her, he was brisk. 'You must hold on a little longer,' he began. 'There are sailors and coastguards and policemen and all sorts of people on their way to you, but they can't land until the storm ends. Now, there's something I want you to do, and I can't tell you why you must do it because the wrong people may be listening to us, but I can tell you that it is *absolutely essential.* Are you hearing me clearly? Over.'

'Yes, go on. Over.'

'You must destroy your radio. Over.'

'Oh, no, please . . . must I?'

'Yes,' Godliman said, then he realized she was still transmitting.

'I don't . . . I can't . . .' Then there was a scream.

Godliman said: 'Hello, Aberdeen, what's happening?'

The young man came on. 'The set's still transmitting, sir, but she's not speaking. We can't hear anything.'

'She screamed.'

'Yes, we got that.'

'Damn.' Godliman thought for a minute. 'What's the weather like up there?'

'It's raining, sir.' The young man sounded puzzled.

'I'm not making conversation, lad,' Godliman snapped. 'Is there any sign of the storm letting up?'

'It has eased a little in the last few minutes, sir.'

'Good. Get back to me the instant that woman comes back on air.'

'Very good, sir.'

Godliman said to Terry: 'God only knows what that girl's going through up there.' He jiggled the cradle of the phone.

The Colonel crossed his legs. 'If only she would smash up the radio, then . . .'

'Then we don't care if he kills her?'

'You said it.'

Godliman spoke into the phone. 'Get me Bloggs at Rosyth.'

Bloggs woke up with a start, and listened. Outside, it was dawn. Everyone in the scramble hut was listening, too. They could hear nothing. That was what they were listening to: the silence.

The rain had stopped drumming on the tin roof.

Bloggs went to the window. The sky was grey with a band of white on the eastern horizon. The wind had dropped suddenly, and the rain had become a light drizzle.

The pilots started putting on jackets and helmets, lacing boots, lighting last cigarettes.

A klaxon sounded, and a voice boomed out over the airfield: 'Scramble! Scramble!'

The phone rang. The pilots ignored it and piled out through the door. Bloggs picked it up. 'Yes?'

'Percy here, Fred. We just contacted the island. He's killed the two men. The woman's holding him off at the moment, but she won't last much longer.'

Bloggs said: 'The rain has stopped. We're taking off now.'

'Make it fast, Fred. Goodbye.'

Bloggs hung up and looked around for his pilot. Charles Calder had fallen asleep over *War and Peace*. Bloggs shook him roughly. 'Wake up, you dozy bastard, wake up!'

He opened his eyes.

Bloggs could have hit him. 'Wake up, come on, we're going, the storm's ended!'

The pilot jumped to his feet. 'Jolly good show,' he said.

He ran out of the door and Bloggs followed him.

The lifeboat dropped into the water with a crack like a pistol and a wide, V-shaped splash. The sea was far from calm, but here in the partial shelter of the bay there was no risk to a stout boat in the hands of experienced sailors.

The captain said: 'Carry on, Number One.'

The first lieutenant was standing at the rail with three ratings. He wore a pistol in a waterproof holster. He said: 'Let's go, chaps.'

The four men scrambled down the ladders and into the boat. The first mate sat in the stern and the three sailors broke out the oars and began to row.

For a few moments the captain watched their steady progress toward the jetty. Then he returned to the bridge and gave orders for the corvette to continue circling the island.

The shrill ringing of a bell broke up the card game on the cutter.

Slim said: 'I thought something was different. We aren't going up and down so much. Almost motionless, really. Makes me quite seasick.'

Nobody was listening: the crew were hurrying to their stations, some of them fastening life-jackets as they went.

The engines fired with a roar, and the vessel began to tremble faintly but perceptibly.

Up on deck, Smith stood in the prow, enjoying the fresh air and the spray on his face after a day and a night below.

As the cutter left the harbour Slim joined him.

'Here we go again,' Slim said.

'I knew the bell was going to ring then,' Smith said. 'You know why?'

'Tell me.'

'Know what I had in my hand? Ace and a king.'

'Banker's pontoon,' said Slim. 'Well I never.'

*

Lieutenant-Commander Werner Heer looked at his watch and said: 'Thirty minutes.'

Major Wohl nodded impassively. 'What is the weather like?' he asked.

'The storm has ended,' Heer said reluctantly. He would have preferred to keep that information to himself.

'Then we should surface.'

'If your man were there, he would send us a signal.'

'The war is not won by hypothesis, Captain,' said Wohl. 'I firmly suggest that we surface.'

There had been a blazing row, while the U-boat was in dock, between Heer's superior officer and Wohl's; and Wohl's had won. Heer was still captain of the ship, but he had been told in no uncertain terms that he had better have a damned good reason next time he ignored one of Major Wohl's firm suggestions.

'We will surface at six o'clock exactly,' he said.

Wohl nodded again and looked away.

THIRTY-SEVEN

The sound of breaking glass, then an explosion like an incendiary bomb:

Whooomph!

Lucy dropped the microphone. Something was happening downstairs. She picked up a shotgun and ran down.

The living-room was ablaze. The fire centred on a broken jar on the floor. Henry had made some kind of bomb with the petrol from the jeep. The flames were spreading hungrily across Tom's threadbare carpet and licking up over the loose covers of his ancient three-piece suite. A feather-filled cushion caught, and the fire reached up toward the ceiling.

Lucy picked up the cushion and flung it through the broken window, singeing her hand. She tore her coat off and threw it on the carpet, stamping on it. She picked it up again and draped it over the floral settee. She was winning—

There was another crash of glass.

It came from upstairs.

Lucy screamed: 'Jo!'

She dropped the coat and raced up the stairs and into the front bedroom.

Henry was sitting on the bed with Jo on his lap. The child was awake, sucking his thumb, wearing his wide-eyed morning look. Henry was stroking his tousled hair.

Henry said: 'Throw the gun on the bed, Lucy.'

Her shoulders sagged in defeat, and she did as he said. 'You climbed the wall and got through the window,' she said dully.

Henry dumped Jo off his lap. 'Go to Mummy.'

Jo ran to her and she lifted him up.

Henry picked up both guns and went to the radio. He was holding his right hand under his left armpit, and there was a great red bloodstain on his jacket. He sat down. 'You hurt me,' he said. Then he turned his attention to the transmitter.

Suddenly it spoke. 'Come in, Storm Island.'

Henry picked up the microphone. 'Hello?'

'Just a minute.'

There was a pause, then another voice came on. Lucy recognized it as the man in London who had told her to destroy the radio. He would be disappointed in her. It said: 'Hello, this is Godliman again. Can you hear me? Over.'

Henry said: 'Yes, I can hear you, Professor. Seen any good cathedrals lately?'

'Is that . . .'

'Yes.' Henry smiled. 'How do you do.' Then the smile left his face abruptly, as if playtime was over, and he turned the frequency dial of the radio.

Lucy turned and left the room. It was over, and she had lost. She walked listlessly down the stairs and into the kitchen. There was nothing for her to do but wait for him to kill her. She could not run away – she did not have the energy, and he obviously knew it.

She looked out of the window. The storm had ended. The howling gale had dropped to a stiff breeze, there was no rain, and the eastern sky was bright with the promise of sunshine. The sea—

She frowned, and looked again.

Yes, it *was* a submarine.

Destroy the radio, the Professor had said.

Last night Henry had cursed in a foreign language.

'*I did it for my country,*' he had said.

And, in his delirium: *Waiting at Calais for a phantom army.*

Destroy the radio.

Why would a man take a wallet of photographic negatives on a fishing trip?

She had known all along he was not insane.

The submarine was a German U-boat, Henry was an enemy agent, and he was at this very second trying to contact the vessel by radio.

Destroy the radio.

She knew what she had to do. She had no right to give up, now that she understood; for it was not only her life that was at stake. She had to do this one last thing for David and for all the other young men who had died in the war.

She knew what she had to do. She was not afraid of the pain – it would be *very* painful, she knew, and might well kill her – but she had known the pain of childbirth, and it could not be worse than that.

She knew what she had to do. She would have liked to put Jo somewhere else, where he could not see it; but there was no time for that, for Henry would find his frequency at any second, and then it might be too late.

She knew what she had to do. She had to destroy the radio, but the radio was upstairs with Henry, and he had both the guns and he *would* kill her.

She knew what she had to do.

She placed one of Tom's kitchen chairs in the centre of the room, stood on it, reached up and unscrewed the light bulb.

She got off the chair, went to the door, and threw the switch.

'Are you changing the bulb?' Jo said.

Lucy climbed on the chair, hesitated for a moment, then thrust three fingers into the live socket.

There was a bang, an instant of agony, and then unconsciousness.

Faber heard the bang. He had found the right frequency on the transmitter, had thrown the switch to 'Transmit', and had picked up the microphone. He was about to speak when the noise came. Immediately afterwards the lights on the dials of the wireless set went out.

His face suffused with anger. She had short-circuited the electricity supply to the whole house. He had not credited her with that much ingenuity.

He should have killed her before. What the hell was wrong with him? He had never hesitated, not ever, until he met this woman.

He picked up one of the guns and went downstairs.

The child was crying. Lucy lay in the kitchen doorway, out cold. Faber took in the empty light socket with the chair beneath it. He frowned in amazement.

She had done it with her *hand*.

Faber said: 'Jesus Christ Almighty.'

Lucy's eyes opened. She hurt all over.

Henry was standing over her with the gun in his hands. He said: 'Why did you use your hand? Why not a screwdriver?'

She said: 'I didn't know you could do it with a screwdriver.'

He shook his head in incredulity. 'You are a truly astonishing woman,' he said. He lifted the gun, aimed it at her, and lowered it again. '*Damn* you!'

His gaze went to the window, and he started.

'You saw it,' he said.

She nodded.

He stood tense for a moment, then he went to the door. Finding it nailed shut, he smashed the window with the butt of his gun and climbed out.

Lucy got to her feet. Jo threw his arms around her legs. She did not feel strong enough to pick him up. She staggered to the window and looked out.

Henry was running toward the cliff. The U-boat was still there, perhaps half a mile offshore. Henry reached the cliff edge and crawled over. He was going to try to swim to the submarine.

Lucy had to stop him.

Dear God, no more, she prayed.

She climbed through the window, blotting out the cries of her son, and ran after Henry.

When she reached the cliff edge she lay down and looked over. He was about half way between her and the sea. He looked up and saw her, froze for a moment, and then began to move faster, dangerously fast.

Her first thought was to climb down after him. But what would she do then? Even if she caught him, she could not stop him.

The ground beneath her shifted slightly. She scrambled back, afraid it would give way and throw her down the cliff.

That gave her an idea.

She thumped on the rocky ground with both fists. It seemed to shake a little more, and a crack appeared. She got one hand over the edge and thrust the other into the crack. A piece of earthy chalk the size of a watermelon came away in her hands.

She looked over the edge and sighted Henry.

She took careful aim and dropped the stone.

It seemed to fall very slowly. He saw it coming, and covered his head with his arm. It looked as if it would miss him.

The rock passed within a couple of inches of his head, and hit his left shoulder. He was holding on with his left hand. He seemed to loosen his grip. He balanced precariously for a moment. The right hand, the injured one, scrabbled for a hold. Then he appeared to lean out, away from the face of the rock, arms windmilling, until his feet slipped from their narrow ledge and he was suddenly in mid-air, suspended; and finally he dropped like a stone to the rocks below.

He made no sound.

He landed on a flat rock that jutted above the surface of the water. The noise his body made hitting the rock was sickening. He lay there on his back like a broken doll, arms outflung, head at an impossible angle.

Something vile seeped out from inside him on to the stone, and Lucy turned away.

She had killed him.

Everything happened at once, then.

There was a roaring sound from the sky and three aircraft with RAF circles on their wings flew out of the clouds and dipped low over the U-boat, their guns blazing.

Four sailors came up the hill toward the house at a jog-trot, one of them shouting 'Left-right-left-right-left-right.'

Another plane landed on the sea, a dinghy emerged, and a man in a life-jacket began to row toward the cliff.

A small ship came around the headland and steamed aggressively toward the U-boat.

The U-boat submerged.

The dinghy bumped into the rocks at the foot of the cliff, and the man got out and examined the body of Henry.

A boat she recognized as the coastguard cutter appeared.

One of the sailors came up to her and said: 'Are you all right, love? Only there's a little girl in the cottage crying for her mummy.'

'It's a boy,' Lucy said. 'I must cut his hair.' And for no reason at all she smiled.

Bloggs steered the dinghy toward the body at the foot of the cliff. The boat bumped against the rock, and he scrambled out and on to the flat surface.

It was Die Nadel.

He was very dead. His skull had smashed like a glass goblet when he hit the rock. Looking more closely, Bloggs could see that the man had been somewhat battered even before the fall: his right hand was mutilated and there was something wrong with his ankle.

Bloggs searched the body. The stiletto was where he had guessed it might be: in a sheath strapped to the left forearm. In the inside pocket of the expensive-looking, bloodstained jacket, Bloggs found a wallet, papers, money, and a little film can containing twenty-four 35mm photographic negatives. He held them up to the strengthening light: they were the negatives of the prints found in the envelopes Faber had sent to the Portuguese Embassy.

The sailors on the cliff top threw down a rope. Bloggs put Faber's possessions into his own pockets, then tied the rope around the corpse. They hauled it up, then sent the rope down for Bloggs.

When he got to the top one of the sailors said: 'You left his brains on the rock, but never mind.'

The sub-lieutenant introduced himself, and they walked across to the little cottage on top of the hill.

'We haven't touched anything, for fear of destroying evidence,' the senior sailor said.

'Don't worry too much,' Bloggs told him. 'There won't be a prosecution.'

They had to enter the house through the broken kitchen window. The woman was sitting at a table, with the child on her lap. Bloggs smiled at her. He could not think of anything to say.

He looked quickly around the little cottage. It was a battlefield. He saw the nailed-up windows, the barred doors, the remains of the fire, the dog with its throat cut, the shotguns, the broken bannister, and the axe embedded in the windowsill beside two severed fingers.

He thought: What kind of woman is she?

He set the sailors to work: one to tidy the house and unbar the doors and windows; another to mend the blown fuse; a third to make tea.

He sat down in front of the woman and looked at her. She was dressed in ill-fitting, mannish clothes; her hair was wet; her face was dirty. Despite all that she was remarkably beautiful, with lovely amber eyes in an oval face.

Bloggs smiled at the child and spoke very gently to the woman. 'What you've done is enormously important to the war,' he said. 'One of these days I'll explain just how important it is. But for now, I have to ask you two questions. Is that, okay?'

Her eyes focused on him, and after a moment she nodded.

'Did the man Faber succeed in contacting the U-boat by radio?'

The woman just looked blank.

Bloggs found a toffee in his trousers pocket. 'Can I give the boy a sweet?' he asked. 'He looks hungry.'

'Thank you,' she said.

'Now: did Faber contact the U-boat?'

'His name was Henry Baker,' she said.

'Ah. Well, did he?'

'No. I short-circuited the electricity.'

'That was smart,' Bloggs said. 'How did you do it?' She pointed at the empty light socket above them.

'Screwdriver, eh?'

'No.' She smiled thinly. 'I wasn't that smart. Fingers.'

He gave her a look of horror. The thought of deliberately . . . He shook himself. It was ghastly. He put it out of his mind. 'Right. Do you think anyone on the U-boat could have seen him coming down the cliff?'

The effort of concentration showed on her face. 'Nobody came out of the hatch,' she said. 'Could they have seen him through their periscope?'

'No,' he said confidently. 'This is good news. It means they don't know he's been captured and . . . neutralized. Anyway . . .' He changed the subject hastily. 'You've been through as much as men on the front line are expected to suffer. We're going to get you and the boy to a hospital on the mainland.'

'Yes,' she said.

Bloggs addressed the senior sailor. 'Is there any form of transport around?'

'Yes – a jeep down in that little stand of trees.'

'Good. Will you drive these two over to the jetty and get them on to your boat?'

'Surely.'

'Treat them gently.'

'Of course.'

Bloggs turned to the woman again. He felt an overwhelming surge of affection and admiration for her. She looked frail and helpless, now: but he knew she was brave and strong as well as beautiful. Impulsively, he took her hand. 'When you've been in hospital a day or two, you'll begin to feel terribly depressed. That's a sign you're getting better. I won't be far away, and the doctors will tell me. I'll want to talk to you some more. But not before you feel like it. Okay?'

At last she smiled at him, and it felt like the warmth of a fire. 'You're kind,' she said.

She stood up and carried her child out of the house.

'Kind?' Bloggs muttered to himself. 'God's truth, what a woman.'

He went upstairs to the radio and tuned it to the Royal Observer Corps frequency.

'Storm Island calling, over.'

'Come in, Storm Island.'

'Patch me through to London.'

'Hold on.' There was a long pause, then a familiar voice. 'Godliman.'

'Percy. We caught the . . . smuggler. He's dead.'

'Marvellous, marvellous.' There was triumph in Godliman's voice. 'Did he manage to contact his partner?'

'Almost certainly not.'

'Well done, well done!'

'Don't congratulate me,' Bloggs said. 'By the time I got here it was all over bar the tidying up.'

'Who killed him, then?'

'The woman.'

'Well, I'm damned. What's she like?'

Bloggs grinned. 'She's a hero, Percy.'

Godliman laughed aloud. 'I think I know what you mean.'

THIRTY-EIGHT

Hitler stood at the panoramic window, looking out at the mountains. He wore his dove-grey uniform, and he looked tired and depressed. He had called his physician during the night.

Admiral Puttkamer saluted and said: 'Good morning, my Führer.'

Hitler turned and peered closely at his aide-de-camp. Those beady eyes never failed to unnerve Puttkamer. Hitler said: 'Was Die Nadel picked up?'

'No.' There was some trouble at the rendezvous – the English police were chasing smugglers. It appears Die Nadel was not there, anyway. He sent a wireless message a few minutes ago.' He proffered a sheet of paper.

Hitler took it from him, put on his spectacles, and began to read:

YOUR RENDEZVOUS INSECURE YOU CUNTS I AM WOUNDED AND TRANSMITTING LEFT HANDED FIRST UNITED STATES ARMY GROUP ASSEMBLED EAST ANGLIA UNDER PATTON ORDER OF BATTLE AS FOLLOWS TWENTYONE INFANTRY DIVISIONS FIVE ARMOURED DIVISIONS APPROXIMATELY FIVE THOUSAND AIRCRAFT PLUS REQUISITE TROOP

SHIPS IN THE WASH FUSAG WILL ATTACK CALAIS
JUNE FIFTEENTH REGARDS TO WILLI

Hitler handed the message back to Puttkamer and sighed. 'So it's Calais after all.'

'Can we be sure of this man?' the aide asked.

'Absolutely.' Hitler turned and walked across the room to a chair. His movements were stiff, and he seemed in pain. 'He is a loyal German. I know his family.'

'But your instinct . . .'

'Ach . . . I said I would trust this man's report, and so I shall.' He made a gesture of dismissal. 'Tell Rommel and Rundstedt they can't have their panzers. And send in that damned doctor.'

Puttkamer saluted again and went out to relay the orders.

EPILOGUE

THIRTY-NINE

When Germany defeated England in the quarter-final of the 1970 World Cup soccer tournament Grandpa was furious.

He sat in front of the colour television set and muttered through his beard at the screen. 'Cunning!' he told the assorted experts who were now dissecting the game. 'Cunning and stealth! That's the way to defeat the Hun!'

He would not be mollified until his grandchildren arrived. Jo's white Jaguar drew up on the drive of the modest three-bedroom house, and little David rushed in to sit on Grandpa's lap and pull his beard. The rest of the family followed more sedately: Rebecca, David's little sister; then Jo's wife Ann; then Jo himself, prosperous-looking in a suede jacket. Grandma came out of the kitchen to greet them.

Jo said: 'Did you watch the football, Pop?'

'Terrible,' Grandpa said. 'We were rubbish.' Since he retired from the Force and had more leisure time, he had taken an interest in sport.

Jo scratched his moustache. 'The Germans were better,' he said. 'They play good football. We can't win it every time.'

'Don't talk to me about bloody Germans,' Grandpa said.

Jo grinned. 'I do a lot of business with Germany.'

Grandma's voice came from the kitchen. 'Don't start him off, Jo!' She pretended to be going deaf, but there was not much she missed.

'I know,' Grandpa said. 'Forgive and forget, and drive round in a bloody Audi.'

'Good cars.'

'Cunning and stealth, that's the way to defeat the Hun,' Grandpa repeated. He addressed the grandson on his lap, who was not really his grandson, since Jo was not his son. 'That's the way we beat them in the war, Davy – we tricked them.'

'How did you trick them?' David asked, with the child's assumption that his forebears did everything in history.

'Well, see, we made them think—' Grandpa's voice became low and conspiratorial, and the child giggled in anticipation. 'We made them think we were going to attack Calais—'

'That's in France, not Germany.'

'Yes, but the Germans were all over France, then. The Froggies didn't defend themselves as well as we did.'

Jo said: 'Nothing to do with the fact that we're an island, of course.'

Ann shushed him. 'Let Grandpa tell his war stories.'

'Anyway,' Grandpa continued, 'we made them think we were going to attack Calais, so they put all their tanks and soldiers there.' He used a cushion to represent France, an ashtray for the Germans, and a penknife for the Allies. '*But* we attacked Normandy, and there was nobody there but old Rommel and a few pop-guns! Cunning and stealth, see?'

'Didn't they find out about the trick?' David asked.

'They *nearly* did. In fact, there was one spy who found out. Now not many people know that, but I know because I was a spycatcher in the war.'

'What happened to the spy?'

'We killed him before he could tell.'

'Did you kill him, Grandpa?'

'No – Grandma did.'

David's eyes widened. '*Grandma* killed him?'

Grandma came in carrying a teapot, and said: 'Fred Bloggs, are you frightening the children?'

'Why shouldn't they know?' he groused. 'She's got a medal, you know. She won't tell me where she keeps it because she doesn't like me showing it to visitors.'

Grandma was pouring tea. 'It's all over now, and best forgotten, just as Jo says. Anyway, not much good came out of it.' She handed a cup and saucer to Grandpa.

He took her arm and held her there. '*Some* good came out of it,' he said. His voice was suddenly quite gentle, all the elderly grumpiness gone. 'I met a hero, and married her.'

They looked at each other for a moment. Her beautiful hair was pepper-and-salt now, and she wore it in a bun. She was heavier than she used to be. For years her clothes had always been fashionable and glamorous, but she no longer had the figure for haute couture.

But her eyes were still the same: large and amber, and remarkably beautiful.

Those eyes looked back at him, now, and they both were very still, remembering the way it had been.

Then David jumped off his grandpa's lap and knocked the cup of tea to the floor, and the spell was broken.

The Pillars of the Earth

Critical acclaim for the worldwide bestselling epic* The Pillars of the Earth, *voted into the BBC's top 100 of Britain's favourite novels

'Enormous and brilliant . . . this mammoth tale seems to touch all human emotion – love and hate, loyalty and treachery, hope and despair. See for yourself. This is truly a novel to get lost in'
Cosmopolitan

'A highly enjoyable tale . . . this book evokes its period brilliantly'
Sunday Times

'A historical saga of such breadth and density . . . Follett succeeds brilliantly in combining hugeness and detail to create a novel imbued with the rawness, violence and blind faith of the era'
Sunday Express